BREAKING NEWS

ALSO BY ROBERT MACNEIL

The People Machine

The Right Place at the Right Time

The Story of English (with Robert McCrum and William Cran)

Wordstruck

Burden of Desire

The Voyage

NAN A. TALESE ■ DOUBLEDAY   New York   London   Toronto   Sydney   Auckland

NEWS *a novel*

Robert MacNeil

PUBLISHED BY NAN A. TALESE
an imprint of Doubleday
a division of Bantam Doubleday Dell Publishing Group, Inc.
1540 Broadway, New York, New York 10036

DOUBLEDAY is a trademark of Doubleday, a division of
Bantam Doubleday Dell Publishing Group, Inc.

Library of Congress Cataloging-in-Publication Data

MacNeil, Robert, 1931–
    Breaking news : a novel / Robert MacNeil. — 1st ed.
        p.   cm.
    ISBN 0-385-42020-X
    I. Title.
PR9199.3.M3363B73   1998
813'.54—dc21   98-19562
                                                   CIP

TO BOB KOTLOWITZ

AND IN MEMORY OF BILLIE

ACKNOWLEDGMENTS

To Nan Talese, for her nurturing and
attentive editing; to all the people at
Doubleday New York and Toronto,
who are tirelessly helpful; to Bill
Adler, my long-term literary agent,
who suggested this book,
my heartfelt thanks.

BREAKING NEWS

1

It began with Grant Munro's speech to the Radio Television News Directors Association.

After dinner in the Waldorf ballroom, he received the RTNDA's presidential award for lifetime achievement, the citation noting that "as the longest-serving network anchorman, and in his many years as a leading network correspondent, Grant Munro has brought great distinction to the broadcast news industry."

Grant rose, smiling—tall, fit, his good looks burnished by the habit of success and admiration—and said he hoped the "lifetime" part was premature, as he hadn't quite finished with it. Warm laughter and long applause.

"As for the achievement side of it, I have a few questions. I've been fortunate, in a long career with terrific assignments, to have done many things I'm proud of.

"I and my colleagues, all of you in radio and television, network, local, or cable news, all over the country, have been the window through which Americans have seen history unfold. We have tried honorably to shape that history and make it understandable to our fellow citizens."

He went on to list some highlights of that history from when he had joined the network in 1963, just after the Kennedy assassination.

"But the picture is not all glorious."

Grant paused, and even the smallest sounds of coffee cups and dessert spoons were stilled.

"We've had several months to digest and consider our behavior since the presidential sex scandal broke last winter. Judging by the immediate soul-searching and breast-beating, most of us felt we went too far.

"Nobody who believes in the First Amendment and the role of the press would deny our legitimate right to examine presidential behavior that affects the public interest. And that was not always clear in this story.

"But what I deplore, and what still sickens me—whatever the president's guilt or innocence—is broadcast news media behaving like the Gadarene swine. You remember, Christ sent evil spirits into a herd of pigs, and the maddened herd raced over a cliff and drowned. I think that in our swollen numbers; in our new and insane competitiveness; in our rising desperation for ratings; our prurient glee in discussing the president's sex life; in our rush to report unsubstantiated rumor, leaks, and gossip; an evil spirit entered *us,* and we became that herd of maddened swine racing toward our own destruction."

The ballroom erupted, exploded with applause, whoops, and cheers, and for more than a minute Grant couldn't go on. He glanced along the head table to Winona, whose eyes were glowing with pride and love.

"Now, where does it stop? In the name of competition, every time a big or sensational story comes along, are we forced to be even more outrageous, more irresponsible, each time ratcheting up the excesses?

Each time jettisoning more cherished journalism values as useless baggage? Where does it stop? And if it does not stop, what happens to our credibility with the public? How do we restore some sense of proportion? How do we bring back a Fourth Estate that can claim to serve the democracy and not just titillate? Those are my questions, as I consider the achievement you honor tonight."

Afterward, as the crowd filtered out of the ballroom, Richard Schoenfeld, the executive editor of *Time* magazine, said to a colleague, "Interesting. Maybe we should think about a profile of Grant Munro and the TV news business. Maybe a cover."

But Grant's boss, Everett Repton, president of the network news division, was murmuring to his boss, the president of the network, "Gadarene swine? Jesus! I think Grant's beginning to lose it."

2

Two months after his prostate surgery, *Time* writer Christopher Siefert wanted an assignment to take his mind off his trembling convalescence.

"First, tell me how you're feeling," Dick Schoenfeld said.

"I'm all right now. I still have to go back periodically and find out if they got it all. You know the cancer drill. First PSA test a month after the operation was a little ambiguous."

"This is the first time I've seen you not twitching for a cigarette."

"Had to give that up, too. I'm on the patch. Third level. I guess it's working. It's either that or stark fear."

"You're looking a hell of a lot better."

"Well, if you've given up everything that makes life beautiful . . . gin . . . cigarettes . . . sex. Anyway, you want to do a cover on Grant Munro, the news anchor?"

"Do you know him?"

"I see him here and there . . . book parties and things. He's not a friend. But why him?"

"I heard him speak recently. He compared his industry to the Gadarene swine for their greedy rush on the President's sex life."

"I saw that in the *Times*. Good line."

"And they all cheered him as though he'd been singing their praises. I'd like us to take a look at network news through him."

Siefert said, "I don't watch it much. Television news people strike me as a bunch of posturing, overpaid mannequins. But if you're going to do television, why not someone like Ann Murrow? She always has the media tomcats scratching at her door."

"She's not really a news anchor. Of course, you can work her into it if you want to . . . work them all in."

"She'd make a hotter newsstand cover than Grant Munro."

"My hunch is Grant Munro's the place to start. And my hunches usually work for you."

True. Dick Schoenfeld was by far the best editor Siefert had written for, with good intuitions in matching stories and writers.

"I guess I'm missing something. I don't feel any edge in it. Too bland."

"You'll find the edge. You always do."

"Unless you know something about Munro I don't?"

"A couple of years ago a close friend of his fell off a mountain and got killed. Remember? Munro had to be rescued by helicopter."

"What was he doing on the mountain?"

"He climbs them for fun. Or he used to. Tough mountains. Doesn't that make him more interesting?"

"Was it his fault?"

"Don't think so. Just one of those accidents."

"So?"

"So . . . how does a guy in the public eye handle something like that? Death of a close friend? Why don't you go through the file and see what you think."

"You thinking puff piece or exposé? The empty suit undressed, or the national hero canonized?"

Schoenfeld laughed. "I'm thinking a nice sound piece of journalism, elegantly written, psychologically penetrating, full of trenchant insights and telling anecdotes! Seriously, I want a cover we can run maybe in late summer, for the fall TV season, with sidebars. We haven't done anything big on television for a while."

"Some corporate jazz involved . . . Time-Warner pushing you to trash the competition?"

"Nope. My idea. The main thing is, it's perfect for you. No rush. Take your time. Very little travel. Most of the players are here in New York. A good way to find your sea legs again."

"Or are the bean counters on your ass to justify all my time off and medical benefits?"

"No way."

"How many words?"

"Doesn't matter. Whatever you need for a good character study, plus some analysis of the trends in an important industry. Think eight to ten thousand and see what you come up with."

3

The first to sense something in the wind was Sherman Glass, Grant's agent. Some correspondents used lawyers for a straight fee, begrudging an agent's perpetual ten percent. But Grant had signed with Sherman in 1965, as a young correspondent off to Vietnam, and had never been quite exasperated enough to drop him.

Sherman had the irritating agent's itch, always craftily half a deal ahead of Grant, whose instinct was to leave well enough alone.

He asked Grant to lunch, making "we haven't had a chat for a while" sound slightly ominous, like a dashboard warning light you don't recognize. Sherman liked to show off his star client and preferred the Four Seasons' Grill Room, where he could see and be seen; and where the clientele was often straight out of Monday's "Information Industries" section in the *Times*.

Even seated, Sherman was unprepossessing. His hair grew low on his forehead, making him look stupid, which he wasn't, and his lips were fleshy and wet, often extruding a huge cigar.

Grant didn't drink at lunch when he was working, but Sherman still had a martini on the rocks, as Grant had in the sixties, when he was eager to emulate the seasoned men at the network. Amazing that they'd done anything useful in the afternoons, but they wrote and edited and cut film and got shows on the air. Their quitting martinis at lunch hadn't improved TV journalism.

Sherman ordered a steak, Grant, fish; and they proceeded to have the usual conversation:

"Great to see you, Grant."

"And you, Sherman."

"How's it going?"

"Pretty well, I think."

"You still running and all that?"

"Yeah, it makes me feel good."

"Winona good?"

"Sure, she's fine."

"How's the vineyard doing?"

"Coming along well."

Sherman sipped his drink and surveyed the room. "You heard anything from the brass?"

"What do you mean? I saw them all at the affiliates' meeting in L.A. They got me out there to do a speech."

"That's good. Hey, your talk at the RTNDA was dynamite!" He chuckled, but there was a faint unease in it. "Sometimes you really let 'em have it."

"Well, someone has too. No one gives a damn what the content is now. Affiliates or corporate. It's all the same bottom line."

"Just don't like to see you biting the hand that feeds you."

"What are they going to do to me, bite back?"

And that gave Sherman his cue; he was trying to open negotiations for a new contract.

"Why now? It's two years away, isn't it?"

"No, it's less, more like nineteen months, and we need to be thinking about it."

"Well, if you want to start talking to them, go ahead."

"The thing is, they won't talk."

"What do you mean?"

"I can't make a date to talk with them. They don't return calls, or only after several tries. They make excuses. Busy. On the road. Other stuff going on."

"Is that anything to get antsy about?"

"It's not like them. It's not in character. Usually they're busting their ass to talk to me to keep you happy. You know what I mean? Now, they're not."

"What do you think it means?"

"I don't know. That's why I asked if you'd heard anything, talked to any of them."

"As I said, we all had drinks and dinner together at the affiliates. Nothing unusual."

"Everyone cordial?"

"Sure, they're business guys, professional glad-handers. There's never anything to talk about with them. They love the latest White House gossip, especially the dirty stuff. Never had a real conversation with any of them."

"Well, just thought I'd ask."

"You worried about this?"

"No, no."

"You sound it."

"Let's just say I'd be happier if they wanted to talk."

"I can call them and tell them Sherman Glass is feeling lonely and neglected. Buy him lunch and make him happy."

"Better not do that."

Sherman unwrapped a cigar that might have unbalanced Winston Churchill and moistened it obscenely.

"I'll cool it for a month or so and then try again. Maybe after Labor Day, when they're back in their routines. There's plenty of time."

Grant left, wondering whether his irritation was worth all the legal mess of dumping Sherman and undoing his exclusive representation agreements. Probably smarter to leave it alone.

IT GRADUALLY emerged that Sherman's hunch was sound. A few days later, Winona said Betty Rosten had told her she'd had a call from a telephone interviewer doing market research, asking about news personalities on television. Grant's name had been among them. The questions were disguised, but Betty, who had worked in advertising, got the feeling that the client was Grant's network. The questions kept coming back to his news team: could she identify that name or this, did she have positive or negative feelings? Betty was a close friend but very direct. Was Grant's show in trouble?

A WEEK or so later, Grant and Winona were at the Spring Gala of the New York City Ballet. Betty Rosten had been on the board for years and always invited the Munros, who made a generous contribution. Then the Rostens would join the Munros' table at the Public Library dinner and contribute in turn. Such mutual back-scratching kept New York culture alive and gave anyone socially ambitious, and with the money, a fast track into a sort of society.

After watching the City Ballet perform in the New York State Theater, the party filtered out of the first tier to the dinner set up on the promenade: a caterers' instant fairyland, subdued lighting, soft music, snowy tables with fantastic centerpieces of flowers and fruit, tall candles, the wall by the bars lined by the handsome pool of out-of-work actors, playing waiters in black tie. Ordinary ballet goers gazed down at the glittering scene from the gilded railings of the upper tiers.

Recognized by many, Grant made slow progress through the familiar faces: a peck from Kitty Carlise Hart; a back slap from Henry Kissinger; a cheek brush from *Vogue* editor Anna Wintour; a blown kiss from Anne Bass; a smile and thumbs-up across the crowd from Walter Cronkite; an arm clench and fierce whisper from a woman convinced Grant was ignoring Myanmar; a joker's grin from Charlie Rose, who was surfing for show guests with an arm on Peter Martins. Grant caught an unmistakably frank look—in a city of frank looking—from a blond woman in a red evening dress. He turned away, then back, as she smiled complicitously.

Grant found the table and Al Rosten, who was talking to another guest. Lithe young dancers with skinny shoulders and long necks soaring from abbreviated evening dresses slithered through the chattering crowd. No one was in a hurry to sit down. He had picked up a glass of white wine when a man introduced himself and asked, "Have you considered what you'll do when you retire from your news program?"

Startled, Grant said, "What do you mean, retire?"

The man smiled knowingly. "Well, assuming that does pass through your mind, I have a suggestion that might interest you."

"I have no intention of leaving the program, but what's the suggestion?"

They had to lean together to be heard in the echoing hubbub.

"To be president of a major university."

"No, thanks. Not interested." Instant response, suddenly heated.

"You don't even want to know which university?"

"Not really," Grant said. The man shook hands and moved away. But the message "when you retire" kept ticking over while Grant made small talk at dinner—difficult, with the noise and the music. What made him think Grant was so old or professionally washed up?

In the limo recrossing the park to the East Side, Grant said to Winona, "Do I look like someone ready for retirement?"

"Not according to the other woman at the table, Betty's friend. Why?"

"A man came up and asked, when I retired, if I wanted to be president of some university."

"Which one?"

"I didn't give him a chance to tell me. Groucho Marx: Do I want to be president of a university that would ask me? More important, who's ready to retire?"

"Not Grant Munro—I take it—is the message." She gave his hand a squeeze.

"That's the message, kid. Pass it on."

"They don't want doddery old fogies nowadays. Everyone's retiring earlier. Maybe that's the message. Revered academic institution seeks revered newsman—vital, dynamic, handsome, vigorous, all his own hair . . ."

"Most of his own teeth . . ."

"Beloved and trusted by the nation."

"Is that all?"

"And adored by his wife."

"Funny, he didn't mention that."

"I'd hold out for President of the United States."

LAURIE JACOBS was head of P.R. for the news department. She was congenial with Grant, hell on wheels to others, a sweetly vinegary New York woman, very sharp, always positive, never defeated. She was good to look at, well built, late thirties, divorced, with a couple of half-grown children.

She had quickly made Grant an ally when she came to the network, and she was smart enough to embrace trouble before it engulfed her. This morning, thirty seconds after he got into the office, was loosening his tie, and looking at phone messages, Laurie leaned around his door, smiling brown eyes, big grin, black curly hair. "Got a minute?"

"Sure. What's up?"

"This." She put down the *New York Post* folded to "Page Six," and with a scarlet fingernail stabbed the headline: ANOTHER RATINGS DIVE: CHANGES COMING? His name stood out in bold type.

Network officials fear *"The Evening News"* with **Grant Munro** is headed for the cellar. After a slight climb last winter, ratings have dived again. News department sources say something's got to change. They can't keep falling like this. **Munro** has held the anchor chair longer than any of his rivals. He'll soon be 60. Some network colleagues are asking: Is **he** what has to change?

"Criminal!" Laurie said, wrinkling her nose. "Absolutely criminal!"

"Where did they get that from?"

"Who knows? But I wanted you to know it's not from me."

"Who are news department sources?"

"Sweetheart, your guess is as good as mine. I think it's awful, but my gut feeling is not to make it worse by commenting on it."

"Well, the *Post* may hype it, but they didn't just make it up. Someone's been talking to them."

Even as he spoke, Grant felt chilled, suddenly and unaccustomedly alone.

"They called and I said we had no comment on stuff like that."

"You knew it was coming?"

"Not like this!"

"What did they ask you to comment on?"

Angela called from the doorway, "Grant, morning meeting. They're waiting."

He had to go. But as he took his place opposite the young executive producer, Marty Boyle, amid all the "Morning, Grants . . . Hi, Grants," he wondered which of these producers and writers, his closest colleagues, might have been the *Post*'s source.

Nobody mentioned it. They went through the usual news budget from Washington, from the bureaus overseas, the scheduled hearings, news conferences, speeches, announcements; Middle East talks, a flood in the Midwest, unseasonably early fires threatening homes in California; nothing earth shattering.

"Nothing to lead on yet," Marty Boyle said, and Grant felt a spasm of irritation to hear him, barely thirty-five, talking about leads as though he'd been in the business forever.

AFTER THE MEETING, Grant sat in his office, trying to fathom that wave of strong feeling.

It wasn't Marty's age. Journalism made instant veterans, like soldiers in wars; innocent, green, and totally scared one day, soon battle-hardened pros. And Marty was very skilled.

No; his resentment touched another level: what they *would* lead the show with—when the time came to choose. That was the heart of the struggle, and Grant already knew what each would say.

GRANT: We should be leading on the Middle East talks; it's the most important thing that happened today.

MARTY: Sure, you're right. But we've got pictures of the little girl in Wyoming who was raped and found dead in the woods; great family videos of her, cute and poignant as hell. What do you show for the Mideast? Guys in suits walking in and out of offices? Maybe for excitement some have no ties on? Or a cute little girl whose brutal rape and murder has devastated the whole country?

GRANT: It's only devastated the country, if it has, because lousy TV news shows have built it up into the latest crime of the century.

No, Marty would say, because her mother's the star of a prime time show, and it's a real heartland story . . . plus movie stars!

And both were right. Unless it was the end of the world, suits going in and out of conferences made boring TV news pictures. Yet every time they led with the cute little girl, Grant knew they were cheapening the show. They were telling the nation this was the most important thing that day, implying that the vulnerability of cute little girls and the prevalence of sadistic sex criminals was a big issue, hyping it, feeding paranoia in the country, feeding the fear, the disconnection between different types of people.

Or, a more discouraging thought: Marty Boyle could have been the one who'd talked to "Page Six," to plant a seed, to start a little buzz. If one gossip column printed it, others would follow, establishing a factoid, until it was a common assumption that Grant was in some kind of trouble.

HE WASN'T going to sit there, stewing. This was his place as much as anyone's, his network; it was by his face and voice that most people knew it. He was still the star, so why was he sitting there in a funk because of one gossip writer on Murdoch's rag?

He got up and marched out, reading in eyes, as he passed the desk, full knowledge of the *Post* story and speculation about his reaction. He deliberately kept his dander up to confront Everett Repton. The president's office door was usually open, and even if he was on the phone or had a visitor, he'd wave Grant in, because it was part of the game to introduce his star. But the door was closed, and his assistant said, "He's with Laurie. Can I call you when he's free?" And Grant had to retreat, feeling like a film being run backward.

In the meantime, the day's news was getting away from him, so he booted up his terminal on the computer system and flipped into the AP file to skim the wire.

Then Marty strolled in and slumped into the chair by his desk. "Busy?"

"Nothing special. What's up?"

Grant leaned back, hands behind his head, and put both feet on the desk.

"Shitty item in the *Post*," Marty said. "I'm sorry about it."

"I'm not ecstatic myself. You know who's behind it?"

"No clue. Honest. Can't figure who'd be so dumb. You're the

butter on everybody's bread, for Christ's sake. But I saw the look you gave me when you came to the meeting after Laurie showed you the piece."

"How'd you know she showed me the piece?"

"She told me she was going to. Didn't want to ruin your day, blind-sided by reporters calling to ask about it."

"Are they calling?"

"Not yet, but I guess they will."

Marty scooted his chair closer, glanced at the open door, and said, "Can I talk confidentially?"

And he turned on the disingenuous, boyish look Grant had seen before. Marty was hefty for a business that seemed to attract slighter, even weedier men. He'd been a running back at college and often still acted like a ball carrier with his head down. But now a sensitive and intelligent look stole over his faded freckles.

"Grant, you and I kid a lot, and I know things between us get a bit edgy . . ."

"Yeah?" Grant wasn't in a mood to be diplomatic.

"You know, they bounced me into this job, great opportunity for me . . . but I guess I can see what it's like for you. You've been here forever . . . been in the business a hell of a long time. Forgotten more than we know. You're one of the icons . . . it's a real privilege for someone my age to work with you . . ."

Grant looked into the open, pudgy face, wondering where the flattery was leading.

"I know we don't see eye to eye all the time . . . but I have terrific respect for your ideas, your knowledge of the business. And I consider it an honor to work for you."

"That's great, Marty. Nice to hear. I think you're a real pro, too. So what's the lead?"

"The lead? I don't know yet . . ."

"*Your* lead. What's really on your mind?"

"Well. I don't know how to put this. I don't want you to think for a second I'd do anything to undermine you. OK?"

"You tell me I shouldn't think it, Marty, I won't think it. I tend to believe people. A bad habit of mine, maybe."

"The *Post* piece made me sick."

"Why? One more piece of shit from the *Post*. We've never paid any attention to them before. Why should we now?"

"You're not upset about it?"

"What'd you expect me to say?"

"All right, I'm glad. Let's forget it and get on with the mission." He snapped his fingers as he did when he thought a scene had gone on too long.

"Fine by me."

"OK, Grant?"

He lurched up and held out his hand. Grant leaned forward and shook it, not knowing why. Marty seemed transparently relieved. He grinned his big grin, slapped Grant's shoulder, and ambled out of the office. His shirt was bloused out of his pants; he was getting fat around the middle.

DURING THE 'eighty-eight Reagan-Gorbachev summit, when the cold war effectively died, Grant had gone outside Moscow to the writers' colony at Peredelkino to talk to the poet Yevtushenko. With his camera crew they went over to Pasternak's house, and Yevtushenko told a story Pasternak had told him. Two young writers, very nervous, came to inform him that the Communist Party had expelled him from the writers' union. He thanked them for delivering such a difficult message, then watched them go down his long driveway, dancing with relief, laughing and congratulating each other for having had the courage to carry the message of betrayal.

Angela's face at the door in her Juliette-of-the-Sorrows makeup. "Marie in Ev Repton's office. Can you do lunch with him? He's tied up till then."

Grant hated waiting two more hours, and lunch overformalized a conversation, when what he wanted was a few hard words and out.

"If it has to be, sure; lunch is fine."

"Quarter to one?"

"Wait, I've got some voice-over to record at twelve-thirty. Better make it one o'clock."

"I'll tell her. And Don Evans is ready with the scripts."

Don put a sheaf of script on the desk, his face cherubic, choirboyish.

"Morning, chief! Time to journey back once again to the days of yesteryear and the glories of steam radio."

They'd been correspondents together in the sixties, but Evans's on-air career had fizzled out and he'd ended up as a senior writer. He also wrote the radio scripts that Grant recorded and were broadcast as "Essays by Grant Munro." One of the minor deceptions of the business. Don was a clever writer—he'd suggested the Gadarene swine bit for the RTNDA speech. Grant liked the thread of irony that ran through his copy and wished he could write as well. But he talked well, and that was what he was paid for. In any case, there wasn't time for Grant to research and write these pieces, along with everything else.

"You want to do a read-through?"

"Yeah, in a sec. You see the piece in the *Post* today?"

"Sure. Required reading. Everyone memorized it, then like good agents chewed up the paper and swallowed it. Under pain of torture no one will confess he's read it."

"What do you think about it?"

"Rupert Murdoch, having bought half the world's journalists, likes to tear down the other half. This week it's your turn."

"Who do you guess put the idea into their heads?"

"Who among your dear friends and devoted colleagues? Who has something to gain? Certainly I don't. At my age"—he smiled—"I'm hooked to your star. If some young dude replaces you, they'll have me out of here in a week. So I don't have anything to gain."

Don Evans and Grant had weathered several personal generations of rivalry, jealousy, and mutual suspicion. Grant had ended up the famous one, paid probably forty times what Evans earned. They were left with a kind of grudging, good-humored modus vivendi, the sharp edges rounded smooth by time.

"Your nose for this kind of thing has always been pretty sharp."

"Too sharp. If I'd spent less time trying to figure out the politics, I'd probably have jumped ship a long time ago . . . when the going was good. No, I'd forget it. If someone here is putting out that kind of suet for the birdies, it'll become more obvious, and we'll know. Fretting about it will just make your life sour."

"You're right. We're running out of time. I'd better read your scripts."

"Hold your applause till the end."

Grant read through Don's scripts, deft as usual, just deep enough to give drive-time listeners the illusion of having heard something, but no more profound. Intellectual slumming for Don; he should have been bending his mind to something serious. But that ambition had left him, and the network paid him more than any newspaper or magazine would.

Grant made a few marks for emphasis, and they headed off to the radio end to record them. Normally he recorded this material in a breeze, one after another, one take, no fluffs. Unaccountably, today, he stumbled a few times and had to start over.

"Mind on something else maybe?" Don asked as he came out of the studio.

The same thing happened a little later, when Grant went to the television audio booth to lay down some voice-over narration for a small tape piece. The young producer, Ellen Siegel, had been recently promoted from associate producer, and this was the first time she'd worked with him on her own. She'd written four small inserts, none longer than twenty seconds, and he read them all smoothly. But she asked him to do two again. Through the glass he saw the audio man, Larry, an old-timer, give her a glance that said: You're going to ask Grant Munro to do a retake when the first one's perfect? He shot Grant a look to see whether he'd noticed, and a tiny smile passed between them. That was fine. Grant didn't believe in bullying the young producers and writers, so he read the two pieces again, stressing what she wanted stressed, but this time she said, over the talkback, "You're a little long on each piece. Let's do another take." Very assured, very much in command.

Grant did another take, but he must have been so caught by the dynamics that he forgot to speed his delivery to make up the extra second.

"Still long," Ms. Siegel said primly but, he thought, with unwarranted satisfaction. He had to take a deep breath to control his rising annoyance; did a third take, remembering to increase the pace, and was rewarded with a crisp "That's fine. Thanks, Grant," as though she had been doing this with him for years.

Why was he annoyed? She was perfectly within her rights. If the pieces wouldn't fit, they wouldn't fit. But something about her manner, a little officiousness to cover her nervousness, making him jump through hoops that the older producers avoided with him—something about her lack of deference compared to theirs. Most of all, it was probably her age and her confidence and her pert little ass as she bent over the console, reminding him of his age. And everything combined to put him in an even sourer frame of mind than before.

He left the recording booth and walked back to his office, people nodding or saying hi on the way, with rising irritation at all the petty stuff he did as part of the job. That and the hundred little negotiations that shaped the day. It would start again with the noon meeting to review where they were on the day's news and their staff assignments.

Years ago Eric Sevareid had complained about being "nibbled to death by ducks." Grant felt that way.

Actually, in order to do the voice-overs and make lunch, he had to skip the noon meeting, and that compounded his mood. They were quite capable of producing the show without him, but when they made the decisions without his input, without his editorial head present, he couldn't complain later if he didn't like their decisions. You were either there in the boiler room or not.

4

Someone had started a web page and chat room specializing in gossip about the business. She, or maybe he, called herself Hollygo Lightly, in homage to Truman Capote, and claimed to be the First Electronic Black Drag Queen Gossip Columnist.

www.hollygo.com

At the BBS (Beige Broadcasting System) handsome but aging news anchor Gregory Peck maybe should rent the movie "All About Eve." That before your time, sugar, you cultural illiterate? Well, it about actress Bette Davis, gettin on in years, finds sweet-as-honey but ruthless little Anne Baxter tryin to steal her man and her role? Well, over at Beige, Gregory Peck (reason I call him Gregory Peck is those eyebrows and soulful eyes and that voice! Make you think of roasted chestnuts, all cracklin by the open fire. Just sayin "good evenin" that voice give a gal the shivers! Know what I mean, sister?) well, Gregory better keep an eye on young Billy Boy Blue. My spies tell me the ambitious Billy Boy, now doing an out-of-town run as White House correspondent, has his cute eyes on the top spot and has friends in high places. Some big dudes at the net think the dynamic Billy Boy was boffo reportin on the president's sex life and want to move him (Billy Boy, not the Prez!) into Gregory's anchor chair right now, but Mr. Peck's contract run till the year 2000.

Some of them network dudes still smartin about Gregory Peck callin them all Gadarene swine. And a good source tells Hollygo that dynamic Power Ranger, Peck's 19-year-old executive producer (I know, honey, but he *looks* 19), is also itching to get the old guy out. Power Ranger is just sick and tired, and stamps his little foot, when he hears *his* new show referred to derisively as "Entertainment Tonight," meaning, muchachas, there may be more entertainment on C-Span! Don'tcha luv it?

GRANT SHOWED the printout to Winona, who said, "Billy Boy means Bill Donovan? But is it malicious, I mean dangerous, or just silly and fun?"

"It could be all of that. Someone's feeding this bird, someone in our shop."

"Does it matter, if it's just a joke? Does anybody pay attention?"

"The whole industry's beginning to pay attention. It's so outrageous they can't ignore it."

"Well, you should ignore it. Although"—she gave him a kiss—"what's so bad about being called Gregory Peck?"

WHEN SOMEONE online asked Hollygo to describe herself, she said:

You want to know what I look like, honey?
Think Ru Paul . . . on a bad day.

It had to be someone who worked in one of the networks. Her information was too in and too current to be from outside. Her nicknames became transparent after a few days. She called the networks Beige, Taupe, and Bisque, and when asked why—and insiders loved to ask her about everything—she said:

Honey, I can't think of nothin stupider than fashion names for lingerie colors. Bor-ing. I never wear nuthin as wishy-washy as taupe, beige, or bisque. That means your mother's underwear— just like the straight news—and I had enough bein straight by time I was seven. When I get run over and they rush me over to the cute interns at St. Vincent's ER, I wanna be wearin nuthin but scarlet silk, black satin, emerald green. I might go for Amber,

Champagne, Peach, Lavender, Ivory, Chocolate, or Cinnamon: stuff like that about somethin real. But ain't nothin real to my mind about evenin news on BBS, the Beige Broadcasting System.

Some of her nicknames were pretty funny, like Nutcracker Sweet for a White House correspondent.

Word reaches me that Taupe Broadcasting Company glam White House correspondent Nutcracker Sweet was out on the lawn doin one of her standuppers? A gust of wind come along and blows up her skirt, showin all she's got. "Don't look, guys!" she squeals with girlish modesty. But the old cameraman says, "It's OK, darlin. We've seen balls before!" Don'tcha luv it?

An old story, but someone must have passed it on to Hollygo. Angela showed him printouts when she thought they were funny . . . or close to home.

It was obvious that young people in various network newsrooms logged on, because they were feeding her gossip about their own generation. It was raunchier than any newspaper column; it had no inhibitions about who was supposedly sleeping with whom, what executive had hysterics in a meeting. One piece claimed someone was caught in an office giving a "sexual favor"; others about who couldn't get it up; who couldn't keep his hands off a P.A. in the edit room; troubles with wives or husbands and kids; outing affairs and imminent divorces; all the chatter that used to be known only to those working closely on one show. Now it was everywhere, and she was often right on the mark.

I was surfin through my Bisque sites hopin for some risqué chatter. (You pronounce that risk-ay, OK? But Bisk, as in Tsk! Tsk! Got it?) How about this? That haughty sister they got as White House correspondent, the one I call Excedrin Headache? You know it took her eleven takes, e-leven! to do her standupper about President Clinton's latest limp-dick appointment so's they could get it on tape in New York? You didn't think, when the anchorman, old Grecian Formula, says so smooth, "And now a report from Excedrin Headache at the White House," that it was LIVE, did you? OK. Her script was so bad, I'm told, her boy producer, Attention Deficit, keeps on makin changes, tryin to goose up her sign-off, tellin her what to say, and ends up dictatin the whole (expletive) thing, it nearly don't get on the air, even when they changed the runnin order four times in the first feed. Anybody don't know what *takes* is, or *runnin order,* don't know enuff to be hittin this web site anyway. Just take it from Hollygo: it big-time teeveenews talk. Language be everthin, chilluns. You got to talk the talk before you can walk the walk, as the preacher says.

O my, speakin a preachers, you cute thing, I was forced, kinda date TV rape, to watch the Reverend Dimmesdale, the saint of television, last night, and I declare, sisters and brothers, I took about ten minutes before I was freed from bondage (not what you're thinking, alas!). And for sheer, unvarnished unction, I'd never seen anythin like it. That boy should be makin millions puttin all them televangelists outta bidness, steda preachin at us and callin it journalism.

Bookish references like *Dimmesdale* and words like *unction* made Grant sure Hollygo was a network writer; a familiar type, feeling burned out, compromised, jaundiced about everything, despising what he did. A terrific game for someone.

Where did a queen like me get so high and mighty bout journalism, you might ask? The Queens School of Journalism, baby! I listens to the I-man. Classes 6–10 A.M. Ever time it's been a slow night on 12th Avenue and I can't pick up nothin by 6 A.M. but WFAN on my Dick Tracy wrist radio. Cost you $20,000 bucks to attend the Columbia J School. Cost you nothin, chilluns, to learn it all from the I-man.

No one could stop it: the anonymity of the Internet protected everyone. A news vice president, a dope who was supposed to keep an eye on the unit managers and administration, fired off a memo forbidding anyone to use the office computer system to call up Hollygo. In about three minutes, she had the memo on the Net.

I hear we've got all the execs at the nets absolutely devastated cos they computer terminals all tied up readin me, passin me the dirt. That means the kids not doin they homework, they not writin the news shows . . . which may be the best news for American democracy since the Stonewall riot. Those tired old queens need to get a new act. Nobody under 65 watches them anyway. Just look at what the commercials are for: Depends, Efferdent, Preparation-H, Dentu-stik. What does that tell you, honey? They ain't products girls our age be usin. Our grandmothers maybe, but my old granny too busy gettin herself bused down to the gamblin in Atlantic City one day and Ledyard, Connecticut, the next, to be worryin bout no network news. She wins too. She's got somethin figured. Does she like her big old grandson struttin around in drag? She doesn't care. She says I look mighty cute and tells me, Just keep your seams straight, darlin! Don'tcha luv it?

As more network types chimed in, Hollygo's chat room became a virtual reality newsroom, combining people from all the rival nets and cable; it was a freemasonry that dissolved inhibitions and shop loyalties. In Grant's young days, network loyalty had been like patriotism; you had your network logo tattooed on your soul. Not these kids. They arrived idealistic from the top colleges and soon they were as cynical as the old hands. Hollygo was an outlet for frustration many felt at the "freak of the week" stories they were doing and at the vanity and pretensions of the highly paid featured correspondents they worked for.

> Miss Clairol, the gorgeous and ambitious risin star at Taupe, spotted again in the ladies' room with Bartlett's Quotations, so she'll have somethin stunnin to drop into the heavy intellectual chat over there. Want to know where that trick came from? Bobby Kennedy. Fastest quotations in the West.

Some of the people on line identified themselves as Taupees or Beigees; others didn't let on, and used names as colorful as Hollygo's. Some were using Hollygo's chat room to ask each other for dates.

The gossip columns now fed on her regularly, and the *New York Observer* tried a mystery profile without divulging her identity—if they knew it. A few years ago it would have been shocking to mock the business so openly, trivialize it, and reduce it to cheap entertainment, but now that seemed to be a game everyone played.

Grant and Everett Repton had both joined the network in the mid-sixties and thus had been colleagues ever since, but not friends. Repton had been a field producer, never creative, but a deal maker, a smooth operator, terrific facilities organizer. Often it wasn't how great your story was but how you got it back to New York and on the air. Ev had always found the way to ship film, the improbable microwave connection, the obscure satellite uplink.

His personal, not professional, cards were engraved Everett B. Repton III. He was a Princeton graduate and had a jovial, unruffled social assurance with his superiors; an air that said: Don't worry, you've got more important things to worry about; we'll get it done. Repton did get it done but, Grant noticed, always mysteriously got it known how hard he'd worked, stayed up all night, driven the exposed road under fire to get through. Everybody did the same things; it was how you earned your spurs at the network. No medals for trying and missing, or even saving money; the medals came only for getting a story on the air. As in war, the medals went to men whose heroism got mentioned up the line and back at HQ, and Ev Repton's story always got told. His self-promotion bounced him up and up, to news manager, to vice president of administration, and, for five years now, to president of the news division, thereby nominally Grant's boss.

Never quite trusting him, Grant had also not wholly outgrown his unease with the Princeton assurance Ev had worn when they first met, implying that he'd been given a private code that deciphered society in ways Grant would never pick apart. In the world's eye, success had since made Grant more than Ev's social equal, but it did not erase the memory of Ev's putting him down when they were young.

"You want to talk about the *Post,* I guess," Reston said in the car. "I thought you'd be along. I spent the morning with Laurie trying to figure out a strategy."

The usual story at the restaurant. The owner of the Union Square Café made a fuss over Grant, steered them to a nice table, and stayed chatting for a minute, so that everyone in the place was turning around. He was being polite but not paying any special homage to Repton. And Ev was grinning away behind the oversize glasses he wore to give some distinction to his long WASP face, lapping up whatever attention spilled over, but—and Grant knew him well—grinding his teeth.

The equation frustrated all network executives. They were the bosses in every usual sense, but a large dimension overflowed their authority. The public couldn't take its eyes off the talent, the on-air stars. Grant had long ago stopped being embarrassed. It paid not only his ridiculous salary but Repton's. So every time he looked past Ev, Grant would catch a knowing look across the room. Part of the routine.

"By the way," Repton said, "I got your note about Sherm Glass. I'll call him and make a date. You know what he wants?"

"Contract talk, he told me."

"God, is it that time again?" Through the big glasses, his pale blue eyes looked so astonished that Grant was sure he'd had the contract out that morning and knew to the hour when it expired.

"When are you taking some time off this summer? It's easy, this year. No conventions or anything to get in the way."

"We haven't decided yet. Maybe some sailing; maybe I'll spend some time in California at the vineyard."

"Pretty hot there in the summer, isn't it?" The well-heeled Easterner's instinctive reservations about California. "You and Win"—nobody called Winona *Win;* she hated it—"should come and spend some time with Edie and me on Martha's Vineyard. Sail your boat over from Maine. Much cooler. Lots of interesting people."

"I know. All the people we see in New York."

As he was speaking, Grant had a vision of Edie, pretty woman with a ripe mouth who always gave him interested looks from very wide, clear eyes. He thought of her in L. L. Bean wraparound skirts, Ev in pants with whales on them; playing golf, tennis (they weren't sailors), having cocktails, dinners. He doubted in a summer they ever met anyone they didn't already know.

Grant said, "Maybe I'll get up into the Cascades for a few days. It'll be cool enough there."

"Not nervous after your bad time there?"

"No, I feel it'd be good to get back."

"Like getting back on a horse that's thrown you? Edie says that. But, jeez, Grant, you damn nearly died that time . . . like your friend. I think I'd be scared off for life. And you've got to be careful. You're not a kid anymore. None of us are, or is it none of us is? Whichever." He laughed. "Let's order."

If he was avoiding the subject, Grant wasn't.

"What did you decide to do about the piece in the *Post*—you and Laurie?"

Repton never answered anything directly. "Well, there are two parts to it, aren't there? One is, who's talking to the *Post*? The second is the substance of it, the facts."

"What facts?"

"Well, the ratings. They're facts, or numbers that we treat as facts. We can't deny them. Everyone else knows them, so we can't pretend they don't exist."

"We can say they're not important. We can act worried about them or we can act not worried. Sounds to me as if someone's been acting worried and the *Post* picked that up. If no one was worried, the *Post* wouldn't have had a story."

"But nobody's been talking to them."

"Well, obviously somebody has."

"Nobody has officially."

"The point is someone's been sounding worried."

"Now, the ratings matter, Grant. You can't just dismiss them. They matter."

"OK, but going down two-tenths of a point doesn't matter unless somebody makes a big deal out of it."

"It's the direction, not the amount. They were going up. They've turned around. That's what they notice."

"Who's they? Network? Corporate?"

"Network and corporate. Both."

"So that's where it comes from? They're making the big deal out of it?"

"Not a big deal yet. Not a major big deal."

"Big enough for someone to tell the *Post*."

"If it came from there . . ."

"And they're giving you a hard time."

"Sure, but I don't bother you about this stuff."

"Ratings always go down in the spring and summer. Better weather, people are outside, they see less television."

"True. But we're having the summer sag from a lower base this year."

"I hear you're doing an audience survey about the show."

"Yeah, the new corporate guys asked for it. It's out of our hands. They've contracted it out to some people they've used before."

"But you know about it?"

"Oh, sure."

"Why didn't you tell me?"

Ev laughed. "Oh, come on, Grant! There's all kinds of stuff we do that I don't bother you with. I don't come running every time they want us to save some more money on foreign coverage, or want to trim another percent off salaries and benefits. That's my worry, not yours. Market research, ratings, all that crap, is what I'm paid to do, so you guys with the talent can put the stuff on the air that earns our keep."

"What's the survey for?"

"Well, since you ask, they want to know why we're losing market share. They say they do it for all their products. Phone surveys, focus groups . . ."

"Focus groups? Great to be just another product out there in the big consumer world."

"Now, don't start coming on naïve and idealistic. There are no white hats just because we're selling news. We're not a protected species anymore."

"So how endangered are we?"

"What d'you mean?"

"Your corporate masters collect all their market research, analyze their focus groups, and decide—what?"

"Who knows?"

"You know."

"I don't know."

"You know what the options are."

"Well, so do you."

"Have they spelled them out?"

"For Christ's sake, Grant, nobody's spelled anything out! They're doing some fucking market research. You want to call a congressional hearing? They do it all the time. Audience research. The network does it. We do it. What's got into you? As long as I've known you, you've always been above this crap."

"What's got into me is the *New York Post* saying some people here want me out."

"That's crazy. That really is crazy."

"Are you going to *say* it's crazy; are you going to put out a statement?"

"Look, you're the big-deal journalist! You want Laurie to put out a press release saying there are no plans to change the anchor of 'The Evening News'? All you do is give the story more legs. The only thing is to ignore it."

"That's the strategy?"

"Don't you think it's the right one?"

Grant might have thought it was the right tactic if he hadn't also thought—more, felt—there was something going on.

Then Repton changed the subject and the tone. "Something I wanted to ask you. Is it true you made a financial settlement when your friend Tony Weldon was killed? For his wife? Somebody told me."

Grant was startled. "Where in hell did you hear that?"

"Someone told me."

"Who told you?"

"Someone we both know."

"Well, tell whoever it is to shut up about it."

"My informant thinks it reflects well on you. I was told in a way that made you sound like a very decent human being."

"And you were surprised?"

"Yes, between us, I think it was a hell of a thing to do. I admire you for it."

"I'm serious, Ev; don't repeat it. OK? It's important to me to keep it private."

"OK, fine."

"Now, when is all this market research supposed to be finished? When do you get the results?"

"A couple of months, I think. End of the summer, probably—after Labor Day."

"This time I want to know what they find out. OK?"

"OK."

"Before I read about it on 'Page Six'?"

"Of course."

As they left the restaurant a young man said to his companion, "Look, it's Grant Munro!"

He shook Grant's hand. "We watch your show all the time."

"Where are you from?"

"Hershey, Pennsylvania."

"Fine. Nice to meet you."

"We hate to bother you, but would you mind if we took a picture?"

"No problem. Happy to do it."

So Ev was forced to take their camera and shoot Grant with the folks from Hershey.

"You don't know how much this means to us."

"It's a pleasure."

In the car going back uptown, Repton said casually, "What d'you think of Bill Donovan?"

"Very smooth. Very green. Still has a local flavor about him, but I guess he's catching on fast."

"I think he's a great find. He really got his feet wet in a hurry on the Clinton story."

Grant's view of Donovan was quite different, but he was still wondering how Repton had found out about Teresa. Not from the bank. The only other person who knew was the broker who'd sold the stock, Tom Wharton . . . who, of course, was Repton's broker! Ev had introduced him years ago.

Back in his office, Grant called Wharton. "Did you tell Ev Repton about the block of stock I sold and what it was for?"

"Gee, I guess I did. He has some of the same stock."

"Well, damn it, Tom, do not tell anyone else!"

"I won't. I thought it was a real decent thing you did and—"

"I don't care. It's nobody's business but mine. I'm serious. I'm tempted to find another broker. I am really pissed off."

"OK, OK! I get the message. It was dumb for me to say anything. I thought you and Ev were close friends."

"Wrong!" said Grant and hung up.

And Wharton wondered what had got into Grant Munro, who in twenty-five years had never shown such anger.

6

The note Christopher Siefert scribbled after his first few minutes in the presence of Grant Munro—and that's how it felt, in the presence—was *Eerie self-possession.* And later, when that first interview for his *Time* profile was over, he added, *Self-absorption like a strong vacuum that has sucked up all curiosity about others, subtracted curiosity, except about himself, a black hole of self-absorption. (Maybe too strong?)*

Years ago someone had said Siefert's long profiles had a novelist's touch, although critics had not admired his only novel. Siefert enjoyed trying to winnow out celebrity's distinguishing traits, its effects on personality. It was a game to discern the psychological tics success had implanted. Often, perversely, celebrity seemed to subtract personality, even from someone as high octane in her manner as Joan Rivers; fame long coveted had scared personality deep into its burrow.

In Grant Munro, it had left on the surface a mask of genial modesty, professional grace under praise. Christopher Siefert was expert in calibrating the vacancies in celebrity personalities, in finding ways to express the subtle signs of manufacture, the seams and joins in their pseudo-personas.

If he felt superior to many of his profile subjects, Siefert had some reason. He was more intelligent than many; his Harvard and Oxford degrees made him vastly better educated and better read; often more discerning and sophisticated.

His own abilities had been recognized quickly. His 1977 book, *Vietnam and the American Psyche* ("brilliant, deeply and achingly insightful"—*The New Yorker*), appearing at the time of the Carter amnesty, had been a *New York Times* best-seller for nine weeks. It had been nominated for a Pulitzer and only narrowly defeated (how narrowly he knew, bitterly, from a friend on the committee), but it was long out of print. Spotting it recently on a used bookstall near Zabar's, Siefert wondered who in the neighborhood considered it no longer essential in his library. Still, it had served to launch him as a writer of promise, assuring that his next book would get serious attention. But that collection of recycled magazine profiles and essays, not original work, fell short of reviewers' expectations. The novel published in 1984 was dismissed by the *New York Times Book Review* as "watery Updike." When the Berlin Wall fell, Siefert had tried to mine the same seam of psychological insight that had worked for Vietnam, but *The Psychic Impact of the Cold War* did not put him back among the authors who were regulars on television. Its failure coincided with, or precipitated—he wasn't sure— the death of his wilting suburban marriage.

The job at Time Inc., twice hopefully abandoned and twice expediently resumed, had gradually become a career. He wrote some criticism, but editors considered him too mordant, too supercilious to use often. At book parties, publicists began noticing that he drank more and stayed until it was awkward not to invite him to dinner. In fact, he was drinking too seriously to work well the night Elizabeth Deegan saw the state he was in at a book party, and hustled him off to eat. Years before, they'd had an affair when she was a *Time* researcher, but she'd drifted off to *Fortune,* then into and out of a Wall Street marriage. The only satisfactory relic of that was a handsome apartment on Central Park West— her ex-husband preferred the Greenwich house. Elizabeth, now a cookbook editor, prettily overweight, nervous at forty-four about re-entering the singles' scene in Manhattan, was grateful to find Siefert and willing to fix him up.

She said he looked awful and insisted he have the medical checkup he'd put off since his divorce. Besides evidence of his drinking, the lab report came back with a high PSA count, and he had to submit to multiple undignified biopsies, which revealed enough malignancy to justify a prostatectomy. He'd recovered, overcome several weeks of incontinence, but sexual function remained unnervingly—he tried to think of a safe word—elusive.

So not only did the Christopher Siefert who faced Grant Munro for the first interview feel personally depleted, but the man he met looked ready to do a commercial for a fitness club: tan, lean, not an ounce of unwanted weight. Siefert knew they were almost the same age; he'd turned sixty in February, Grant would do so in October. Yet Siefert believed he looked older by fifteen years.

So, added to the formidable armor of self-confidence Grant presented to the world was this athletic body, taller than Christopher by several inches, with thick brown hair, only tinged with gray, where Siefert was half bald. And Grant's clothes added yet another layer to this packaged confidence: discreetly, casually expensive.

From reading the file, Siefert knew approximately what this "fellow journalist" (he put derisive quotation marks around it) had been paid for the past two decades. Adding all this up, he was there to profile one of the richest, best-looking, most successful men in America, on whom assurance sat like a silk hat . . . No, that was his own defensiveness and probably literary condescension; there was nothing cheaply ostentatious here, nothing in dubious taste. Whatever his humble background (and Siefert needed more information), Grant Munro carried his success sleekly, with a disarming modesty (well, a practiced modesty), and every sign of gentility.

In short, everything conspired to raise the bile in Christopher M. Siefert, and that was just as he liked it. He knew that the jealousy, envy, and antipathy a subject initially provoked served to energize him as a writer, give him a force to work against; an emotional polarity that would run through the finished piece, with the negative charge neutralized as balancing admiration leaked in along the way. That's how it had worked for Siefert in characters as diverse as Muhammad Ali and Newt Gingrich.

He set the small tape recorder running. He liked early questions that seemed innocent.

TRANSCRIPT:

CHRIS: Grant Munro interview. OK. Let's start. Is being a household name, a celebrity, an advantage for a journalist, or a disadvantage?

GRANT: It's both, of course. Great for access, getting calls returned. But that's more the influence of the program than of me. It's a disadvantage, though, if it gets in the way.

CHRIS: I read that in the last campaign, covering some primary races, you attracted bigger crowds than some of the candidates. In New Hampshire, right?

GRANT: Well, that's an old story, and exaggerated. I went out for one day to observe. I wasn't there covering the campaign; we had correspondents with each of the candidates. I just wanted to get some flavor.

CHRIS: But you did attract bigger crowds than the presidential candidates?

GRANT: In a couple of places. You know those events in New Hampshire. Very intimate, and the media tend to overwhelm them now in any case.

CHRIS: You're not bothered by this?

GRANT: Yeah, I'm uncomfortable with it.

(Siefert wrote: *NH campaign—smart, disarming.* With the tape recorder providing a full transcript, his notes could be sparse.)

CHRIS: But the advantages. Air travel, for instance, gets to be more of a hassle all the time; your name must smooth the way for you . . .

GRANT: Sure. It does.

CHRIS: Private jets instead of airline schedules.

GRANT: Sometimes. The networks are a lot tighter with dough than they used to be.

• • •

GRANT HATED questions touching the privileges of his position, although he was practiced at answering with no appearance of guilt. But as the phrases left his mouth, he knew they could be turned into positive statements. He could see the caption under a picture: *Anchor: Celebrity gets in the way of journalism.*

Siefert was trying to imagine what life must be like for a man in Grant's position. His thoughts kept coming back to the money, reportedly six million dollars a year! How much did Grant keep after taxes, and what did he do with it? In his notebook, Siefert jotted down: *Tax Lawyer.* He wanted to know everything about it. He wanted to see inside Grant's apartment on Fifth Avenue, his house in Boothbay Harbor, his boat, his vineyard in California. He wanted to know just what else Grant spent his money on; but, fundamentally, for his personal curiosity, Siefert wanted to know what it felt like to have that kind of money. Besides a tax lawyer, he needed somebody who advised the rich, some private banker or investment expert. Elizabeth might have some ideas from her days at *Fortune.* Or the *Time* researchers could dig one up.

Other than the wealth, it was a stretch to think himself into a role where one was paid so much court. Siefert had felt waves of deference and courtierlike awe emanating from Grant's sanctum on his first visit to the network. The atmosphere in the corridors had the democratic, free-spirited casualness of journalism (shirtsleeves, first-name camaraderie) that gave it a surface ease, but he sensed beneath a stronger current, magnetic lines of force coming from the star, growing stronger as he was handed from the lobby security desk, to P.R. assistant, to Laurie Jacobs, to Grant's assistant, Angela. Then Grant, perfectly unaffected, charmingly informal, in an office large enough to accommodate a conversation area with sofa, two easy chairs, and coffee table, away from the work area of desk and computer terminal. There were two walls of floor-to-ceiling books and one of photographs of sailboats and mountains.

His shirtsleeves rolled up, tie loosened, like any newsman, rising athletically to shake hands, Grant was first to say what Siefert had intended: "I think we've met a few times. I see you at the Century now and then."

Smooth. He managed, politely indicating a chair or the sofa, then sitting down after Siefert, to make him feel that he had Grant's total attention. He scribbled: *Eerie self possession,* but sensed no curiosity, or perhaps curiosity only about what Siefert intended to do to him.

Grant said, "I really admired your *Vietnam and the American Psyche.* I read it when it first came out and I was trying to explain the strains the war produced. I still have it up there . . ." With the special eyesight of an author's vanity, Siebert instantly spotted the spine on one of the shelves across the office. "I've gone back to parts of it a few times, and I've quoted it in commentaries. You're meeting a fan."

And a diplomat, Siefert decided, enjoying the awkward first steps in the dance of mutual seduction that always defined the roles of profiler and profilee.

"Laurie tells me you want to do a profile?" As though it was the first time Grant had focused on the reason, when Siefert knew his approach had thrown the network into a little tizzy of excitement and anxiety. Nobody was blasé about a *Time* cover.

"Right. A substantial piece about you and your show . . . possibly a cover, depending on the flow of news . . . you know how that is. We never commit our souls absolutely to a cover in case it gets bumped by major news, but that's the intention right now. We'd like to run it at the end of the summer, just as the new season begins."

"Is that the peg, the new season, or is there another angle?" Grant asked.

"No angle. More an exploration of where television news is and where it's going."

Grant laughed. "Well, it's going to hell, of course. And if you want to talk about that, I'd be happy to. I haven't made any secret about how I feel."

"I know. I read your speech to the Radio TV News Directors. Gadarene swine was strong stuff."

"I meant it to be."

"Did that image come from your familiarity with the Bible as a child?"

"No. Don Evans suggested it—he's the senior writer on the show—and it expressed what I felt."

"I sensed from Laurie Jacobs that the network wasn't thrilled . . . they hope we won't dwell on that view of things?"

"Of course. They'd prefer we emphasize the positive."

"Is there a positive?"

"Well, if you're Everett Repton—the news president; you'll talk to him—he'd probably say something like: We're running the most serious news operation we can in this media environment . . . can't be the purists we thought we were twenty years ago."

"And what's your take on that rationale?"

"My take? Even bowing to the spirit of the times, if we had the confidence to treat the audience as adults, not children who'd throw tantrums if they got spinach instead of ice cream, and promoted that heavily, we might get a good audience. But nobody dares; no network is willing to make a radical change from the way it's done now. All news shows have to seem user friendly, touchy feely, minimum spinach, max ice cream."

"And yet you go on doing it every day."

"Oh, sure. I don't want to leave it yet. I don't want to abandon even this defensive, fall-back position. I think we should resist day by day: block the pandering lead when we can, insist that important foreign and political stuff gets covered adequately, kill the sillier notions for audience-building gimmicks."

"Well, I'd like to explore your feelings about the business more thoroughly, looking back at your own career, some personal things about you, you know the kind of thing . . ."

"How much time do you need? I want to make sure I'm free."

"I don't want to hurry it. I'd like to talk for a couple of hours, on the record, talk to people in your shop, observe your news operation, then have time for more interview with you. If you're willing, I'd like to meet your wife. Winona? See you in your home setting, maybe have a lunch or dinner, other words, time to get to know you."

"Sounds more like a book than a magazine piece."

"I like to feel my way into a subject. Not rush at a story with ready-made conclusions."

"Nice luxury. I wish I could practice that kind of journalism."

As he was leaving, Grant said warmly, "I hear you've recently been through a prostate operation. I guess we all worry about that now." It was said with such apparent sincerity, it was impossible not to feel warmed by the empathy, eyes, smile, friendly handshake.

"Oh, I'm fine," Siefert said, wondering where in hell Grant had picked that up.

"I saw Dick Schoenfeld at a dinner party the other night, and he told me confidentially, knowing I was going to be seeing you. I'm glad it's OK."

IT WAS A pleasant June day, not too hot, and Siefert decided to walk. The doctor had said walking was the best therapy to counter the aftereffects of the surgery.

If Grant was as self-absorbed as most of the celebrities Siefert encountered, he masked it well. After a half-hour conversation, Siefert understood why he'd reached the top. Journalistic and broadcasting skills aside, he had personal qualities that would have carried him far in politics, the military, anything where personality underlay achievement. Seemingly unaffected, affable, open—and smart.

"Well . . ." Elizabeth greeted him affectionately, "you look better for being back at work. Tired?"

"No, I feel fine."

She led the way into her spacious kitchen. "Come and taste something." She held up a wooden spoon. "What do you think?"

"Am I allowed to know what it is before I say?"

"Say first, know later."

"It's good. Tasty. Garlicky. Salty. Fishy. Good."

"Too salty? Too garlicky?"

"No, pretty good. Makes me want a drink, though."

"Well, that's fine. It's an appetizer. Brandade de morue. Cookbook I'm working on. It's a spread made from salt cod, potatoes, olive oil, garlic. You like it?"

"If I say yes, do I get a glass of wine?"

"You get that anyway." She pulled some white wine from the fridge and poured each of them a glass. "Tell me, how was the—what did you call him—the posturing, overpaid mannequin?"

"Certainly overpaid, but no mannequin, and no posturing. Very impressive, in fact. Smart. Candid. Unaffected." Siefert settled into a chair at the broad scrubbed table that served for cooking and dining. "On top of that, he loved my Vietnam book."

"Smart guy. I'd love your book too if you were coming to do cover on me."

"It sounded genuine. He had it there, on his bookshelf."

Elizabeth laughed affectionately, kissed her fingers, and reached across the table to touch his lips. "You writers! Praise my book and you got me. What an easy lay!"

"He knew about my operation. Dick Schoenfeld told him at a dinner party. In confidence."

"You upset about that?"

"No, I guess not. But this is going to be more interesting than I thought. His self-confidence is amazing. But there have to be some chinks there."

"So you like the assignment now?"

"Yes. It's an amazing phenomenon, when you come to think of it, that our society has created these news gods . . . and made them so famous . . . and so rich! Imagine being paid six million bucks a year!"

"Well, it's just a market, like everything else. You're supposed to eat this on toast or bread. Try it. I'm glad you're working again. It's put a sparkle in your eye."

"You know, according to the network P.R. handouts, Munro has won every award known to man, except maybe the Nobel Peace Prize, and there wasn't a sign of them in his office; no autographed pictures of our hero mingling with the great and famous; only pictures of sailboats and mountains."

"With our hero on them, I presume."

"I guess so; I didn't look that closely."

"And what's that a sign of, Dr. Freud? Indifference to fame? Or inverted snobbery? Got so many, don't need to show them off? What did he say about it?"

"Didn't ask him."

"Oh, you should! Ask him next time. I'd love to know what he says. It must have been a conscious decision, putting them away."

"I suggested getting together for dinner with his wife. Would you like that?"

"Sure, I guess so. What's she do?"

"She's a social worker."

"Well, that's kind of down to earth."

"But what else could it mean—the absence of trophies? I've got so many I don't need to show them? You're supposed to take them for granted?"

"Genuine modesty? I'm not worth all the fuss they make over me?"

"Or what we do isn't worth the fuss, doesn't deserve the celebrity, the money . . ."

"You're obsessed by the money!"

"Well, try to imagine getting by on six million a year. How can anything be worth that much?"

"Ask yourself how can Demi Moore be worth twenty million a picture. He's cute."

"He's what?"

"Grant Munro's cute. He's appealing. It makes you feel good to watch him. You obviously got some of that in person. He's a nice guy. And he must be smart, because he found your G spot."

"I'll tell you something else about him: he speaks in complete sentences."

"Did you assume he was illiterate? You've never watched him on the air. It's not just the news. It's all the stuff they do at conventions and election nights, and things. I've listened to him a lot. All the Princess Di funeral, I watched him. He's pretty smart. At least he *sounds* smart to me."

7

www.hollygo.com

Question for the day, babes in teeveenewsland, come to me from a gorgeous sister at Taupe (well, I don't xactly know she gorgeous, but she kinda sound gorgeous, know what I mean?). Anyway this gal work her butt off I'm guessin for Excedrin Headache at the White House. She don't say so right out but I'm gettin the vibes. She sure soundin like someone singin the Excedrin Headache blues. Her question to me: Hollygo, you talk about the I–Man all time like you got somethin goin wit him. So tell me, how come he keep hittin up on the boy correspondents, makin fun of they accents, and all that jive, and he never hit up on da wimmins? The I–Man always pickin on Grecian Formula, Lone Ranger, and Gregory Peck, and he give da wimmins a free ride. Why is that? Only hollygo willin to tell these star broadcastin broads where they get off. Some of the girl friends at Taupe want to know?

Well, darlin, I print your question but I ain't no Ann Landers with a bag full of answers. So I just put it out there for the I–Man, Dean of the Queens School of Journalism (don't that have a nice ring now? Dean of the Queens? Dean a da Queens? Don'tcha luv it?).

Now Hollygo like to state for the record, like they say in them congressional hearins, she ain't got nuthin goin wit the I-Man. Nu-thin! Hollygo listen to him in her bed of sin, lollin back on the black satin sheets under her leopard-skin throw (faux leopard, Brigitte!) lettin my boyfriend bring me a coffee but keepin my eyemask on cos Hollygo let nobudy, no-body, see her without her makeup, darlin, and that take an hour . . . I think we slippin away from the point here. Anyway, Hollygo listen to de I-Man for the penetratin interviews, man he get to the bowels of politics and stuff, and the I-Man picks Hollygo off the Internet for the real inside stuff on teeveenews. Synergy is what we got, nuthin else. Hollygo never met the I-Man, and he sure as hell never met me, so how could we have anythin goin, less it phone sex, and the I-Man gave up phone sex when he went national.

But she got a point, don'tcha think, the sister at Taupe Broadcastin? The I-Man been goin after Grecian Formula somethin awful for the way he talks. He pickin on the Lone Ranger for his weave. So the brother got a weave? But the anchor takin the real slings and arrows right now (slings and arrows, that Shakespeare, darlin . . . you never heard tell of him? Honey, for a dead white male that dude had the moves, like a loong time ago, he invented the drag queen, made cross-dressin into high art, with a whole theater full of she-males to act them out! Talk about avant-garde!). Anyway, like I was sayin, the anchor takin the worst hits just now is Gregory Peck. He gettin it all ways; all the gossip queens on his butt, sayin he too old. People inside his Beige network must be feedin the rumors (you heard it first on Hollygo) they want Gregory to ease on down the road and make way for Billy Boy Blew, sorry, I mean Blue, in Washington.

Now *Time* magazine (you heard of that? You grandaddy maybe had some wit his *Playboys* in the attic), now *Time* magazine has sent a big-name writer over to Beige to write a cover story on Gregory. Gregory friends worry, that ain't gonna do him no good. Does that have the smell of death about it to you?

You get on the cover of *Time* and you either end up as President of the United States or in jail. Folks at Beige all linin up, hopin they goin be interviewed by the big-time *Time* man, Christopher M. Siefert, so's they can diss Gregory or luv him. Hollygo hope some they dudes gonna say somethin nice about him, cos, like the I-Man say, it don't get any better than that. So now I waitin for the I-Man to get old Gregory on his show and give him one them sweet-talkin, buddy-buddy, locker-room, male-bondin interviews he so good at, and give Gregory a chance! The I-Man sell everthing else. Sell Gregory! Sell decency. Sell family values! (Ain't no one ever talked about Gregory Peck havin trouble keepin his zipper zipped, unlike some dudes in teeveenews—or the White House maybe.)

Anyway, good question, darlin! Keep em comin and tell Excedrin Headache to buy longer skirts, willya? I'm tired of seein those bony knees in her White House Lawn standuppers! Don'tcha luv it?

By the time Ernie Schmid got to the diner these mornings, his stomach wasn't just growling, it was almost barking at him. Making it on unemployment money meant only two solid meals a day, and he always woke up ravenous. It was hunger that propelled him out of bed, out of the dingy room, to buy the paper and get a jump on the help-wanted ads. Most of the creeps he saw in the jobless line were probably still asleep. A lot more blacks and Asians on the line than there used to be.

At 6:15 he dropped his coins in the vending machine for the *Minneapolis Star-Tribune* and crossed the street to the cheerful chrome of the diner. He was the first customer, and it took the waitress a few minutes to plop down his eggs, hash and potatoes, toast and coffee. While waiting, Ernie salivated so copiously he had to pull a paper napkin out of the metal dispenser to wipe his lips. Only when the food arrived and he had gorged two mouthfuls did he open the paper, expertly, to the classifieds. He could skim it now like a pro, flash a glance down the column to see, once again, no one looking for photo lab technicians.

More relaxed, Ernie then read the column systematically from top to bottom, automatically skipping ads demanding stuff like college degrees. Fuck it. Nothing new. Another long empty day ahead. Slow down. Taking his time, Ernie poured a generous blob of ketchup onto his plate and dipped a fried potato. He was turning toward the front page when he recognized a picture under the caption *John Wheatly Admired St. Paul Photographer Dies.*

No kidding! As quick as that? Because it was . . . what? Only five months since John had let him go. After fighting it for years, taking all the newest stuff, John would begin to feel better, definitely look better, and ease up on the drugs; then it would come back and slam him until finally nothing worked. He got so weak, he couldn't run the business. And now the paper said just like that: "The cause of death was AIDS."

If only he'd been more interested when John encouraged him to take pictures instead of just running the negatives through the developing and printing machines and making occasional enlargements. As far as he knew, John had no one to leave the business to, so it was probably all sitting there, all that good equipment. If he'd known what was going to happen and had applied himself, maybe John would have let him take over. Then he'd have something substantial. His own business. Easy enough. Passport picture? Sure. Stand here. Watch the light. OK, just a few minutes. Wipe the twin Polaroids, put 'em in the cutter. Eight dollars and seventy-five cents. And the portraits people always wanted. Not that hard. Big studio camera. Just have to get the focus sharp. The rest was all running customers' film through the processing machine and packaging up the automatic prints. If he'd shown a spark of interest . . . John was really a nice guy and might've . . . Trouble was, Ernie always felt a little uneasy in there with him in the dark room, knowing John was gay . . . although nothing ever happened. John never bothered him. Hey! Now Ernie remembered something John had said one night when they stayed late to process hundreds of high school prom pictures promised the next morning. Routine stuff, so they'd printed the enlargements assembly-line fashion, John loading the negatives and paper into the enlarger and making the exposures, Ernie grabbing the exposed sheets, slipping them into machine . . . so automatic that John was talking about all kinds of things to relieve the tedium.

What would the kids think of their photos thirty years later? How embarrassed people often were by how they looked when they were young and unguarded.

Then he said, "Ann Murrow would probably give a fortune to hide some pictures I took of her years ago, when she was the weather girl on the local station here—"

"Ann Murrow—the woman on television? The big star?"

"She was a runner-up in some beauty contest, Miss Minnesota or Miss Minneapolis; I can't remember. She came from here."

"I didn't know that."

"Well, she changed her name after that. Her real name was Anna Malakoff. She changed it to Ann Murrow when she became a news person. Probably thought it'd make people think of Ed Murrow."

"Who's Ed Murrow?"

"God, Ernie, everyone knows that! He was a big newsman when I was a kid . . . anyway, there was this guy she was hanging out with, young businessman on the make, I think he owned the TV station, and she said she wanted some provocative shots to give him a kick. So she brought a lot of sexy underwear and did all kinds of hot poses, the stuff you see in *Penthouse* and *Hustler*. I bet they'd pay a hundred thousand bucks for them now. Imagine: Ann Murrow girlie shots."

"What was she like?"

"Back then? She was all sweetie-pie to me when she wanted some pictures, but I didn't like her much. One of those people who would do anything to get ahead."

"Anything? Like what?"

"Like . . . anything."

Awed by the sum mentioned, Ernie had asked, "Would you ever sell them to a magazine?"

"No, it wouldn't be fair to her. She must have forgotten about them long ago. But if she remembered, she'd probably pay me to burn them."

"So you could make a lot of money that way?"

"No, that's blackmail. I'm not that hungry."

"But a hundred thousand dollars!" Ernie said.

"I'm just guessing."

Now Ernie repeated to himself: A hundred thousand dollars. And a delicious excitement suffused him; he could hardly contain it. Still before seven on the diner clock. No one would be around this early. He paid and walked rapidly down the street, trying not to run. It was only a few blocks away, in a row of old buildings restored, shopfront on the street, studio and darkroom at the back where you entered from an alleyway. No one in sight. He slipped in easily, remembering the four-digit code for the keypad lock on the door and the other one to disarm the security system.

It was strange to be in the place after so many months, and knowing John was dead, but nothing looked changed. He peered into the empty shop for a moment, noting the venetian blinds pulled down over the glass door and the display window. Carefully shutting the door to the back, he turned on a light. He knew exactly where John filed his negatives, and the system—simple and alphabetical. He was perspiring as he walked his fingers through the *M*'s, didn't find Murrow, then remembered the changed name and looked back for *Ma*'s. And there it was, under Malakoff, a manila envelope containing not only negatives in their own plastic envelopes but two proof sheets. Ernie took them to the table, turned on a light, and grabbed the loupe. They were sensational! Artfully lit and perfectly exposed, two-and-a-quarter-inch square, fine grain, shot on the Hasselblad—and the poses! Wow, this gal had no shame. She was young, and her body was terrific. But the knowing way she posed, it was like she was teasing someone to fuck her. She had a Santa Claus hat and red panties, more or less on, like offering herself as a Christmas present. In one shot she was sucking on a giant candy cane. Easy to figure what that meant. Incredible, knowing who she was now, that dignified broad that interviewed the president, for God's sake! Who went around the world doing heavy investigative and political stuff. She was a big star. She got paid millions a year. She was on the cover of magazines. They even wrote about her in *People* magazine! And these pictures—wow! Looking at them closely made Ernie gulp and feel horny.

He reached for the color negatives to check them and put a strip on the light table. Perfect condition.

Jesus, I'm going to be rich.

Ernie put everything in the manila envelope, closed the file drawer, and turned off the lights. He opened the door a crack and checked the alleyway: still empty. He closed the door and punched in the code to reset the burglar alarm. The signal turned from green to red. Then he let himself out the back door. Still not a soul in sight. Easy!

He walked home, shaking with excitement. No one would miss them. Who else knew they were there? No need to worry about finger-prints. His prints were all over that place anyway. It was almost like John meant him to have them. Like compensation for getting AIDS because he screwed around with guys, finally getting real sick and throwing Ernie out of work. For five months he'd found nothing. His girlfriend had gone off with some other guy. He'd sold his car and pawned his stereo and had to move into this godforsaken rooming house, where everything stank. But not much longer. Ernie closed his door. There was no chair to sit on, so he lay down on the bed. He pulled the pictures out to have another look. He needed to be real careful planning this, real careful—and smart.

First, he had to have some prints. Had to prove to her he had the pictures. Maybe send her a couple of prints. Or he could cut a couple off the proof sheet . . . but then she'd have to look at them with a magnifying glass. She wouldn't see the real whammy shots these could make. But go up to full color eight-by-ten, and she'd get the message. The grabbier the prints, the more she'd be likely to pay. To make prints, he'd have to crank up the darkroom and mix fresh solutions. But that was easy; he'd done it almost every day for two years. And there were plenty of chemicals in the store cupboard; wouldn't cost him nothing. Easy enough to get in. Who'd know if he slipped in and made a few prints? And there were photo-mailing envelopes there, with stiffeners built in—official-looking—and labels—all that shit. No. Not smart. Those mailers and labels were printed with John's shop name and address. Better use plain envelopes, like the Priority Mail envelopes John had sent him to get at the post office for rush jobs. Make it look more important, more urgent.

But maybe it'd be safer at night, with no one around? Maybe not, because the lights'd show. Sometimes cops came by, checking when he and John were working late. Maybe early morning, like today. No one around, but less suspicious if someone did see him slipping in or out.

Jesus, there was a lot to think about. He needed to find her address in New York. Her home address would be best, but how would he ever get that? Her office? That had to be in the phonebook. A New York phonebook? Maybe the public library.

Then he had to have a return address. Not this dump, where mail was left on the front hall floor and got walked on, and everybody pawed through it. He needed a mailbox. Heard about that from some guy who'd been having an affair with a married woman. Rented a mailbox in another name. That's what he needed. A mailoffice box in another name, so they couldn't trace him if she decided to get lawyers on to him, or got the cops involved. Although maybe she wouldn't want lawyers or cops looking at these pictures.

He sat up on the edge of the bed and examined the proof sheets again. Wouldn't he love to make out with a gal like that! Perfect body and obviously dying for it. Probably did everything in the book. Hell of a lot classier than Maria, who had ditched him. It had been months since he'd had any.

No wonder he could feel a little horny looking at these shots even in the miniature proofs. But this wasn't getting the work done. Had to get on with it. Before anyone began asking what to do with John's business. What happened in a case like this? Did he leave a will? If he knew he was dying, he probably did. So, somewhere some lawyer would soon be getting busy—doing what? John had given the impression he didn't have any family, or any he cared about, like Ernie himself, with his parents gone and only some cousins he saw once in Duluth and didn't like. He liked being alone. Since his mother died, he'd been back over there only once, driving by the house when he got his car . . . just to see how the neighborhood looked, now that he had no connection with it. Her will had taken months to sort out, and when her furniture and stuff was sold and the lawyers were paid, he got a measly $2100. He'd expected it was going to be a lot more, like about $6000. Like, she was always talking about saving money and she never stopped working. He could hear her saying, "Don't just sit there all day, dreaming." True. He had to get a move on.

First, where to leave the photos. He didn't trust anyone in this dump. Some of the boarders he saw on the stairs looked like they'd just come out of prison, and the women he wouldn't touch with a ten-foot pole. He pulled out the bottom drawer in the chest, which always stuck so he had to seesaw it back and forth to get it open. He put the manila envelope under his sweaters and sports shirts and closed the drawer with a squeak. But as he stood up to look in the mirror and comb his hair, he thought better, wrenched the drawer open, and put the envelope under the mattress, right over by the wall. Maybe safer.

His hair needed cutting, and the cheapest was about five bucks. The thought of money made him hungry again—and it wasn't even ten o'clock. Maybe there was still some cash in the register. He should look when he went back. He wet the comb under the tap of his bedroom sink and combed his hair carefully, rehearsing the conversation about a mailbox.

"I'm in and out of the city, moving around."

But you couldn't look like a slob downtown. Ernie changed to a dark sports shirt with a collar, worn just a couple of times, put on his pale windbreaker, then checked it out. He looked OK.

9

Christopher Siefert had been forcing himself to watch television, starting with "The Evening News with Grant Munro," and the competition on the rival networks, all news channels, and syndicated tabloid shows. He'd planned a few days' immersion, but it took a week to cover the network magazines, morning programs, news of showbiz and entertainment, the Sunday talk shows, and public television.

What a relief it was finally to turn the set off, to have silence! How restful to read, be able to focus his attention, not have it driven by the manic pace and noise of the television mind.

Watching had been exhausting, eyes and ears so overstimulated that he kept falling asleep. And this was the utility the average American household—whatever that was—ingested for a statistical seven hours a day?

It was wearing to watch so many dynamic, brightly smiling, perky-eyed, pumped-up, well-coiffed people of both sexes: constantly yapping, shouting, selling, promoting, informing, disclosing, confessing, in an endless adrenaline rush. It seemed the national personality had lost all ability to relax, to be quiet, to be thoughtful. This hyperkinetic pace wasn't confined to the sillier shows; it drove the news programs as well. Trying to analyze it, Siefert supposed the motive must be fear; fear of not being bright and entertaining enough in this hectic, mad, jumpy world in which everyone seemed to have snorted coke or taken vitamin E shots. To be bright, to be dazzling, to effervesce; the effort made him think of vaudeville, the desperation of borderline acts fearing the hook.

He thought of the enervated people out there on the fringes of working America, daytime television addicts: unemployable ghetto dwellers, the discouraged, the incompetent. How could they feel viable in a world that looked like a continuous Miss Personality test in a non-stop beauty pageant? Only the thin, the beautiful, the perky need apply.

Once, in the early sixties, Siefert had reported a story about the grim dichotomy in Washington, life for blacks a few blocks east of the dazzling Kennedy White House. In one row house, with brazen rats staring through a hole in the rotten kitchen ceiling, he remembered going into the darkened front room, surprised that it was full; perhaps a dozen black people sitting in the shadows, saying nothing, watching television in their Plato's cave, observing the shadows of life.

And yet television had the power to put all those forlorn people more in touch with life than any previous generation. They could be illiterate, indifferent, incurious, but the tube routinely showed them things previously known only to the educated and well traveled.

So, what to make of the journalism he had found? In fact, a surprisingly wide range: if people wanted to follow long sessions of the House or Senate, or see news conferences and speeches by American and foreign leaders, they could do it on cable. At the other end of the spectrum were shows as sensational as supermarket tabloids. The last time Siefert could remember watching television extensively, the three networks had had a virtual monopoly and had driven most national print magazines, like *Look* and *Collier's,* out of business. Now, with so many new channels, television had broken up like the magazines, its content, no longer homogenized for a national mass viewership, catering to every sliver of taste and interest. Probably it was healthy in the long run . . . but it certainly produced a lot of crap at present.

He'd been absorbing the research. Almost half the audience that had previously watched one of the network news shows, like Grant Munro's, had adopted the lighter, more sensational, and entertaining shows as reasonable sources of information. More Americans still said they got news from television than from newspapers; but what they called "news" might be a breezy half-hour of showbiz gossip hosted by a woman whose short skirt and crossed thighs were serious program content.

Since many of the defectors constituted the most desirable demographics to advertisers—young consumers aged eighteen to forty-five—it wasn't surprising that the networks were worried. Not surprising that they were dumbing down their flagship news shows to recapture errant viewers.

Siefert thought Grant's news show agreeable to watch, not offensive, but not compelling. You could see and hear the newsmakers, but in brief flashes, like being offered a lick of ice cream from a passing car.

It was also condescending, transparently trying to ingratiate itself with socially alert features on diet and life styles. Even these pandering stories were maddeningly unsatisfying. They breezily cooked up your interest by teasing astonishing information to come, but when it came, it begged too many questions, the examples seemed staged, too neatly contrived to be plausible.

Grant's producers were saying, in effect: This'll do for you, because our market surveys and focus groups tell us precisely what you're capable of absorbing. As Pauline Kael had put it, the true rot set in when you began thinking of "the jerk audience out there."

10

Whenever Joseph Steinman looked down like this from the General Motors Building, his eyes gradually lost focus on the seething activity around the square in front of the Plaza Hotel. And he would feel he was looking down on the affairs of his clients; sometimes like the puppet master who pulled their strings, sometimes like a scrutineer at Vegas, monitoring the croupiers and gamblers from hidden screens, alert to all the weaknesses displayed.

He had good reason to feel benign about his clients. He had made them, and they had made him, very rich. His ten percent of Ann Murrow alone brought his little agency a cool $800,000 a year. And he had others—TV personalities, names printed boldface in the gossip columns—although none with quite the celebrity candlepower of Ann Murrow.

Joe had been working out a scheme to make her a more valuable commodity still. She didn't know yet. He wanted it to be watertight in its logic, dazzling in its simplicity, before she turned those cold blue eyes on him. Her claque in the press thought those eyes full of sincerity and human empathy; Joe Steinman knew them to be windows to a granite soul.

It still amazed him that a woman so feminine, so feline, was driven by such ferocious and unresting ambition. Even now, at forty-five, if she sat in this office, her miniskirt displaying a silky wealth of leg, her mouth cushiony and inviting, her good breasts, shining blond hair, her seductive perfume, all so artfully employed, she could still make him breathless. And sad. If only . . . but she was indifferent to him as a man, he was perfectly aware, although when she wanted something she could still deceive him just enough to sharpen the sexual edge, as she did with the men she interviewed, and her employers—anyone who could be useful to her. Steinman was always useful and knew better than most how she turned on the sexual lights, like an aircraft at night, when she wanted to land. Like her call just now.

"Joey?"

He loathed being called Joey, the nickname his mother had used, but the way she breathed *Joey* made him feel good, like being hugged, and aroused . . . just enough. She could probably calibrate the intensity in hundredths. And he knew that too.

"Joey? Someone in Minnesota has sent me some photographs taken years ago. Taken as a joke. Stupid photographs. He says he has two whole rolls. I'd forgotten they were ever taken. Now he wants me to buy them. I want you to take care of him. Whatever you have to do. Get rid of him. Get rid of the photographs. All of them. He wants a hundred thousand dollars, or he says he'll sell them to *Penthouse* or somewhere. You figure out what to do."

"Are they embarrassing?"

"Joey! Why would I care if they weren't embarrassing? When you're young, you do dumb things, and I did that time—as a joke. I'm embarrassed to have even you see them . . ."

Even you made him wince, relegated to court eunuch.

". . . but I have to trust someone to handle this. I think a lawyer's the wrong person."

"OK. I get it."

"And no police. No blackmail investigation. I want to keep it private. I'm sending the stuff over by messenger."

"OK. Don't worry, I'll handle it. While I've got you, I have an idea I want to run by you . . ."

"Not now. Get rid of this first. It's got me really spooked. If these got published—you'll see."

"Fine. Stop worrying. I'll take care of it."

"I knew you would."

"Who took the pictures?"

"Some little gay photographer in Minneapolis. It was a long time ago."

"Can you remember his name?"

"No. I certainly can't!"

And she hung up. Never said goodbye or thank you. She didn't have time. She worked the phone like a president twisting arms for votes on a tough bill. If someone she wanted to interview wouldn't play, she'd phone two dozen prominent people and persuade them to intercede. Fanatical. Obsessed about giving any rival the slightest advantage by failing to try a hundred and fifty percent.

Her package arrived marked *Confidential,* to be opened only by him. Steinman locked his office door and spread the prints out on his desk. There were six, and he stared at them very hard. If Ann was beautiful now, she had been dynamite then, but unpolished, amateurish, and crude in poses clearly designed to drive some guy crazy. He felt little stirrings of desire and humiliation: that she did not care if he saw them—*even you, Joey.* He left the photographs and walked to the window to look down at the constant traffic, the horse-drawn carriages waiting, the foreign flags stirring outside the Plaza.

The pictures had to be suppressed. At any cost. Well, almost any. There were limits, but they were obviously high. These wouldn't necessarily kill her career, but they could derail his plan to raise an eight-million-dollar property to ten or twelve million.

Who was this guy who sent the pictures, and what would it take? He went back to the desk and read the letter again. It was typed but not professionally, the address hand-printed. The return address was a box number in Minneapolis–Saint Paul. A name, Anthony Zabricki. No phone number. Sent by Priority Mail, deliver only to addressee, return receipt requested. The network had probably run the package through the bomb-screener in the mail room before sending it up to Ann's office. Surprising that her assistant hadn't opened it.

The letter was mild.

Dear Ms. Murrow,
I am a fan of yours. I have photographs of you taken years ago. I'm sure you'd like to have them safe in your possession. For the sum of $100,000, I will sell them to you, the two rolls of negatives, two proof sheets, and all prints that have been made. Or I'll sell them to a magazine like *Penthose*. Please reply quickly.
                                        Sincerely,
                                        Anthony Zabricki

The signature, immature, someone who didn't sign his name very often. *Penthouse* misspelled. The letter paper was plain, unfolded, paper-clipped to the photographs and cardboard backing. An expert might find fingerprints.

Joe dropped the letter and, without touching them, bent again over the photographs. Hard to be cool and objective. They were so calculatedly personal. They were intended to arouse, or infuriate, one person, presumably a man, although, like a lot of rejected men, Steinman had never excluded the possibility that Ann might turn her sexuality on women, too, if she found that useful. What a piece of work!

So . . . he could reply immediately to the box number and offer a meeting, go there, size the man up, and negotiate. Joe's great skill: making deals. Or find out about Anthony Zabricki first . . . might be worth a few thousand dollars. A precautionary investment.

One of his clients had ghost-written a book with a New York police detective who'd left the force under corruption charges, dropped when he plea-bargained himself out by testifying against other cops. Not a popular fellow in New York, he wisely lived in California. A few phone calls found him, and through the skein of ex-cops and two more calls, Steinman got in touch with a private detective named George White, in Minneapolis.

"Could you do a small investigation for me immediately?"

"Depends what it is, depends what's immediately, depends what you'll pay."

"I want a brief profile of a man who's rented a mailbox in Minneapolis–Saint Paul. He'll probably be checking it several times a day for a response to a Priority Mail. Where he lives, what he does for a living."

"Blackmail case?"

This guy was pretty sharp.

"No . . . not as complicated as that."

"Meaning you don't want the cops involved."

"I mean there's no need for that."

"You a lawyer?"

"Yes."

"Criminal lawyer?"

"No, I just represent business clients."

"We're pretty busy. What does 'immediately' mean?"

"I mean right away."

"You mean today, this afternoon?"

"Yeah. Right away."

"Yeah, we can probably do that."

"What's the price?"

"A thousand a day. That'll cover it. See where we get in a couple of days. If it looks like a longer job, we can talk."

"A thousand a day's OK, like you say, for two days; then we'll consider."

"You want to fax me the particulars?"

"Better if I tell you on the phone."

"All the same to me. You'd better give me a credit card number. Just for insurance."

11

The idea came to Grant as a formed conclusion. No preparatory debate, no agonizing pros and cons. He knew exactly when . . . a couple of days after the "Page Six" story and lunch with Repton, and Marty Boyle asked casually when Grant was taking a summer break.

"Haven't fixed a date yet. Does it matter?"

"No, just for planning back-up."

Grant said he'd come back with dates, assuming Marty meant that Bryce Watson wanted to plan his summer. Bryce, the network's senior political correspondent, had been back-up anchor on weekends and vacations for four years.

The next day John Carmody's column in the *Washington Post* reported that "Bill Donovan, the hot new White House correspondent, has also landed the job of substituting for Grant Munro this summer, replacing Bryce Watson." A line of background about Bryce, well liked in Washington, and a line somewhat dismissive of Donovan, saying that until his "sudden appointment to the White House job, he'd been a news anchor in Atlanta."

Bryce called Grant at breakfast.

"Grant, did you know about this?"

"I certainly didn't."

"Do you approve of it?"

"I do not, and I'm going to tell them right now. I'll call you back when I've talked to Repton."

But Edie Repton said Ev was out of town, and Marty Boyle was locked on the cell phone in his car. Carmody didn't print rumors, and this sounded like information from a good source, from Repton or Marty.

When Grant reached him, Marty said, "How the shit did that get into print?"

"But is it true?"

"Well, it's something Ev and I have discussed—"

"Not with me, it hasn't been discussed."

"Well, come on, Grant."

"Don't 'come on, Grant' with me! This is important. It's always been discussed with me. That's how Bryce became substitute anchor. Because I wanted him."

"That was long before my time."

"It still applies. I'm not having some inexperienced kid replacing me. If any local TV anchor can step into this job, what's the point of pretending any longer?"

"Grant, please, calm down. I think you'd better talk it over with Ev Repton."

"You mean it's his idea."

"You'd better talk to him."

"Don't play games with me, Marty."

"Nothing's settled, Grant. There was talk about it. I don't know how Carmody got this. We wouldn't put anything out without talking to you."

"But this was put out; someone leaked it."

"Not me."

"That's the second time you've told me that in a week."

"Well, it's true both times."

"Marty, I'm getting to the bottom of this. Bill Donovan will be substitute anchor over my dead body."

"Grant, take it easy, will you? Look, got to talk to London. Nothing'll happen until we talk it over . . . when Ev gets back."

"Where is Repton?"

"In Washington. OK? Sorry, got to go."

In Washington, where Bill Donovan was! Grant was beginning to feel something he'd not felt since his first days in the business, when a boss could scare him with a dirty look. Fear. Things out of his control, coupled with anger and a creeping sense of impotence.

The first time Grant had seen Donovan on the air, he felt an instant dislike, and it had intensified as he watched Donovan's smirky reporting all through the White House scandal. Grant had a visceral reaction to people on the screen he considered phony, and Donovan was phony in spades; a walking puppet manipulated by his hunger for celebrity.

He had riveting eyes that commanded attention even in long shots, but particularly in the medium close-ups, which were ninety percent of the business. Donovan's dark eyes reflected light brilliantly, and the expression framing them was impertinent. He seemed to be looking at you brazenly, assuming an unwarranted intimacy. They said he tested well with younger females.

The look irritated Grant because it subordinated the content of what Donovan was reporting; transmitting his personality, his presence, as more important than whatever he was saying. In Bryce Watson, personality was subordinated to the news; in Donovan, the opposite.

Marty would probably say, "But Bryce hasn't *got* any personality! That's why he comes across so gray and bland. Watch for half an hour when he's substituting for you, and you won't remember who was there."

The truth was, today the industry didn't want people who merely delivered the news; it wanted people who delivered themselves, who captured viewer eyeballs.

At their peak, networks had commanded the eyeballs plus the hearts and minds of the nation, because there was a compelling story to tell every night—Berlin Wall, Cuban missile crisis, threat of nuclear war, Vietnam, Watergate—something fundamental to the nation, vital to the people.

Now, capturing eyeballs was a different game. The industry wanted personalities to fit a newly disrespectful television, the medium that had made and broken presidents, the medium that slavered over the sex scandals, as Donovan seemed to be slavering when he reported from the White House.

The more Grant stewed about it, the angrier he got. He left messages with the Washington newsroom, but Ev Repton was out of touch all morning. Finally he called Laurie Jacobs and got a straight answer.

"What do you know about the Carmody story?"

"About Bill Donovan? I gave it to him. Is there something wrong with it?"

"Who told you to give it to him?"

"I was talking to Donovan, and he asked if I knew he'd be substituting for you this summer. First I'd heard, so I checked with Ev, and he confirmed it. I said I'd prepare a release and he said there were a couple of details to button up, but I could slip it to Carmody."

Grant exploded. "One of the details to button up was Bryce Watson and the other was me!"

"Oh, Grant, I don't believe it! How could Ev do that?"

"I intend to find out."

"Look, darling, I really didn't know. I'm sick about it. I thought I was doing the right thing. Didn't Ev ever ask what you thought about it?"

"He did not."

"Oh, dear! Oh, dear! I'm beginning to see. A little game of *fait accompli?*"

"That's what I'm talking about."

"What can I do? I feel awful."

"Don't do anything. Just don't confirm it to anyone else until I get to Ev."

"Grant, please understand, I would never do anything to hurt you."

"Thanks."

If that was true, why hadn't she checked with him before calling Carmody? Because she'd naturally assumed he was on board? Or because she didn't think? But Laurie always thought; she was always three steps ahead of everyone else. So how had Ev pulled this off so smoothly? And why? Why would Repton want to leak it first to Carmody? *Fait accompli.* But in Washington, not New York.

Morning meeting. Grant thought the group around the table was avoiding his eyes. Through the news budget for the day. Special prosecutor, nothing new. Middle East peace talks stalled. Fire still raging in California. Marty Boyle came on like his Hollygo nickname, the Power Ranger.

"Can't we get some different pictures? It's always the same stuff. Same crap they've all got." He waved up at the monitors tuned to the cable news channels.

"Jeez, Marty," the assignment editor said, "it's tough getting what we got. Those helicopter shots were great."

"Sure, sure, but why can't we get something different?"

So Grant said, "You can get someone killed. The wind turns suddenly and our guys are as much at risk as the firefighters, without the training to survive."

"I don't want people to get hurt. I just want more dramatic stuff. That's the business we're in: getting the most dramatic shots."

Grant was about to say it, but Don Evans put in dryly, "I thought we were in the news business, Marty."

Sly smiles around the table. Evans hid his smirk in his coffee mug.

"OK, OK," Marty said impatiently. "Let's move it along. Little Wyoming girl. What're we coming up with today?"

"No new angles, Marty. Nothing happening."

"Something's got to be happening. Come on! Let's get moving. What're they offering?"

"All they suggest is another take on local reaction . . . shocked small town still reeling from horror—"

"We've done that," Marty said contemptuously.

"We've done everything, Marty. Her grandparents in Florida . . . friends of the family . . ."

"What about school friends? Tearful little girls mourning their playmate?"

"Parents won't let us."

"How hard have we tried?"

"Pretty hard. They're adamant. No publicity for their kids."

"Try harder for the kids!"

"They're scared, Marty."

So Grant weighed in. "Knock it off, Marty! Leave the story alone for a day. No news is no news."

Exaggerated patience: "Grant, if that's the way you want it, it's your show. But I'll guarantee you the other networks will be all over it again today, and what'll we look like?"

"Maybe like journalists, Marty."

Cheap and obvious, but he couldn't resist. Grant was imagining the same editorial meeting with Bill Donovan in his seat and the Wyoming sex murder blazing over the top of the program.

Marty recovered cheerfully. "OK. Grant wants us to lay off Wyoming for a day, we lay off. But unless something good comes along, we'll have to play the hell out of the California fires. OK?"

In the hallway, Don Evans said, "Didn't know you were so high on Bill Donovan. What's the score there? Why are you dumping Bryce?"

"I'm not dumping Bryce."

"End run by Marty?"

"You think so?"

"I think he'd love to have the kid in here instead of Old Reliable. Make it his kind of show."

"Over my dead body!"

"Fill me in when you can," Don said. "I'll let you know what I pick up."

"Thanks."

Suddenly Grant felt comforted by Don, who had been such a bitter rival years ago.

NOTHING STOPPED the news or the flow of letters he had to respond to. He had to swallow his rising anger and spend an hour with Angela on the mail. Even weeding out junk invitations, complaints, and flattering comments, which got printed cards, plus requests for autographs and signed pictures, which they handled in batches, still left a pile to be dealt with every day.

"Commencement speech at George Washington. Honorary degree. A Wednesday morning?"

"Means a trip to Washington and back for the program."

"Shall I regret? You've turned down those two others."

Washington. Strands of anxiety came together. Washington platform. Maybe he should.

"What day is it? Anything else special?"

"Lunch . . . Council on Foreign Relations."

"I can skip that. OK, let's accept George Washington."

He could hear Winona saying, "How many honorary degrees do you need?"

"I don't *need* any." Her question always irritated him a little. "It's figuring out how to say no."

"You can always say no—if you mean it."

Having a psychiatric social worker for a wife didn't leave a lot of room for comforting self-deception. This was different. Emotionally, he needed the Washington platform.

"Dinner at the Plaza to honor Ken Walden, our distinguished new corporate chairman. They want you on the honorary committee, and to say a few words. You're free that night."

"Sure. Have to do that."

"Speak to World Affairs Council in L.A. Would mean a special trip. It's a Friday. You could go up to the vineyard for the weekend."

"Give me that to take home. I'll check with Winona. No. The hell with it! I don't want to work up a foreign policy speech." As he said that, Grant had a fleeting image of Bill Donovan being asked instead, of his accepting, and . . . Should he reconsider?

"If I want to go to the vineyard, I don't need to make a speech as an excuse. No."

"Conference at the Kennedy School on how to improve presidential election coverage. Two days, Tuesday and Wednesday."

He was tired of these conferences but had to go to some of them to show that he was concerned and involved.

"Who else are they inviting?"

"News anchors, White House correspondents." Angela looked at him. "That means Bill Donovan." Her East Village, heavily mascara-ed eyes looked absurd, but they communicated full comprehension.

"Am I free?"

"Nothing on those days."

"Put it aside. I'll think about it."

She registered nothing while making a note on her pad, but he knew she was thinking: He's never as indecisive as this.

"Next?"

"Affiliate in Cleveland. New owners switching networks to us. Want you to speak at a ceremony to mark the change. June twenty-third. You haven't given me any vacation dates yet, so I don't know whether you'll be away.

"Maybe. Tell them sorry, no." Trying to be more typically decisive, but privately he was waffling about that one, too. The network anchor was a symbol of everything. Everyone wanted a piece of you and you needed to be wanted.

"Laurie came by about that. They've contacted her and Affiliate

Relations. Everyone says it's a big deal. Very important. First affiliate to switch our way in a long time."

Affiliate loyalties had become a real factor in network journalism. Some local stations had shoved Grant back into late afternoon to give better slots to more profitable local news or the syndicated tabloid shows that were sucking away the younger audience. A happy affiliate proud of its network connection might—might—keep Grant in a preferred slot. An unhappy affiliate—and they were more typical—might tell him to buzz off.

"You reconsidering?" She read the silence. His eyes kept flicking over to a monitor showing a police chief, must be the Wyoming guy, talking to a clutch of mikes.

"Let me talk to Laurie. What else?"

"Carnegie wants you to join an advisory committee on U.S. world goals in the twenty-first century."

"Regrets. I've got too many of those things."

"Sure? It's here in New York?"

"Sure."

"Dinner at the White House, to celebrate Independence Day. July Fourth is a Saturday."

"I'll check with Winona."

"There are these to sign. And these drafts to check. You've got ten minutes before the noon meeting. And remember, lunch with Shirley Trattner."

"Oh, right."

"Twelve forty-five, Jean Lafitte. Meet her there. Want to do phone calls till the noon meeting?"

"How many calls?"

"Seven or eight."

"They find Ev Repton in Washington?"

"Not yet."

"I'd better read the wires. I'll do the calls after lunch."

Grant Alt-tabbed his computer keyboard over to the AP wire and skimmed the top stories. Of course! Police in Wyoming had been forced to hold a news conference to feed the hungry media dogs. No arrest. Investigation continuing. Had some hopeful leads. Everyone on the force as eager for progress as the whole town. Couldn't rush a criminal investigation.

MARTY GLOATING, "So . . . Wyoming makes fresh news."

"Not news, just a police department covering its ass because we're hounding the hell out of them."

"Hey, it's a news conference! It gives us a peg to hit the story again."

"Why do we want to hit the story if there's no real development?"

"Because it's got the whole country on the edge of their seats. CNN and Fox did the news conference live, Grant. *Live!*"

Giving Grant a change of tack. "So we're letting Rupert Murdoch drive our news judgment?"

"CNN too!"

"Marty. Listen to me, buddy. I'm saying no to Wyoming today. OK? Clear?"

"If that's the way you want it, Grant. It's your show."

"Sometimes," Grant said. He pulled Marty aside. "Listen, I haven't got to Repton yet, but Laurie says he told her to leak the Donovan story to Carmody."

"No shit? Without running it by you first?" Sarcasm and irony were not the Power Ranger's standard equipment, so Grant wondered whether he'd read it right.

"You didn't know? Really?"

"Grant, I don't know how Carmody got it. I thought the discussions were still going on. I assumed with you included."

ONLY 12:20, early, but Grant wanted to walk to clear his head. He was letting this thing tie him into knots. He hadn't run that morning because of the Israeli prime minister's breakfast at the Regency. A ritual all the anchors usually attended, because not showing up implied a lack of interest and registered with the government in question, bad when you wanted key access or an interview in a hurry. Also because it was a way to see newsmakers in the flesh, and such background briefings, commonplace for reporters on a beat, gave you some confidence when you later unraveled the strands of political spin.

Grant felt the lack of exercise clogging him up emotionally and physically; no chance this evening because they had to go out to a dinner.

It was in that mood, arriving at Jean Lafitte, glancing in the mirror, that Grant suddenly saw himself differently. For the first time, he looked old.

Perhaps it was the overhead lighting, but there was no mistaking what he saw. Old! He turned to another mirror: the same. He felt profoundly different as he spotted Shirley and went to her table.

They'd been professional pals for years. Hollygo called her the Tylenol Lady, and she did resemble the cool actress who'd pitched Tylenol. A wholesome mature blonde, with that mid-fortyish way of being pretty and comfortable with it, a quiet, intelligent sexiness. They had often eyed each other speculatively over the years, never more than an appreciative glance or smile, both well married.

"How are things?" Shirley asked.

"Your lunch. You tell me."

"Aren't we supposed to have a little polite chat before we interview each other?"

"Habit's too strong, I guess. Winona says I do it too much."

"How is Winona?"

"Fine. Very busy."

"It must be hell to be married to you—"

"Thanks."

"No, married to a guy in your job, married to—"

"Careful!"

"Married to all the attention. You can't see it, but practically ev-

eryone in the restaurant noticed when you came in and they keep dart-
ing little glances over, wondering who's the blonde Grant Munro's having lunch with."

"If they watch enough to know who I am, they know who the
blonde is."

"Not the same thing. Some of them may think they've seen me
somewhere on television, but it'll be vague. Anchors are different; everybody knows you."

"We'd better order something to eat."

As she studied the menu, Grant sneaked a glance in the mirror. An
alien feeling had gripped him. His whole attitude to life had altered in
that second of recognition. Look again. Yes, he looked old. He glanced
down at the menu, then quickly to the mirror again. Beside him, Shirley
looked glamorous and young. He couldn't shake off the strangeness.
He'd always assumed he was young. But, with no sense of a change in
body, no sudden ache or weakness, he was older, not by a few days but
by a generation. A man looked up and caught his eye in the mirror.
Guiltily, Grant turned his eyes away.

"I think the monkfish sounds nice. What're you having?"

"Sounds good to me."

"I need some friendly advice."

"You have an offer from another network?"

"Who says men aren't intuitive! That was true a couple of years
ago, but then they gave me the magazine show. More exposure. More
money. And that's been fine—to a point. I like the traveling, and I get
more time with Herb. But should I go on doing it?"

"What are the alternatives?"

"The first will make you laugh. Anchor local news, here in New
York, six and eleven, five days a week. You're sneering!"

"I'm not!"

"They want somebody mature—believe it or not—someone solid,
or so they told my agent. What does solid sound like? Chunky? Overweight?"

"Not your problem, I'd say."

"The other possibility would be a radical change. How do you like president of Bryn Mawr?"

"Did you go there?"

"I did. And it's very tempting. If I wanted, I could teach on the side."

"What would you teach?"

"History. I have half of my doctorate from the University of Pennsylvania."

"I didn't know that."

"I was going to be a historian before I fell into television. At Bryn Mawr I could finish the dissertation."

"And what about Herb?"

"He's willing to work it out. It's not far from Philadelphia. He could commute at first, and he's sure eventually he could settle there. The teaching hospital picture in New York is lousy for doctors like him, with all the amalgamations and the managed-care thing."

"It's funny; somebody just asked me if I'd be interested in being a college president, and I immediately said no."

"Which college?"

"I didn't wait to hear."

"But, Grant, you're in a totally different situation from mine. Anyway, this is why I wanted to talk over my options."

"What d'you feel about them?"

"Let's start with my general feeling. I'm forty-four. Forty-five soon. And you know it's far tougher being a woman in the business—all the way, getting in, getting the assignments, getting promoted—and not getting shoved aside as you get older. It doesn't matter for a man. How old are you . . . honestly?"

He was astonished at how hard it was to say. "I'll be sixty in October."

"Well, you could pass for ten years younger. I can't pass for a minute less than my age. To hold the line as it is, I have to color my hair, I work my butt off in the gym, watch every mouthful of food, and count every glass of wine. Because every year there's another batch of gorgeous, smart blondes coming out of the J schools, and the producers salivate over them. I think they get prettier and smarter every year."

"And the producers get younger."

"Tell me about it! The kid who's my field producer now is only a couple of years older than my son, David, and the executive producer, Tom Wiseman, is in his mid-thirties. The other day Wiseman said to me, not wasting any tact on the old lady, 'Shirl, can you do something about your roots? They're showing up on the studio camera.' "

"Jesus!" Grant said, resisting the urge to check her hair.

"But he's right! I could kill him but he's right. I'd been too busy to keep my usual appointment. Why am I telling you this? You don't do anything to your hair, do you?"

"Not yet." He chuckled to make it sound light.

"And it looks great. A little gray. Very becoming. But a little gray doesn't work for a forty-four-year-old correspondent whose competition is made up of Barbie dolls straight from the factory."

"Barbie dolls don't have half a doctorate in history."

"Don't be so sure nowadays! Even so . . . that doesn't matter a damn to the network. Four years ago I had my eyes done."

"I didn't know."

"You weren't meant to. I went to the best guy I could find and got a subtle job. Now, if I'm going to stay in the business, I'll have to go for the whole facelift. That's the reality. Everyone in the business does it."

"Every woman."

"And a lot of men. You'd be surprised. Maybe you wouldn't. Who's surprised about anything anymore? I don't know. But it's a way of life. They're starting in their thirties, and keep nipping and tucking all the way. So I've faced it. If I stay, the big lift. Disappear for a month. Tell you all I'm on vacation in Tibet and come back to astonish you with how much good the Himalayan air did me."

"*If* you stay?"

"Well, that applies to the local news job too, though I'm not taking that too seriously. Just something to put Bryn Mawr and my present job into better perspective. A halfway house. I'd probably get the heave-ho from there in a few years, facelift or not. Mature may be their flavor this month, but that can change in a minute. New news director, new flavor."

"Let's put your present job in the best light. You've got one of the top half dozen network jobs, on a high-rated show. You always have a major role in conventions, election nights, and you must make—"

"Sure, more money than I can admit to anyone."

"Then why think of leaving?"

"Because—I don't know—a lot of reasons. Some are atmosphere. You know it. You breathe the same air. The business has lost its seriousness. It's a game—a self-important, cute game. Look what I do really: for every interesting story that offers a bit of insight into what makes this country tick, I have to do some utterly crass freak story or sob-sister pulp nonsense. That's not work for grownup people. When I try to take it seriously and lend the people some dignity, Wiseman says, 'Shirl, you're making it too highbrow.' I think I could do it only one more season this way, but that isn't an option. Wiseman wants to go under cover—"

"Oh, God!"

"He's been itching to follow the other magazines with their hidden cameras and all that phony exposé, all that hype and very little that matters. Honestly, I can't do that. I'm not going to leap into the shot at the end of the piece, like some avenging angel: 'We've got the goods on you because we've had'—dramatic pause—'hidden cameras!' It's all too cheap. I can't do it."

"Well, I applaud you for that."

"Anyway, I went to see Ev Repton in confidence—my agent thinks I'm crazy, incidentally—I went to good ol' Ev and said, 'What else could I do if I quit the magazine?' And he said, 'Why would you quit the magazine?' And it went nowhere from there. No constructive analysis of my career, what I'm good at, what I might be interested in doing."

"Come back to Bryn Mawr, because I sense it's what you're leaning toward."

She sighed. "Maybe. I guess so."

"There are bound to be disadvantages there, too. You'd have to spend a lot of time raising money and sucking up to the people who'll give it. And speaking of money, I assume you'd take a huge cut in pay."

"I don't need so much money."

"But the other thing I wonder about, can you, at forty-four, forty-five, take up the academic life you dropped twenty years ago and get professional satisfaction?"

"Get satisfaction? Sounds like a soap opera concept. But it's a good question."

"There's plenty of competition in the academic world. Must be bright young women coming along, already with doctorates in history, with tenure or close to it."

"You ought to be a guidance counselor for midcareer malcontents."

"Well, I wonder whether it would be as attractive as it sounds? Can you really be a college president and pursue your studies?"

"But, Grant"—she said this vehemently—"it would be respectable . . . respectable work!"

"Respectable . . . that's a hell of a word."

"I could respect myself for doing it. Often, now, waiting around while the crew sets up in some scene of misery we're about to shoot, seeing what those people are going to have for supper, knowing that we can stop at a good restaurant as a matter of course and have a meal they'd consider a fabulous banquet; doing all that now, I don't feel respectable. I feel exploitative. I'm not airing their grievances, their plight, for any redeeming social value. I'm doing it to titillate our audience and get ratings. I came into this business thinking that what we put on the air really mattered—that it played some role in the democracy . . . I don't know. I'm sorry."

Her eyes had filled with tears, and she raised her napkin to blot them. "I shouldn't drink wine at lunch. It makes me maudlin."

"It makes you damned eloquent." As he said it, he realized how unctuous it sounded.

"You can escape that stuff, you see? In the hard news, you can still tell yourself it matters, the country needs to know what's going on."

Grant said, "Sure, and we'll lead on the Wyoming murder again tonight."

"What are we coming to?" She looked at him very candidly. "Well, you said it for all of us. Gadarene swine. I loved your speech."

"Thanks for the note you sent me."

"Are you all right?"

"Why?"

"Because you look a little funny."

"A lot of what you've said rings a bell."

"You mean Bill Donovan? Am I right?"

"Between us—yeah. Now I've got to get back before the Power Ranger makes all the decisions."

"You call him that too? I thought it was just us minions in the field."

"Thanks for lunch. How long will Bryn Mawr give you?"

"I've got a few months."

"Time for a facelift. Maybe college presidents need them now, too."

"A facelift isn't a joke. It's finding the right surgeon and getting on his schedule. For some of them, you have to wait a year. It's serious stuff."

On the way out, Grant again saw his face. He checked the disturbing reflection in store windows as he passed. He looked old.

12

www.hollygo.com

Any you web surfers out there in teeveenews been doubtin the reach of Hollygo, just read on. Hollygo now got so many spies in place, we able to compare reactions to the same story in two newsrooms at the same moment. Journalism schools, log on! Take note! Organize classes round this web site, give the professors a rest, less y'all too busy givin public relations and teevee makeup classes, like we hear goin on in them so-called journalism courses. Don'tcha luv it?

What you wanna be, chile? I wanna be Walter Cronkite, ma'am, cos my mama tole me Mr. Cronkite a great man and Martin Luther King trust him. Well, chile, you just step over here, and learn yo makeup. This here eyeliner what you put on give you *authority,* see? This bitty rouge high up the cheekbone, that make you real *trusted* like. What'you mean, real men don't wear makeup? Like the Pope don't wear skirts? Where y'all hear that? You need makeup in teeveenews like you need good hair. And good hair be the course next week. And you need good hair like you need sharp clothes, man, and sharp clothes is a special seminar next month. And you need sharp clothes (don't worry bout price; you get em free an credit the designer at the end of the show) like you need a voice got balls in it, and that gonna be your major next semester: we gotta voice coach could a put balls in Marilyn Monroe voice, if she'd a wanted. That get your bachelor degree. Step after that for the masters is intensive prompter readin, so you stop lookin like some frightened lil rabbit. You graduate all them courses, chile, and you qualified be Walter Cronkite any time you like and you got the diplomas to prove it!

So, here the scene, chiquita linda. At the Taupe network news this morning, executive producer Attention Deficit says to Grecian Formula, the anchor who look like he been bungee-jumpin or somethin worse last night, "Big day in the Wyomin story. Cops held a press conference. Nothin else to lead on so we goin with it big." And Grecian says, like his mind is off in some bedroom (not his own), "Great! Fine. I like it when we stick with the hard news! Terrific! Who've we got on the scene?"

Attention Deficit kinda sighs and rolls his eyes and says they got Miss Clairol, who everybody know, cept maybe Grecian, been twitchin her cute little butt out there ever since the chile got herself killed dead, and filin them heavy intellectual reports. "Oh, yeah! Terrific little reporter, isn't she?" And that's the way it is, folks.

But not at BBS. At Beige, Power Ranger tries the same deal, but Gregory Peck say, "No way!" Hollygo informant who was there say it remind him/her (you think I'm gonna give y'all clues?) make her/him think of *To Kill a Mockingbird,* when lawyer Gregory Peck stand up there in court like Abraham Lincoln hisself. "Listen to me, buddy," Gregory say in that voice make a gal shiver, "I'm sayin no to Wyomin today. OK? Clear?" And the Power Ranger caves. "If that's the way you want it. It's your show."

"Sometimes," Gregory mutter ominously.

The lesson, compañeros de me vida, be this: responsible journalism, like liberty, equality, and virginity, gotta be defended ever day, and sometimes it wins. Sometimes. Don'tcha luv it?

13

At 4:45, told Repton was back from Washington, Grant marched in uninvited and closed the door hard.

"OK, I want to settle this. Here's the deal: you put Bill Donovan on to replace me and knock out Bryce Watson, and I quit—publicly and noisily, with full explanations."

Repton acted like a man who had rehearsed the scene. Unflustered, he pushed his big glasses up and reclined in his spring-back chair.

"Sit down, Grant. You're upset. I'm a little upset that you come barging rudely into my office and slam the door. But I'll overlook it. Suppose we tackle this like gentlemen."

"A gentleman doesn't treat Bryce Watson as you have."

"And?"

"A gentleman doesn't engineer a *fait accompli* he knows I will resist. A gentleman discusses it with me, cleanly, first. This is sneaky stuff personally, quite apart from what it does to the network."

"And what does it do to the network?"

"It makes us look like fools, replacing Bryce, one of the most respected journalists in Washington, with a nonentity like Donovan."

"A nonentity who got cheered by the Washington press corps when he spoke at the National Press Club today?"

"I didn't know he was speaking at the press club. What about?"

"About the difference between being a local anchorman and suddenly finding himself covering the President, at a time of great drama. Very funny, very self-effacing. Very perceptive on the ways of Washington. They found it charming."

"So you got it leaked to Carmody because Donovan was speaking to the press club today?"

"Not very subtle, is it? But while I was there at the head table, the press club president told me they'd asked you several times in the last few months, and you turned them down."

"It's true. I've had too many things on my plate."

"Like having lunch with Shirley Trattner? When I tried to return your calls, Angela said that's where you were."

The sarcasm made Grant angrier. "All this is beside the point. You couldn't have expected me to roll over and lick your hand when you pull off this little P.R. coup. I repeat, if Bill Donovan replaces Bryce as my substitute, I'm out of here."

"Let me point out that you have a contract that lasts two more years. Besides the fact that Sherm Glass is about to negotiate another."

"Contracts can be broken."

"They can, but you might be smart to talk to your agent about that."

"I will!"

"I'm sure he'll advise you not to do anything foolish."

"Never mind the contract! I want to talk about Bryce and Donovan and where you get off with this sneaky, underhanded behavior. In the thirty-five years I've been here, in everything I've done I've tried to maintain the network's prestige and keep earning the respect of the public and the journalistic community." Grant heard his voice rising, but did not lower it. "And now, with no warning, you take a step that severely undermines that respect, and you go behind my back to do it. And you talk about behaving like a gentleman!"

Repton adroitly shifted to the mollifying tack. "Grant, sit down. Talk reasonably. You're taking all this too seriously."

"I won't talk reasonably until you stop diverting me into tactics and start discussing the substance."

"All right. Let's talk substance." As if on his cue, the intercom buzzed and his secretary said, "Ev, Marty needs Grant to call him about the show." Very deflating.

"I'd better call."

Repton pushed the phone over with a smile. Grant called Marty's extension, heard the self-important bark he used to underlings: "Marty here. Yeah?" Which oozed into the deferential when he recognized Grant's voice.

"Grant, we got two lead-ins to redo. Stuff's coming in different than we expected. You coming to do it, or you want us to?"

"You do it, Marty. I'm tied up."

"OK, buddy." And he pictured Marty like Hal in *2001*, happily pursuing his own agenda, perhaps connecting intimately to Grant's talk with Repton.

"So, substance. Here's what matters, as I see it. Priorities. Number one." Even the shape of Repton's spread fingers as he began counting irritated Grant. "The News Department needs your show to remain dynamic and competitive. It's in some trouble, as we know, even when you're on the air. Number two priority: you need time off. Vacation. Very important to recharge your batteries. OK? Number three: vital that whoever replaces you maintains as far as possible our competitive position. Number four: Bryce Watson doesn't. Abysmal. The establishment may love him in Washington, may invite him to the Gridiron and all that, but with the American public, Bryce doesn't get it done."

"Where do you get that from?"

"From the same market research we discussed."

"You didn't tell me it was finished."

"It isn't. It's part of the data they sent over early. Reaction to various personalities on the air. Bryce Watson is below acceptable."

"And Bill Donovan?"

"Too early; hasn't had enough exposure to register yet."

"So why the rush to promote him?"

"Playing a hunch. Studying the audience survey material, which was part of the reason we hired him in Atlanta. Someone did it with you when they gave you the breaks a long time ago. I remember a lot of people who didn't see it then. Now back to today. Forget my interest, whatever that is. What about your interest? Surely it's not to come back from a summer vacation, which you fully deserve, and find that Bryce Watson has left you with an even smaller audience?"

A long pause. Grant felt outsmarted, trapped by his own anger.

"Whatever your survey data, two things you haven't addressed. Bryce Watson is a seasoned, reliable journalist; he's brought nothing but dignity to our show. Donovan is a green kid. We don't know what embarrassments he could cause us. Suppose there's a big foreign crisis?"

"I presume you'd come back . . . no?"

"Sure. But that's no reason to push Donovan—because I can back *him* up . . ."

"And dignity, Grant. Come on! The age of dignity in our business went out with . . . take your pick. Dignity doesn't buy us anything today."

"You still haven't addressed the way you did this. It's a hell of a slap in the face to me, and it's a devastating professional blow to Bryce."

Repton held up both hands in surrender. "Guilty!"

"What do you mean?"

"Guilty both counts. I offended you. I'm sorry. I'll make it up. I devastated Bryce Watson? I regret it. Maybe he'll leave, go somewhere else, if they'll have him. CNN, maybe. The corporate people keep urging me to dump high-overhead guys like Bryce and hire in younger, less expensive. They look at the cable networks—I know, I know—but they don't know the difference; they just see the bottom line. We're a high-cost operation; they're low-cost. Watson is high-cost, but if he wants to stay, he's still senior political correspondent. He's got lots to do."

"That's it? Sorry. I'm guilty. Too bad?"

The intercom buzzed. "Grant? Marty says they need you in three minutes, no later."

"Better go and do the show and sleep on it. Come and see me tomorrow. You'll see I'm right. Tactics unprincipled? I agree. But strategy, correct."

NOT ONLY was the Wyoming child murder leading the show, but Marty had added an analysis segment. Two legal commentators—part of the legal subprofession spawned by the Simpson case—disputed how much right the public had to know what the police were up to. This concocted issue was no more news than the police news conference. Simply feeding the public fever to justify incessant updates. The little murder victim had told her mother of having a dream that she would be killed. And now they were following this crap, like everybody else.

Still furious, Grant flung himself into the chair in the makeup room, astonishing the placid Cynthia, who said, "What's up? You look ready to kill someone."

"Right."

He tried to relax, breathing slowly, but in doing so, he was staring at the reflection of his face, looking for the signs he'd noticed in the restaurant, and he saw them. He watched as Cynthia followed her routine. She was hiding what she could, or disguising it, putting a darker color under his chin line.

Grant had come to use these ten minutes to calm down and put himself in a good frame of mind to go out and do the show.

In the old days, he'd bring all the tensions from the newsroom, all that hyped-up jazz that television people liked to create, as though the whole organization were collectively winding its alarm clock to go off and wake up the world when the opening titles hit the air at six-thirty Eastern time. He'd march out so wired up, sometimes, he'd notice his left thumb trembling involuntarily. Too hyper. Not his natural style, but part of the mental goosing the atmosphere induced when you first realized you were all alone out there, in the lights, and it all depended on you. They made you the BFD, paid you millions, put you out there, and it boiled down to something very simple.

Subtracting commercial time, you had twenty-two minutes. Subtracting correspondents' reports, voice-overs, sound bites, and interviews, you had about five minutes a night for actually talking to camera, looking the nation directly in the eye, making your number. And it was not continuous; not like an actor coming on stage, using the first few minutes to warm up and relax. You had to do it in bursts of fifteen or twenty seconds, and each time it came back to you, you had to jump-start the energy again. You had to make it pour out of your eyes, your voice, and the language of your body from the belly button up, some sense of vitality, urgency, empathy, to hold their interest and carry the program. And, in every scripted lead-in and lead-out, you had to adapt your delivery to the sense and mood, the affective part of each story, to be in tune with the spirit of each. You couldn't come stony-faced out of a tragedy, or humorless out of a lighter piece, nor did you want to sound stupidly mawkish or goofily amused. No crocodile tears, no forced yuks. That was what separated the guys in local news, even most of the network correspondents, from the few pros who sat in the top chairs at the networks. Restraint. Vitality in restraint.

You had to hit the precise tone that expressed your own style, not something you'd manufactured for television; the tone of your news department, which you personified, plus something intangible and undefinable that made the audience like you, trust you, and want to come back night after night—all in bursts of a few seconds, like squeezing the trigger on an M-16, the rounds blipped off before you knew it. You were left staring at the unseeing camera eye while the audience watched a field correspondent's report or a commercial.

Some hit it very easily. It grew out of their personalities; they didn't seem to be trying to prove something, and the audience sensed that. Others—and it was obvious—manufactured it and kept tinkering with it, fine-tuning, or changing the tone altogether. Some never got all the parts in sync. Walter Cronkite was a natural. Eric Sevareid was a bundle of nerves. In some, it seemed totally contrived, a persona, a voice, a demeanor, a look concocted for television that, however glamorous, made people uneasy—waiting for the trapeze artist to fall.

Grant had finally made it work, and it took some doing, to relax, to be himself, to stop *delivering* the news and simply tell it, conversationally but forcefully. But he had to think himself into that each evening, wind himself down from the high-tension setting the producers liked.

The producers got younger all the time, and every mini-generation brought a new sense of pace. Every few years, it seemed, the internal stopwatches these kids had in their souls got recalibrated to new speed settings.

Marty Boyle talked in bursts of broken phrases, the way they wrote scripts for TV . . . no punctuation . . . no complete sentences, staccato phrases with three dots between them.

Marty's most eloquent communication was his finger-snapping. When he snapped his fingers in the newsroom or editing room or control room during the show, you could hear it everywhere. The snaps unnerved the producer whose piece was running at that moment. Marty thought it was dull. Right there! Snap! He snapped the second he got impatient at the length of a shot, the duration of a sound bite, or when someone was pitching a story to him. He snapped. Something had violated his inner sense of the contemporary tempo needed to stop the erosion of younger viewers, which threatened to drive network news at suppertime out of business. Snap. Boring. Snap. Too long, cut it back. The reflexive impatience of the MTV-trained generation.

The previous afternoon, Marty said, "Grant, your lead-in's too long."

"Come on! It's nineteen seconds."

"I need thirteen."

"I need nineteen to say it."

So Marty said, cooperatively, "OK, Grant. Read it to me and I won't put the watch on it."

So Grant read, his habitual delivery sounding too loud and self-important in the office. And after twelve or thirteen seconds, Marty snapped his fingers.

"There! That's how long it should be."

"But I need that many words to say it."

"Drop the stuff in the middle about what happened last week."

"You need that background to understand it."

"The audience doesn't listen to that stuff anyway. You don't want to lose them *before* you get to the piece."

"The piece won't make sense if there's no context."

"OK. I'll get the correspondent to work the background into the piece."

Perfectly reasonable. Civilized discussion. A trimmed-down version of editorial negotiations everywhere. But the result was this: Grant's on-camera lead-in was cut to thirteen seconds, and when the story appeared on the show, there was no background.

After the show, he stopped Marty. "What the hell happened to the line of background?"

"Oh, yeah. She didn't have time to put it in. Her piece was running long."

IF YOU WATCHED any television with the sound off, a music video, a commercial, a news program, and concentrated on the number of shot changes, never mind the content, you could see it. Flip, flick, flip. Every few seconds, sometimes faster. If the shots lasted longer than a second or two, you were probably watching an old movie. The heartbeat of America was being driven by a pacemaker constantly set faster and faster by this collective, generational impatience. And that drove the pace of his show, whether Grant liked it or not. That impatient snap of the fingers. The finger-snappers might be idiots, might have little idea of traditional journalism, might be cultural barbarians; or they may be bright, Ivy League–educated, with private intellectual tastes. But the Zeitgeist haunted their souls; they vibrated to it like one tuning fork in sympathetic harmony with another, and they drove the aesthetic of television, which affected everything else.

News executives like Ev Repton would say, "Grant, I'm sorry. I feel the same way. But this is how the industry's going, and we have to go with it." And then, leaning back from their big desks, or from the lunch table, they'd indulge the special talent of network news people for serial rationalization. Whatever was good for ratings and share was good for journalism and good for the country. They were the last redoubt of serious journalism on the nation's most persuasive medium; if they lost their audience, the cretins in tabloid television would take over. So they backed the latest Marty, the latest Power Ranger.

NOW . . . fifteen minutes to air. Grant took a few deep breaths as Cynthia removed the makeup cape. He put on his jacket, snubbed up his loosened tie, and went into the studio, where the script lay ready on the anchor desk.

"Evening, Grant." "How're you, Grant?" The studio crew gave the usual hi's. The audio engineer dressed the microphone around his tie and the earpiece cord inside his jacket. The routine was calming, and Grant settled down to read through the prompter segments, matching the handscript on the desk to the segments on the prompter screen. If the prompter crashed, as it did occasionally, he could find his place on the paper script.

The stage manager asked for quiet, the prompter operator asked if Grant was ready, a stagehand quietly slipped a glass of ice water onto the little shelf below the desk level. From the control room the audio man checked the IFB level in his earpiece, and Grant counted to ten for a mike check.

As smoothly as the captain taking over the bridge of a ship, everything quietly, efficiently, and untheatrically clicking into place.

"Ready when you are, Grant," the prompter operator called.

"Five minutes to air," from the stage manager.

For the first time that day Grant relaxed and read quickly through the prompter copy.

"Two minutes to air. Two minutes."

Here at least he could feel in charge.

BEFORE GOING home, he left a message on Bryce's answering machine. "This is Grant. Sorry I couldn't call back sooner. I finally got to Repton in late afternoon and had a dust-up. Nothing settled. I'll call you tomorrow."

AT HOME Grant shrank from having to drag himself and Winona through it, but once he started, it all unraveled, from the Carmody titbit to Repton.

"I really blew it with Repton, barging in there, ranting about quitting."

"Honey, you lose your temper so seldom, they never see you angry. Chances are Ev Repton has gone home thinking *he's* blown it. Look what he's risking. Your position is a lot securer than his. I'll bet he's bluffing with those survey figures and he's really worried about it tonight."

"You sure know how to make a guy feel better."

"Sure." She kissed him in the cute, comradely way that had evolved over their marriage. "He's my guy and I love it when he shows a little temperament with those people. You know what I think . . . ?"

"Sounds like a professional opinion coming."

"I think you're so careful not to be the temperamental star, not to be the eight-hundred-pound gorilla they expect you to be, that you're too nice to them. That's why it's so effective when you blow your top. Think of Repton's position—if you're really serious about leaving."

"And if I was serious about leaving, what would you think?"

"I'd cheer. I was cheering when you thought about it over O. J. Simpson. Remember?"

She always helped him. No wonder she couldn't reduce the number of clients she saw but kept collecting more. She always came up with a rationale that let him see behind the looking glass of his own emotions.

All the same, tired as he was, Grant lay awake, haunted by Bill Donovan's smirking mannerisms on camera.

To create the illusion that you were not reading from the prompter, you moved your head a little so that viewers wouldn't notice your eyes fixed on the words. Some made it look quite natural, but Donovan had adopted a set of irritating tics. He'd drop his chin and, as he looked back up, for an instant, would keep his eyelids lowered, then flick them open, as though in a flash of candor. It was unrelated to the sense, but every so often it was repeated. So was his habit of cocking his head to one side and delivering a sentence at an angle. To Grant it looked arch. If he watched Donovan with the sound off, the head seemed to be wagging in a meaningless rhythm, as though the mind of his puppet master had wandered. It reminded Grant of the nursery rhyme, "Wynken, Blynken, and Nod." That was Donovan: Wynken, Blynken, and Nod.

And his inflections! Donovan spoke in little bursts of words, pausing as though pondering what to say next. Pure affectation, which further drew attention to him and away from the import of what he was saying. And he'd fallen into the pattern of emphasizing certain words where no emphasis was needed, giving the strange impression that he knew something he was not conveying, or knew less, that in fact his mind had become divorced from the meaning.

Grant noticed it in flight attendants reciting the formula texts of their craft. "The flying time to Denver *will* be three hours and twenty minutes at an altitude of forty-*two*-thousand feet," as though someone had challenged both the duration and the altitude.

But also Donovan's language. With English teachers for parents, Grant had absorbed grammar by osmosis, and his inner ear protested when he heard Donovan say, "The president acts like he's got a second wind," or "It's not that big of a deal."

Would he care if Donovan were charging up the ladder at another network? But it was *his* ladder Donovan was climbing, and Grant was furious that they could think him a suitable replacement. What were thirty-five years of experience and seasoning worth if he could be sub-bed by a smarmy young jerk no different from the hosts of the tabloid TV shows? What difference would the public see in the programs?

Tomorrow he'd go back to Repton and insist.

14

Christopher Siefert sat at his computer, sketching in some preliminary ideas for his *Time* profile: "Phenomenon of anchor person central to television industry, therefore the culture.

"In the history of Western culture, has there ever been anything like it, these figures to whom all defer? To whom the high and mighty, the lowly and the damned, feel they must confess or appear to confess?

"TV hosts usurp many traditional roles—confessors, inquisitors, prosecutors, therapists, debriefers, moderators; the voice of fate in Sophocles' chorus, the pert-impertinent fools in Shakespeare, exorcists in the Inquisition, the accusers in Salem, the inquisitor in Dostoevsky, as well as the fawning courtiers of the Sun King, the eunuchs of the Great Khan, the flatterers and toadies of tycoons and politicians. Extraordinary that television has created an entire profession of intermediaries.

"But if society makes stars and monsters of these television hosts, treating them like princes, it also makes them hugely vulnerable. Those adored can rapidly be spurned. Now, apparently, Grant Munro is vulnerable.

"Perhaps he's like the king selected in the ancient fertility rites. Chosen and enthroned to guarantee successful crops, every luxury and indulgence afforded him in wealth, food, drink, palaces, jewels, women, until the season turns and the gods require propitiation. Then, whatever his honor and prestige, he is ritually killed to ensure that the seasons continue to turn, the crops grow, the Nielsen ratings prosper another season. Like Richard II:

. . . for within the hollow crown
That rounds the mortal temples of a king,
Keeps Death his court . . .

"And now, like reincarnations of sacrificial kings, sit Grant Munro and his rivals, in their golden anchor chairs, resplendent in the riches and fame showered on them, with every indulgence the society can offer, as long as the crops thrive, the ratings stay competitive and rate cards high, network coffers brimming, and Wall Street analysts satisfied with quarterly performance.

Allowing him a breath, a little scene,
To monarchize, be fear'd, and kill with looks.

"When the ratings decline, then sacrifice him to the gods of fleeting popularity."

Too much, Siefert thought, saving his copy in the computer. Way too much, but he liked the conceit. Might be a few lines he could use when it came to writing the piece.

15

Joe Steinman had been doing a lot of thinking while waiting for the detective in Minneapolis to call back.

A successful agent needed a mind constantly inventing possibilities, weaving the personalities in his care into fresh little dramas. Like a playwright, imagining what could be. Especially in television, where the whole game was a shadow play, a circus sideshow of illusionists' tents. It was the same game; the tent that drew the biggest crowd was the winner. The trick was figuring out what drew the crowd. It didn't matter whether you called it news or sitcoms or cooking shows or wild animals on PBS; it was personality that got people into the tent . . . right now, Ann Murrow's tent. The other trick was knowing when it was time to move the tent to another location. The circuses always knew when to move on, and when they came back, they always had new gimmicks, some fresh razzle-dazzle among the old favorites.

Murrow was not getting any younger. That was the starting point. Still gorgeous, and sustained that way with every assistance money could buy; constant little attentions by nutritionists, dermatologists, artful cosmetic surgeons, masseurs, personal trainers. As far as Steinman knew, she'd had everything possible lifted, tucked, enhanced. All the magazines and gossip columns knew was that she went regularly to Canyon Ranch, of which she was an original shareholder. It was good cover for a multitude of professional services; she could be said to be hiking at Canyon Ranch while ducking over to L.A. for a couple of days of minor surgical attention or colonic irrigation. The bills for these services he saw, because he managed her personal finances. She didn't want more people knowing her business, which might be one reason she had never married. As for children, only Steinman was entrusted with that information. "A stupid mistake, Joey," privately put up for adoption years ago, several miscarriages, D and C's, one actual termination of pregnancy.

Joe Steinman knew a lot about Ann Murrow, and he knew that she trusted him completely. Why else would she simply send over the photos? She could have told him what to do without letting him see them. She trusted him and, he also knew, she despised him. Funny. You'd think—well, he'd thought for years, enduring many painful rebuffs—that all the services he had performed; all the deals, the private arrangements, career-related and personal; the embarrassments he'd extricated her from; the nuisances he'd eliminated; the obsessed, half-crazed fans diverted; the stalker he'd quietly frightened away with some ex-cop private security men when the NYPD were going to make it too public. You'd think that for all this she would like him, would occasionally invite him to dinner or lunch, or at least take a meal with him, or accept one of his repeated invitations to a Seder. You'd think, he'd thought for a long time, if he did all this and helped make her unbelievably rich, she'd be nice to him. But she was not. Ann Murrow treated Joe Steinman, the man who kept all her secrets, like dirt. Only when she wanted something would she flick on the charm for the necessary few minutes, then flick it off.

Years ago, he thought he was in love with her. His shrewd wife in Tenafly would say, "You be careful of that woman. You'll fall for her. She's the type that has every man eating out of her hand." And his wife was right. Looking at the photos had revived all those thoughts. He used to fantasize that one day, out of boredom, perhaps, or kindness or whatever—she'd had so many men—Ann would have offered him once, or a few times—but never! She would tease the hell out of him when she wanted something done, but she was not destined for his bed or for the couch in his office, on which others had occasionally been more generous. It was strictly a business relationship. He and his wife no longer asked Ann to Seders; he did not invite her to lunch.

And the funny thing was, he often remarked to himself, he did not despise *her*. However she treated him, Joe Steinman admired Ann Murrow. He liked her style, he liked the way she had the balding guys who owned the network drooling over the blond *shiksa*. No, he did not despise her; what's to despise in a great business arrangement? And now his percentage of her—eight hundred thousand; could be an even million or more, according to his new plan.

The photos had upset the plan, at least put it on hold. And he hadn't been able even to raise it. She wanted the photos eliminated first. Understandable, and smart. As usual, smart.

But some curious thoughts had been turning around in Steinman's head while he awaited word from Minneapolis. Sure, the photographs would be an embarrassment. She'd left all hint of tawdry beginnings behind in her remarkable advance from weather girl to local news anchor in Milwaukee; riding the television markets up to L.A., then to the network as co-host of the morning show, then co-host of the magazine in prime time, and finally knocking the male co-host out of the box by constantly upstaging, outshining, outsmarting him. At each stage (and Steinman had a tape of each stage so that he could compare the style changes), she had become cooler, more dignified, more elegantly chic, more understated. New York and her own show had completed the process, the final layer of polish and sophistication. You could take her anywhere now. He knew she was angling to get an exclusive with Prince Charles, and he'd bet she wouldn't be out of place. The Prince of Wales might look awkward; Ann Murrow wouldn't. She talked to kings, presidents, prime ministers, and movie stars as equals, and they all called her Ann, as though using her name lent them some charisma.

So, the photos were an embarrassment. But disaster? Once again—he'd done this several times—Joe locked his office door, unlocked the safe, and arranged the photos on his desk. Then he walked around the desk to study them. Each day, as they'd become more familiar, his reaction to them had evolved.

They were still provocative. He could feel their sexual force, but by today's standards they weren't really smutty. There was no actual nudity, certainly none of the shameless genital display the models considered routine for *Penthouse* or *Playboy* . . . had for years. Nothing pornographic. In fact, by current standards, her bit of provocative flirting for the camera was tame, in good taste. It wasn't keyhole stuff, like being photographed *in flagrante* . . . Not as if she'd been a gal so hard up or dumb she'd acted in a porno flick. No, by all such measurements, these were mild. Yet if they were published, no doubt they'd create a sensation. Could probably get more than $100,000 for a full set. The money wasn't important; it was the publicity . . . and that could be played. It would have everyone talking about Ann Murrow for a couple of weeks, one cycle of *People, Time, Newsweek,* all the TV talk shows, Ann saying, with dignity, "I was in love with a guy, and I wanted to kid him a bit." She wouldn't have to say that the guy owned the station that soon promoted her from weather girl to news anchor without any news credentials. Wouldn't have to say the guy was married.

Take it a step further: what would it do to the plan? Of course it would bring out all the gray old farts, the journalism dignitaries, who bleated constantly about the news being turned into showbiz, but what would be the result? For several weeks the most talked-about TV journalist in the nation, probably on earth, would be Ann Murrow, and the most watched. Notoriety was one of the few things that predictably goosed ratings. And when you wanted to reopen the bidding for talent, when you wanted a bidding war, ratings said it all.

And that was what Steinman had in mind. Reopen the bidding war that had had all the networks thrashing around during the last Ann Murrow contract crisis. Daily stories in the columns. She may go here. She may go there. Daily items on "Entertainment Tonight." Leaks about this network offering x mill, that network offering x plus y.

He didn't need sexy pictures to engineer that, but if worse came to worst, he could make the pictures work too. It was even possible— nothing was impossible with Ann Murrow—that she'd figured it the same way, which may be why she had sent him the pictures. Maybe not figured, just sensed. Nobody had a better P.R. sense than Ann Murrow.

16

In the morning it was raining, but Grant needed exercise, so he ran twice around the reservoir. Coming home, waiting for the traffic light on Fifth Avenue, he knew what he wanted to do. Out of the shower, he called Sherman Glass at home.

"Hey, what's up? You never call me. I always call you."

"There's something I need to know about my contract. What does it say about my right to approve who substitutes for me?"

"Well, it's there. I don't remember the exact wording; I'll have to look at it. But it's there."

"When you get to the office, will you look it up right away and call me? I want to know the exact wording."

"Sure, but what's up?"

"They're trying to put Bill Donovan in place of Bryce Watson. I'm not going to let them."

"Hey, Grant!" And Grant heard an odd note in Sherman's voice. "I think you and I should talk this over before you do anything. I'm just starting a negotiation, remember? We better not get our wires crossed."

"Sherman, call me when you've got the wording and we'll discuss it then, OK?"

"OK, OK. But don't do anything rash before we talk. I think we've got a chance for a great five-year package here, Grant. We don't want to blow it on side issues. Bill Donovan shouldn't be a deal-breaker."

"I hear you. Talk to you later."

A deal-breaker, Sherman's term, was exactly what Grant thought Donovan should be, but he should have been smart enough to look at the contract wording before charging into Ev Repton's office.

He felt clear-headed and loose after the run. He caught the headline news on WCBS, skimmed the *Times* while standing at the kitchen counter, eating his Special K and coffee, and was in the office by nine-thirty; Sherman called a few minutes later.

"I got the wording. It's open to interpretation, but the operative stuff is this: 'Network will not assign a correspondent to substitute for Talent without consultation.' It doesn't say approval, just consultation."

"So, it *is* a breach of contract? They didn't consult me."

"It's a technicality. Probably an oversight."

"It wasn't an oversight, Sherman. Repton as much as told me; it was deliberate. They leaked it to Carmody to make it a fact before they talked to me."

"What did you say to Repton?"

"I said I'd walk out if they made Bill Donovan my substitute."

"Oh, no! You should have called me! Let me handle this. You shouldn't be doing it directly."

"Sherman, I don't want you to handle this. You say Donovan shouldn't be a deal-breaker. I say he is."

"No, no! We can talk this over with them. It's the wrong time to put their backs up."

"What about my goddamned back? You represent me. It's my back you're supposed to care about, not theirs."

"Sure, sure. But there's another way to handle this than you making threats in person. We can find a way to negotiate it. We'll get them to ease off on Donovan for now."

"What do you mean, *for now?*"

"Donovan's a hot property. I know another network was looking at him. Your guys were smart to get him. But they'll have to develop him. Find anchoring slots for him."

"Why do they have to do that?"

"Because that was the understanding when they signed him."

"How do you know that?"

"Because we represented him. It's our contact."

"We means who?"

"It means us—our agency."

"But who specifically, Sherman. Who?"

"Well—it means me."

"You're Bill Donovan's agent?"

"That's right."

"Since when?"

"We signed him about nine months ago, when he was getting restless in Atlanta."

"You never told me."

"Well, I guess it didn't seem relevant, Grant. We sign lots of young talent. Who knows where they're going? But that's the name of the game. Spot them before they're big stuff."

"You don't see a conflict of interest in representing Bill Donovan and me?"

"No. Why? Bill's a young guy. His career is no threat to yours. It's a whole new generation. Nothing I do to advance him is against your interests. In fact, by representing both of you, I can dovetail the two interests. Far from any *conflict* of interest, I see it as *protecting* your interests. Seriously."

"Sherman, listen to me. I think Bill Donovan is a smirking asshole. He's everything I hate seeing our business turn into. I don't want him sitting in my chair. If he does, it sends the message that any handsome empty suit can do this job. And if that's true, what happened to credibility, what happened to experience in the field? What happened to news judgment? I didn't get this job till I had nearly twenty years in the field!"

"I know, I know. But times are changing—"

"You don't make some handsome kid who's been a reporter for a couple of years the editor of the *New York Times*. If you did, everyone would die laughing."

"They didn't laugh at Bill yesterday when he spoke at the National Press Club."

"So you know about that too? What in hell's going on here? I suppose you set it up."

"As a matter of fact, I know someone there who thought it'd be a good idea to invite him. Give him some exposure to Washington insiders."

"Sherman, the people who go to those press club lunches, unless you have real newsmakers, are not Washington insiders. Many are not working journalists. They're P.R. people, lobbyists, advertising people."

"So why's that so bad? Grant, I beg you to leave this to me. You've got a lot riding on this with Ev Repton. Let me handle it."

"Not this time, buddy. You sort it out later. I—"

"Grant, please!"

Grant hung up and went straight to Repton's office.

"I've slept on it as you suggested. And this is my position. According to my contract, you have to consult me before assigning any substitute. Clearly you've breached the contract. If you withdraw Donovan and re-instate Bryce, I'll overlook it. If you persist, I will not honor the contract. Is that clear?"

"Grant, we don't want this to escalate."

"Neither do I. Now, tell me you're continuing with Bryce and will be telling Carmody it was a misunderstanding about Donovan."

"Look, I think we can work this out."

"Tell me!"

"OK, OK. For this summer, Bryce is in. Then we have to talk."

"And you'll tell Carmody."

"OK, OK."

"And I want to see the survey data you mentioned."

"It's very preliminary. Still raw stuff."

"Not too raw for you to use it to drop Bryce ten thousand feet without a parachute."

A calculating look clouded Repton's pale blue eyes. "Grant, I was a little hasty yesterday. So were you. Let's both calm down. We've got to work this through together."

"That's just what I wanted to hear, Ev. I'll watch Carmody's column."

Repton said casually as Grant left, "You want to see the survey? Why not? I want to be open with you. But I trust you to keep it to yourself. You'll see why. Remember, it's just preliminary analysis." He handed Grant a document in vinyl covers.

The pleasure Grant felt was tempered by the hunch that this was a small and temporary victory. He called Bryce to reassure him, but personally had no confidence that it was more than a stopgap. Then he called Winona, who said, "What did I tell you? You scared him yesterday."

"Only for a moment, I think. Only for a moment."

He did not call Sherman Glass. Let him find out on behalf of his new client. His betrayal was the biggest shock of all.

And it was that evening, when he had reason to feel he had gained some ground, that the idea of the facelift suddenly came into his head. It sprang at him from the audience survey. One page told the story. It was headed AUDIENCE REACTIONS TO NEWS PERSONALITIES, broken down into demographic groups, comparing the well-known figures on all the networks and cable with Grant and his colleagues.

First, simple audience recognition, and Grant scored very high: 79 percent. Not surprising. He'd been a network anchor for so long. Interesting who scored higher: Ann Murrow was the top. Eighty-seven percent of the U.S. television audience could say who she was. Then columns for subjective attitudes: *Authoritative, Pleasant, Comfortable to Watch, Arrogant,* lists of positives and negatives. Grant's positives were high but, again, lower than Ann Murrow's. It stung him to notice she scored higher than he did in *Credibility.* But when the audience was broken down by age and education, there was a difference. *Viewers 50+* scored Grant very high. So did *Some College Education.* When he looked at *18–49,* the difference was obvious. His score was much lower, like that of the other news anchors, but, curiously, not Ann Murrow. She rated very high with younger viewers too.

Grant looked for Donovan's name and found it. As Repton had said, the numbers were too small. An asterisk pointed to a footnote saying "too few responses for reliable analysis."

There was another page of personal qualities viewers perceived, and there the message was unmistakable. Grant Munro was considered fatherly, grandfatherly, a trusted older figure. It translated: too old. It translated into facelift.

Later, as he was brushing his teeth, looking at himself in the mirror, he saw what he had seen at Jean Lafitte, probably reinforced by Shirley Trattner's story. Brushing forced the muscles along his jawline to exaggerate his jowls. He closed his mouth and put the toothbrush down. The medicine cabinet had three mirrored doors. He opened the side doors and studied his face in the right and left profiles. Then, with his thumbs, he pulled the skin of his jawline upward and saw how it improved the look. He did the same with the saggy skin of his neck. Finally, with his fingertips, he lifted the puffy skin over his eyelids.

Then he realized how ridiculous he looked, holding up the wings of his eyebrows. Worried that Winona might see him, he closed the mirrors.

Even entertaining the idea for a moment was a little surrender to the trends he thought he was fighting, that the appearance of youth was the commanding value, outweighing experience, wisdom, or knowledge.

But! He was not going to use comforting rationalizations about the society to mask his epiphany: he would be less vulnerable if he appeared less old, and he could achieve that with a facelift.

HIS BARBER, Graham, called himself a stylist and charged appropriately, but was willing to come to the apartment. It was private and was economical of time, and Grant had rationalized away the embarrassment years ago. In order to keep Grant's hair looking the same, Graham came every Wednesday unless Grant was away, and then they rescheduled.

The next Wednesday morning came two days after Grant's lunch with Shirley.

Graham said, "A little more gray showing on top now. If you wanted to, it would be simple to put a little color back in."

"You mean that Grecian Formula stuff they advertise on TV?"

"Oh, dear, nothing as crude as that. I mean proper salon coloring, but very subtle."

"I don't want to do that."

"I didn't think you would, but lots of men are doing it these days. That and many other things to keep the beast of age at bay—facelifts, eyelids, chins. All the things women have done for ages, men are doing now. Lots of men in television. You'd be surprised! And hair transplants, and hairpieces, of course."

He was busy snipping away through his monologue, knowing Grant preferred to let him chatter without responding. But his phrase "the beast of age" sounded so heartfelt that Grant looked at him in the mirror.

"Have you had any cosmetic surgery, Graham?"

"Why certainly!" He pirouetted his face back and forth in the mirror.

"Surely you're too young to need it."

"You're delightful to say so. How old do you think I am?"

"I suppose late thirties or early forties."

"Bless you! I'm actually almost fifty. But don't tell a soul!"

"And you're happy you did it?"

"I can't imagine living without it. In a few years I'll go back for some tightening up." His fingers pulled the skin around his jawline. "If I can afford it. But they say it's better to start younger and do a little at a time, small adjustments. That's what the actors do. Some start in their thirties. It's a terrible expense, but I think it's appropriate in my life. And in my work. Smart people don't want someone doing their hair who looks a mess. And just for myself in my life. How I feel about myself. How my partner feels about me. I feel young. I want to stay looking young. I want to look as good as I can for as long as I can. I can't stand the thought of letting it all go and just getting old. I'd die. There! Done!"

"Thanks, Graham."

"Don't mention it. Same time next week?"

"I think so. I'll get Angela to call if there's any change."

Graham packed his scissors carefully in a soft leather case and rolled up the drop cloth spread under the Windsor chair they used. Grant put on a shirt and tie, chosen from the side of the wardrobe devoted to plain blue or stripes too fine to moirée on television, the sober uniform of his trade, nothing too loud or conspicuously stylish.

Graham finished tidying up.

"You know, if you ever thought about cosmetic surgery yourself, you'd make an excellent candidate."

"Why?"

"Because you have such a strong bone structure—cheekbones, jawbones. And I could give you a referral."

"Well, thanks, Graham."

Grant couldn't bring himself to admit it had even crossed his mind. And given that Graham was gay, Grant obviously felt a clutch of defensiveness, unwilling to concede any relevance to himself. But as when Shirley had mentioned a facelift, it was as though there was a conspiracy afoot to plant the idea.

Winona came downstairs, dressed for work, looking, as always, smart but not so fashionable as to make her female clients uneasy.

"Graham, what do you think I should do with my hair?" She fluffed out the short ends of the same Audrey Hepburn cut she had worn for years. "It's so practical, but I get tired of it now and then."

"Darling, I'd be very reluctant to change it. It's your look! It suits you perfectly, and it's always contemporary. A very young look. You might wear it a trifle shorter or longer here or there for variety. Or frost it, or color it a little. I've just been suggesting to Grant that he could wash his gray out with a little coloring."

Winona turned from the mirror, laughing. "Oh, Grant would never do that!"

"That's what he said," said Graham in mock despair. "But seriously, if you'd like me to think about options for you, I will. Though I think you'd be crazy to change what works so well."

"I guess I think so too," Winona said, and opened the front door. "Thanks. Just hearing that has made my day." And she turned her dazzling wide smile on Graham. "Bye-bye, honey. Talk to you later."

Grant said to Graham, "I can drop you, if you like. The car's downstairs, as usual."

"All right! I love it on the days I walk into the salon straight out of Grant Munro's limousine."

They got into the wood-paneled elevator that served one apartment on each floor.

"Not limousine, Graham. Just a car."

"But it has a chauffeur."

"It has a driver."

"You make it sound so prosaic. If I had a car and driver in New York, I'd play it to the hilt. I'd make sure everyone knew."

www.hollygo.com

Yesterday, girlfriend (say, did you know the Japanese say that? Only they say it garufrendo? Imagine all them Japanese drag queens got up like geishas callin each other garufrendo?). Anyway, yesterday hollygo reported one small victory by Gregory Peck over the forces trashin the teeveenews bidness. Well, he on a roll. Remember, they tryin push out Old Reliable as Gregory Peck's summer replacement anchor with young White House correspondent Billy Boy Blue? Even leaked it to John Carmody in the *Washington Post,* like it already a done deal? Well, hollygo is reliably informed Gregory had a fit, said no way José! You put some know-nuthin kid in my chair and what's the point a pretendin any longer? And management backed down cos he got it in his contract that they have to consult him on substitutes. Old Reliable stays in place and God's in his heaven, like the preacher says.

But stay tuned, or stay logged on, cos this ain't over yet, no way! We got miles to go, and clothes to buy, before we sleep.

Don'tcha luv it?

18

Before the morning meeting, Marty Boyle stopped Grant to mutter, "Need a word," and they stepped back into Grant's office.

"The *Time* writer Christopher Siefert is here already. Wants to observe the morning meeting before he talks to you."

"So?"

"So I thought maybe we should cool it on the Wyoming murder story . . . you know . . ."

"How do you mean, cool it, Marty?"

"It won't look good to have you and me arguing like yesterday in front of him."

"So you want me to say, fine, go for broke on the girl who dreamed her own murder?"

"It's a big story again. They've found definite evidence of sexual assault."

"I thought it was rape all along."

"Yeah, but the autopsy results show semen in her vagina and they're going to do DNA—"

"Jesus, Marty! I don't care. I'm not going on our air talking about semen in some little girl's—"

"It's a huge story, Grant! Bigger and bigger. We can't ignore it. I just don't want us to have a fight about it in front of Siefert."

Grant turned around at the door. "OK, Marty, I agree!"

"You agree? Wow!" A big smile widened his freckles.

"We won't argue in front of him. Just forget the Wyoming story."

"We can't do *that!*"

"Sure we can. When the desk raises the story, we say give it a rest today. We did enough yesterday. No argument. No fight for *Time* to play up. Clean, see?" And Grant walked out, with Marty's agonized stage whisper in his ears: "But we can't just ignore the story!"

"We will, Marty," said Grant over his shoulder, "or I'll fight you every inch of the way and make sure Siefert's tape recorder gets every word. OK?"

Grant felt alive and confident as he took his seat, to the usual chorus of "Hi, Grants, Morning, Grants," the energy heightened by *Time*'s presence.

When the Wyoming story came up, Grant looked at Marty. There was a pause, and Marty said quickly, "Naw, we played it hard enough yesterday."

"We didn't have the autopsy yesterday, Marty."

"I know. But it's in questionable taste, all that seamy detail. What d'you say, Grant?"

"I agree. Fine decision, Marty."

Whether Siefert noticed, the meeting rippled with little gestures of incredulity.

When they settled in Grant's office, Siefert said, "I thought it would be good to begin with some basics—how you started in the business, stuff like that."

"Fine with me."

Siefert started the small tape recorder.

TRANSCRIPT:

CHRIS: Just make sure this is working . . . (Sound recorder stopped, rewinding, playing again)

MARTY: . . . in questionable taste, all that seamy detail. What d'you say, Grant—

CHRIS: Oops. (Sound of fast-forwarding) Well, anyway, we know it works. By the way, would you describe what the relationship is between you and Marty Boyle, the executive producer?

GRANT: Sure. It varies from show to show, and with the individuals. The executive producer runs a program. He hires and fires, controls the budget, makes assignments, brings the raw product into the shop, and shapes it into a show. The anchor can be very passive. The old joke in the business is: Just tell me where to stand and what to say! Or he can be deeply involved. On network news shows, the anchor's usually more involved. We're all called editors or managing editors. In our shop, Marty and I share the running of the show.

CHRIS: Is that smooth? No friction with two bosses?

GRANT: Oh, yeah, there's friction sometimes.

CHRIS: Seemed smooth this morning.

GRANT: You should have been here yesterday.

CHRIS: When you disagree, what's it about?

GRANT: News philosophy. A program has an identity, and that's shaped by what it puts on day after day. As I told you in our first talk, there's a tug-of-war between those who want to make it more appealing to hold on to audience, and those who don't want to sell its soul.

CHRIS: You're in that group, and Marty's in the first?

GRANT: Well, it's subtler than that.

CHRIS: He's young, I notice.

GRANT: They're all young these days.

CHRIS: So there's a generational tug-of-war too? Over style? Over content?

GRANT: Sure, there's some of that.

CHRIS: How often, to use your phrase, do you feel them trying to sell your soul?

GRANT: Take today. If we'd decided to play up the autopsy results of the little girl murdered in Wyoming . . . the lurid details you know will be all over cable and the syndicated shows . . . that would have been a piece of soul for sale.

CHRIS: But you all agreed on that.

GRANT: We did.

CHRIS: Suppose you don't agree? Who has the last word?

GRANT: Editorially, I do. If I exercise it. That means I have to be here, fully involved, up to speed. If I'm not—and this job has many demands on my time—then I have to accept what they do.

CHRIS: And is that different from what you'd do?

GRANT: Occasionally. Remember, we're all part of the same news organization. We breathe the same air, same traditions.

CHRIS: So who's really the boss on "The Evening News"? I'm not clear.

GRANT: I am, if I choose to make choices.

CHRIS: But if you let them do it all the time, it wouldn't be your show?

GRANT: Right. It would be in name, but less in spirit.

CHRIS: And how important to you is it to have the show yours in spirit?

GRANT: Very important.

CHRIS: Because, you told me last week, you feel you're defending something, resisting, you called it, "the pandering lead." I wondered about that. What's a pandering lead?

GRANT: The lead that appeals to the supposedly low tastes of the public—for sex, violence, crime, scandal.

CHRIS: If, say, you were to lead on the Wyoming sex murder tonight?

GRANT: That's right.

CHRIS: But you *did* lead on it last night. I saw the show.

GRANT: We did. I was distracted by some meetings, and they thought it was the strongest story.

CHRIS: And you didn't?

GRANT: The way the day worked, I had to accept their judgment. It's what I just said. The editorial judgment is mine to exercise, but I have to exercise it or . . .

CHRIS: Or lose it?

GRANT: To some degree.

CHRIS: Well, anyway, I got you off on a tangent. I wanted to talk about your early days. I've seen your bio and the handout stuff from Laurie. But I'd like to hear some of it in your own words.

(And Grant relaxed, because this was easy to do.)

CHRIS: People are always fascinated about how famous, successful people got started. They love to hear it. So tell me how it began for you.

GRANT: I was out of college . . .

CHRIS: University of Connecticut, right?

GRANT: Right.

CHRIS: Major?

GRANT: English.

CHRIS: OK.

GRANT: I'd saved some money . . . I worked every summer through high school and college on boats, sailboats.

CHRIS: What kind of work?

GRANT: Everything: scraping, painting, sanding, varnishing, engine maintenance, crewing for races, permanent crewing, skippering, yacht delivery, all that stuff. My second year out of college, the summer of 'sixty-one, I was crazy to go to Europe. It amazes me today that my kids' generation doesn't seem as curious, as hungry as we were . . .

CHRIS: Sorry to interrupt. Just tell me their names and ages.

GRANT: Our son, Sandy—Andrew is his real name—is twenty-seven, and his sister, Heather, is twenty-five.

CHRIS: You were dying to go to Europe . . .

GRANT: I felt I wouldn't be fully alive until I'd been there. I'd been trying to get a journalism job after college and couldn't land one, so I worked as much as I could on boats that fall, winter, and spring. By June I had two thousand dollars, and I took off on Icelandic Airlines, the cheapest fare. Had a wonderful time with my first taste of England, France, Italy, and, by a stroke of good luck, Berlin. You know, big flashpoint; Ed Murrow had done a documentary calling the city a "frying pan with a handle a hundred and ten miles long."

CHRIS: Was Ed Murrow a big role model for you?

GRANT: Not so much. Sure, in general terms. But personally, I guess I came a little late to feel the mystique. So . . . anyway, you remember, East Germans were streaming out through Berlin. I wasn't paying much attention until I met a guy with a motorcycle, a Swede, at a café in the Piazza Navona in Rome. He asked if I wanted a ride to Berlin. He was going home that way and was curious about what was happening. Three days later, we were in Berlin—a place full of spooky associations from all the war movies. In the youth hostel there were students who knew cheap places to eat. We went to the zoo, the ruins of the Reichstag, but particularly I hung out in East Berlin, my first taste of the drabness, the uninviting stores, the shoddy new construction. I was a kid who'd grown up in the cold war, and this was all exciting to me.

In the middle of one night, one of the students banged on my door. "Come quick. They say the Communists have started building a wall."

CHRIS: Amazing! To fall into that story.

GRANT: I know. I threw on my clothes and we walked rapidly through the Potsdammer Platz and along the edge of the Tiergarten to the Brandenburg Gate. It was about four-thirty in the morning, already light, and a beautiful day. A handful of people were gathered, silent in the dawn, on the boulevard leading to the gate . . .

(He was telling this well, Siefert thought, wondering whether it was polished from frequent telling.)

In the center of the huge arch, scruffy East German Volkspolizei, the people's police, were using cranes to unload large cement flower-pots, filled with flowers in bloom. They were lining them up to block the street. To one side, toward the Potsdammer Platz, they were stretching barbed wire and unloading cast-cement sections. They were cutting the city in two. The stunned crowd watched quietly. News photographers and cameramen moved along the crowd, taking pictures of the East German actions and the West Berliners watching. A cameraman with a sound camera came in front of us. I complained that we couldn't see. He turned and said, in an English accent, "Do you speak English?"

"I'm American," I said.

"Could you hold this a sec?" I took the bag he handed me. He lifted the camera off his shoulder brace, broke off the magazine, and said, "Can you unzip the bag? There's another mag inside. Quick. Can't waste a sec."

When he stopped to consider the next shot, he said, "Do you mind sticking with me for a bit, hanging on to my bag? My sound man's gone back to the office for more film. And I don't know where the bloody correspondent's got to. Just till one of them gets back? Thanks."

He worked for the BBC in London, and I became his unofficial assistant. By the end of that feverish day, after I had run, carried, shot-listed, brought wurst, sausages, for them from a street vendor, he said, "This looks like a biggish story and we need help. If you'll stick with us for a day or two, I'll see they pay you for your time."

(Siefert let his tape recorder do the work. Grant was a good story-teller. Let him tell it his way.)

Well, a day or so turned into six weeks of the most excitement I'd ever had, working all day and half the night seven days a week. We filmed the East Germans building the wall through streets, into the brick walls of existing houses, across the middle of bridges, through squares, through the British, French, and American zones. The BBC men were great to me, and I worked my ass off for them, in a kind of demented joy. I learned how to load magazines, how to keep shot lists, drive film to Templehof Airport and ship it to London. Day and night, Nigel, the cameraman, and I and his soundman, Rufus, patroled the growing wall, looking for stories, and always found them: dramatic confrontations when West Berliners stormed the East German police, tense moments when U.S. tanks met East German tanks cannon to cannon on Friederichstrasse; pathetic stories of East Berliners in the upper-story windows of their houses, weeping as their lower doors and windows were bricked up.

It gave me a more concentrated course in television news than a year in graduate school. We existed on wurst and sauerkraut and Pilsner, seldom a sit-down meal. I met their colleagues, the correspondents. I ran whatever errands they asked me, made phone calls for them, and listened carefully and watched what they did. I wanted it never to end, but eventually even that story calmed down, and they didn't need my help anymore. We parted good friends, and they gave me a recommendation. Their Berlin bureau chief typed it out on BBC stationery, a letter saying, "In my opinion, Mr. Munro is born for a career in television news and I have every confidence he will succeed in it. He has all the necessary qualities."

CHRIS: Do you still have that letter?

GRANT: I guess so. I can look for it.

CHRIS: If you would. I think we can use it; a box, maybe.

GRANT: When I flew home in October, the letter got me a job in the newsroom at the TV station in Providence. Remembering those days makes me think—nothing we did as television journalists exaggerated or overplayed the significance. I was still a kid and knew nothing of world affairs that summer, but I got the feeling that we were doing something important in letting the world see this monstrosity. We still show monstrosities, but from different motives. It's that loss of innocence I mourn in our business, and I'm uncertain about why and where it happened.

CHRIS: Where do you think it happened?

GRANT: I don't really know. In the Cuban missile crisis—that came next—television played a different role. There was little to show once Kennedy announced the presence of Soviet missiles and said they had to be removed. I remember watching in Providence, after my Berlin experience, dying to be at the center of the action. But the loss of innocence . . . I'll have to think about that.

CHRIS: I didn't know about Berlin. It's a good story. But your bio says it was the Kennedy assassination that launched your career. Tell me about that.

GRANT: Well, it did more directly. I was in the Providence station. Fortunately, I wasn't out to lunch. When I heard the first bulletin, I had a very simple reaction. If Kennedy had been shot, what must his mother think? That probably sounds pretty naïve, but it's what I thought. Twice that summer I'd been up to the Kennedy compound in Hyannis on weekends when the president came in by helicopter.

Dave, one of the Providence cameramen, was a friend. I found him eating a sandwich and I said, "Hey, the President's been shot in Dallas. Let's grab the mobile unit and run up to Hyannis and see what we can get from the family."

He said, "The mobile unit's supposed to go over to the state capitol; something with Senator Pastore."

I said, "Come on, Dave, this is history! The President's been shot. Who cares about Pastore?"

"The station cares. Pastore's on the communications committee. What about Steve?" Steve was the news director.

"He's out to lunch. There's no time to get him. Come on, Dave, we've got to go! It's the story of a lifetime!"

My hunch was a lucky one. We got to Hyannis first and got a position right by the fence of the Kennedy compound before the police cordoned the area off. And when they did soon after, we were inside the cordon. Because Dave was a hell of an engineer, and we'd done it before, we quickly got a microwave signal out.

We couldn't see much action in the compound, but it didn't matter. All the Kennedys' neighbors came out and told me what they'd seen. After getting the news, Rose Kennedy had gone for a long walk on the beach all by herself. The neighbors talked all that long beautiful afternoon about the Kennedys' comings and goings, the brothers, the sisters-in-law, Jack and Jackie. It became a neighborhood wailing wall, and it fascinated the network. New York kept coming back to the Providence station asking for more cut-ins from Hyannis, for replays of our taped stuff and requests for more moody talk from me. The Hyannis crowd took to me. They wanted to pour their feelings out to someone—and I was there.

CHRIS: What happened about your taking the mobile unit?

GRANT: The news director was furious, but the station manager and owners were basking in the national network attention; you know, their call letters repeatedly sounding across the nation, and it all rolled forward from there for me.

I learned, maybe I knew instinctively, maybe I learned it from sailing, there are moments—in the news business, as in wars, as in politics, as in love—when you have to commit instantly and go for it, on gut feelings. Those heady moments when your gut tells you it's the right thing to do, even if it runs over a few toes, because in the long run they're going to see it. You just had to be bolder than the rest. I guess that sounds boastful, but it isn't, because these aren't fully conscious decisions. That day, I got the scent of it; it made me feel bolder, smarter, quicker to see the opportunity and seize it. It's happened to me since then. A moment of pure clarity, as if the lights have gone down on all the irrelevant detail, leaving the obvious course of action brilliantly lit, like a flare path. On the right occasions I've known just what to do. It's seldom let me down. And whenever I've felt it, the adrenaline's surged and it was a joyful moment. There haven't been any such moments for a long time. That's the penalty of sitting here.

(Moments of pure clarity, Siefert noted. *Good stuff!)*

Inside, back here at HQ, behind the lines, it's all committee and consensus—you must know what it's like—hundreds of little negotiations every day. The bold stuff is for the freedom of the field, and even that's screwed up now, because the news managers and the money people make so many decisions back here in New York.

In the old days, no one at the network complained, never even mentioned, the flights charged, the chartered planes, the hotel bills, the rented cars, the crazy, exotic expenses, like "rental, two camels." If you got there and got what you needed to be competitive—better if you got what no one else did, because you'd followed your hunch away from the pack—no one ever mentioned money. No one got to be a hero in the field saving dough. Now there's so much second-guessing in New York, I think the system kills initiative.

Anyway . . . my piece of the Kennedy story that day was obviously a tiny part of the whole. But I was excited to be part of it, to have my face and name and reporting up there with all the big names that filled television that weekend, and it launched my real career.

CHRIS: How did it do that? What happened?

GRANT: Actually, the first thing it did was reunite me with Winona. We'd gone together in college, then had broken up. She saw me on television that weekend and called.

CHRIS: Want to tell me more about that?

GRANT: I guess not.

CHRIS: Perhaps Winona might?

GRANT: Maybe. You can ask her.

CHRIS: But, anyway, what happened in television?

GRANT: Well, the network phoned and offered me a job on the

news desk in New York. I spent a year there getting basic training. Then they moved me to Washington and then Vietnam—

CHRIS: What period were you in Vietnam?

GRANT: December 'sixty-five to March 'sixty-seven.

(Angela opened the door. "Noon meeting, Grant.")

CHRIS: I'd like to hear about Vietnam separately. And there's still a lot of other ground to cover. Maybe we'll need more time than we figured. Is that OK?

19

In two and a half days, the Minneapolis detective George White produced solid information.

"The name isn't Zabricki, it's Schmid. Ernest Schmid, goes by Ernie. Zabricki was his mother's name, Anthony his father's. He's young, born 1971, not what you'd call an important citizen, but no trouble either. Smart enough to get a high school diploma with average grades. No arrest record. Never been fingerprinted. Has a valid driver's license with no violations. He's unemployed, drawing unemployment. Lives in a cheap rooming house. Had to sell his car, pawn his stereo. Was a technician or assistant in a small photographic store over in Saint Paul until he was laid off. I staked out the place where he rents the box. It's one of those private mailbox places. He's hitting the box two, three times a day, obviously waiting for something. Am I right, something he expects you to send him?"

Steinman ignored that. "What's he look like?"

"He's OK-looking, ordinary, dark hair slicked back, could use a haircut; thin, probably weighs about a hundred and fifty. Looks like a thousand guys his age. Not a real tough kid but kind of scrappy-looking, like he could take care of himself. Has nothing to do with his time. Guess he needs money. Eats a big breakfast at a diner, then skips lunch or has a bag of potato chips, and fills up at dinnertime. Walks a lot. Hangs out in the library, and keeps checking that mailbox. So, what d'you think? You want us to find out more?"

"You have his address?"

"Sure, I told you, a rooming house. Couple of women who could be hookers. A truck driver. Not where you and I'd want to stay."

"Any chance you could have a look in his room?"

White chuckled. "Surreptitious entry?"

"Is it possible?"

"What would we be looking for?"

"A flat envelope, probably." Well, what the hell, Steinman thought. "Some photographs, in fact."

"Thought it was something like that. Well, I can tell you they're not in his room. We already had a look while one of us kept an eye on him downtown at the mailbox. Nothing there. If he's got them, he's stashed them somewhere else. All he's got there is some clothes. Not even a claim ticket for a baggage locker, or anything like that."

"I see. You went to a lot of trouble."

"You too. Anybody willing to cough up a thousand a day has got something big on his mind."

"How about the photographic store where he worked? What about that?"

"It's closed. The owner was sick. Died of AIDS recently. That's why Ernie got laid off. Owner was too sick to run it."

"What was the owner's name?"

"Let me look here. It was in the paper. Yeah, John Wheatly." He read Steinman the small obit.

"Could this Ernie get into the store even though it's closed?"

"I don't know. We could keep an eye on it and find out."

"Why don't you do that for a couple of days."

"You keeping the meter running? A thousand a day?"

"Yeah, but for that, you can watch the store and keep an eye on Zabricki too."

"You think he'll go back to where he got the photos, right? Well, he might. That's OK. I guess you want them pretty bad. Anyway, I'll call you in a couple of days."

Steinman felt a little uneasy about the rising interest in the detective's voice. Not impossible a savvy guy could watch Zabricki, retrieve the photos, muscle him out of the way, and . . . no, most detectives stayed clean. More or less clean. A lot of ex-cops, a whole network of ex-cops, who knew shortcuts without breaking the law. Unauthorized searches were not exactly kosher, but not exactly unknown.

He dialed Ann's private number, and she picked up.

"Hi, Ann. It's Joe."

"I'm tied up. Call you in a minute."

She had a phone manner, when not pouring on the charm, that was so impersonal and indifferent that he always felt a tingle of offense; even his voice wouldn't produce a little warmth in hers. But that was Ann.

When she called back, obviously anxious, he passed on the information and asked, "Does the name John Wheatly, a photographer, ring a bell?"

"Sure. That's the little guy who took them. I don't need his name, Joey. I need the goddamned pictures!"

"OK, OK. We'll get them. We've made a good start. We'll get them. But I thought it'd be smart to find out something about this creep before we deal with him."

"It *was* smart, Joey. You're right. I'm just worried, the longer it goes on, he'll get nervous and do something else with them."

"Don't worry. We'll get them. I'll call you."

Again she hung up with no polite phrase.

Tomorrow he should think about getting out to Minneapolis himself.

Ann Murrow wasn't someone for half results. She didn't want progress reports. She wanted final reports. Case closed. Success. Put-it-out-of-her-mind reports. That's what she wanted.

20

www.hollygo.com

You win one, you lose one, muchachas. It like that in war, in love, in teevee. But Hollygo think the Beige net losin it bad makin a respectable correspondent like the Tylenol Lady talk to the trash she had on that magazine show last night. What they tryin to do, make it the Rocky Horror Picture Show? No way. Not camp enough, just stupid. It pathetic to be hustlin for ratins with the likes of O. J. Simpson—AGAIN? Who they think wanna watch that shit?

It like that stuff they doin last winter about the president's dick and the foxy intern, furrowing they brows with heavy discussion: Is oral sex technically adultery, professor? News programs just like tabloid trash. Like that poor white trash Paula Jones got put up to this just to make the President of the United States pull down his pants in public so's everone can have a laugh? That why she doin it, cos them Clinton haters put her up to it, financin her, stoppin her makin a deal when she could of. But back to O.J., that black trash . . .

Hollygo confess right off she ain't one those blacks that went crazy with joy when O.J. got off. No way. Hollygo like Chris Rock. You hear that brother? All his black friends say what a great win for black folks but he been goin to the mailbox ever since lookin for his O.J. prize? And nuthin. I think O.J. killed them both, as simple as that. And to keep draggin him on teevee to milk another few drops of his celebrity? Forget it! That juice been sour a long time, and the Tylenol Lady shoulda knowed better.

I had to drink the whole mess a margaritas my friend brought over just to get over my huge disgust. On what happened then, hollygo just gonna draw the curtain.

Don'tcha luv it?

21

Christopher Siefert left his large apartment on West End Avenue and walked east on seventy-seventh, on his way to lunch. He was feeling better, sleeping better, urinated less often as his bladder control improved. Being back on a job seemed to have toned him up physically and mentally. Elizabeth said his color was improving, probably from the sun he got with all this walking.

He was enjoying the intellectual challenge Grant Munro presented. Two forces, like opposing electrical fields, made the professional dynamic interesting. The guy was impressive; still surprising Siefert by how well he talked. This was no empty suit, no mannequin. He knew a lot about journalism; he talked about his own experiences fluently and movingly. A natural storyteller, the sentences unrolling in that arresting, authoritative baritone voice. And he'd covered decades of important stories.

On the other side—nice as Grant was, apparently unaffected—was this wall of self-assurance, and it put Siefert off balance, irritated as much as it impressed him.

Different from Muhammad Ali. Siefert had done a long profile when the boxer was only thirty-six, on the verge of retiring, but not able to. Ali's physical presence in those days made Siefert think of a sleek jungle creature momentarily tame, like a young panther, a perfect animal. It gave him pleasure just to watch as Ali lounged sleepily around his French château in Chicago, the grass uncut outside, an unwashed Rolls-Royce in the driveway, insisting that Siefert take his shoes off to walk on the thick white rugs Ali's wife prized. You wanted to stroke this man because his body was so perfect, like that of a healthy animal in a free-range zoo.

Grant Munro's aura was nothing like that. Ali's grace came from the physical perfection and animal sleekness. Grant's from the habit of confidence, the patina that gradually formed on those accustomed to success and admiration. It conditioned them to abbreviate conventional manners. They appeared to move more slowly, expend less effort—even if they wanted to put themselves out, they didn't, because they were used to others doing the putting out—in small things, reaching for something, adjusting a chair, advancing for the handshake. Gradually, as in royalty, the necessary gestures became miniaturized in effort, the royal hand wave reduced to the motion of screwing in a lightbulb.

Obviously, Grant was unaware of this, but it had become habit, a stillness about him as if he were waiting, part defensiveness, because he was importuned so much by strangers, part expectation that the world and everything he needed would come to him.

When Grant stood up, he stood erect so that his six-feet-one appeared taller. That was it: Grant used all his assets; he made the most of everything he had been given by nature.

And that's where Christopher Siefert felt himself irritated. Walking home from the interview about Berlin and JFK, he realized that Grant had made the most of every gift, every experience, every opportunity. As in so many successful people there was an element of opportunism, snatching at chances, intercepting the crucial pass. Siefert had dropped passes, figuratively and literally. He was lousy at sports and not interested. But if he compared their starting advantages in life—his comfortable Manhattan home, private school, Harvard, Oxford—with Grant's apparently modest beginnings and a nothing college (well, that was snobbish; better avoid that), Grant had used everything he'd been dealt to maximum effect, while Siefert had dribbled advantages away.

Still, behind the masterly confidence Grant conveyed, that appearance of everything knitted together, like a suit of chain mail, all links closed, there must be loose ends. Everybody had them. Siefert had investigated enough successful people to have dispelled the common illusion that their lives must be perfect. There had to be a raveled sleeve of care somewhere in Grant's emotional wardrobe, and Siefert would find it. There was the mountaineering accident—he'd get to that—and these elusive rumors that people were scheming to ease Grant out. Siefert wanted to explore that line before he talked to Grant again, to give him something to chew on besides Munro's composure, his complacency.

He needed to talk to the people around Grant. Today he was having lunch with Everett Repton, who wanted to go to Daniel, so Siefert gave himself time to walk across the park.

Repton was scrutinizing the menu so carefully, Siefert thought he'd been forgotten, or that Repton was nervous and stalling. But eventually the oversize glasses pushed up to the forehead fell back to his nose, making Repton's flat blue eyes larger. He looked familiar, someone Siefert had known slightly and happily forgotten.

"I think we've met before somewhere."

"Didn't you live in Bronxville? Some years back?"

"That's it. I lived there until seven years ago."

"You spoke at the club. About a book you'd written."

"Yes, that's right." Bronxville. That fitted Repton.

"I think it's great that you're doing a cover. These are difficult times for those of us trying to maintain standards in a business that changes so rapidly. It's true in network news, as I'm sure it's true at Time Inc."

"You don't mind the recorder? Easier than taking notes at lunch, and I get accurate quotes. If you want to go off the record, just say so and I'll stop it."

In fact, most people forgot the tape was running, or feared to seem pretentious by asking that it be stopped.

Repton waved urbanely. "Nothing I have to say is secret. I'm proud of what we do. We're a serious news organization, with a great tradition of service to the American people. And we've got the best team in the business."

Siefert thought, why beat about the bush? But he approached the question conversationally, unthreateningly.

TRANSCRIPT:

CHRIS: OK. Everett Repton interview. You've been in the business a long time—

REPTON: Nearly thirty-five years.

CHRIS: Yes; I've studied your bio. You've had a lot of experience . . .

(People loved to know you'd read their bios. Spared them the immodesty of reciting their own achievements but assured them they hadn't been ignored. People hated it when reporters didn't know how important their lives had been.)

. . . going back to the Kennedy era—

REPTON: Well, Johnson. Just after Kennedy. I left Princeton in 'sixty-four, the Johnson-Goldwater year.

CHRIS: What I find difficult to understand, coming new to your business, is all the rumor, the public speculation, sheer gossip that swirls around you. Nobody's guessing who our next executive editor's going to be, or if they are, it's kept within an enclosed world or in specialist trade publications. But TV news is out there with Hollywood and showbiz generally, the columnists pumping up rumors. I've even seen stories in the *National Enquirer* about what this or that anchorman is getting up to.

(Repton smiled, uncertain where Siefert's question was going.)

REPTON: We ignore it. Let's face it, we're in a business that creates stars. We try to keep our feet on the ground as journalists, but it's a star-making business and a starstruck audience. So we sometimes attract the kind of attention Hollywood does.

(Vamping until he found Siefert's drift.)

CHRIS: How do you explain the speculation that Grant Munro is on the way out, that some people in your shop think he's been there too long and the only way to stop a further ratings slide is to replace him?

REPTON: Oh, that! The only thing I've seen like that was a silly story in the *New York Post*. If we took that stuff seriously, we'd all be in the loony bin—well, delete that—we'd all be—

CHRIS: In therapy?

REPTON: Something like that.

CHRIS: So you don't take the "Page Six" story seriously?

REPTON: Not for a minute!

CHRIS: Don't you wonder where such an idea comes from? I mean, you must have a huge investment in Grant Munro. He's the identity around whom your whole operation revolves, a five- to six-hundred-million-dollar-a-year business, right?

REPTON: That's in the ball park.

CHRIS: And a respected newspaper prints a story saying that guy may be for the high jump. You don't take that seriously?

REPTON: Well, I'm not going to bite on *respected newspaper,* but the answer is, I ignore it.

CHRIS: You ignore it? Laurie Jacobs told me you and she spent half a day figuring out how to respond to it.

(Repton looked irritated.)

REPTON: Oh, well, sure, we kicked it around a bit, but we decided to ignore it.

CHRIS: Was it damaging to morale in your shop?

REPTON: Nah! We're all seasoned news people, too. We take all that gossip-column stuff with a big grain of salt.

CHRIS: What about Grant? He must have been upset.

(Repton lowered his forkful of quenelles de brochet, trying to read whether Siefert had already been to Grant, as he had to Laurie.)

REPTON: Yes, he was a bit.

CHRIS: I guess you reassured him.

REPTON: On what?

CHRIS: That you aren't planning to replace him.

(Repton beamed.)

REPTON: He knows that. We're in the middle of negotiating a new contract with him.

CHRIS: When is his present contract up?

REPTON: The year two thousand.

CHRIS: So his position is secure till then, and what . . . how many years beyond?

REPTON: We're discussing that.

CHRIS: Three years, four years?

REPTON: That's really confidential.

CHRIS: And the money he makes?

REPTON: Very confidential.

CHRIS: Is it safe to say that he'll be making more money in the new contract?

REPTON: That's often the way it goes.

CHRIS: I see stories that Grant makes nine or ten million a year.

(Siefert had seen actually six or seven million, but wanted to see Repton's reaction.)

REPTON: No, no; that's wildly exaggerated.

CHRIS: What wouldn't be wildly exaggerated? How can I get an authoritative figure?

REPTON: We never discuss that sort of thing.

CHRIS: Not for attribution?

REPTON: Off the record?

CHRIS: Off the record, I can't use it. Not for attribution, I use it but don't say where I got it.

REPTON: I'll think about it.

CHRIS: But just to be sure I've got it, Grant Munro is secure as your anchor for two more years, right?

REPTON: Right.

CHRIS: And you want to extend that. So he's your anchor for the millennium? To take you into the twenty-first century?

(He could see Repton disgesting *anchor for the millennium,* perhaps imagining it as a banner, as Siefert could, across Grant's face on the *Time* cover.)

REPTON: It's up to Grant. Sooner or later he's going to want to step down, take on something easier . . .

CHRIS: And then what?

REPTON: Then we'll assess things, choose a successor, and have a smooth transition—

(Was Repton giving him a hint, Siefert wondered, or hoping to give Grant a hint in print?)

—but he'll always be part of our team . . . . as long as he wants to be.

CHRIS: Where would such an idea come up? How would a gossip writer in the *Post* hear of such a thing?

REPTON: You mean hypothetically?

CHRIS: Yeah, hypothetically.

REPTON: Oh, some disgruntled colleague, someone's agent—not Grant's, obviously—someone in sales, network sales, who'd like a different package to sell . . . I don't know. Someone in an ad agency, for that matter, the wife of a rival correspondent tattling to her hairdresser . . . You're a sophisticated print reporter; you tell me how such stuff originates.

CHRIS: But this did not originate with you?

REPTON (laughing): Hey, I thought we were dropping the subject.

CHRIS: OK. How did the network feel when Grant called broadcast journalists Gadarene swine? Did you agree with him?

REPTON: I think he was just using a figure of speech. We were all disturbed by the presidential sex story and how to cover it. But the situation forced us to be competitive. We couldn't stand back from it.

CHRIS: So you think Grant's criticism was wrong?

REPTON: I wouldn't have put it that negatively. I mean, look at *Time*. You guys were all over the story, just as we were.

CHRIS: Another subject. How did Grant take that tragedy on the mountain? How did it affect him?

REPTON: It was an awful business . . . the death of his friend, the publicity, the rescue, the shots from the helicopter of that body swinging . . . I kept seeing it on cable, on local news. It was everywhere, again and again.

CHRIS: Did you run it on network news?

REPTON: We had to. Couldn't ignore it when it was everywhere else, and it was our star half-frozen on that mountain.

CHRIS: But how did Grant act when he came back?

REPTON: I don't know . . . he doesn't show his feelings much. I guess you'd say he was very down. We suggested he take some time off, but he wanted to work, thought it the best way of getting over it.

CHRIS: He hated the publicity?

REPTON: He hated becoming a news story himself and he hated something from his private life becoming public. We don't even mention his kids in publicity material . . . He wants their lives kept private.

CHRIS: That meant as much to him as the death of the climber?

REPTON: I couldn't say that. But I'll tell you one thing . . . this has to be unattributed, OK?

CHRIS: Sure.

REPTON: Well, you haven't turned the recorder off.

CHRIS: Oh, OK. There!

Transcript ends

Repton said, "I was told Grant made a financial settlement on the guy's widow. A big settlement. So obviously he felt very strongly."

"How much was it?"

"I heard half a million dollars."

"Indeed? So he felt responsible?"

"You'd have to ask him. But I didn't tell you this."

"The way you didn't tell me how much he makes. The recorder's still off. Unattributed?"

"Not for attribution, no 'network official' sourcing. OK?"

"OK."

"Five million."

"Less than I thought," Siefert said.

Ev Repton was crumpling his napkin, about to push back his chair, but he leaned forward. "Your question about how it affected him?"

"Yes?"

"I think somehow it made him act older."

"Does older mean too old for the business?"

"Oh, I'm not saying *that!* I have a car; can I drop you?"

"No, thanks, I'm walking."

No, Siefert considered, waving to Repton's car, the president of news wasn't the kind of ally he'd like to have. Certainly no unqualified testimonials to his big star. And why had he told him about Grant's giving money to Teresa Weldon?

22

Grant went to Sherman Glass's office but refused lunch. He sat down calmly, looking at his agent's piggy eyes under the martini-crashed pouches of the upper lids, watched him wipe his wet lips with the thumbs of his clasped hands.

"Did it never go through your mind that signing Bill Donovan would upset me?"

"Nope! Not for a minute. Never did. Why should a guy at the top, the king of the mountain, care if I sign a kid that has years and years of paying his dues until he's in your class? Why? Tell me."

"Because Repton and others see him as my replacement, and I'll bet you do, too."

"Honest to God, Grant, it's possible, I guess. Years from now, when you've decided to step aside, take on a different role. Yeah. Maybe I could see Bill Donovan being a contender—way down the line."

"I'd hate to think you were bullshitting me, buddy."

"That's crazy! I'm your agent. I've negotiated the best contracts for you of anyone in the business. Better. I'm working on the new one, better than ever. You'll soon be so secure financially, you'll never have to think about working, or money, for the rest of your life. That's an enviable position."

"Why would I want to think about not working?"

"Well, everyone looks forward to that."

"I don't look forward to it *now*."

"Hell, I'm not talking about *now*."

"You're raising it now, and in the same breath you're talking about the brilliant future for the kid."

"What d'you want me to say, Grant? You're our most important client. Your needs come first. But it's not a conflict of interest for us to build a stable of young talent. We'd be out of business if we didn't. We have to take 'em on spec. Some may work out big, some won't; we know that. We took you on when the network first got interested in you. We didn't know how far you'd go. But taking on Grant Munro then didn't bother the established stars on our roster. So you should see it the same way they did. OK?"

Against Grant's will, almost, Glass was relieving his suspicions.

"You got the network to sign Donovan with a promise of anchoring?"

"Promise, no. Intention, yeah, if the right slot comes along. Possibility, yes; promise, no."

"So—bingo! the right spot magically comes along: dump Bryce Watson!"

Sherman separated his hands in a so-what-can-you-do gesture.

"Whose idea was it?"

"Oh, his, Repton's."

"They discussed it with you?"

"Well—sure."

"Was that part of the possibility, as you call it, in the agreement you negotiated?"

"No! Come on, Grant! I can't discuss my negotiations for a client with other clients, even you. It isn't—"

"Ethical?"

"Kosher."

"Ethical."

"Right."

"Well, there's your conflict of interest. You can't tell me something that directly affects my interests, because it violates your confidentiality with another client. Answer? You shouldn't have the other client!"

"This doesn't directly affect your interests."

"You bet it does! Who substitutes for me is a real interest. I told you that, and it's in the contract."

"Consult, not approve."

"From now on, Sherman, it's going to be *approve*. I want the next contract hardened up. I want it to say I have to *approve* of anyone they propose as my substitute. Veto power. I want it in there, or I don't sign. I don't want to go through this every time they bring in some new airhead. Get it?"

"OK, OK. I'm not sure they'll go for it, but I'll try."

"You're not listening. I'm not asking you to try. I'm telling you what I want! No prior approval, no deal!"

Sherman looked weary of the conversation but still sly.

"I think I can get them up to ten mill. Best in the business. What d'you think of that?"

"It's less important than what I just told you."

"Jesus! You lost interest in money? I tell you this is *the* important contract. Two-thousand to two-thousand-five, if I can swing the five-year deal. Bring you to sixty-seven. And you'll have options after that. But it's a push to get the five years."

"Why?"

"Because—come on, Grant!—because you're getting older, like all the rest of us. You look great, but eventually . . . you know . . . after a while . . ."

"So how many years do they want to renew for?"

"They're not saying yet. Look, don't start getting into the negotiations, Grant. It's just the early stages. I'm still feeling my way. Leave it to me and we'll be all right."

"How did Donovan take being bounced in and bounced out of substitute anchor?"

"He was pissed. You would be too. But he's OK. He's a real nice guy. You should get to know him. He thinks the world of you."

"Really?"

"Yeah, really. You're his model."

"When I was his age, my models were the correspondents, the reporters, the guys in the field who did the actual stories, here and overseas. I didn't even think of myself as an anchorman. It seemed too elevated, like gods on Mount Olympus."

"Sure, but today kids come straight out of communications school wanting to be anchors."

"And they make them anchors on cable news. I see them. Half of them look and sound about fifteen."

"You can't knock youth, Grant. It's better to join it. Make it your partner. Help it along; get youth to do the work for you. That way you sleep at nights. You know what's happened to you?"

"What?"

"I'm just getting it. It's the first time in your whole career you've stopped thinking of yourself as the promising young guy. You've never worried about young competition before. Well, I'm telling you, stop worrying. By the time Bill Donovan, or anyone, is ready to take over your job, you'll be so glad to leave it, you'll pay them to get out."

SURPRISINGLY, shockingly, Winona had the same reaction.

"It's natural they'd want to try out young people in the summer when fewer people are watching. Sure, Donovan seems callow and inexperienced to you, but he has that new look they all seem to have now. It's becoming the TV look, gazing at the audience personally and intimately. Your style—it's kind of the style of your generation, our generation—looks at us more impersonally, as an audience, friendly but distant."

"Is that a bad thing?"

"No, it's just a question of changing generational styles, as in anything else. Look how different Clinton's style is from the presidents before him. It's like clothes. It's less formal. It's like everything. Everything changes."

"Donovan's style gives me the creeps. He looks all for himself. And, to be honest about it, I look old. I've just really noticed it."

"You're crazy!"

"I'm not crazy. I look old. When I shave, what I see in the mirror is this older guy, with sagging jowls, a flabby jaw, and puffy eyes."

"And I see a man who looks younger than sixty has any right to look. Look at your figure. All that running. You're always the same size. You've used exactly the same belt hole for so many years, your two favorite belts are cracking across that line."

"I'm not some guy working for Lazard Frères or Merrill Lynch. I may look OK to you; the question for me is, is OK for sixty going to work on television?"

"Of course it is."

And at that moment it came back into his head. He was going to get a facelift. Why hadn't he said it aloud?

Winona was saying, "That's part of the age. I have clients younger than you, men in their forties and fifties, feeling threatened by younger rivals. Sexual rivals, professional rivals. It's classic, part of the male menopause. And with all the corporate downsizing, it's worse. But they're in a very different boat. You're the top guy. You're the guy they build the whole image around. *The man you can trust, The Evening News with Grant Munro.* You've become their icon."

"So why were they trying to sneak Bill Donovan in and push old Bryce Watson off the gangplank behind my back?"

"Because they were looking for someone with more sparkle than Bryce. I can understand that. He's a friend and all that, but he's pretty deadly on the air."

"You've never told me that."

"Honey, I've said it a lot. You haven't been listening. He's color-less. Maybe that's why you like him, because he's so blah, you look fabulous by comparison. When he's on, people long for you to come back."

"Honestly, I never thought of that."

"Maybe not consciously . . . but isn't it pretty terrific to have as your substitute a guy who's no real rival?"

"No. I've always thought that someday he'd naturally succeed me."

"Not very realistic. How old is Bryce? Fifty-one, fifty-two, something like that? Say you wanted to retire at sixty-five—"

"I don't."

"I know, I'm just using it. Say you left at sixty-five; he'd be practically sixty. And all he'd be is drabber, a less vital version of you, another white male person of the same generation, and they'd have to replace *him* in another five years or so. No, I'm sure they'd want someone who's a whole fresh image—a new generation—new style—as you were in 'eighty-one."

"Repton showed me the preliminary stuff from the audience surveys they're doing. The younger demographics already think I look over the hill."

"Maybe you shouldn't be looking at that stuff."

"Too late now. But what really gripes me is what it says about our journalism—if you pop up with this guy, who isn't thirty yet, and all he's done is anchor the local news in Atlanta."

"He's been covering the White House."

"How long? Six months!"

Winona flashed her big grin, clasped Grant's face in both hands, and gave him a warm kiss. "Honey, I love you. You're smart as hell, but if you really believe it's Bill Donovan's lack of experience that bothers you more than his youth, you're fooling yourself. I think you're scared because he's young."

"That's exactly what that creep Sherman said. First time I've heard the footsteps of youth coming up behind me."

"Sure, and that's perfectly natural, but as I said, you're in too secure a position to worry about it."

But he did worry.

Had he been kidding himself all these years? Unconsciously securing a nonthreatening back-up, one who would make Grant look good when he came back? The minute it was out of Winona's mouth, a little bell of recognition had dinged in his mind.

But what about Winona's point about the new style, Donovan's intimate look, Grant's distant? Did he seem too distant? Should he try to bridge that intimacy gap? To project himself differently? Or would the facelift help by opening his eyes wider?

23

By the time Grant got the appointment with his internist, Michael Rosenberg, every magazine he turned over seemed to be advertising cosmetic surgery.

He felt in perfect health, weight steady around 178, one or two pounds more than he'd like, but fine. Rosenberg insisted on a PSA check to give early warning of any prostate danger. With Christopher Siefert's example, and cancer in the family, a sensible precaution, like the colonoscopy now recommended every few years. And it didn't hurt to have an electrocardiogram once a year. All that running hadn't saved Jim Fixx.

Grant liked Michael Rosenberg, who was medically conservative, thoughtful, thorough, a pleasure to talk to. Only a few years older, he seemed fatherly, just intimidating enough that Grant wouldn't want to do anything he'd be embarrassed to tell Rosenberg about.

"Would you think I was a jerk if I considered getting a face-lift?"

Not a flicker of surprise. "Not at all. Many of my patients have cosmetic surgery, for a variety of reasons. Tell me what you're thinking."

"I want to do it and I don't want to. I'd be very embarrassed if anyone knew I was considering it."

"I know businessmen in their forties and fifties who do it because they're afraid they'll be pushed out for younger-looking men. Are the people at the network asking you to do it?"

"No, it's my own idea. I've just been noticing how much older I look."

"No particular reason for anxiety?"

Grant sidestepped. "I'd like to know more about it. Can I count on the doctor to keep it private? How serious is the operation? How quickly would I be back at work? What are the risks?"

As usual, Rosenberg made him feel better.

"Look, there's no moral stigma. It's not something to be ashamed of. It is medically sound and more sophisticated than it used to be. Our profession isn't nearly as censorious as it was, although I think the heavy advertising is distasteful. But I could find you someone who'd do an excellent job, with the least risk—and it isn't risk free—and who'd be completely discreet.

"In New York?"

"Sure. New York or L.A. are where most of the cosmetic surgeons are. I can refer you to someone you can talk it over with, quite privately; a consultation."

"But if I go to the office of a cosmetic surgeon, someone's going to talk about it. It'll end up in *New York Magazine* or the *Post.*"

"We can make sure that won't happen. For someone in your position, an arrangement could certainly be made. Perhaps a doctor could come to your apartment."

"Then I'd have to tell Winona."

Now Rosenberg was surprised. "You haven't discussed it with her? Well . . . knowing you both all these years, I wouldn't recommend anything as serious as cosmetic surgery without consulting her. I'd speak to her before I consulted the surgeon."

"Well, I'm embarrassed to. But you're right. I wanted to know a bit more before I raised it with her."

"You think she's going to object?"

"She spends a lot of time with people who barely have any medical care. She feels even more than I do that medical resources are unfairly distributed in this country."

"We all feel that."

"But it really gets her when people are using up doctors and facilities just because they can pay for them. And whenever she says that, she mentions all the rich women getting liposuction, or their fannies or breasts lifted, while the poor don't get basic vaccinations or Pap smears."

"But if you feel it's important professionally, she'll understand. I'd be happy to talk to her myself. She's very sensible, and a social conscience in a woman in her position is a wonderful thing. With your money and success she could turn her back on the world."

"I know. I'm very proud of her."

"And your children. They've taken the same direction. They're not down on Wall Street, burning up the bond market."

Winona was upset.

"Why are you letting them do this to you? Honey, it isn't worth it. Get out while you can with some dignity left."

In fact, he'd flirted with that during the O. J. Simpson circus. But it was still his franchise. He wanted to fight the drift to sensation; to hang in there, try to keep the place honest. In 2000, he'd see. At least he'd be taking TV news into the twenty-first century.

Winona kept bringing it up.

"Sweetheart, why can't you just look like yourself? If you give in to this, you're making it harder for everyone else. You're a role model for millions of other men. If *you* have to pretend you're younger than you are, then they'll have to. Don't you see, it debases the currency? It helps companies justify laying off seasoned workers and hiring young ones, at lower salaries and no benefits."

• • •

THAT NIGHT more intimately, curled up with him just after turning out the light, Winona said softly, "Think of the facelift from my point of view."

"OK."

"Say you look fifty, now . . . which I think you do. And you do this surgery and it makes you look forty. Where's that going to leave me? A sixty-year-old woman, who already looks her age? I don't care much how other people think I look, but I care what you and I think. Aren't you going to start thinking I look awfully old, too old for you? Can you stop yourself from thinking that because you look younger, you *are* younger. And start comparing me with women who look the age you think you are? And then shame me into getting my face lifted, and my behind lifted, and everything else?"

"No, sweetheart, your behind is terrific." He patted it affectionately. "I like you the way you are."

"But I like you the way *you* are, and you're not giving my opinion any weight. What's driving you is what some imaginary person thinks. Or even worse, the jerks who run the network. If I didn't know you and trust you completely, I'd think you had a young girlfriend and were doing this for her."

"You know that's crazy."

"I know. But at least that'd be something tangible on which to pin such a decision. Mean as anything to me, but understandable. What you're doing is based on such an abstraction, the hypothetical opinions of hypothetical people, who you *think* are dying for a younger face."

"The whole business is going to younger faces. Look at the all news cable channels and the local news, and the newer network correspondents."

"Well, kiddo, I seem to recall you were a new network correspondent once when you were barely out of the cradle. So were the others of your generation, the guys who had done some great local reporting, or who'd done time in Vietnam. But Cronkite and Huntley and Brinkley didn't all commit suicide when you came along—"

"Yes, but nobody was pushing me in to replace them."

"—and they didn't get facelifts. Can you imagine Walter Cronkite getting a facelift—or Edward R. Murrow?"

"Murrow I could imagine. Pretty image-conscious, a real dandy with his clothes . . . and he was a big ladies' man. He might have a facelift in today's climate."

"Well, Cronkite didn't."

Her personal argument touched him more. Had she read something in him that hadn't seen himself?

He wasn't worried about getting older, just the look of getting older. Sure, he noticed the signs they wrote about in magazines: harder to stay asleep at night, longer to take a leak, erections less frequent and not as good. But for the first time, instead of only noticing, he'd stopped and read one of the sleazy ads for pills supposed to increase male stamina: some lean muscled guy with a bushy mustache shown above the waist but looking down at—what?—his success or his failure?

No, it was the combination of things that had got to him, all coming at the same time, with Christopher Siefert's profile bang in the middle of it all.

TRANSCRIPT (Christopher Siefert interview with Sherman Glass):

CHRIS: Five million. Very good source. Authoritative.

GLASS: No, I won't confirm that. It's full of shit. I negotiated the contract; I should know how much it's for.

CHRIS: Then what's your figure?

GLASS: It's not *my* figure. It's the correct figure. It's the figure written in the contract in my files.

CHRIS: Then what's that figure?

GLASS: I can't tell you. I don't discuss my clients' finances or contracts. But I can tell you your figure is nuts.

CHRIS: It's the best figure I have to go on. I repeat, it's from a very good source.

GLASS: Then it's a very good source who's playing games.

CHRIS: How do I get it right, if the people who know are playing games?

GLASS: OK. You want it right? Off the record?

CHRIS: Off the record, I can't use it.

GLASS: But no names, no hint about agents?

CHRIS: Right.

GLASS: The honest-to-God figure is seven million.

CHRIS: Higher than I thought. I thought the real figure was six.

GLASS: Seven million. On my mother's grave.

CHRIS: OK. Seven million.

GLASS: Which is where the new negotiations start.

(The disgusting way Sherman Glass twirled the unlit cigar in his wet lips made Siefert wonder why Grant had a guy like this as his agent.)

CHRIS: What are you asking for?

GLASS: I don't discuss a client's negotiations.

CHRIS: Still, not for attribution, I assume more.

GLASS: You assume right.

CHRIS: I assume a lot more?

GLASS: Sure. And then you ask me what's a lot, and we go on kidding each other. Look, Grant Munro is one of the most valuable commodities any network's got. Proven journalist, great anchorman, honorable guy; public trusts him. He's been with them for thirty-five years. The other networks have tried to lure him away. Cable would kill to get him. Big offers. But he's stayed loyal. You add all that up: years of loyalty, commitment, trust, credibility, plus the investment the network's got in him, promoting him, all the years of national exposure, he's a big star . . .

CHRIS: The anchor for the twenty-first century? For the millennium?

GLASS: Great line! You going to use that line?

CHRIS: I don't know. But you're saying Grant Munro's worth a lot more than seven million and you're going to try and get it.

GLASS: You got it!

(He pulled the cigar out and looked at it.)

You know, I can't even smoke in my own office anymore! Building regulation. The city of New York says they can set aside smoking areas. This fucking building won't do it. It's a shitty world. You want to go grab a drink and some lunch?

CHRIS: Sure.

GLASS: Come on over to the Four Seasons.

CHRIS: Then everyone'll know I talked to you.

GLASS: They'll figure it out anyway. Come on. I'm buying.

CHRIS: I'm interviewing you. I have to pay.

GLASS: So there *is* a free lunch!

(At the Four Seasons' Grill Room, when Sherman Glass had shaken enough hands and ordered a martini, Siefert restarted the tape.)

CHRIS: If you had the chance to represent anyone, who is the hottest talent on the air, in your view, right now?

GLASS: After Grant Munro, of course . . .

CHRIS: Of course.

GLASS: You don't quote me.

CHRIS: Right.

GLASS: Ann Murrow.

CHRIS: Why? She's not a news anchor. She does that magazine show, all that exposé, celebrity stuff.

GLASS: You must be joking, putting down magazines. All the networks are doing is making out like bandits in television like you guys have made out in print forever!

(Between the waiter's hand and Sherman's, the martini appeared not to touch the table.)

GLASS: I'll tell you why she's hot. She's probably making eight million plus now. Contract's due soon. She's worth ten, eleven, maybe more, for the next contract, if she stays where she is. Her shows are up in the top ten or twenty most weeks. But the demographics are as good as the share.

CHRIS: Meaning, she pulls the audience advertisers want to reach?

GLASS: You said it.

CHRIS: Which Grant Munro doesn't?

GLASS: Different game. "The Evening News" gets great audience, but it's older.

CHRIS: Would she pull that audience if she were anchoring the news?

GLASS: I don't know. The patterns are changing. But if I was her agent, it'd be a good question.

CHRIS: What can you tell me about the Donovan business?

GLASS: What Donovan business?

CHRIS: The White House correspondent. The story that he was going to be Grant Munro's substitute, then not going to be. Do you know about that?

GLASS: Sure. Donovan's my client.

CHRIS: As well as Grant?

GLASS: Sure. I have a lot of clients.

CHRIS: So what's the Donovan story?

GLASS: No story. Just some confusion, a misunderstanding about a press release. No big deal.

CHRIS: Was Grant involved?

GLASS: Well, of course. He has a right to be consulted on who substitutes for him.

CHRIS: Is that a veto?

GLASS: No, just a right to be consulted.

CHRIS: Is Donovan being groomed for Grant's job?

(Glass looked at him, sharply.)

GLASS: I think Bill has a great future. He's young. He's getting network experience and he's a terrific talent. They were smart to hire him.

CHRIS: With your help, I gather.

GLASS: Sure, that's our function as agents. We spot talent, help bring it along and mature. That's what we did with Grant Munro back in the sixties. Look where he's gone!

CHRIS: Is Bill Donovan going that far?

GLASS: If you offered me a bet on it, I'd take it.

2 6

A day later, George White in Minneapolis called Steinman.

"We confirmed that he's going into the photo store. Early in the morning, when no one's around. He uses the back door in an alley. It's got a key pad combination, which he obviously knows. Was there this morning around six-forty-five. We were watching his house and followed him. He went to the diner for breakfast, then walked over to the store. It's only a few blocks. He stayed inside about ten minutes and came out."

"Was he carrying anything?" Steinman asked.

"Like a package of photos?" Almost a smile in the detective's voice. "No, nothing. Empty-handed."

"Maybe they're in the store?" Steinman suggested.

"Could be. But that's not easy to check. There's not only the lock but probably an alarm, and since he worked there, he knows how to shut it off. And even if we got in and you told us what photos to look for, there are bound to be thousands in there. Needle-in-a-haystack kind of thing."

"Is the store still closed for business?"

"Yeah, I checked. No will's been filed for the owner. 'Course he died only a couple of weeks ago. Or maybe there's no will. Who knows?"

"But Zabricki's using the place like it was running?"

"Hard to know how he's using it."

Steinman asked, "Where else did he go since we talked yesterday?"

"Back to the mailbox twice. Nowhere else. Except Burger King. He went in there for lunch. Big burger, fries, a Coke. So he must have a little dough, because he was skipping lunch before."

"No other sign of where he has the stuff, what you said yesterday, luggage lockers, nothing like that?"

"He hasn't gone anywhere like that. He went to his house, the diner, the photo store, the mailbox, Burger King. 'Course, it could be he spotted us. Even when we're careful, people can spot a tail. Especially if they're worried. And he could be a worried kid, if he's trying to blackmail you and not getting a response. Know what I mean?"

"Yeah, yeah, I know."

"Or, you know, maybe he's got the photos on him. We could accidently bump into him, jostle him in a crowd, give him a quick frisk."

All of this sounded too unsubtle to Steinman. "Could you leave a message from me in that mailbox?"

"Sure. What're you thinking? Setting up a meeting?"

"I'm just thinking out loud. Considering the next move."

"We could meet him for you. I could do it myself. Save you coming out here."

Even if these guys were discreet, that meant widening the number who would know Ann Murrow was involved, and why.

"I think I better handle it myself," Steinman said. "Where could I meet him?"

"Well, you could use this office. 'Course, it might scare him off. It says *Detective Agency* on the door, and a lot of people think detective means police."

"Where else?"

"He could suspect a trap anywhere you suggest. I presume he's asking for money."

"Yes."

"He probably wants a drop-off then. You deliver the money; he delivers the photos. No one meets. That's been my experience."

"I was thinking of negotiating with him." It sounded weak. Steinman felt himself losing the initiative. The detective obviously knew his stuff.

"If he'll sit still for that. You know, there're places . . . hotel lobbies. Or rent a hotel room and set a time. Not the room you use yourself; another one for the meeting. Harder for him to find you later. There's the train station. There are bars. Take a drive in a car. All kinds of ways."

"I want to think about it," Steinman said. "Keep an eye on him one more day—and night too. Same terms. Call me tomorrow this time, and I'll give you an answer. Think of some places in the meantime."

27

Laurie Jacobs came by to twist Grant's arm about the Cleveland affiliate.

"Darling, they're devastated you said no. They're big fans. One reason for switching networks was to get *you!* They can't stand the Lone Ranger!"

Like everyone, Laurie was adopting Hollygo's nicknames for the opposition.

"The station manager wanted to talk to you personally, but I got around that. Anyway, *if* you agree to do it, they'll fly you out early that morning in a private jet and schedule the ceremony for midmorning. They've worked it out. You'll be back here by two. You've made the show later than that lots of times."

But he hated doing it; leaving everything to Marty Boyle.

"They have another plan. They're desperate to make this work. Night before, after our show, private jet, overnight there.

"And I spend the evening flying to Cleveland."

"Lousy, I know. Anyway, if you could possibly do it, Grant, it would be a huge deal for the brass, and for me."

"What's the date again?"

"June twenty-third."

He turned over the diary, and that day was empty.

"OK, I'll do it."

"That's wonderful. Wonderful!"

Grant was thinking he'd have to schedule the operation soon and clear time for the recovery, before other dates started peppering the calendar. Summer was the only time he could take off that long.

"I'll make all the arrangements. You won't have to think about it until that day. I promise."

"OK, great."

Winona would say, "Why do you have to do all these favors? They don't own you." No, they didn't, but they did. It was part of the job.

Laurie, who'd been standing by his desk, sat down and dropped into her confidential mode. "How'd you stiff them on Bill Donovan?"

"I'm supposed to be consulted on substitutes. I reminded them."

"And young Billy Boy Blue is not on your list of eligible candidates?"

Grant smiled. "Bryce Watson is my candidate."

"That's pretty clear."

He asked her, "How did you handle it with Carmody?"

"I took the fall. Said my info was wrong. My fault. Bad girl. Slap, slap." She tapped her pretty face. "Sorry."

"So naturally he got more curious."

"Naturally. All the usual routines. Wrong because it was premature or wrong-wrong?"

"What did you say to that?"

"Nothing. I blamed it on bad information. I blew it. Profuse apologies. Never steered him wrong before, never will again."

"What about Donovan?"

"He was mad."

"What'd he say?"

"He shouted at me. A lady of my refinement cannot repeat to a gentleman what he said."

"I thought he was such a nice fellow, a great guy. That's what everybody tells me."

"A nice, pissed-off fella."

"I'm sorry to hear that."

"You look it!" Laurie flashed her big smile, then wholly surprised Grant. She got up, leaned over, and kissed him on the cheek. "Thanks!" And left.

He was pleased but a little unsure of the message.

He looked at the time. He had to go to the eye doctor. For ten years or so he'd been using contact lenses, and it was time again to increase the magnification. Menus and newspapers were getting hard to read, except in bright light.

While the doctor checked for glaucoma and cataracts, Grant was calculating how much maintenance his body was beginning to require. Stronger lenses periodically to keep him seeing; a partial upper denture, maybe some implants pending, to keep him chewing; caps to make his own teeth cosmetically passable; and the hearing aid he'd need sooner or later. The left ear, in which he'd worn the studio earpiece for years, with occasional bursts of high-decibel tone, was gradually failing. So far, his legs and feet were all right, and he had none of the knee problems of so many runners.

So, at sixty, EKG all right, lungs OK, blood pressure good, cholesterol moderate to bad, prostate a little enlarged but no cancer signs. No polyps in lower colon, other blood work OK. He could run, walk, chew, see, drink, digest, pass water, have bowel movements, and keep his weight at 178. So far, so good.

And this sixty-year-old, in good health, now thought he could slow time down with cosmetic surgery, stop the clock? Wasn't this tempting fate, which had always been so kind to him? But why was a facelift tinkering with destiny any more than having his teeth capped? That was cosmetic surgery of a kind, like having the dermatologist freeze off enlarged moles. He hadn't felt he was cheating or deceiving anyone when he'd had his teeth done; a sensible investment for a profession that required reasonable-looking teeth. But the facelift seemed on a different moral plane, surrounded by a cloud of disapprobation.

Whom would he have to tell? Winona knew, and Michael Rosenberg. The kids? Needed to think about that. At work, Angela? Not sure. Marty? No. Repton? No. But would they notice? They'd certainly notice something; no point in going through it if they couldn't see a difference. Ideal if they just thought he'd had a great vacation; looks years younger. That's what he'd like to hear. But if anyone in the office knew, it'd be bound to get into print.

And if the thought of reading sneering comments about a facelift made him shudder, should he be doing it?

It amazed Grant that he'd become so much a worrier. Never like him to think about the negative possibilities. But screw this up, come out with his face looking even slightly weird, and he'd have no future at all. Of course, that might have been true after a lot of the things he'd done in the past. As life got shorter, was he going to become more nervous about everything?

Rosenberg had recommended a woman doctor in San Francisco. Perfect for privacy, and an hour's drive to the vineyard house for recuperation. He had to pick a weekend to fly out for a consultation.

28

Christopher Siefert hated eating in restaurants by himself, but Elizabeth was busy tonight, so he was waiting his turn at the cooked-foods counter in Citarella, trying to decide between lasagna and salmon, when the counterman said, "Next? Twenty-eight, twenty-nine?"

A woman beside Siefert said, "I'm twenty-nine."

"Don't you wish! So what'd you like?"

"One lasagna!"

"You having a party?"

She turned to Siefert: "Such a comedian!" And he recognized Laurie Jacobs.

"Hi, Chris Siefert."

"Oh, hi!" He liked how her face lit up.

"I was thinking of lasagna too," Siefert said.

"So, two lasagna now?" the counterman said. "A date already!"

"My kids are out," Laurie said.

"Well, instead of reheating lasagna, how about coming to dinner with me, somewhere close."

She hesitated a second.

"Lady, it's a good offer. He looks nice. You don't want to, I'll go with him!"

"It's a great idea."

"So, no lasagna now?"

"No, I'm sorry."

"I hope you'll both be very happy."

"He doesn't joke like that with me," Siefert said as they headed past the long fish counter to the exit.

"It's a girl thing." As they came out on Broadway, Laurie said, "Hey, I love this! But I need to leave a message for my kids. Could we go up to my place, just three blocks, have a drink, and I'll leave them a note?"

They began walking north. "How old are the kids?"

"Thirteen, fifteen, but, you know, New York kids. Older than we were at twenty-five."

Siefert liked the *we*. Laurie couldn't be more than forty, perhaps younger. Her eyes sparkled. His spirits, depressed by the evening alone, lifted.

She plunged into the baroque gloom of the Apthorpe.

"Rent controlled, naturally. They're always trying tricky ways to get me out. My husband hated it. So it was him or the apartment—and he lost. One of those things, you know?" Expecting he'd know.

"Yeah, I know."

Her apartment, with its bright colors, wallpapers, materials, pictures, all seemed to sparkle as she did.

"It's so cheerful!" Siefert said. "I really should do something about my place. It's gloomy."

"Cheaper than therapy! Not that I haven't tried that too. You near here?"

"West End and Seventy-seventh."

"Right around the corner!" Everything out of her mouth was an exclamation. "Give me a second and I'll get you a drink."

"Where would you like to eat?"

"God, anywhere but here, by myself!"

She disappeared and came back, her outfit changed, her lipstick brighter. She poured him a Scotch and herself a glass of wine.

"Is this work or fun?" she asked.

"You mean it won't be fun if the magazine pays?"

"Yeah, but then I can't be indiscreet. Watch what I say, watch what I drink."

"No notes, no tape recorder, OK?"

"Fine by me." She was scribbling on a pad and saying aloud, "Stepping out on the town with famous writer. If you need me, I'll be at—where?"

"Café Lux? You like that?"

"I love it! Wonderful!"

"Going to be a bit of a comedown when they find out who the famous writer is. They'll be expecting at least Norman Mailer."

"Nah, they've met him already! Come and look at this." She led him into a study with floor-to-ceiling bookshelves, and pointed. "You have to bend down over here. S's there."

On the shelf were Siefert's Vietnam and cold war books and, remarkably, his novel, *Old Attitudes*. How could a writer resist a woman who read him?

"You can tell by the accumulated dust that I didn't rush out and buy them to impress you."

"I'm impressed."

"I'm a fan."

"That's what Grant Munro said, at least about the Vietnam book."

"He is. We talked about it when we heard you were doing a story. Everyone was thrilled that it was Christopher Siefert."

They walked down Broadway to the restaurant, Siefert answering her questions. Was he working on a book? Had he given up fiction? She'd loved one of the characters in the novel, and so he was talking about himself with this friendly woman who made him feel young and optimistic. Yet who, beneath her attractive exterior, seemed somewhat sad. Interesting contrast with Elizabeth, who was unfashionably large, and comfortable with it. Laurie was thin and sexy, but wistful, perhaps depressed, belying the enthusiasm she radiated.

"Would you like white or red wine?"

"I really prefer red, if you don't mind."

"Me too. Wine is one of Grant's big interests, I gather. His vineyard in California."

"They don't make wine themselves. Just grow the grapes for wineries nearby."

"They?"

"Guy Ferris, the cameraman Grant worked with for years, runs the vineyard. In fact, they're partners."

"That's interesting." Siefert hadn't heard of Guy. "Is it open, his vineyard, one of those you can go and visit?"

"I guess. I don't know. But I can ask Grant. Or you can."

Siefert was thinking that if he went out to Seattle to talk to Tony Weldon's widow, once on the West Coast he could visit the vineyard.

"What do you make of Grant?"

He wasn't expecting such a direct question. Usually P.R. people were coyly devious in asking how their boss was coming across.

"He's a bit overwhelming to meet at first."

"Tell me! The first few months I was there, I thought, I can't work for this man! I'll fall in love with him! I'll make a fool of myself. I mean, what a gorgeous hunk! You know Hollygo calls him Gregory Peck? It's perfect! *And* he's smart. *And* he's nice. *And* he's successful. *And* he's famous—"

"—and he's rich," said Siefert.

"Exactly. My mother would kill for a combination like that."

"But when you got used to him . . . ?"

"I'm still not used to him, if you mean it's ho-hum being around him. I adore him! Oh, by the way, he's also a great husband. I mean, never any hint of fooling around—and there are plenty of hints in this business about stuff like that. I'd know. And a terrific father. Millions of people watch him every night and trust him before their own relatives. And then how many men have such romantic hobbies?"

"But he's not happy the way the business is going. It's no secret. His Gadarene swine speech, for example?"

"No. He makes my life hell every now and then, sounding off. I'm supposed to make our news department sound like the second coming of Edward R. Murrow, and he implies we're selling out like everyone else."

Siefert was listening carefully, but was aware, for the first time since his operation, of a sexual current in his body, perhaps only a premonition. It felt good.

"Who else besides Guy Ferris knows him really well? Friends, colleagues, you know, people with anecdotes about him? Maybe who've covered big stories with him, been sailing with him?"

"Well, Don Evans has been there as long as Grant. He's our senior writer. Very smart. He'd be interesting. Besides, he's very funny."

"And Grant isn't?"

"No! I didn't mean that. Grant has a good sense of humor and he gets off some good shots. Everybody in the office kids; it's part of the culture. You'll hear it if you hang around a few weeks. It's an edgy kind of kidding."

"Edgy—ill natured?"

"Edgy—ironic. Part New York, but part network. Bitter ironic."

"Is that jealousy? Of people who are paid so fabulously and become famous while others remain anonymous and are paid ordinarily?"

"Could be, some of it. But it's hard to be bitter about Grant. He isn't the kind of guy who makes people jealous. He doesn't rub his success in your face. He doesn't flaunt it. In fact, he doesn't really show it at all."

"So what happened about falling in love with him?" Siefert asked, smiling.

"Oh, well, you know, I was partly kidding, trying to tell you the impression he made on me. He's very straightforward. Not devious."

"Ingenuous?"

"Too strong. But there's a lot of fake sincere in the business. Do you know what Walter Cronkite said at Charles Kuralt's memorial service? *'All that's necessary to succeed in television is to fake sincerity.'* He was quoting Fred Allen, and boy, is it true! But Grant doesn't fake it."

"Who does fake it?"

"D'you think I'm going to be dumb enough to tell you that? Anyway, Grant doesn't need to fake anything. He's been around a long time, all the big jobs, foreign correspondent, Washington. You don't pull the wool over his eyes as a journalist."

"But as a person? Is he too trusting, too unsuspicious for this business?"

"Maybe, but then, when he finds out, he comes back so strong, he wins out in the end."

"Like when—?"

"You know, you should talk to his wife. She's one terrific woman. If Winona will talk to you—I bet she will—she'd be great on this stuff. She's not one of those corporate wives afraid to whisper her name. She says exactly what she thinks."

Siefert decided not to push the questioning; he liked being with Laurie, and he'd picked up quite a lot.

29

Winona was out at a benefit Grant had chosen to avoid, and he found himself wandering restlessly around the large apartment. The next evening after the show he'd fly to San Francisco to consult the doctor, visit Guy at the vineyard, and fly back on Sunday. Despite Winona's objections, he was determined, though a little uneasy.

He wandered into the library, a beautiful room, well-made floor-to-ceiling shelves, deep chairs with good reading lights. Years ago he'd seen this room in Italy, when he was interviewing the writer Luigi Barzini. His library made Grant want one like it, and, making more money than he knew what to do with, he indulged his whim. He got a decorator to ask Barzini's permission to copy his library for Grant on Fifth Avenue. Where Grant and Winona came from, that would have sounded absurd, but not in New York. For all he knew, Barzini had used the money he made from *The Italians* to do the same; what Grant admired as his taste might have been copied from the library of some aristocratic Roman family. So now it was Grant's taste.

Every time he passed this room on busy mornings, or at the end of the usually busy evenings, he regretted not being able to spend more time in it. One of his recurrent fantasies was to begin a systematic course of reading. And in those little daydreams he'd always see himself in one of these comfortable leather chairs, undisturbed, tasting the sweet pleasure of losing himself in a book.

Winona would say, "Why don't you read in the mornings before you go to work?" And he'd say, "I have to watch the morning shows, listen to some NPR, and read at least the *Times,* or I won't know what's going on and I'll be out of the loop." She'd say, "You have an office full of people who are paid to be in the loop. Why can't they just tell you?"

She didn't understand: if he wasn't up to the minute on every current happening, the executive producer would make all the assignments and decisions about the show. Grant had pushed too hard to be managing editor to let the power slip away because he didn't know what was going on. And three mornings a week, he went for his run.

Well, Winona would say, as she would to one of her clients in therapy, "You make your own priorities, and you can change them." And so on. Old discussion.

Tonight there were no other claims on his time. Winona wouldn't be back for two hours, and the beautiful room—intentionally located at the back of the apartment, away from the traffic on Fifth Avenue—was richly, invitingly silent.

But he couldn't settle to anything. He'd pull out a book, sample a page, read a blurb on the jacket, and put it back. Again and again. Many of the books had been sent by publishers' publicity departments, and most of them he hadn't read. But on one side were books he and Winona had always owned, from college onward, and some of his father's. He hadn't opened them for years, but now he felt the presence of his father in the room.

Who had never seen it, of course. Cancer took him years before Grant got where he was and the money that went with it. What would his father have felt, so deeply embittered in his own life, about having a son who made six million dollars a year? Grant would never have told him. When he died, network anchors weren't even making a million. Adding up everything his father had possibly earned in his abbreviated working life—twenty-three years of teaching high school English, ending at forty-eight—he had probably never made more than a quarter of a million dollars. In total. His life's work. Maybe only half that. Grant was glad he'd been spared the embarrassment of knowing. His mother knew, but really didn't. She wanted to stay near Old Saybrook, Connecticut, so they'd bought her a nicer house out on Fenwick Point, where Katharine Hepburn lived, and when the kids were growing up, they'd make the two-hour drive up there. They'd take her to lunch at the Griswold in Essex, or the Bee & Thistle in Old Lyme, somewhere like that, and she considered that quite grand enough. She had seldom come into New York.

His father's death had mercifully ended the bitterness between them, his resentment that everything seemed to come so easily to his son—everyone said it—and came only with pain to him.

The financial mess Grant's grandfather had left meant that following two previous generations to Yale was out of the question for his father. Scraping through teachers' college at night was the best education he could get in the thirties. So he was reduced to peddling his literary tastes to high school students, few of them readers, most headed for blue-collar jobs.

He died of lung cancer in those terrible days after the Kennedy assassination, in November 1963, when the exhilaration of Grant's work had worn off and he felt compelled to keep making the ninety-minute drive to the VA hospital outside New Haven. His father died with a distant prospect of Yale University—and probably knew it. Grant wanted it to be over with his father, and felt terrible that he did want that. And this shrunken man, looking at forty-eight like a skeletal eighty, never softened.

"You don't know what work is," he said one afternoon, the awful, sandpaper whisper suddenly loud in the silence, his mouth slack under the oxygen tube that fed his useless lungs. When Grant turned from the window to the bed, his father's eyes, huge in his shrunken, waxy face, seemed consumed with envy of Grant's youth, his health, what he saw as his son's casual success at whatever he did. On the covers, his large hands lay inert, skin drawn tight over the big bones, a catheter taped over the almost invisible vein it fed with glucose and pain medication. The hands, too weak to grasp anything, had already let go of life.

"You don't know a damn thing. Everything comes too easily to you."

He'd always had to guess why his father disliked him; whether, in fact, it was dislike or a pose hardened into habit, always there in his black moods. In other moods, usually when he was drunk, he could be sentimental. Those were the moods that gave his mother, Grant, and his sister a maudlin semblance of affection.

Grant would have been ashamed to have his father know what he was about to do. He could almost hear his father's derisive, boozy laughter descending into his chest, where it turned wheezy and liquid-sounding, like a laugh half under water. At sixty years, he lived with the superstition of his mother: any boastfulness invited doom. Don't even whisper that you think you've done well, or you'll pay for it. Celtic foreboding. She thought it was bad luck to call him Grant Munro, seeming to pair the names of two presidents, suggesting too much pride.

Grant Munro. Some people thought he'd made it up for television. It was what people had come to expect from television. Made-up names. Made-up personalities. Made-up life.

By the ninth day with no word, Ernie Schmid thought the pictures hadn't got there. He had vision of stars like Ann Murrow getting tons of fan mail, which waited until someone got around to it. Or—he shivered at the thought—she'd gone straight to the police: Someone is blackmailing me. Please investigate. Arrest him!

Naw, she wouldn't want the police looking at pictures of her posing like a floozy. Her picture was in the paper again today, talking to the First Lady, both in elegant evening gowns, at some flashy ball, with Hollywood stars. Ann Murrow was still a great-looking woman, firm tits, nice ass, one of those smiles that lit up even a newspaper picture. She wouldn't want these cheesy pictures getting out. Maybe she was ignoring him, testing him to see what he'd do? See if his threat to show them to a magazine was empty. Maybe she was waiting to see if he'd send another message, a follow-up?

Maybe he should make some prints while he still could get into John's store. If the six he'd sent were lost or were sitting in a huge pile of fan mail, maybe he should have a full set, a couple of sets, just in case.

Besides, there was the money in the till. He'd thought of it only after he'd made the first prints. He'd noticed the cash register but hadn't thought of it until he was out of the shop. He'd sneaked back in a few mornings later and, sure enough, John had not cleaned it out. Ernie counted 94 bucks and some change. And underneath the cash tray, a couple of checks and a bank envelope with ten crisp new $100 bills! Jesus, a thousand bucks! John must have had it there for some emergency. A thousand bucks. It scared him, it was so much. He put it carefully back into the bank envelope and replaced the cash drawer. Before he closed it, he slipped a twenty into his pocket. He celebrated by getting a hamburger and fries at Burger King. He felt rich. Today he was going to get a haircut. It gave him a warm feeling that all that money was just sitting there. John was dead. Who would know?

An older man in a suit came into the diner right after him and sat at the counter. Even though Ernie was there first and was a regular, the waitress took the man's order before his. Bitch.

It'd be a little risky, like the time he'd made the first prints. He'd had to stay a while to mix the developer, stop bath, and hypo and bring them up to the right temperature, adjust the enlarger, make the exposures, and process the prints through the washing and drying. But nothing had disturbed him, and he'd slipped into the alley with no one the wiser. The mailbox place wouldn't be open until nine. He could get into the photo store, make the prints, then go check the mailbox. If the alley was empty, he could slip back into the photo store to tidy up—and pick up some cash. If there were people around, he could wait until the evening or the next morning.

He finished his breakfast, pleased at having something purposeful to do, knowing he'd enjoy seeing the pictures again. This time he'd do them all. Two sets; one for himself, just in case.

HE WAS SITTING on the darkroom stool, waiting for the solutions to warm up. For only two rolls, it wasn't worth loading the processing machine, so he was using open trays. The first negative was loaded in the enlarger and focused. He could see the young Ann Murrow's tits with the nipples registering white in the negative image on the easel. It was so easy doing all this. What if one day he simply rolled up the venetian blinds on the street door and display windows and opened the store for business? People would start coming in to get film developed, passport pictures and portraits taken, to buy film and frames. It could go on just like before. Money'd come in and he'd have a job. He'd have the same job as before, but he could pay himself more. He could pay himself a couple, maybe three hundred a week. He knew there was an accountant; John had said someone looked after taxes and stuff. His name must be around. Maybe John had left no will at all. No, that was unlikely. He was getting carried away. But supposing he did open the store, and after a while someone came along and asked what he was doing? Could he say: John asked me to keep the store open? Who would know any different? John was dead, and how would anyone know he hadn't told Ernie that? And if someone took over the store, because they were in John's will or something, maybe they'd want Ernie to stay on as the technician, like before. So the worst that could happen, he'd have his job back. But maybe nobody would come along and he could just keep on running it like it was his. And make money like John had. He must have made plenty from all those weddings and school proms.

A little *ping* from the timer. He checked. The developer was ready. Time to make his prints. He didn't need to make test strips, since he'd exposed these negatives already. He worked quickly, taking unexposed print paper out of its lightproof box, lining it up on the easel, dropping the eight-by-ten frame into place, making the timed exposure, lifting the frame, pulling the paper out, and sliding it into the developer. He had that timed, too, but he checked the margin to make sure, then slipped the wet print into the bleach and then the wash. Then he removed the negative holder, slid the film strip along to the next exposure, snapped it into place, and checked the focus on the easel. No changes. All standard now. He worked methodically through both rolls, gradually advancing prints through the solutions and finally into the dryer. The finished pictures began accumulating—two sets of perfect prints.

He was so far along, he might as well finish. He took the time to empty the trays of chemicals and wash them out while the last prints were drying. He tidied up, drying the trays and work surfaces with paper towels. He retrieved the last negative strip from the enlarger, holding it by the edges to keep it free of his fingerprints, then placed it with the other negatives and the last prints, still warm from the dryer, in a large manila envelope.

He went quietly through the door to the front of the shop. Even with the blinds drawn there was plenty of light to see the cash register. He removed all the bills from the cash drawer. He lifted it and put the envelope of $100 bills in his pocket. He left the checks. Too risky.

He closed the door to the front of the shop and, with his large envelope, went to the back door and listened. All quiet in the alley outside. He turned off the lights and cautiously opened the door slightly to check. Instantly, it was forced violently inward, knocking Ernie on his back. A large man pushed into the room, closed the door behind him, turned on the lights.

He had a gun.

Terrified, his heart beating wildly, Ernie sprawled helplessly on the floor. The man, pointing his gun, bent down and snatched the envelope out of his hand.

"Security guard. Get up. Face to that wall. Hands on the wall. Legs apart. Quick, move!"

Stunned, Ernie obeyed. The man ran a hand over his body and stepped back.

"What's your name?"

"Ernie Schmid."

"What're you doing here?"

"I work here."

"This store's been closed for months."

"The owner asked me to do some work while he was sick."

"The owner's dead."

"I know, but he asked me to finish some work for a customer."

"This property's sealed. Nothing's supposed to be removed from it. You can be charged with breaking and entering."

"I didn't break in. I worked here. I know the codes."

"Well, I'll be easy on you. Beat it now before I call the cops."

"You mean go?"

"I mean go. Fast!"

Ernie turned around. "The pictures. I got to deliver them."

"Nothing's supposed to leave this store. Court orders. Now get out."

Ernie opened the door and ran. Jesus, lucky escape! Then two streets away, thinking: All that work, and I don't have the fucking pictures! But it could have been the cops, not a security guard. And I have a thousand bucks. More. A thousand and eighty-four bucks. He didn't find that. And even if they check the cash register, who knew the dough was there?

They must have been following him. The guy with the gun looked like that man in the diner at breakfast. Came in after Ernie, left before him. But why would a security guard be following him?

31

"Tell me about the Donovan business" was Siefert's first question. He felt on a different footing with Grant's writer, Don Evans, who seemed out of place in network news; laid back, facetious, his mainspring wound more loosely than his colleagues'. It made Siefert more direct.

"My dear fellow, if I told you on the record what I think, I'd be out of a job. And I need to hang on a few more years. I can't bite the hand that affords me luxuries like this." He indicated the Century, where they were having a drink. Respecting the club rules against appearing to work, Siefert had left the notebook and tape recorder in his briefcase downstairs.

"Well, talk to me off the record, and if there's something I need to use, I'll check back with you."

"No direct attribution."

"Fine."

Everything about Evans seemed from the generation past: narrow lapels, slight English intonation, the martini glass he now raised fastidiously.

They had met for drinks because Evans didn't eat lunch; he went for long walks instead.

"You asked about Bill Donovan, my esteemed colleague with the peachtree fuzz still downy on his cheek?"

"A reference to Atlanta or his youth?"

"Both. He was a local anchor in Atlanta until touched by the magic wand, and behold, he was a fully fledged network correspondent covering the biggest White House scandal since Watergate."

"Sounds as though you think that was an inappropriate transition."

"Not anymore. It's the way the world turns now. What used to be called paying your dues, learning the craft at different levels, like the newspaper business—"

"You started in print, I notice; the AP and the *Times*."

"I'm complimented that you do your homework even on your sources. Yes, my head got turned by television in the sixties, and you might say I ran away with the circus."

"Was it a circus then?"

"Well, I didn't think so. Anyway, I don't know any newspaper, or a magazine like *Time,* that would put a reporter on the White House beat with so little seasoning. At least until he'd covered a presidential campaign."

"Why do they do it?"

"It's become a recognized route. It confers instant credibility and national exposure."

"A route to . . . ?"

"The anchor job in New York."

"Donovan is being groomed for that?"

"Of course."

"What happened about his being the summer replacement for Munro, and then not being? Everyone seems to dodge that question."

"They arranged it without telling Grant. He blew up, and they backed down. But I think there's another shoe to drop."

"Well, what's going on? Why fool around behind Munro's back? He's their star."

"Whom the gods wish to destroy, they first make mad . . . perhaps."

"Like leaking stories to the *New York Post*?"

"Perhaps."

"Like telling the *Washington Post* Donovan is going to be the summer replacement?"

"Maybe."

"What else?"

"By injecting into the climate of the newsroom, particularly around the evening news, a mood of insecurity, like an invisible nerve gas."

"You think someone is doing that deliberately?"

"I know there are people who think it's time for Munro to move on. That we won't get back to number one with him. He's fine, a great guy, but it's time for younger blood . . ."

"Do you think that?"

"Oh, leave me out of it. I'm an observer, not a player anymore. I watch, I listen. I talk to people."

"Are they right, the people who want to replace Munro?"

"What is right in this context now? What is the purpose? Is it to provide a respectable news service to the public? Is it to build and retain credibility? Then you should hold on to Munro. Or is it to do anything that will improve the ratings? To try to claw back some of the youngsters who are ignoring network news in droves? Then maybe you take a gamble with the MTV generation."

"But who are the people who want him out? How powerful are they?"

"I know some. Higher up. I know them in a different context."

"Above the news department?"

"Yes."

"At the network level, or corporate?"

"I can't give you that."

"But they're powerful enough to get someone in the news department to make it happen?"

"Yes, but no. Not that powerful. Because there are other people up there who think Munro's terrific. People he knows personally, has for a long time. He has a solid constituency of his own."

"So it's a power struggle at the top?"

Evans sipped his martini and smiled. "You *Time* writers have such a felicitous touch with cliché."

Siefert laughed. "OK. Which side are you on?"

"I told you, I'm not on a side. I used to think of Munro and me as deadly rivals, when we were correspondents at the same level. I thought I was a better reporter and a better writer. The network thought he was better, and he was. Better voice, better presence, very good at those big occasions where they had to ad lib for hours. Like the coverage of Princess Di's funeral. Did you watch any of that?"

"In and out."

"Well, Grant Munro was terrific. Better than anyone. He has style. He's a serious journalist but doesn't take himself too seriously."

"You sound like an admirer."

"I suppose I am now. But it's quite objective. We're not close friends. I used to resent the way he got pushed up the ladder and I didn't."

"On what basis? Why resent it?"

"Simple career jealousy."

"And you felt better qualified? By what? By education? I notice you went to Harvard. Munro went to the University of Connecticut. Did that make a difference?"

"Probably. This is all very unseemly, but there's a point to my telling you."

"I can understand your feelings. I was at Harvard."

"I know. I read your bio. And Oxford. Rhodes Scholar?"

"No," Siefert said. "I paid to go. Indulgent parents. You wanted to make a point?"

"Right. It took me a long time to realize. It wasn't until I saw my own career in perspective that I could see how his abilities outshone mine, in the network context. If I was unhappy about that, and I was, I could have left and gone back to print, where I probably belonged. But I didn't, and here I am, writing for him."

"You write his scripts?"

"I work on 'The Evening News.' And I write a radio commentary he does every day. Little essays on this and that."

"You write them and he reads them?"

"Yes, and I get paid extra for doing it."

"How do you feel about it, as a writer?"

"No worse than I did ghost-writing a couple of books."

"Can you tell me which ones?"

"I'd better not."

"It was you who suggested the Gadarene swine image in his speech about the Monica Lewinsky coverage. He told me."

"Oh, he told you? Yes, I worked with him on that speech. 'Prurient glee' was another phrase I liked."

"Why did the whole industry applaud him so rapturously for trashing them like that?"

"It's an old story. They could feel remorseful and not have to do anything about it. It's like going to confession."

"What can Munro do about it himself—to resist all this?"

"Probably what he's doing. Oppose them when there's some overt move. Cultivate his own friends in the media and high places. Keep his head, not get paranoid when he suspects people are plotting against him, and go on doing the show every day. Go on being Grant Munro."

"What else can *they* do?"

"There are other things. Young Bill Donovan isn't the only arrow in their quiver."

"Who do you mean?"

"I heard someone seriously suggest that Ann Murrow would be a good move—a dynamite move was the actual expression."

Curious, Siefert thought. The other person who had raised that name was Sherman Glass, Munro's agent. And Donovan's agent.

"Ann Murrow. How would you feel about that?"

"Like George Bush when he lost his dinner all over the Japanese prime minister."

Siefert laughed. "Is she even a remote possibility?"

"Not if you compute the equation in any traditional way. Apart from her style and her taste, there'd be the objection that she's not a trained journalist. But she likes to call herself a journalist, and she gets people to watch. They might think that outweighed everything else. But I'm cynical."

"Do you and Munro talk about all this?"

"We're not that close. We allude to it."

"So why are you telling me?"

"I think it might help him if their machinations are exposed."

"Why do you want to help him? He's probably got millions stashed away. He could quit anytime and live like a king. Why does he need help?"

"Because he's a decent guy. He may not be the smartest or the most original or the most creative person I've ever known, but that's irrelevant. He stands for something a lot of us took seriously for many years, took for granted. That's funny. I mean professional integrity. Sounds corny, but cynical fellow that I am, I believe it. And I'll deny everything if you attribute a word of it to me."

Evans stood up, slight and dapper. "And now I have a date for dinner and a rubber of bridge."

32

When they knew, the airlines usually made a fuss, and tonight a passenger relations agent came on board to welcome Grant.

"We're delighted to have you flying with us, Mr. Munro. Is there anything I can do for you? Do you have ground transportation arranged in San Francisco? Since you're traveling alone, and first class isn't completely full, we'll keep the seat beside you empty for the flight so that you won't be bothered."

All of this more or less sotto voce but not, he was sure, completely unheard by other first-class passengers, probably irritating them, as it would him in their place. Celeb envy lay just the other side of celeb worship. Yet he was hardened to it now and could rationalize it, a class system as cringing as that of the British, fawning over titles. Most Americans seemed to accept this louche aristocracy, probably considered such deference appropriate, as London restaurants did when Lord So-and-So booked a table. They may have got some pleasure in telling their wives, "Grant Munro was on the flight out." And if he'd let that go to his head all these years, assuming that *news anchor* conferred some special grace, he knew they would be just as thrilled by Ed MacMahon. And he didn't even want to think about O. J. Simpson. Americans would curtsey to anyone famous—or infamous.

THE PRETTY flight attendant stopped again, a dazzling creature. With first class half empty, she had a lot of time to pause and chat. He'd look up and she'd be there, offering drinks, nuts, fruit, cookies, and, he began to suspect, more. He hadn't encountered such a come-on in a long time. She was very gushy, with the routine wide-eyed stuff: "What a thrill it is to meet you! My roommate's not going to *believe* you were on my flight! Would you mind terribly signing something to her so she'll believe me? Her name's Mary Jo. Everyone respects the work you do so much! I'd love to hear you tell me all about the interesting people you've interviewed."

All of this from a dark-haired honey with great legs, devouring green eyes, and a charming Alabama accent. Deborah Jones from Montgomery, University of Alabama, loved flying, meeting people, good books—majored in comparative literature. Lived in San Francisco, broke up with her boyfriend a couple of months ago, shared an apartment with another flight attendant, Mary Jo, who happened to be away on vacation; and Deborah had three days off until her next flight.

To get clear of the aisle, each time she came back she stepped into the space in front of the empty seat, and, amazingly, her knee, not easily ignored, always seemed to come to a stop close to his.

Over years of high-risk exposure, and inevitable lapses, Grant had developed immunity to cute flight attendants. The lapses dated mostly from the days when they were still stewardesses, and very young; when they seemed like the candy they gave out on landing or takeoff. His own gradual education in restraint just about bracketed the years of feminist re-education of the entire culture, even the television industry. Not long ago men whose names were still household words would go through the newsroom snapping bras—and getting laughs. One newsman amused himself by tweaking the nipples of a woman correspondent through her dress. But on this Friday flight, hovering around him was the old temptation, on a platter; beautifully packaged candy, in shiny paper. Just pull the ribbon.

He found himself wondering whether she'd be showing the same interest if she didn't know who he was. Said something about his state of mind, the difference between being fifty-nine and forty-nine. The younger the women, the less they noticed, because fewer of them watched the network news programs.

Why was he coming to San Francisco? Was there an important story? Would he do the program from there? No?

Somewhere in his brain a cassette from years ago began to play, and he could hear the sure formula. If you're by any chance free this evening, so am I. Would you care to have dinner together? But he had the sense not to say it aloud. He did say he was going to stay at his vineyard in the Russian River district, and her eyes lit up like the big score bumper on a pinball machine.

"A vineyard! What's it called?" She made *called* about five syllables.

"We don't make wine. We sell our grapes to wineries."

Guy Ferris was in his mind, and he began telling her about stories they had covered together as a correspondent-cameraman team and the hundreds of evenings they'd spent after shooting the action in various places—Vietnam, Afghanistan, Lebanon, South Africa, Europe—

"You were in all *those* places?"

—often talking wine, because they were drinking it, and because Guy began teaching him what he'd learned about wine growing up in South Australia.

By this time they were on the last forty-five minutes, beginning the descent into San Fran, and she had slipped into the empty seat, her trim knees twinkling at him, devouring his story.

"And we made a decision that one day we'd have our own vineyard. Some Aussie told Guy that California was the best undeveloped potential for great wine anywhere. When assignments brought me out here, I'd run up to the wine country. In the early seventies I found a place abandoned during Prohibition. The winery was really a mess, but I fell for the land and the old house. The price was low; it was well before the California wine boom. When Guy quit shooting wars and revolutions, he moved there full time, and he runs the place."

IN THE Clift Hotel, even with the time difference, he had trouble going to sleep. He couldn't get Deborah Jones or the doctor out of his head, the implications of one running into the other. He'd decided long ago that he was going to play it straight with Winona, and he pretty well had. He was glad he'd had the sense not to take the bait, but his imagination had.

For a few minutes, as the plane coasted down over the Sierra Nevada into San Fran, his imagination had been conjuring up a little apartment on Telegraph Hill, drinking wine with her . . . and so on. In the end he got up and had a couple of Scotches from the mini-bar to calm himself down.

www.hollygo.com

Hollygo don't know whether she usin the wrong deodorant or what, but she ain't pickin up any real good gossip. Come on, y'all, dish the dirt with me! Gotta been someone misbehavin at the Radio TV Correspondents' dinner in Washington. I know, nothin like when the I-Man rocked em all a few years ago, but I mean, come on! Five hundred ruffled shirts and five hundred off-the-shoulder dresses, and a dozen hospitality suites pumpin out the booze, and no one got *anythin* to report? Y'all too drunk to remember? Or too embarrassed? Tell y'all what. Next year, you put the arrangin in my hands, and hollygo'll fix you a party like you'll *never* forget. A compulsory cross-dressin, everyone-in-drag, party. Call it Shakespeare to get it past Jesse Helms, an As You Like It party. See what comes out of the teevee closet. Don'tcha luv it? Imagine Bill Clinton and Hillary both in drag. Dominatrix for her and maybe a Paula Jones or Monica Lewinsky outfit for him! Then watch Hillary crack her whip! If it wasn't bent before, Lolita, it would be then!

Speakin of Paula Jones and the like, I think the teeveenews people missin a bet there. If you gonna keep signin up outsiders like Susan Molinari as news anchors, why not go for it big? Get Paula! Get Monica! Get Gennifer Flowers. Go, baby, go! Get the women the Kennedy men all been hittin on. Ask not what your country can do for you, ask what you can do for your country! Too late for Marilyn Monroe, but get Anita Hill! Get all the women been workin under them officials and put them in the anchor slots! Who knows more about politics than they do? They know all the distinguishin characteristics of politics. You gonna make politics into entertainment teevee? So go for it!

Old Gregory Peck been a surefire subject of gossip for weeks now, a steady boldface name in the columns. He slipped away to California to look at his little-bitty vineyard, but next week he back where the grapes of wrath are stored. Maybe it'll stir things up. Right now, hollygo just dyin on the vine! Don'tcha luv it?

George White in Minneapolis was engaged in some elementary analysis.

On his desk were the two packages of negatives, two sets of prints, and two proof sheets, the last, he judged, made sometime ago. He had checked and counted. The negatives matched up perfectly with the frames on the proof sheets. None missing.

It had taken him about a minute to recognize the weather girl from Minneapolis TV back in the early seventies and another to recall Anna Malakoff, her name before she moved to Milwaukee and changed it to Ann Murrow, now one of the most famous names in America. He remembered Anna Malakoff vividly.

He was a young cop on the Milwaukee police force. Presidential election year, and the local police augmented the private security and Secret Service personnel protecting the candidates. Late at night, the night before or the night of the Wisconsin primary, he'd been patrolling the parking lot behind one of the headquarters hotels. It was full of vans and RVs used by the candidates and the media. All was dark and quiet, but as he passed one of the RVs, George heard a small noise. Thinking someone might have broken in, he tried the door, found it unlocked, quietly swung it open, and shone his flashlight inside. Its beam caught a man and a woman engaged, in police parlance, in an act of sexual intimacy—to George, screwing. Two faces dazzled by the light. George recognized the press secretary to one of the presidential candidates, and the woman was Anna Malakoff, Ann Murrow.

In a voice George knew from television, the press secretary shouted, "Get out," and he complied.

George, comfortably married for many years, looked at the pictures. Provocative little bitch, she was, the grand lady millions knew now as the avenging reporter, exposing crimes of petty miscreants, or cooing over celebrities. Amazing to George what they got away with on television. Fun to imagine what her fans would think of these pictures, not explicitly pornographic, not like the stuff sad girls were lured into on the verge of active prostitution. A far cry from that.

Obviously Ernie knew who she was and was putting the squeeze on her. No wonder Steinman was so anxious, willing to pay a thousand a day, no questions asked. George looked at the new prints, still arranged in pairs as they must have come out of the dryer, not yet collated into separate sets. When he'd snatched the envelope from Ernie in the shop, it was still warm. The kid must have worked in the store, known about the pictures, and when the owner died, decided to cash in. Must have been making the new prints while George was waiting by the door in the alley, waiting nearly two hours, almost ready to give it up, when the door opened a crack and he was able to ram his way in, scare the hell out of the kid, flourishing the pistol, unloaded because George didn't like risking mistakes. The kid, an amateur, easily frightened by talk of calling the cops. Put up a feeble effort to get the pictures back, then scuttled out.

He leafed through the sexy poses, which already looked dated. Steinman was going to be a happy man. George had done far more than expected, actually retrieved the incriminating stuff with little violence, nothing he couldn't defend, and scared the kid off, probably for good. Steinman would want to know if he'd got it all, but how would he know whether the kid still had a set hidden? He might fear it, but he wouldn't know.

He called Steinman's number.

"Got some good news for you. I got the pictures, the negatives, and the two proof sheets."

"Fantastic!"

George recounted his moves, waiting before dawn outside the rooming house, following Ernie to the diner, then to the photo store, waiting outside till he cracked open the door, surprising him, seizing the envelope.

"Said I was a security man, threatened to call the cops, and he ran off. He's a kid. I think he's out of it."

"Is it possible there are more prints inside the shop?"

"I looked around after he left. Nothing obvious. I think we got it."

"That's great news. I want to have them in New York as soon as possible."

"I can Fed Ex them."

"I don't trust it."

"How about a personal messenger?"

"You've got someone you can trust?"

"Me. I get on a plane and bring them to you in New York."

"You'd be willing to do that? I'd pay your expenses."

"First class?"

"Sure, first class. When could you come?"

"I'll call Northwest right now, get the first plane in the morning. Be there probably by noon. Where are you in New York?"

"General Motors Building across from the Plaza Hotel."

"Fine. How about getting me a room at the Plaza? I'd enjoy a night in New York."

"It's done."

"But we have to discuss this a minute. I've saved you a hell of a lot of trouble. No fuss. You don't have to come here, negotiate with some punk. You're clean. What are you going to do for me?"

"Well, you get a thousand a day. We agreed."

"The thousand was for tailing the kid. No agreement about recovering the stuff."

"I'll give you ten thousand," Steinman said, "besides the thousand per diem."

"Fifty thousand," George said.

"No way! That's fucking blackmail!"

"Oh, no, Mr. Steinman. Blackmail is illegal. I'm not threatening you. I'm asking for a suitable fee for recovering the pictures free of hassle for you."

"Twenty-five thousand," said Steinman.

"Fifty," George repeated.

"No. Twenty-five! That's it."

George made his voice very low. "I know who the lady is, Mr. Steinman. I remember when she was the weather girl here a long time ago. I remember some other things about her."

"OK, fifty thousand."

"It's a deal. I'll call you when I know which flight."

George put the phone down, smiling, thinking he could have held out for a hundred thousand.

Steinman hung up delighted. Fifty was a lot less than he'd expected to pay. And it was clean. He hadn't enjoyed the prospect of negotiating with a blackmailer.

Ann Murrow answered her private line.

"I have some good news. The photos, negatives, prints, and two proof sheets will be in my office tomorrow."

"All of them?"

"All of them. There's a negative for each shot on the proof sheets."

"How much?"

"Fifty thousand, plus a few thousand expenses."

"Good work, Joey."

"What do you want me to do with them when they get here? Destroy them?"

"Joey, I'd hate to think of you keeping them to sneak a look at every now and then—"

"Come on. For God's sake, Ann."

She laughed her throaty laugh. "Just kidding. Bring them over yourself when they arrive, plus the prints I sent you, and I'll deal with them myself."

So she didn't trust him. "If that's the way you want it."

"Oh, and you know what, Joey?" When her voice turned cute and alluring like this, no good ever came of it. "The fifty thousand?"

"Yes?"

"Would you pay it, and we'll settle up later?" And before he could answer, she'd hung up.

A corner of his mind was almost disappointed that the pictures had turned up. Of course, before taking them over to Ann he could run a set through the color Xerox. Just for the record.

35

"Hello. I'm sorry I kept you waiting. I'm Maureen Friedland."

"Dr. Friedland. Grant Munro."

"It's always intriguing to meet such a famous face in the flesh. Please, sit down and be comfortable. My consultations usually start with a little talk, then move on to the clinical side."

Immediately, he liked her; blond, fortyish, California youth prolonged, probably still trim in a bathing suit: good advertisement for her work.

"I'm curious." She smiled almost shyly. "Most of the leading cosmetic surgeons are in New York and L.A. So why San Francisco—and why me?"

"You were warmly recommended. San Francisco because it's important to me to keep this private—out of the newspapers. I thought San Francisco might be less obvious."

"Don't worry. No leaks from here. I do lots of well-known people—" her smile had a tiny edge of humor "—*very* discreetly."

"The other consideration is where to go after the operation. I'm told it takes several weeks—"

"More or less. We'll go into that fully."

"—and my wife and I have a place in Sonoma County, where we grow some grapes. Our house there would be a private place to—"

"Hide out while you convalesce?" She smiled.

"Exactly. It would be logical to tell the office I'm staying there, and it's completely private."

"And you've flown out from New York just for this consultation?"

"Yes."

"So this is more than exploratory. You've really decided to go ahead with the surgery?"

"Yes, but I'd like more information—what you think it would achieve, what would actually be done. And I didn't want to get into all that until I'd chosen the doctor. I didn't want to go shopping around in New York."

"You haven't talked with any other cosmetic surgeon?"

"No, only my internist—"

"Dr. Rosenberg. Michael Rosenberg. Yes, I talked to him."

"—and he made the inquiries that led me to you. I've read that you can't fly for a while after the surgery. Is that right?"

"Yes, it's inadvisable."

"And I can get to our place by car. But once I'd heard more about your work, it seemed fortunate that I'd chosen San Francisco for the other reasons."

"Well, that's very flattering. Certainly I'll answer the clinical questions, but I'd like to ask a few personal ones first. In your case, knowing your public persona, I feel less confident than usual . . . I don't wish to intrude . . ."

"Don't worry. Ask whatever you think is necessary."

"I've admired your work for many years and I can appreciate your special need for privacy. Everyone must feel they own you a little."

"No, please. Go ahead."

"I usually ask why a patient *wants* cosmetic surgery."

"Why do you need to know that?"

"So that I understand their expectations. If too much is riding on the results—if a woman who thinks it will save her marriage—I may advise her not to do it. I'm not in the business of saving marriages. I can make suitable patients look better. I can undo, or postpone, some of the effects of aging. But I can't mend lives."

Her left hand was prominent on the desk. Engagement and wedding rings. A woman who seemed comfortable with herself.

"So, if I may . . . Why?"

"It's obvious, I suppose. It's a business full of young people. I'm about to be sixty and I've recently noticed how old I look."

"Well, let me tell you that you look fine for sixty. Much better than seventy-five percent of men your age. People might take you for mid-fifties or younger."

She looked at him, smiling, considering. "A lot of men your age, and younger, do this because they want to seem attractive to much younger women—or men."

Grant laughed. "That's not my motive."

"No, I imagine that's never been a problem!" Dr. Friedland laughed easily, then, realizing her remark might have seemed flirtatious, began to blush. She said crisply, "Well, what precisely do you want to know about the clinical side? You've been reading about it?"

"I want to know exactly what you do. Where you make incisions, what you eliminate. What are the risks."

"Fine, but first you have to choose which parts of what the layman calls a facelift—jawline, neck, cheeks, eyes, and forehead. I have these diagrams to show you."

She opened a looseleaf notebook with plastic-covered illustrations.

"Tell me what parts of your face you think you want worked on."

"The areas that I think make me look old are around my eyes and the jawline, the double chins. Mostly it's the puffiness around my eyes and the sagging jowls and neck."

"Well, that's quite usual. I wouldn't touch your forehead. It's not necessary. The eyes, yes. That's the most common procedure. I can remove the fatty tissue that's causing the pouches."

"Tell me exactly what you do."

"Well, if you follow these illustrations, I'll start with the eyes. Above the eye, I make an incision like this, and separate the skin from the layers underneath. Then the skin flap is pulled up to the incision, any excess is cut off, and it is stitched closed. In the lower lid, an incision is made, here, just under the lash line, extending out into the natural crease. Again, I lift the skin away from the underlying tissue. Usually there are fat globules, and they're snipped out; the skin is pulled up and a little outward toward the corner; the excess is cut away, and the wound is closed with fine stitches."

"What are the risks?"

"Well, in inexperienced or careless hands, there's a danger of damaging the eye, and below, here, the skin may be pulled too tight, dragging the lower lid down so that it shows too much of the white, or the eye never quite closes. I assure you, you don't run that risk with me. Two to three days after the surgery, I remove the stitches. You'll have swelling and discoloration, perhaps black eyes, for a week or ten days, and then it will begin to look normal. For example, if you wanted to do only the eyes, you could be back on television, wearing makeup, in two weeks."

"Now tell me about the neck and jowls."

"Two parts to this, and it is more serious surgery. I do it—with the eyes—under general anaesthesia, and the healing time is longer. The first part is what people think of as a facelift: tightening the skin over the cheeks. But modern technique involves two layers to make it last. First, an incision following this line, in the scalp above the ear, down the front of the ear, behind the tragus, this little cartilage bump, under the ear, and down into the scalp. The skin is dissected away, carefully separated from the underlying structures, out to here, below the corner of the eye, and over the cheekbone almost to the nasal labial fold here, and down to the jaw and neck on the side. Same on the other side. Then I move down to the neck. Another illustration. Just under the chin, I make a small incision, large enough to admit a cornula, a tube connected to a vacuum—"

"That's liposuction?"

"Right, a liposuction tube, and that sucks away some of the fat from this area. Then, going back to the incisions on the sides, I cut away the fat along the platysma, a large muscle that comes up from the collarbone to the jawbone. On both sides. Then through the incision under the chin I put several stitches where the muscle divides to make it a stronger support for the neck tissues. Now back to the first illustration. Under the skin flap I've raised, in front of the ear by the cheekbone, I excise a triangular section of the muscle and connective tissue underlying the skin layer, the subcutaneous musculo-aponeurotic system. And pull the new edge up to this line and suture it. That pulls the facial muscle structure tighter and lifts the underlying neck tissues as well. All that remains, then, is to drape the loose cheek skin layer over the new structure, secure it to create the proper tension, cut off the excess, and suture along the line of the original incision so as to leave the least visible scar, and it's all done."

"What are the risks?"

"I feel there are risks only in incompetent hands. The surgeon must be careful when dissecting the skin layer to leave enough thickness so that the blood supply remains adequate when the skin is re-attached. If you elevate too thin a layer, there can be narcosis, or skin death. And if we dissect too deeply, we risk injuring the nerves or muscles that control the face. And you can have a bad result if the surgeon pulls the skin too tight when closing the incisions. These are not mistakes that happen with me."

"Tell me about after the operation."

"When the incisions are closed, the face is enclosed in a pressure bandage to hold the tissues tightly in place, and ice packs are applied to reduce postoperative bleeding. During the surgery bleeding has been controlled by a local injection of a vasoconstrictor solution. The pressure bandage comes off after twenty-four hours. Then you need to stay physically inactive for a few days, keeping your head elevated, not bending over, and not stretching your mouth; taking liquids through a straw, not chewing. I'd advise having a nurse for a few days. We can recommend some who specialize in cosmetic surgery patients. By three weeks to a month, you should be well healed, and people will think you look refreshed and rested, and more youthful—"

"But not startlingly so? I don't want people to think immediately: He's had a facelift."

"Because, in your heart, you're a bit embarrassed to be doing it?"

"Well, I'd be embarrassed if people knew."

GUY FERRIS drove into San Francisco to pick up Grant, and his reaction was characteristically salty and direct. Getting into the Toyota Land Cruiser, marked inconspicuously *Russian River Vineyard,* Grant felt as though they were off on a story, as so often in the past, when the back would be full of Guy's camera gear.

Guy had changed little in thirty years: stringy, weather-beaten, as sun-baked as now; a dried apricot of a face and vivid blue eyes, of which, outdoors at least, you saw only slits through manifold squint lines and bristling eyebrows. For a little chap—he'd probably never weighed more than 150—with small hands and feet, he had the arm and leg strength of a much bigger man.

"Why the magical mystery tour? You sneaked into town to see a plastic surgeon."

As usual, he was driving like a madman down the roller-coaster San Francisco streets.

"Let's find a place for lunch and I'll tell you."

"Lunch I've fixed. Great Chinese place. Upstairs in the Embarcadero. All dim sum. Chinese take their families there on the weekends. OK?"

"Great."

"You don't want to make the big confession, but I've figured it out. Facelift, right?"

"I guess I gave it away when I told you where to meet me."

"Easy. Cute little sheila at the reception desk. I say I'm your partner, waiting for you. We get to talking. Saturday, so she hadn't much to do. I put two and two together. It's facelift."

"Right. But I came out here to keep it quiet . . . out of the gossip columns."

"You know what I think?"

"I can guess."

"I think you're barmy. Or in straight American, out of your fucking tiny mind, or you wouldn't be waltzing across America for a consultation, getting the doctor to come in specially on a Saturday . . ."

"Well, I'll tell you why and see what you think about it."

"I don't need to know why. Why do aging sheilas and pooftah actors get their wrinkles trimmed away? Only one reason, mate. Scared of looking their age, wanting to look younger. What other reason is there? Unless you're going for an implant to make Percy stand up better. I hear that's the rage these days of declining American glory! Never had the problem myself. D'you know what else they're doing? At least, before Viagra. Sticking needles in it and injecting something to make it jump up and salute. Can you imagine it? Sorry, luv, little tired, need my tiny injection. Are you ready, sweetheart? Here goes! Oooh! Aaah! That stings! Then they wait. Takes fifteen minutes. Maybe she runs out to buy some cold beer—can you imagine it? Meets a mate, gets to talking, forgets Arthur upstairs. Rushes back up. Sorry, luv. Sorry? It just bloody came and went! Twenty minutes ago, Captain Marvel; now just a shadow of his former glory. Oh, well, she says, cozy and companionable, let's have a beer and you can try it again!"

Guy was laughing and wiping tears with the back of whichever hand was not squealing the Land Cruiser around a corner. And while he was off on his scatological riff, Grant thought of Guy with a Saigon bar girl, murmuring endearments, making her laugh with his plausible Vietnamese.

Early in 1966, he'd ambled into Grant's network office in Saigon, saying he was a free-lance Aussie, and could Grant use another cameraman. Only two months in Saigon, Grant felt he'd been wasting time attending briefings, trying to smoke out where it would be smart to go in the interior.

Guy was amazing. American troops loved him because he seemed like one of them, not "media." And when they did follow one of his hunches and found the action, often more than they wanted, Guy was cool. They were all scared, soldiers and journalists—only an idiot wouldn't have been scared—but Guy put his fear away in some compartment while he was filming, then brought it out and laughed about it afterward.

Robert Capa said, "If your pictures aren't good enough, you aren't close enough." No long lens, no zoom, was a substitute for getting up close to the action. Guy took the risks that were fatal to many, including Capa. From the first rolls Guy shot and shipped back to New York came the praise that flowed the whole time he was there.

Guy had been around Asia, and with his guidance Grant came of age as a Vietnam hand: where to eat, what girls to see, what to buy in the blackmarket and what in the PX; Guy knew it all. There was a lot of macho crap in any war. Everyone wanted to seem knowing, hardened, savvy, brave, unsentimental; no one wished to appear confused, scared, bewildered, childlike, and there was a lot of faking it. Guy made faking it unnecessary. He became closer than a brother.

Grant got Guy transferred to London when he was posted there, and almost everything Grant did after that he tried to have Guy shoot it with him. Finally, when Guy'd had enough, they collaborated on the vineyard. They had pooled Guy's knowledge and savings with Grant's money, giving Guy's experience an equity value to make them equal partners.

As in Saigon, the Embarcadero restaurant hostess greeted Guy as if he owned it, and soon they were drinking beer and picking dim sum from the moving steam trollies.

"What does the lovely Winona think?"

Grant felt good, being able to talk openly, to lay it out to the only person, besides Winona, he could trust completely.

"She doesn't like it, but she's getting used to it. So? What do you think, seriously?"

"How long is the recovery before you dare show your face back at the office?"

"Three weeks; maybe a little longer."

"No sun, though. So you couldn't work outdoors."

"Right."

"You know, if you'd forget the bloody operation, spend a month working the vines with me, we could go up to the mountains for a few days climbing—gentle climbing, I mean—you'd get yourself in shape. Drop in on Teresa—"

"Put that out of your mind for a start!"

Guy laughed. "Anyway, it's amazing how you'd tune up. Bit of sun, lose ten pounds, you'd go back slim as a whippet, everyone'd think you'd *had* a facelift. A bloody sight cheaper and a bloody sight more fun. Maria Luisa's a great cook. So's Rosita. We'd stage a little test on our trial Merlot. Get bottles from all the premium wineries and compare. We'd have a hell of a good time; you'd go back looking ten years younger. If you wanted to be fanatic about it, you could even slide into the gym in Healdsburg and work out."

Looking at Guy's lean, tanned face—no double chins, jawline like a Marlboro model, eyes clear and unpuffy, now that they were out of the direct sunlight—the argument made some sense. But his gaunt, weathered look had had a lifetime to gel.

"Tell me straight out, why no operation?"

"Because it's undignified, that's why. Hacking around, mucking about with the face God gave you. That's what chaps do who have no identity of their own, don't know inside who they are."

"It won't be *that* different. It'll be subtle."

"It seems false, somehow. Not like you. And you don't need to do it. Fuck them and the young twerp you say they want to bring in. You've built up a nationwide following. Took you years. They're not going to throw that away for someone no one knows."

"That's what Winona says."

"Smart lady. You should brazen it out. Sure, get yourself in shape if you want, but you look fine now. I think you've had a jolt to your confidence. Not surprising, with sixty sneaking up on you; it can get to a chap. But if they'd do that to you—bounce you for a kid—why would you want to work for such arseholes? Let 'em rot in hell. Take your money and run. Have a good life."

"I don't want to run. I love the work. I can't imagine giving it up. What would I do with myself?"

"Come out here. Make the best wine in California. Or get the boat of your dreams and sail it around the world. I'd go with you, provided we had a few creature comforts of the Rosita variety to warm up the bunks."

"That's all great, but I don't want to give it up yet. For one thing, it's money."

"You're not in it for the money."

"No, but we can use it here."

"And you're not in it for the crumpet like some of them. Back in a moment. Got to point Percy at the porcelain. All this beer's overflowed me wooden leg."

Everything he'd said made good sense, yet Grant didn't buy it. He wasn't changing his identity; he was preserving it a bit longer, putting time on hold.

THEY DROVE out to the vineyard, walked over the vines examining grapes until dusk came, and the green haze of summer growth, the sweet pale curves of hillside, vanished down into the little fog creeping up the Russian River from the Pacific.

The old house, with its quaint siding, was dark in the shadow of a eucalyptus grove. The cough-drop smell of eucalyptus mingled with the sea smell of the river mist. He had strong feelings of being at home in this house, perhaps stronger than in any other place he'd lived. Seeing the first lights gleaming from the old curved windows was deeply reassuring, a sudden feeling of wholesomeness. Coming into the front hall, with its aromatic cedar paneling, was like being embraced by an experienced, loving woman.

Maria Luisa, the housekeeper with the luminous black eyes, cooked her best Cal-Mex meal; Rosita came with Guy and they drank a lot of the wine the neighbors had made from their grapes. The facelift was not mentioned again. And Sunday morning Guy drove Grant to the San Francisco airport, saying, as they shook hands, "Give it some serious thought before you go for it."

3 6

In his briefcase on the plane were Dr. Friedland's lists of preparations for surgery and care afterward, but he didn't read them now. Despite Grant's denials, Guy's reaction had reawakened doubts.

Imagine the *Time* story mentioning a facelift! Not just mentioning, but highlighting it, as inevitably would happen if Christopher Siefert found out. Grant worried, because he was beginning to trust him.

But at the core of his anxiety was Winona. They had not disagreed so fundamentally since their earliest years together at college.

THE FLIGHT attendant leaned over. "I'm serving a breakfast now, Mr. Munro. Would you like the Spanish omelette, or cereal and fruit?"

"The cereal, I guess."

"And coffee?"

"Yes, please."

· · ·

HE'D MET WINONA at Thanksgiving in their freshman year, when they shared a lift home for the holiday, and they became inseparable.

Winona was a serious student. At first she treated Grant's lazier ways with affectionate tolerance, lending him notes for classes he missed, marking key passages in required reading. Then his ways began to irk her.

They would meet for a sandwich and coffee at lunchtime, often when he had just crawled out of the sack, and she had half a day behind her.

"How can you sleep so long?"

"I just do. I guess I need it."

"I think it's because you're bored. You aren't interested enough in what you're doing to wake up."

"I'm interested in you."

She'd ask, "When you're working on boats in the summer, do you sleep in like this?"

"No way! There's too much to do. I get up at six."

"You see! When you like what you're doing, when you're not bored . . ."

"I'm not bored with everything. Some of the lectures are interesting."

"When you get to them!"

Her dad was a fitter in the Electric Boat Company's works in Groton, where they made the nuclear submarines. Winona, the first in the family to go to college, insisted on paying her own way. She had a full scholarship and waitressed at a hotel on the shore in the summers.

From the time he was fourteen, Grant had been employed every summer on sailboats, and now he was crewing one boat for the whole season, keeping the yacht's working gear in shape and the cosmetics sparkling. He loved that boat, a Concordia yawl. The wooden hull, the varnish, brass, and teak decks were killing to keep up, but rewarding.

Back from a month of cruising in Maine, the Concordia owner let Grant ask Winona out for a sail on her day off.

"It's glorious," she said. "Beautiful."

"Of course this is just a day sail," Grant said. "You don't get the real experience until you make a longer trip. Sleep on the boat, wake up in the morning in a different place."

"So you can sail away and leave all your problems behind. Isn't that what sailors have always done? They go away, and their wives stay behind to do all the unglamorous things."

"Like waiting on tables?"

"Don't be mean!"

"I'm sorry."

"It's OK. Only it seems unreal. Lovely but unreal. I don't see how you could do it all the time."

The subtext was beginning to be familiar.

"What you didn't see today was all the scut work behind the scenes. It's as hard and unglamorous as waiting on tables for jerky tourists."

"But it isn't real life, is it? It's a game. It's like playing golf. Like Ike going out to play golf. It's not his real life."

"Well—some people make a good living out of golf; the pros who teach people . . ."

"But, Grant, do you see yourself, for your life's work, helping other people play games?"

IN THEIR junior year, they had Thanksgiving with her family. Very warm. Everything was fine until they began talking of Winona's major, psychology, and what Grant thought of it.

Winona laughed. "Don't ask Grant! He hasn't a clue about what he's going to major in."

Her dad turned to him with real concern. "You're not interested in your major?"

As they drove back to college, Grant said, "Whew! It's not only you nagging me about my major, about my career. Now it's your father, too."

And she said, "Nagging? You think I'm a nag?"

"On that subject, I do."

Winona let him drive in silence, then suddenly said, "Grant, I'm not going to do this anymore. You're not interested in going anywhere. You don't make real effort at anything, because everything comes easily to you; you float along. You don't try. I want to be with somebody who tries hard. Someone who's going somewhere." And they broke up.

THE LIGHT in the aircraft cabin was changing as the day advanced and they moved east.

WINONA AGAIN: "Is the facelift a good thing to do, if you can't tell the children about it?"

"I didn't say I can't. I said I don't want to right now."

"You're worried they won't approve."

"They don't have to approve. I didn't consult them when I had my teeth capped."

"But you didn't keep it a secret, either." Winona, always honest, always direct. "I think you should examine why you feel uncomfortable about telling them."

Typical therapist's remark. Sometimes a little less clinical analysis would be welcome. He pushed it aside then and since; childish, but he didn't want to discuss why he didn't want to tell the kids.

Because you're embarrassed. Because they'll think you've surrendered something they admire, or you hope they admire. Deep down, you suspect you've let go of something you always held tight, the lifeline that ties you to yourself. It's the lifeline you see many others abandoning in the rush of exposure, celebrity, money, and you despise them for it.

What did he imagine his kids thought of him anyway? Heather ending her first year of medical school at Johns Hopkins, Sandy in

Wyoming as a wilderness camping instructor for the National Outdoor Leadership School. Grant hadn't the slightest idea what his image was in their eyes. Look how he'd seen his father, a vision he felt changing now, twenty-four years after his father's death. But if his view of his own father had been distorted, what might Heather and Sandy think of him?

He was evading the issue. What would go through Heather's head if he told her right out that he was going to have a facelift? Try to imagine.

First, she'd think medically. Who was the surgeon? Who referred you; who recommended? What credentials? It was a serious business. There were risks; did he know that? All that left-brain activity to give her time to explore her emotional reaction. That's how she was.

But why, Daddy? You look perfectly good to me. You're not too old. You look great. Some guys I work with can't believe you're my dad because you don't look old enough! Do you really need to? What if it comes out badly . . . they do, you know. Some people have to get them done again. Real horror stories. They can make mistakes . . . Again to give her time to feel. Then: Do you want my advice? Don't do it. Tell the people at the network to stuff it. I don't think you should let them change a thing. Grow old gracefully. It'll make you look desperate, willing to do anything to stay there. Anyway, enough from me. What does Mom think? Maybe if she had one too, you'd both stay even. But I like you both as you are. OK? Gotta go.

Something like that from Heather. She'd accept it. Surgery was not frightening to her, but she'd probably feel he'd surrendered to the crasser values of television.

Sandy? Vaguer, harder to get him to focus. Well, gee, I don't know what to say, Dad. Sounds a bit drastic. What do they do exactly? Wow, that's pretty radical! If you're feeling a little flabby and slack, why don't you work it off? Come out on a course; hike it off. Climb it off. Seems more natural.

Echoing Guy Ferris. In his present phase, which had lasted since Yale, Sandy saw everything in terms of what could be done naturally. He wasn't mystical or silly. Grant suspected he'd come out of this in a few years and find a career in environmental work. He'd hinted at going for a higher degree in environmental studies. Right now it was hard to get him to come to New York. He felt he was himself in the mountains and open skies of the West.

Winona said, "It was easier for you. Your dad was a failure in your eyes and his, and he made that easier to accept because he was unkind to you. He never was to me, incidentally. So it was easier for you to do better than he did. No competition. Look what Sandy competes with out in the world. Not easy to better his father."

Grant didn't want to get into that. She handled these concepts every day. He didn't. He knew that when he looked at Sandy, he felt some envy. He was lean and ruggedly good-looking. He'd never smoked. He had a clear, faraway look in his eyes, and he was doing what he loved. It was as if Grant had kept on with sailboats as a profession, out of doors, healthy, constantly surrounded by unspoiled nature, peace in the soul.

Whenever he thought Sandy had no ambition, Grant had to remind himself that he'd always had to be spurred into competition, sometimes only if he'd felt challenged, someone trying to grab his story, a guy from another network running faster for the plane. Grant had not been aggressively ambitious. Just in spurts, when he'd sensed someone's hot breath on his neck and felt his position threatened. Like his reaction to Donovan. He couldn't swing around and knock the young upstart off his horse with the flat of his sword, but he felt the emotion. He did feel competitive. He was damned if he was going to be pushed out of the way by some young twerp!

BUT ONLY a few moments later, he felt his mood darkening. If this plane crashed, if he died now, how would his career be remembered? Grant had a quick image of the *Times* obituary page, and could almost see the highlights from his network bio.

He could feel the impermanence of what he had done for thirty-five years, the evanescence, which contributed directly to Americans' transient sense of history. The more that history comprised fleeting moments on the screen, the more it would flicker away. This great advance in civilized communication, allowing every citizen in his own home to watch history being made, was a medium that seemed to erase history as fast as it showed it.

Reagan's people said the nightly network news drove his White House; each day revolved around feeding and shaping those three nightly assessments of the presidency. But now that reality existed only in books, the outspoken memoirs of the Reagan staff. Electronic media might drive the news, might catalyze history hour by hour, but they didn't preserve it. Television might provide raw materials—videotapes, voice recordings and scripts—it provided them, for the most part, to people who *wrote* history.

"MR. MUNRO, I'm going to be serving a late-afternoon snack, Fruit and cheese. Would you like a glass of wine, or something else to drink?"

He looked out the aircraft window where the day looked older.

"I'll have a glass of red wine."

"Would you prefer the Merlot or a French Bordeaux?"

He chose a potential competitor's Merlot. She leaned closer. "I haven't said anything because I know celebrities enjoy their privacy. But I wanted to tell you, I'm a great admirer of your work."

"Well, thank you. You're very kind."

"And it's an honor to have you with us today."

Quite different, hearing it from this matronly woman instead of the dazzling, green-eyed Deborah Jones. He sipped the Merlot.

He often had a little shriveling of conscience when he read what the P.R. people had written; exaggerating, heightening, coloring, to make it seem more important than Grant thought it was. Like his being wounded.

He'd been in Vietnam for sixteen months when, covering a firefight, a single round carved a neat but bloody channel on the outer edge of his left thigh. He'd been running and noticed only a sharp sting until he and Guy hit the ground behind some cover, and he saw the bloody pants leg. The medevac people were close by and free, so, with Guy filming, Grant was quickly bandaged and put aboard.

The wound began to heal quickly, but New York decided it was time to bring him out.

The network press release and resulting stories overdramatized it. Obviously ambivalent, he'd shied at the initial exaggeration, but privately enjoyed the extra fuss. Network programs put him on, and each time "wounded by enemy fire" became part of the setup piece, with the footage Guy had taken. Grant liked it and he didn't like it. It enhanced his worth at the network. When the news department took a full-page ad in the *New York Times,* lauding their correspondents who had been wounded, arrested, imprisoned, or killed in the line of duty, Grant was included.

Over his thirty-five years, there had been several such—what should he call them?—silly little deceits, and this coral of micro-exaggerations had grown and solidified into his public persona.

What was the real truth about him? What he was telling Christopher Siefert felt like a recitation of the same P.R. highlights.

IT WAS 5:35 in New York. He put his watch forward. A half-hour to go.

He pulled the phone out of the seat back, ran a credit card through the slot, and dialed his home number. Winona answered with the cheerful "Hell—ooo" that always made him feel good.

"Hi. It's me. I guess we're on time and I should be at La Guardia in half an hour or so."

"Oh, good. How'd it go?"

"Just fine."

"She didn't make you change your mind, hearing all the gory details?"

"No. But Guy was pretty negative."

"Did you like the doctor?"

"Yes. Very reassuring."

"Too bad! I was kind of hoping she'd scare you off."

"No. I'll tell you about it. I should get to the apartment at six-thirty, six-forty-five; something like that. You want to go around to Grazie?"

"Sure. You may be a little later, with all the Sunday night traffic. I'll call them and say seven."

"That's great. See you soon."

"Bye."

He put the phone back, thinking: What if that was our last conversation? What if the plane crashed?

Why was he so gloomy? He was coming home. His spirits always rose when he was coming back to Winona. And he had a date in the kind of unpretentious little Italian restaurant he liked. He'd never lost the pleasurable lift that prospect gave him, the thrill of living in a city in which you could never know all the restaurants.

Working down his interview list, Christopher Siefert had reached Marty Boyle, Grant's executive producer. Compared with the subtle and diminutive Don Evans, Marty was a beefy, sandy-haired, overgrown schoolboy. Bursting out of his rolled-up shirtsleeves were large freckled arms that had probably sacked quarterbacks in high school. Marty had a communications B.A. from the University of Ohio and a journalism master's from Northwestern.

He seemed a little nervous. For that reason, or to impress Siefert with his importance, Marty let phone calls constantly interrupt the interview.

CHRIS: I guess you're aware everyone calls you the Power Ranger around here?

BOYLE (laughing): Oh, sure. And the Kid from Hell. Yeah, I know. Ever since Hollygo started on the Internet—you been following that?—it's everywhere. I have friends at the other networks who call me that now.

CHRIS: Well, since you mention it, I was going to ask about some of the things Hollygo says.

BOYLE: Don't put too much importance on that stuff. It's all a joke, really.

CHRIS: Do you have any idea who it is?

BOYLE: No. Someone in this shop, because she picks up gossip from here. The guys at the other networks, even cable, say the same.

CHRIS: Aren't you dying to know who it is?

BOYLE: No, I'm too busy. (Phone rings) Yeah, Marty. Hi. Well, tell her to take the earlier feed. Pay the five hundred. Sooner we get it, sooner we can chop it down.

(Siefert noted the wide colorful suspenders on Marty's loud, striped shirt.)

CHRIS: Looking back through the Hollygo columns, I see she says, quote: A good source tells Hollygo that the dynamic Power Ranger . . . is also itching to get the old queen out and replace those drooping jowls and eyebags with some firm young flesh. The old queen I presume means Grant Munro. Is that the way you feel?

BOYLE (laughs): God, no!

CHRIS: Well, where would Hollygo get that idea?

BOYLE: Beats me. Makes it up, like she makes up other stuff about us.

CHRIS: But isn't that piece a reference to Bill Donovan?

BOYLE: Could be. Who knows?

CHRIS: And you're one of those who wanted Donovan to come in as Grant's summer replacement?

BOYLE: We had some talk about it, but it's not going to happen.

CHRIS: Because Grant objected, I gather.

BOYLE: Well, you'd have to ask him.

CHRIS: Let me put it more directly. You're the executive producer. That's a lot of responsibility. You're facing another fall in the ratings. The numbers fell, you brought them up, they've dropped again. No longer number one. Do you personally think the show would be saved if it had a new anchor, someone younger, more vibrant, a more with-it style, to attract younger viewers?

(Marty looked stolidly at Siefert's small tape recorder.)

BOYLE: I think we've got the best anchor in the business. I'm behind him, I mean Grant, all the way. We're a team. We're all in this together.

CHRIS: You agree that the problem is younger viewers?

BOYLE: Yeah, it's a problem, but not just for us. The other networks. Even cable. More people over fifty watch news. It's a problem across the board.

CHRIS: So changing the anchor is not an option—even if you'd like to?

BOYLE: God, no. Anyway, Grant's contract has two more years to run.

CHRIS: And after that?

BOYLE: It's not my job to think contracts. I've got to put on the best show I can every night. It takes twelve, fourteen hours a day. There's no time to think about two years from now. Running a show like this means solving a hundred little problems a day, day and night.

CHRIS: But there are people here who would like someone different fronting the show, isn't that true?

(Marty looked at him, giving no secrets away.)

CHRIS: I mean, people have told me that's true.

BOYLE: Oh, sure, some people may feel that way, but that's not my job. My job is to work with the talent.

CHRIS: Talent . . . ?

BOYLE: The on-air talent.

CHRIS: Then how *do* you get around the age problem? You've got a talent, an anchor, old enough to be your father. At your age, you must feel an affinity for the younger viewers. How are you trying to bring them in? Story selection? Avoiding some stories? Tell me how.

(The phone rang and Marty barked instructions to someone obviously reluctant to receive them. His manner with subordinates was rude, overbearing. Listening, reviewing what had been said, Siefert conceived that Marty wasn't going to say anything negative about Grant. Obvious. But you could feel the strain in him, like a drunk trying to walk a straight line.)

BOYLE: (on phone): Yeah, but do it anyway, OK?

CHRIS: One of the day's hundred problems?

BOYLE: Producer in London. She and the correspondent see the piece one way, I see it another. They want two-fifteen. Two minutes, fifteen seconds. They can't have it. The Second Coming isn't worth two-fifteen these days.

CHRIS: I was asking what you do to make the show attract younger viewers. Is that it? Keep items short?

BOYLE: Nothing new about that. That's our business. Keeping it brisk. (Snaps fingers.) It's knowing when people are going to get bored.

CHRIS: That must affect story selection, too.

BOYLE: Sure. You see the show? We're heavily into making the news mean something personal to people. Not just some stuff their parents told them they should watch. It shouldn't feel like a duty, watching the news, like taking medicine. It should be interesting, it should be fun, be relevant to your life. If you're a young mother trying to do it all these days . . . you've got only so much time. You're interested in what's happening right around you in your world, not so much way out there . . .

CHRIS: Quarrels in a faraway country between people of whom we know nothing?

BOYLE: You got it. That's a good way of putting it.

CHRIS: That's what Neville Chamberlain said to calm the war fears in Britain when Hitler annexed the Sudetenland in 1938.

BOYLE: Oh, yeah? (Phone rings.) Marty here.

(This time Marty rummaged on his desk and found a script. Siefert could see parts crossed out, scribbled lines replacing the cuts.)

BOYLE: No, it *doesn't* work yet. All you did was take out the bit I wanted and shove it lower down. Get rid of it! (Snaps fingers.) Look, I'm looking at the fucking script! Page three. OK? Cut it from your lead-in . . . yeah the whole lead-in, right down to the bottom of the sound bite . . . No you *can* do without it!

(Siefert had worked with every kind of editor. Marty was the type he disliked—arbitrary, overbearing, and probably insecure.)

BOYLE: Let me tell you something about the audience now. They all sit with remotes in their hands, especially the men. The research shows men click an average of every five seconds, women less. If we want to keep the men watching, something's got to be happening every five seconds. But not only that. The new ratings can sample the audience every few seconds. You can tell right away if interest went up or down on a particularly story.

CHRIS: If men clicked off?

BOYLE: Yeah.

CHRIS: So you drop the stories that make them click off?

BOYLE: Not that simple, but that's the idea.

CHRIS: Have you analyzed which stories make them click off?

BOYLE: We're working on it.

CHRIS: What would you say were the biggest successes of your show in the last couple of years?

(Marty looked at him, sensing a catch.)

BOYLE: Successes?

CHRIS: What did you do better than the competition, and why? What did you have that they didn't?

BOYLE: Besides Grant Munro, you mean?

CHRIS: Of course.

BOYLE: Princess Di story. We did real good. Got Grant over and anchored our show from London all week. Fantastic story. And we fleshed out all the London stuff with vignettes all over America on what Di meant to ordinary people.

CHRIS: Did it make a difference in the ratings?

BOYLE: Well, everyone's ratings spike up on stories like that. It's why the cable news guys go ape-shit. And so do we. Like O.J. Like the President's sexcapades. Public can't get enough. And I think we've been real competitive on Michelle Robbins.

CHRIS: The rape murder in Wyoming??

BOYLE: Yeah. We've hung in there.

CHRIS: Why is that important?

BOYLE: It's their little girl they see at risk. It's news that touches the most precious things in their life.

CHRIS: Even if, statistically, the possibilities are very remote for them?

BOYLE: They don't believe that. They don't think statistics. It scares the shit out of them, and they want to know every awful detail.

CHRIS: I gather you and Munro have had some big disagreements about that story.

BOYLE: Oh, sure, we argue. It's healthy. Keeps it dynamic. I'm sure you guys argue what to cover big, what to ignore. Every news organization does. But we come out in the same place in the end.

CHRIS: Even on the White House sex scandal? Grant blasted the whole industry on that.

BOYLE (laughs): Oh, sure, the Gadarene swine. Look, the anchors, like Grant, they all sound off now and then. Op-ed pieces, speeches. It's good. It shows the public we've got a conscience.

CHRIS: But it doesn't change anything?

BOYLE: What can it change? It's the business we're in. You get a story like the President's extracurricular stuff, and the public can't get enough of it. You go with it. You pull out all the stops.

CHRIS: The polls showed the public thought it was too much.

BOYLE: The public! Sure, they complain, but they lap it up.

CHRIS: You've been executive producer—what? A year and a half?

BOYLE: Right.

CHRIS: How have you put your mark on the show in that time? (Phone rings.)

BOYLE: I'll see him in, let's see, five minutes. We're nearly done.

CHRIS: I was asking, how is the show different because Martin Boyle is sitting at this desk?

BOYLE: We've cleaned the show up, improved the pace. We cut down on the kind of news we know viewers don't care about, less foreign stuff, much less Washington. And we've developed a line of regular features . . . you've seen it? . . . called "Close to You." That can mean economic news or medical developments or education or crime or life-style stories . . . where they matter, closest to their lives.

CHRIS: Is that your trademark on the show? "Close to You"?

BOYLE: Yeah, you could say that. It was my idea. We developed graphics to give it a uniform look across the week. I've reworked the budget to assign crews and correspondents and producers to keep the pipeline full. I like it. I think it's fresh. I think it's what people want. It tests well.

CHRIS: Tests well?

BOYLE: In focus groups and surveys; it looks good.

CHRIS: But the ratings don't respond to it?

BOYLE: Well, that's mixed, and it's early. We were up right after we started "Close to You." Now we're down a bit. But it's summer. I think we'll pick up in the fall, when the audience has had time to get used to the format. And we're trying something else, although it's still in the early stages . . . interactive news.

CHRIS: How does that work?

BOYLE: Using our home page, we run a series of options on some stories, like a computer menu? Viewers can click on the options, more detail on this story, or this part of the story, and it comes up on their screens. Usual Internet stuff. But most of our viewers aren't on line. So our software counts the hits on the menu options, feeds it to us, and we can hit the most popular preferences the next day on the actual show.

CHRIS: Sounds ingenious. Like instant feedback on your news judgment.

BOYLE: You got it!

CHRIS: How far can you go in asking people what news they want? At what point do you start giving up your authority as journalists?

BOYLE: Good question. I don't think we're there, anywhere near there. There're too many other places they can get it now . . . cable, the Internet. If network news doesn't go a lot farther to please the public, it won't have a public to please. That's my philosophy.

AND THAT was a line Christopher Siefert could already see boxed in large type in the center of a page.

The Cleveland station had booked the governor, senator, local congressman, and mayor. Their speeches made network switching sound like an act of broadcasting statemanship, not crass bribery by a network desperate to improve its presence in a major market. And Grant played the game, praising the journalism values of his news department in a competitive environment more zonked out on entertainment every day. "Zonked out on entertainment" made the wires and got played across the country with headlines like GRANT MUNRO SEES NEWS RIVALS ZONKED OUT.

But it was the night that made the trip notable. For ruining his evening with travel, the station had promised dinner when he arrived. And waiting in the limousine that met the plane was the local woman anchor, Fran Whitman, thirty-ish, lean, and polished. It began with what sounded like routine gush.

"May I call you Grant? I feel as if I know you so well from watching you . . ."

But she was something, her good legs crossed in the back of the limo, as though she habitually rode in one, her line of welcoming chatter falling muted on his jet-buzzed ears and pressure-swollen head.

"You're wonderful to do this for us. And to make it nice for you, we've arranged a quiet little dinner, at a decent restaurant." She did not gild the restaurant with provincial hyperbole. "And you can be at the hotel in an hour and a half."

They were bowed into a little French restaurant, greeted like royalty, ushered past candlelit tables and staring diners to a private room, with a table tastefully set with silver, crystal, candles, flowers, white napkins, for two.

In her hair, clothes, and manners, there was something pleasantly refined about Fran.

"They appointed me to be your hostess, so if there's anything you want, please ask. A drink, some wine—they have a fantastic wine cellar—or we can leave it to Henri."

Grant left it to Henri, who produced good food and excellent wines, if too many courses for the time of night. But the meal was not the message, as became clear after a little more small talk.

Fran had moved up several markets, starting in Pittsburgh, and wanted to keep climbing. That was the message after her little toast, when the Château Margaux was presented and tasted and poured. A worldly young lady, Ms. Whitman from Pittsburgh.

"I'd like to drink to you, Grant, for giving us at the station and for giving journalists—"

Bracing, Grant assumed his grace-under-praise smile, but it was unnecessary.

"—the finest model to follow and to aim for in our own careers. I heard your RTNDA speech. I was there and I was inspired."

She said that mouthful with enormous sincerity, her regulation blue eyes wide open under her regulation blond coif, regulation gorgeous teeth gleaming in the candlelight, and her promising lips parted. They clinked the delicate glasses and sipped.

"This is very good."

"Isn't it wonderful? Do you know France? I suppose you must."

"Yes, I've been there quite often."

"Well, France is my secret passion. I sneak off there every chance I get to refresh my soul."

Grant couldn't tell much about her soul, but the physical package it came in was appetizing. He wondered how provincial she would seem to the French, or simply how American.

"And after all my forays there, and the marvelous food, I can still enjoy what Henri creates right here in Cleveland."

Neatly done, because the gentleman being complimented was within earshot, expertly removing the bone from something. Perhaps Chez Henri was a major advertiser at her station. Between courses, she got to the point.

"I have to confess, Grant, that I had an ulterior motive in wanting to see you alone, so I jumped at this chance."

She made it sound like a Girl Scout volunteering, but he could imagine the maneuvering that had brought her here.

"I'm just a little nervous that you'll think I've cornered you unfairly this way."

"Not at all. I'm grateful for your hospitality."

"You're so nice! I've been sure all along that underneath your formal personality on the air, you'd be a really nice guy—and you are!"

"If I wasn't a nice guy, would that kill the ulterior motive? What if I'm really a rotten bastard!"

"You couldn't be! Well, anyway, I thought, I'll never get a better opportunity for some serious career advice than meeting and talking with you. I hope you'll forgive me for using a nice occasion like this."

"Sure, no problem." Grant took another appreciative swig of the remarkable wine, wishing Henri hadn't swaddled the bottle too heavily in the napkin for him to see the year. Either the wine or Ms. Whitman or both were making him feel mellow, and he'd begun to speculate—as one would—what she would be like to go to bed with. But he couldn't tell yet whether that was the bait she intended.

"My problem is this: where to go next? And it seems to come down to L.A., Chicago, or New York."

She talked, very reasonably, he thought, about her résumé, her experiences, her hopes and ambitions. "My real goal—it may be completely impossible—but my real goal—" She took a tiny sip of wine and managed to convey with a little toss of her head that she was feeling it and being reckless "—is to become a network correspondent."

"Have you applied to any network?"

"Oh, sure, all of them! But you must know what it's like. 'We have no openings but thank you for sending your résumé and tapes.' They probably get so many they don't even look at them all."

"What about your agent? Do you have one?"

"Yes, I do. And he's putting out the word and telling me to be patient. But I'm not the patient type. I'm already thirty, and at thirty, you can't hang around too long. And I figured—" Again the sip of wine and the charming, what-the-hell tilt of her chin "—I figured I'd come right out and ask you. I know there are hundreds of women out there, all as eager as I am. Of course, I think I'm special and have a lot to offer, but, you know how it is, you can't get their attention at a network unless someone *tells* them to pay attention."

"And that someone is me?"

"Bingo! There, I've said it, and I've probably made you think I'm a jerk or the obnoxious female from hell—but yes!" She took another defiant sip and exclaimed, at the arriving dessert, "Oh, crème brulée! I adore crème brulée. *Henri, j'adore crème brulée et vous . . .*" And Grant began to like her a lot.

"Well, I have no problem getting someone to look at your tape and your résumé. That's not a problem."

"Really? That would be fantastic!"

She put a tiny spoonful of crème brulée in her mouth. "But you wouldn't be able to say anything about them—recommend me, that is—unless you'd seen them yourself. I mean, what if I look absolutely dumb on camera?"

Grant laughed. "I take it that's not the case?"

"I think I look great on the air. I do good interviews. I write sharp copy. I can edit tape. Good standuppers. All that stuff. But you won't know unless you see it."

"You could send me the tapes in New York. People do that all the time."

"Or you could see them tonight?"

"Where?"

"At my place. Not far from here. On the way to the hotel. And I have some fantastic cognac."

"Do you think that will improve my judgment?"

"Look. I win either way. Either you love my tapes and I get hired, or—"

She did not wait for Henri to reappear but confidently poured the last of the Margaux, sharing it equally between their glasses, as assured as the young Katharine Hepburn.

"Or?"

"Or I can say I had Grant Munro back to my place for a drink and you won't believe what happened."

"What did happen?"

"Nothing! He looked at my tapes and said he didn't think I made the grade. Thanked me for a nice evening and went to his hotel . . . and called his wife, like a good husband."

"Maybe you should be writing scripts for Meg Ryan. Sounds as if you compose great scenarios."

"You'll come?"

"Sure. Nobody's ever done this number better than you."

"I hope not. I've been rehearsing it for days. Or more honest, right?"

"Right."

"Even down to the husband, right?"

"What husband?"

"Mine. The one who'll be there when we get home."

"That's a detail you didn't mention."

"I was getting around to it . . . saving it for the right moment . . . the *pièce de résistance?*"

"Is he a nice guy?"

"A very nice guy. He'd have to be, to be my husband."

"I guess he would. Maybe we'd better go and meet him. He may be getting worried about you."

"So you're a nice guy, too."

"You don't give me much choice, do you? And I'm old enough to be your father."

"I know. I wondered when you'd say it."

He liked her more the bolder she became, liked the cool appeal, and was even relieved that his libidinous speculations had become pointless. But Fran was like an Agatha Christie plot . . . always another twist.

Escape from Monsieur Henri, with much ceremony and thanks, signing his book of honored guests, promises to send friends who came to Cleveland. Then to her modern apartment, the home of transients, little accumulation on their way to bigger things, and, she said, a message on the answering machine in the bedroom.

"Oh, damn, Dale's had to go out of town. He's a reporter for the *Plain Dealer*. He was dying to meet you."

To Grant's skeptical look, she said, "Honestly, I thought he'd be here. Now, I'm really embarrassed."

"Too embarrassed to show me the tape?"

"I am *not* Meg Ryan!"

"You're prettier."

"Really?"

"About your acting, I can't tell."

"If I were acting, you could tell!"

They sat in her den, looked at her reel, anchoring the local news, interviewing newsmakers, reporting on an investigation into supposed payoffs at a construction site, and the usual "reporting live" standuppers at fires, murders, and heartwarming missing-child-found stories that filled the local news. She was as good, or better, than any Grant had seen, her pretty looks put to the service of the same feeling of spontaneous candor she had turned on him all evening. Then another surprise.

She plugged in a second cassette, and there she was in the same anchor position but reading stories that sounded familiar—national and international news—until he recognized it as the program he had done a week or so before.

"I transcribed all your copy and got it put on the prompter; then they just cut in all the rest of your show . . . with me instead of you. What do you think?"

"I don't know. Wind back to the start and let me see some of it again."

Which she did, and again Grant had several feelings at once. She did it well, calmly, authoritatively, and intelligently. Not very different in emphasis and intonation from his reading.

"What do you think?"

"I'm trying to figure that out." He looked at her, an attractive woman in a tailored suit. Very smart. Well spoken, as his mother used to say. As ambitious as any one of these women he had encountered, yet entirely likable too.

"What I think is, that at your age and experience, I wouldn't have looked or sounded half as professional as you do. I know, because every now and then I see myself on some tapes from the sixties, and I cringe."

"You're not just saying that to be nice?"

"No, I mean it."

"Then what should I do about it?"

"How much reporting have you done?"

"The usual stuff. What you saw. Dale gives me pointers. He's a good reporter."

"What happens to his job if you move on?"

"He'll come with me and find work."

"Nice guy."

"I told you."

"Let me take the tapes to New York. I'll call and tell you what people think."

A little notion was forming. This woman had just as much experience as Bill Donovan, apart from his time at the White House.

"What do you think they'll think?"

"They'll wonder how much longer they have to put up with me if there's talent like you around."

"No, come on!"

He let her drive him to the hotel, to go chastely to bed, musing about the conflicting feelings she had aroused. For moments he'd thought himself caught in the most obvious ploy, a scene in a sitcom; yet he had been tempted physically. She was delicious to look at. Another piece of candy. But he'd been impressed with her. She was one cool lady.

THE NEXT morning at the station ceremony, she greeted him circumspectly, and he liked that. With her tapes he took the private jet back to New York, now thinking it was quite plausible to put some confident young television personality into his chair.

Fran Whitman showed none of the smirky, self-important mannerisms that so irritated him in Bill Donovan. She had the good taste to be straightforward, with no gimmicks. And, despite the cute tactics, amazingly straightforward with him. Nothing else would have persuaded him to take some local station tapes back to New York.

Now he had to calculate how to make them work.

Of course, she might be a flower that bloomed in secondary markets but wilted in New York.

They had tried that with Jessica Savitch, one of the most cynical moves in the business, and long before today's drift to entertainment. Egg on their faces, humiliation and tragedy for her. Well, some thought she was an ambitious, scheming broad who brought it all on herself. But it took some cynical calculations to promote a woman with so few basic skills (Savitch couldn't write a script competently, or shape a field piece) all because she lit up like a movie star when they turned on the camera. A movie star could be as dumb as dirt. Television anchors and correspondents couldn't be and get away with it for very long. The minute they began ad-libbing, or reporting on a complex story without strong producer back-up, or doing a key interview, it all fell apart. They gave Savitch the star treatment, put her on the air during election coverage, and it was pathetic. And that was before she hit the cocaine and blew it on the air.

OK. Take Fran Whitman; how did you avoid the Savitch debacle? Grant's hunch was that Fran was a far more centered personality. For that matter, how did you avoid doing a Jessica Savitch to someone as inexperienced as Bill Donovan if you pushed him too fast?

Forget Donovan for the moment. He was the B scenario. Go back to A: Grant helps a plausible successor to emerge. Maybe even buys the line that Bryce is too dull. OK, say it needed to be someone younger, as Winona said, to avoid a changing of the guard twice in five years. Made sense. And buy the line that it had to be someone as personable and dynamic on the air as Donovan. Well, Whitman was exactly that, in a nicer, less exploitative way.

No anchor of Grant's generation had got there unqualified or un-seasoned as a reporter. Every one of them had been through the mill; had earned it. How did you get the new generation to earn it when the people who ran the industry today didn't even care whether they earned it? If they got ratings without the investment—great! If they screwed up and looked dumb on the air and got a few days of lousy commentary—so what? Soon forgotten. Couldn't be as bad as Jessica Savitch, and whom did that kill? Only her.

Well, what about the existing stable? Shirley Trattner had a solid background, but her reserve, an air of diffidence, her manner, were soft; her voice didn't punch through the background babble. The quality she seemed to lack was elusive, but the young woman in Cleveland had plenty of it—a nice pushiness, aggressiveness that was not abrasive, an eagerness that made people listen, because her sense of urgency was infectious.

Christopher Siefert had talked to enough network people. Now he needed the personal stuff on the coast, then back to Munro himself.

He'd expected more resistance from Teresa Weldon, refusal to discuss her husband's death, to reopen all that pain. Instead, on the phone, she was quiet for a long moment and then said, briskly, but with some edge, "Sure, why not?"

The Cascades bookstore near Pioneer Square in Seattle was a narrow, high shop with a pressed-tin ceiling. When he opened the door, the air smelled spicy, like apple-cinnamon tea.

Teresa was thin, with luminous dark eyes and long black hair in a single braid. She wore a scooped-neck T-shirt, revealing a flattish chest.

Above the tall bookshelves were posters and spectacular photographs of snow-capped peaks, glaciers, and of climbers clinging to perpendicular rock faces.

"Tony started the store for climbers and hikers. I've broadened a little to other outdoor interests—wildflowers, wildlife, forest lore of the Pacific Northwest"—she pointed to different sections—"camping, fly fishing, cooking in the open, survival, some regional fiction."

She led him back through the shop to a nestlike office up some stairs on a cluttered loft level. As he followed her up, her springy step, her lean buttocks under the long cotton skirt suggested vigorous outdoor activity. The warm spicy smell, the narrow spaces and shadows between the shelves, made her shop feel like the lair of an animal that knew how to heal itself.

"We can talk here. There aren't many customers on weekday mornings. I'm making tea; would you like some?"

He accepted and watched as she put a teabag in a mug and switched on the electric kettle. Her braid swung attractively over her shoulder, and she tossed it back with a flick of her head.

Siefert asked, "Are you a climber yourself?"

"Not a serious climber. I did some ascents with Tony and others. I'm more a hiker than a climber."

"I take it Tony was a very good climber."

"Yes. He was buddies with the guys who write all the good books. He loved it. He came out from the East and got hooked. That's why he started the store. It became a kind of hangout for climbers."

"How good a climber was Grant Munro?"

"Tony thought Grant was good. A natural feel for it. And pretty fearless."

"Fearless?" Siefert repeated. "To someone like me, knowing nothing about it"—he glanced at the photographs behind her—"it looks so terrifying I can't imagine anyone not being afraid."

"Well, everybody's afraid, of course." She settled into her chair, crossing her legs, holding her knee through the skirt. "To begin with. But you start to overcome the fear little by little, build up confidence that you can do this bit safely and then the next. The first time you set a nut—do you know anything about climbing?"

"Nothing."

"Setting a nut—it's placing a device in a crack that will hold your weight, protection if you fall. The first time you do it and clip your rope into it, you never believe it'll stay, but it does, and you get used to it; and you know from the way it sits and the kind of rock, whether it's safe. So you build up confidence. All the same, the best climbers seem to have a special place where they put their fear. I don't know how to explain it . . . Why are you doing a story on Grant?"

Siefert noticed it a second time. When she said *Grant* she used the name possessively, as she did *Tony*. Grant was her friend too.

"The magazine felt it was time to look at television news, which is changing—"

"Changing for the worse."

"A lot of people think so, including Grant. He's something of a critic, and he's the anchor who's been the longest in that job, so it makes sense to focus on him."

"What does Tony's death have to do with all that?"

"When I do a profile of someone, I really want to know the person."

"I don't think anyone knows Grant."

"Oh? That's a surprising thing to hear from a close friend."

"Maybe, but it's true."

"That day was obviously catastrophic in your life. It must have been traumatic for Grant too."

She surprised him by smiling derisively. "I'm supposed to say how sad I am for him?"

"Tell me whatever you want to, or don't want to, that will help me understand him. He's a man the world sees as highly successful, invulnerable. I wonder how you see him?"

"Your tea will be too strong." She pulled out the teabag and placed the mug on the edge of the desk within reach, near the tape recorder. "It's complicated. I could talk a lot better if you turned that thing off."

"Fine. Let's talk." Siefert switched off the recorder and settled back to sip his tea.

"I don't want to be quoted as saying any of this. You promise?"

"I promise."

"I liked Grant a lot. So did Tony. Tony knew him a long time before I did. Grant started coming into the store. He'd done some climbing in Europe, in the Alps, South America. You know, climbing with professional guides. But he got taken with the Northwest and the mountains here, as many people do. A special place. Great peaks, some very hard to get to. Much less climbed than the stuff he was used to. They began climbing together. When Grant could get away for a few days, he and Tony would go off. When Grant got his vineyard in California, he came out West more often and would slip up here. I came to work for Tony in the bookstore, a refugee from publishing in the East." She smiled. "I remember a couple of your books . . . and then Tony and I became a thing and we got married. Very simple. New Age, outdoors on a mountain. Grant came to the wedding. There we are!"

She passed Siefert a picture in a standup wooden frame, a small group on a ridge, snowy peaks behind them, all raising champagne glasses. Grant, in shorts and boots, taller than the others, his handsome features standing out from the crowd. Teresa was wearing a wraparound cotton skirt like the one she wore now.

"My wedding dress! I put it on over my shorts, with hiking boots."

"When was that?"

"Six years ago, in August."

"So you were all close friends?"

"Yes. He'd stay with us when he came up; it was more private for him. And he asked us down to the vineyard. Have you been there?"

"I'm going there after this."

"It's lovely. Paradise. Gorgeous old house."

"What was Grant like with you and Tony?"

"A sweet guy. All that serious, sort of pompous manner the newsmen have—and he has it too, maybe less than some—it evaporated when he was here. He was good company. He told good stories. He'd done some amazing things in his career, and both Tony and I had led pretty quiet lives."

"What was it like, being a close friend with someone who's so famous, such a celebrity?"

"It's like nothing. No different, except now and then, you're out in public—he'd take us out to dinner sometimes—and jerky people would want his autograph, want to take his picture. Otherwise, it was like being with anyone else."

"So?" Siefert looked expectant.

She looked back, uncommunicative. "So?"

"I thought you wanted to say something else."

"You want me to talk about that day."

"If you want to."

"Of course I don't want to. If I talk about it, I have to feel it again, and in two years I've just about got to where I can deal with it calmly."

Siefert noticed there was light fluffy hair on either side of her jaw. She was very thin. Was she anorexic, starving herself in her grief? Her anger? Or athletic? Her thinness made her brown eyes huge.

"It wasn't Grant's fault that Tony died. He didn't mean to do anything like that. Tony was his friend. Grant was our friend. Extremely considerate. The last thing in the world he would have wished would be to risk . . . all that. I've said that to myself over and over."

Siefert waited, looking at her thin fingers clasped so tightly over her knee that the knuckles stood out as if skinned.

"But in Grant's world, when you want anything, you get it, or you do it, or you buy it, when you want to, when it's convenient for you. It's habit. It's the way his world works. Everything is possible."

Siefert noticed the present tense and then the switch to the past.

"He wasn't a selfish man, far from it, very considerate. I mean, it was obvious that he had a great deal of money and we lived very simply; he knew how to make that easy and graceful. Lots of little things I noticed . . ."

And listening, Siefert wondered whether she had been in love with Grant as well as with her husband.

"Everyone knows you have to climb when conditions are right. Right time of year for a particular peak. Stable weather. You have to be prepared for delays when things change. Be ready to wait, or give up if it turns bad. And you have to allow enough time to get in to the mountain. Some of the peaks in the Cascades are very remote. You have to hike in a whole day, or two days, through rough country just to get to the base of the mountain. It's very tiring. So you have to be in perfect condition, for that and then for the ascent. You have to be in training. Grant knew that. He amazed us, what he'd put himself through, given his other life in New York, to get in condition. He'd increase his running. He told us he had a knapsack loaded with small sandbags, a few pounds each. He run up and down the stairs in his apartment building, ten floors or something, wearing the knapsack, gradually increasing the number of sandbags. And he had a climbing wall in his apartment."

"What's that?"

"It's for practicing handholds and footholds. They're made in various typical shapes and you fix them to the wall. For a man of his age, Grant usually came out in fine condition."

"His age?"

"Well, Tony was thirty-six when he died, Grant was fifty-seven. That's a lot of difference in what the body can do."

"You said *usually* he was in fine condition. Not the time of the accident?"

"He'd been working very hard, extra programs, special programs, a lot of travel, no time off. He couldn't have had time to train. He called us suddenly to say he had several days free, was coming to California, and was dying to climb for a couple of days. There was Chianti Spire, a peak he'd wanted to try for a long time. There's a row of tall peaks east of the North Cascades National Park, and they're named for different wines—Burgundy, Chianti, Chablis—and maybe that attracted Grant. Tony said you couldn't do it in that time; it'd take most of a day to drive over and another back. Grant called again a few hours later. He'd found a helicopter pilot who'd fly them in, drop them in position early in the morning. They could climb the peak and make the descent. He had it all worked out, so many hours up, so many down, so many spare, and they'd radio for the copter to pick them up. If they were late coming down and it was too dark, they could bivouac one night and call in the copter the next morning."

"What did Tony think?"

"Tony was very methodical. He didn't like to be rushed. And this felt rushed. And he thought it was early in the season for Chianti. The weather was still changeable. Maybe some ice that melted in the daytime but only partly froze again at night. He told Grant it'd be better to wait until late June for Chianti, and try something simpler now if he wanted a quick climb. He suggested some other locations. But Grant was very keen, and the idea of the helicopter ride really turned Tony on. He thought that was great. Avoid all that driving and hiking to the base of the mountain. He checked the weather forecast and it looked OK. So he said yes."

"With misgivings?"

"Not after he'd decided."

"Did you have misgivings? Did you try to talk them out of it?"

"No. I accepted Tony's judgment. And, like Tony, I wanted to please Grant. It's a big high, conquering a new peak, especially one that not every climber gets to. Not that it was the most difficult. Grant wasn't up to the most extreme difficulty. But it was hard. Up to five point ten."

"Explain that."

"They grade the climbs for overall difficulty, Grades One to Five. I can give you a book that explains all this and also describes the actual mountain. Grade One means you can kind of walk up the mountain. Grade Five is the most difficult. But within Grade Five, they grade the pitches, different parts of the climb, by technical difficulty, how steep, how exposed, how much overhang, how good the holds, quality of the rock, vertical rise. Most difficult is five point fourteen. Easiest is five point zero. Chianti has several pitches of five point ten, and it was on one of those where they got into trouble."

"I read about that. The wind came up."

"It's always a danger, but that's where Tony's instinct was right. It was early June. Perfectly clear sunny day, not a cloud in the sky, when they flew in and started up. Everything went fine. They got so warm, they stripped down to their shirts. There are six pitches and they'd reached the fifth, a five-point-ten climb on a two-inch crack."

"Meaning?"

"Meaning a vertical crack two inches wide. You slip your hand in . . ." Like an instructor, she made a crevice with her thumb and fingers, and slipped the fingers of the other hand into it. In another part of his mind the gesture felt erotic.

". . . like that. To get a grip, you make a fist or a wedge with the hand, then the other hand, and you try to get your toe in. Every so often, a body length or so, the leader places protection in case of a fall. Stuff you carry hooked in the rack on your harness—nuts, or chocks, or wedge-shaped devices, different sizes and shapes that will fit different cracks, and with loops of wire attached. He places it, attaches a runner of webbing, with a carabiner—that's a kind of D-shaped aluminum ring with a spring-loaded opening—and then snaps his climbing rope into it and moves up. If he falls, he'll only fall until the last protection stops him, because his partner is belaying him, letting the rope out little by little, ready to brake it if there's a fall."

"Why doesn't the partner fall, get pulled down too?"

"Because he's tied to an anchor, a secure place where they've placed a strong holding device, or several, or used a tree."

"An anchor?"

"It's just the term they use, something that can't let go."

"What I remember from mountaineering books is that they pounded pitons into the rock, then hooked their rope to those."

"They used to, now much less. There are so many climbers, and pitons are hard to remove, they chew up the rock. The new protections can be removed and leave the rock clean for other climbers."

"Would you go on with what happened?"

"Even when you're young and very fit, it's extremely hard work. Even when it's cool, you're sweating. Tony was leading and they were going fine until the day clouded over; a strong wind came up, with some rain in it, and they were freezing. With the wind chill, the temperature must have fallen forty or fifty degrees. They decided they had to give up and go down. The descent from Chianti is by rappelling. You loop your rope into a strong anchor so it's doubled, then you slide down it, using a braking device on your harness. When both climbers have rappelled down that pitch, they pull the rope through, then start down the next pitch in the same way. It's not difficult in good weather, when you can take your time, but they were freezing and in a hurry to get down. Grant went first down pitch five to a ledge, and Tony followed. Grant started to set his rope for the next rappel while Tony cleared his own rope from above, but it was stuck on something and, reaching out to free it, he must have moved too close to the edge, because he slipped off and fell about seventy feet. He hadn't tied in on the ledge. Apparently only the safety knot in the end of his rope stopped him when it got jammed in the anchor on the pitch above. Grant looked over and called to Tony, but there was no answer. He was hanging there, lifeless-looking. Grant radioed for help, then went down to Tony, but when he reached him, there was no pulse. He'd hit going down and broken his neck. By the time the helicopter pulled them out, Tony was dead and Grant had hypothermia."

"How bad was that?"

"He was all right after two days in the hospital."

"Did his wife come out? Winona?"

A guarded look from Teresa. "Of course!"

"Did you see him much afterward?"

"A few times."

She glanced toward the posters of mountains. Siefert looked at this woman, whose breasts showed scarcely more than nipples through her dark shirt; she seemed to be mourning as much as her husband the man responsible for his death.

Laurie Jacobs said it was difficult to be with Grant and not to be in love with him. A remarkable charisma. With these women, Laurie and Teresa, you could feel Grant's attraction through them. Teresa blamed him; she didn't blame him. She missed him. She had lost him too.

Everett Repton said the accident had made Grant act older, seem older. Must explore that more. But what could you call Grant's behavior, badgering Tony into the climb? An act of hubris?

"I'm not clear about something you said. Tony should have tied in to the anchor?"

"If he'd tied in properly—even if he'd slipped over the edge—he would have fallen just a few feet. They do it all the time. That's why they spend so much time setting protection."

"Does it make sense to you that he forgot?"

"Grant thought Tony was so cold he wasn't thinking clearly."

"Obviously, you know all this from Grant."

Teresa said, "The moment I saw him in the hospital, he said, 'Terry, it was my fault. It was my fault!' "

"Meaning?"

"Meaning it was his fault that they were on the mountain."

"Not Tony's fall."

"He meant if he hadn't insisted, they wouldn't have been there, in those conditions."

"And what did you think?"

"Tony could have said no, but Tony couldn't say no to Grant."

The last phrase hung in the air, because she paused, and behind her dark eyes on his, Siefert could sense the whole passionate complexity of this woman, knowing he'd never understand more than scraps of it. She took her eyes away and added, "And Grant was so used to people doing what he wanted, he felt he could make anything happen."

"When did you see him in the hospital?"

"Oh, right away, when they brought them back. They showed me Tony's body; then I asked to see Grant."

So she went from her husband's body to see Grant.

"What did you feel about it? About Grant? Anger?"

"Don't ask me what I felt. I don't know. I felt a great sorrow. A great hurt. Bewilderment. How could this happen so fast? How could everything wonderful be spoiled in a few hours? And anger. Why did these stupid men have to do it? Not just Grant; Tony too. I'd always known that someday, something would probably happen to him. Or Grant. In dreams I saw them falling." She looked away and took a tissue from the box on her desk and blew her nose. "I still do."

Siefert said, "I was told that Grant made a financial settlement for you."

She looked at him. "Did Grant tell you?"

"He hasn't told me anything about this."

"I didn't think so. I didn't think anyone knew."

"I haven't talked to him about it yet. This comes from another person. He thought it was an admirable thing for Grant to do."

Teresa sighed. "I guess when you have so much money, it's the way you solve things. It means everything, and it means nothing. And he didn't know what else to do."

"What did you do with it?"

"Nothing. It's there. In a bank. They told me it should be invested, so I said, 'OK, invest it!' "

"I was told it was half a million dollars."

"I'm not going to discuss that and I doubt Grant will. I was tempted to send it back. But I didn't. I don't know. If I got married again and had children, it would be great for them, I suppose. But I don't think that's going to happen. I could do things with this store, but I don't need to. It's big enough as it is."

"It sounds to me as though you'd rather have the friendship."

"And I don't . . . obviously." Teresa said.

As he was leaving the shop, she gave him a paperback book. "It's by friends of ours. You'll find Chianti Spire in there. And if you want to see it, they've got the tape at the TV station, Grant's affiliate. The news director's very proud of it. They won awards for it."

At the door she said, "I'm going to trust you to keep your promise. No quotes from me. OK?"

"OK. I'll keep it. But I'm grateful. This has been very helpful."

"You came expecting to find an angry, bitter woman, ready to tear him to pieces, didn't you?"

Siefert laughed. "Well, perhaps something like that."

"Another day I might have been. You picked a good day."

The full horror unfolded to Siefert as he watched the tape at the TV station, horror intensified by the self-importance of the reporter aboard the TV helicopter, declaiming, "They're winching Grant Munro up now," the pleasure of reporting this tragedy involving a star colleague too sweet to disguise. Siefert could feel Grant's professional as well as personal humiliation.

The place itself to Siefert looked like hell, like an illustration from Dante, cliffs so awful and steep, only in nightmares could he imagine testing himself as Grant had wanted to do in such a place. Seen from the air, the two climbers looked like helpless insects, like flies caught in a spider's filament, almost still, then oscillating slightly, given life and movement as the helicopter rescue team winched them up. This ghastly scene had saturated the news two years ago, but, like so much that television depicted, Siefert had missed it. Had Grant's career in one sense ended then?

And she went directly to his hospital bed.

Such conceit to think you could begin to understand people whose lives you entered for a moment. No wonder the constant search for metaphor, sifting the black earth for usable diamonds. He was doing it now . . . perhaps this was how to lead the piece . . . the image of this powerful man hanging there, helpless . . . even the anchor terminology the climbers used.

Also, Siefert wondered, how did one simply give another person half a million dollars? Where did it come from? What were the tax consequences?

But his emotional curiosity remained with Teresa.

40

While Grant was in Cleveland, Sherman Glass had called, and Grant was purposely unprompt in calling back.

"New wrinkle. Got to talk. Can you do lunch?"

"No. What's the mystery?"

"I'll tell you. You want me to come over to the office?"

"No, I'll come over there."

He didn't want Sherman seen in the building.

"Now I see why you stay so thin. You starve yourself. No lunch? At least can we order a sandwich?"

The drooping upper eyelids, falling at an angle, made him look like a child denied a treat. A hell of a candidate for a facelift.

"So what's up?"

"Little bird told me Ann Murrow's in play."

"In play for what?"

"That's the puzzle. I thought we needed to talk. I think she's itchy, casting around for new worlds to conquer."

"Why should that bother us?"

"Your show could be a new world."

"Oh, come on! Maybe they're dumb enough to think Bill Donovan might get my job someday. But they'd never go for her. Not a real newsperson."

"But a big star. A hot property. Her present contract's worth about eight million, and it's almost up. She'll get a lot more wherever she goes."

"Goes to do what?"

"To do anything she likes. She can write her own ticket. There's a couple of cable channels would probably pay the freight just to get her and attract some attention. Ten, twelve, fifteen million, maybe."

"You're kidding."

"Not at all. Maybe a new kind of deal. Profit-sharing deal. Percentage of the gross, like Hollywood stars. Share options. A business stake."

"What's that got to do with me?"

Sherman paused, took his unlit cigar out of his lips, and said, "Ev Repton's been talking to her."

"How do you know?"

"I know. No question, it's true."

"OK, it's true. What can it mean? He wants to beef up our magazine." Shirley's fate darted into these thoughts. "Or start a new magazine."

"What if they're talking to her about your show?"

"Now I'm sure you're nuts. That's crazy."

"Maybe not."

"Sherman, the last time she moved, there were rumors for weeks about where she'd land. Somebody must have been putting it out with a shovel."

"Like her agent, Joe Steinman."

"He's probably started the same game. Get all the managements excited, fantasizing a bit. Drive her price up, and she's sitting there, laughing at what an easy game it is to play."

"What if Repton's the highest bidder?"

"OK, Sherman. Obviously you want to tell me something. If all this is remotely true, what are you trying to get me to do?"

"Nothing. Leave it to me. I want to get your deal sewn up. New contract. Big break clause."

"I thought you were doing that anyway."

"I am. But I need something to play with."

"Like what?"

"Like Bill Donovan."

"We settled that, Sherman."

"Sort of, sure, between us. But if you'd reconsider your rigid stand—which they're pretty bitter about, incidentally, having to climb down with Carmody and everything—I think we could sew this up fast."

"Either you're trying to scare me . . . or it doesn't make any sense."

"On my honor, I swear! Straight balls. No curves."

"If the Murrow story is true, assuming you're not just using it to soften me up on Donovan . . . Oh, don't look like wounded innocence! . . . Why would Repton sign me for five more years? If he's willing to sign me for five years, Murrow's not an issue. And if she's not an issue, I don't have to give in on Donovan, and if I don't have to give in on Donovan, why are you trying to make me? Your biggest client, remember?"

Sherman Glass punched his intercom button and shouted, "Where're those fucking sandwiches?"

Obviously missing the lunchtime martini.

"Nice way to talk to the young lady."

"She's used to it!"

"I'll bet. Look, either your information is plain wrong, or her agent is trying to fake everyone out to see what the numbers will do . . . or it's very serious. And if it's very serious—I mean if Repton could consider her for 'The Evening News,' your two-bit stuff with Donovan is a joke."

Sherman sat with his elbows on the desk, pushed the wet cigar into his lips, and smiled. Grant didn't want to hear anything more; he was tired of playing this stupid poker with his own agent.

"Not 'The Evening News' as it is, maybe. But what if they figure these early evening news shows are over? All the news departments' big growth is magazines in prime time. The more they put on, the newsier they get. Maybe they're thinking, put Murrow on five nights a week, strip the magazine, give it a hard news top, and gradually let the evening news audience disappear. Give you a five-year contract, but nobody replaces you. What if that's the game?"

"They'll never kill the early show. It drives the whole news department. It's like dropping the first section of the *Times* and publishing only the other sections."

"Some newspapers are going that way already."

Grant got up. "I'm going back to the office—I've got work to do. We put on a fucking news show every night, remember?" And he walked to the door, regretting the word *fucking*. Not his style; descending to Sherman's.

But Glass's latest idea worried him as he walked back. It was so radical that it was crazily possible.

41

www.hollygo.com
Media chilluns, as they say on the big teeveenews shows, first a little background!

When the Blond Bombshell, as I used to call her, was havin a journalism credibility problem over at Taupe, she calls this older and wiser media sister for advice. "If I cut my hair short, would they take me more seriously as a news person?" she cooed, runnin her fingers through her famous silky tresses, the kind of hair you can't fake in a wig, girls, as I know well. Someone I know was havin a power lunch at the Four Seasons and in a center stage booth was the Bombshell with a Big Hollywood Star (Male

Extra-Hetero, if you're curious). And she is leanin on one el-bow, rapt, fascinated to death, or pretendin to be, by whatever bullshit he feedin her. Ever so slightly she's observed tiltin her head one itty-bitty bit, and gradually all that hair begin to slide down, almost like you could hear old Milton Cross intonin, "The golden curtain descends on Act One," hidin her face. Then she has to make a big show of swoopin up this terrible annoyance and puttin her errant locks back in businesslike for-mation. Great display! Veronica Lake (before my time, of course) couldn't have done it better. You stayin up late watchin her old movies?

But I'm losin my drift, chiquita . . . anyway, she get it cut. She get that Vivien or Vivienne, or whoever hairdresser to the upwardly mobile, to lop off the stuff. (Hope she burned it, cos a woman I know from Haiti might be usin it to mess with her fate.) And she comes back on the air lookin like those simperin choirboy shots they used to fake up for the 1950s Christmas cards. And bingo, lookin like a cute boy, suddenly she's a serious journalist. And everyone's amazed! Cep me. OK? I just started callin her BRENDA STARR. One more lil titbit for you media trivia junkies. Did you know that Ann Murrow came into this vale of tears as Anna Malakoff? Was Anna Malakoff when she was weather girl in the Twin Cities? Then she got herself a job as local news anchor in Milwaukee and guess what? Her name became Ann Murrow, the revered surname of the patron saint of teeveenews. Don'tcha love it?

42

As much as Grant disliked Sherman Glass's style, his hunches were often smart, and this one was not easy to dismiss. Grant saw Don Evans for the weekly radio session.

"What d'you make of all the buzz about Ann Murrow?"

"Brenda Starr? Steinman must be one hell of an agent. She fills up the columns just by letting it out that she might be available. Very clever."

"What d'you think she's after?"

"Looking at her work, my guess is she's after nothing more than being a bigger and bigger commodity. A presence, the subject of endless comment. Celebrity as celebrity. She doesn't do any of it very well. But she makes herself such a celebrity, people watch. Millions of suckers for that faux-journalist, faux-moralist, faux-intrepid girl avenger. The hum of celebrity. Television has perfected the art of making people famous for being famous. Present company excepted, of course, they don't even have to have professional skills. But you have to have something to pull that off, and she's got it. Chutzpah unlimited!"

"I was wondering whether she wanted to get serious about being a news person, wanted to get into hard news."

"You've picked that up? So have I."

"Where from?"

"Ah, you know, just seems to be in the wind. And there are a lot of straws in the wind. Talk of the killer ploy you used on Bill Donovan, for instance."

"No killer ploy. My contract. They have to consult me on substitutes."

"And they didn't?"

"They didn't."

"So you reminded them in a forceful manner?"

"I did."

"Congratulations!"

"Thanks."

Evans looked at Grant with a half-smile. "Perhaps you'll have to do it again."

"How?"

"I've heard they're thinking of young Bill for the weekend slot."

"No kidding?"

"Your contract give you any say-so there?"

"I've never thought about it."

"It isn't substituting, strictly speaking. It's a different show. But the guy who does it has always been the main substitute for the anchor . . . you might say by hallowed tradition."

He meant that Grant had been weekend anchor before he got the nightly slot.

"You hadn't heard this little rumor?"

"No."

Grant pretended not to take it too seriously, but inside he was seething again. Each time he turned around, there was another leak in the dike.

"We'd better go and record."

They went to the radio booth, and Grant read Don's scripts, divorcing the mind that drove his professional performance from personal emotions, to get through the immediate task. He could read just about anything cold and have it make sense. Between scripts, anger and anxiety fluttered back into his prime consciousness, but with a new effort of will, when the cue came, he pushed the feelings away and recorded the next piece.

After the recording, Don said, "That was quite good info I gave you about the weekends. Good source. Worth a little follow-up."

"I hear you. Thanks."

After all the years of edgy relations, Don was sounding like a friend.

• • •

NOON EDITORIAL meeting. For once, nothing to get hot about. No negotiations or battles with Marty. Grant watched the editors and producers
around the table, all much younger, each wearing that crust of bored
indifference over the little volcano of ambition. The network style.
Cool, sardonic shorthand.

"Rundown holds? Nothing new?"

"Nothing that matters. Slow day."

"Washington?"

"Nothing different."

"Overseas?"

"Same."

"What'd the Minnesota piece come down to?"

"Two-nineteen."

"Still sounds long. Let me look at it."

Like those on a boat sailing along in a light breeze on a smooth sea,
they all relaxed, thinking about lunch, about overdue expense accounts,
haircuts, the Korean nail parlor the women used, or simply going for a
walk.

Grant rang Laurie Jacobs after the meeting. Not only was she an
ally; her face always cheered him up.

"Got a second?"

"Always for you, darling. What's up?"

"You hearing anything new about Donovan?"

"Like he's gone back to Atlanta—don't I wish? No. Ev Repton's
away. Our schmuck VP doesn't talk since he thinks I leaked his brilliant
memos and got him laughed at. Why?"

"Nothing special. Just thinking I should keep my ear to the ground
a little more."

"So you don't get blind-sided again? I thought that was absolutely
criminal. Anyway, it's not Billy Boy Blue everyone's whispering about,
but Brenda Starr!" She said the name in italics with a big starry-eyed
smile.

"What do you think all the noise means?"

"It means the lady is restless. You know I used to work over there?"

"Oh. I'd forgotten . . . if I knew."

"She really ran me hard, as if I worked just for her, not the whole department. Biggest thing she wanted from me was to get her on ten-best-dressed-women lists. Not just one year, but again and again, and not just on but up. Get her on the lists and magazine covers. Nonstop."

"Did you succeed, with the best-dressed lists?"

"Oh, sure, but why not? She had the fix in . . . all the designers dying to hang their stuff on her, for the privilege, and she looks great in clothes. But you know what she does now?"

Laurie grinned conspiratorially and leaned closer. "Friend of mine works over there. Brenda breezes in, wearing these to-die-for, drop-dead outfits. Very simple, fab materials, throws her jacket on a chair, I mean, leaves things lying around. The gals can hardly miss it. And you know what? No labels. All removed. Obviously designer stuff made for her. No labels."

"Maybe she doesn't want to embarrass her colleagues, make them feel uncomfortable."

"Darling, if the lady worried about making people uncomfortable, she wouldn't go on the air. I think her phoniness stands out a mile. She opens her mouth, and I reach for a bucket."

"Obviously the fans don't think so. Aren't her shows right up there?"

"Yeah, depending what celeb she's bagged. And there's a lot of competition. Maybe that's why she's peddling her ass again, if you'll pardon my French."

"If you were peddling her now, what would you be thinking of?"

"You mean after she's first woman President of the United States? Don't underestimate Brenda. Well, let's see . . . maybe she just wants to get filthy, stinking rich. It's a great American pastime. And it's legal. Milk the network suckers . . . all those old goats. I've heard them drool over her, in front of me, as if I'm chopped liver! So milk 'em for every dollar you can get while you've still got your looks, then buy yourself a designer island in the Bahamas or a hilltown in Tuscany, and live like a princess."

"Do you think that's what she wants?"

"Darling, it's what *I* want! Just a little innocent projection. If you were living with two sulky teenagers and no husband on the Upper West Side, you'd think so, too."

"But seriously?"

"Seriously? Unless you're naïver—is that a word, naïv-er?—than I thought, you've got something on your mind. Better tell Laurie. Our fifty minutes is almost up, and I've got another patient coming."

"Someone suggested that Ann Murrow might be after my job." Grant tapped the desk.

"Sure! And gentleman that you are, you'll stand up and hold the chair for her. Well, she's got the chutzpah and the balls, but I don't think even the jerk-offs we hold in such high esteem down the hall would go for that. They'd be laughed out of town. Last time I looked, there was still something called the news department. She doesn't know anything about news, unless she's been taking night classes at the New School. Only paper I ever saw her reading was *W*."

"But a woman after me in this job wouldn't be a bad idea."

"It'd be swell, unless one of the other networks does it first. It's amazing nobody has. You gotta candidate?"

"If I gave you some tapes, would you give me an opinion? A woman in Cleveland."

"Cleveland?" She immediately registered cynical calculation. "Is this a conspiracy, or what?"

"Confidentially, I mean?"

"Confidentially from your wife, or confidentially—"

"No leaks to Carmody."

"He wouldn't believe what I tell him anyway."

Angela came to the door. "The crowd from Korean television are here. You ready?"

Foreign broadcasters on State Department junkets wanted to go home saying they'd shaken many famous hands. Grant hadn't figured out how to say no. There followed fifteen minutes of smiling and bow-ing and shaking hands, having pictures taken, exchanging business cards, while the interpreter made everyone understand how pleased and hon-ored they were to meet. They bowed out with big smiles, invitations to visit them in Seoul, and Grant didn't bother to ask anything about the political situation on the Korean peninsula.

Laurie popped back.

"Got the answer on Ann Murrow."

"What is it?"

"At the moment—the Prince of Wales."

"Prince Charles?"

"There's still only one, darling. My friend over there tells me Murrow's been trying every trick in the book to land him. He won't play. Must have more sense than I thought—or better taste. She won't give up. She's got herself invited to a weekend at some English country house where he'll be, and she'll Concorde over and back. Thought that would amuse you. Of course she only wants an inter-view. But who knows? With Di out of the way, maybe she sees a tiara twinkling in her future. All she has to do is slip the mickey into Camilla's tea—and what a miniseries! Rambling gloomy English manor house, royalty, sex, murder, and Brenda. Better than 'Dallas'; run for years. But why am I wasting all these concepts on you when I should be calling my agent?"

At the door she turned. "I'll look at your tape tonight. OK?"

"OK. Thanks."

GRANT AND WINONA almost never watched television, but this was the night of Ann Murrow's magazine, so he got Winona to watch with him.

Winona said, "You know, the minute she looks at me in that serious way and wags her head and starts talking in that phony-baloney voice, she turns me off. I don't believe her. I don't think *she* believes it. It's all an act. And it's so pretentious! I think she's a jerk. And I think we're jerks to be wasting our time watching her."

"What would you think of her in my job, doing 'The Evening News'? First woman solo anchor."

"I think she'd give women a bad name."

"Sherman Glass thinks the network's talking to her."

"If they really are, then it's time for you to leave. I mean it. If they're that crazy, who'd want to work for them?"

"That's what I told Sherman."

Grant went to sleep wondering why Ann Murrow turned off so many people, yet pulled in millions and millions of viewers. Authority figures changed with the decades. There were fashions in everything. But were people so naïve, millions of them, that they didn't see through this crafted performance?

She made as much show of herself as she did of the subjects she talked to. Mugging for the camera, playing her repertoire of attitudes, shaking her head in sorrow, disbelief, responding with indignation when some sleazebag celebrity crook, child abuser, whatever, had passed some threshold of disgust, she recoiled. All calculated. In the interview cutaways and in all her pieces to camera, she attitudinized, pounding a delicate fist into an exquisite palm, sighing at the impossibility of ever conveying how depraved, sick, or unprincipled was the wretched creature she had exposed for the viewer's delectation.

When they had her in a long shot with the celeb de jour, invariably she arranged herself for maximum prominence of calf, thigh, butt, bust—all admittedly great to look at.

But why should that bother him? Lots of people in the business hammed it up in the reverses, taking off and putting on scholarly-looking glasses, pausing with the end of the frame poised thoughtfully on a lip, frowning severely, shaking the head in reportorial amazement. In others it was charmingly transparent.

And the grandstanding questions she asked! The knockout question calculated to produce some outrage or confession that could be released in advance to make news and build audience for the show. It was clever, well calibrated, and cynical. The question was usually one no other journalist would have the bad taste, or the naked cupidity, to ask.

She acted as though she'd been appointed to express society's repugnance as well as its fascination, titillation, its lip-licking prurient identification with this monster.

If Prince Charles were dumb enough to appear with Murrow, Grant could imagine her asking him, and suggesting in her demeanor that the question had to be asked, "Why did you enjoy sex with Camilla Parker-Bowles more than with Princess Di?"

If she and her producers wanted to deal in such crap, fine. There were lots of TV channels now and people to watch. Fine! Room for everything. But when one of the principal network news departments let her fly their flag, it created expectations. A taste for tabloid values was a taste of honey. Others served this schlock, but they did it on syndicated programs that stations could buy or not, as they chose. It didn't come with the imprimatur of network news.

43

www.hollygo.com

The *New York Post* had the picture, but Hollygo has the dirt.

Y'all seen that picture on "Page Six" of gorgeous Brenda Starr, girl reporter? I know all you politically correct dominatrixes want to say Woman Reporter. Well tie me up, put me in bondage, walk on me with your high heels (whatever pleases you, darlin), but Hollygo don't mess with that p.c. shit.

Anyway, Brenda is wearin that slinky black Armani dress. Wearin it? She just about fallin out the front of it! You seen? What does that Murdoch trash tell you bout it? Nothin, sister. "News star Ann Murrow at glamorous Museum of Broadcasting dinner last night." So what? Does it tell you who Brenda's talkin to? Do you want to know? Sure you want to know, or you wouldn't be hittin my site. Hittin my site, that's clean, conchita, that's big boy web talk. So pay attention!

Everybody in broadcastin was at the museum dinner last night. All the network anchors, old Grecian Formula, the Lone Ranger, Gregory Peck, all the TV correspondents we love to watch, Miss Clairol, Nutcracker Sweet, Excedrin Headache, the Tylenol Lady, the Reverend Dimmesdale, our favorite boy producers, Lil Attention Deficit, and the Power Ranger. Everyone. If you weren't there, honey, you toast, and you better forget showbiz and get into somethin honest like hustlin.

In case some you pathetic outerboro bridge-and-tunnel wannabes don't know, the Museum of Broadcasting a skinny little marble buildin on 52nd street, right beside "21." Handy for a quick martini. It kinda like William F. Paley's monument to hisself, like the ancient Egyptian pharaohs built they pyramids so the world wouldn't forget how big and powerful they was. Well, just like that, Mr. Paley, the man who built a lil cigar business into CBS, worried sick that his legend might fizzle out like them sitcoms runnin too long in syndication? So he put up this tall dick of a buildin to show the world who got it up in broadcastin. If you ever get a dose of nostalgia and just have to see the TV show that gave you wet dreams as a boy (I'll send you Hollygo's list if you send me yours), you can go in there and they'll dig it out and run it for you. Provide the Kleenex, too, for tears or whatever. They tell Hollygo that Paley's horny ghost (he was a lascivious old goat) hovers between there and Black Rock, the CBS building down the street. Paley paid for it, but all the same the museum has these big black-tie dinners ever so often to raise money, make the people feel good, and get they name in the papers. So, back to Brenda, intrepid newshen.

Won't surprise you none to know Hollygo had a spy in their midst. A dressed-up spy, lookin chic and sleek to mingle with that fatcat teeveenews crowd (which by the way has worse taste in ruffled tux shirts than a Tuskeegee funeral). So I heard the whole story.

Here's what happens. Cocktail reception, you know, buzz buzz buzz, pretty standard. As usual a dazzled crowd around the ever-popular Brenda Starr, when the lady suddenly slips the adorin throng and heads off, parkin her drink on a waiter's tray. Hollygo's agent in place thinks even Brenda's human enough to have to go to the ladies' room, but no. All alone, our heroine opens the door to the dinin room and slinks in. Naturally our informant follows. Inside, Brenda heads for the table she supposed to sit at, makes a quick circuit lookin at the place cards, picks up one, picks up another, and switches them, then heads back to the cocktails, unaware of our ever watchin eyes.

And then they all go in for the dinner, usual thing, borin speeches, lots of table hoppin, those folks love to schmooze, kiss, hug, shake hands a lot, to show theyselves off to each other. Not Brenda. People come up to her and she makes nice but cool, because, darlin, she so absorbed with the man who just happens to be her dinner partner. Have you ever watched her? This Brenda is a leaner. I mean a lean-er. She leanin and listenin so hard, she like goin to swallow that man. Then she tellin him and he listenin and noddin like he gettin divine revelation firsthand. Can't hardly pry them apart when it's time to go.

Now here's the pay-off. The man she havin all that soul-talk with? Her boss maybe? A big wheel from her Taupe network? No way! She was monopolizin the CEO of MegaTrash—they the robber barons that now own BBN, the Beige Broadcasting Network, home of Gregory Peck. So as my good friend Don Imus would say, and probably will tomorrow mornin, what's that all about?

Sorry, chilluns, Hollygo's gotta go. Gotta dress up for my act at Whips 'n Chains, 12th Avenue. After 1 A.M. Sleep tight!

Don'tcha luv it?

44

"**H**e's definitely interested, Joey. He glowed with the idea."

"Fantastic. You carried the ball a lot farther than I did. I'll follow up with Ev Repton. He sounded interested, but now he'll get the word from God, his own CEO."

"Joey, I think you should wait a day. This Hollygo stuff doesn't hurt, although I'd love to know the little bitch who was watching me. Has to be someone in my office."

"Not necessarily. Everybody knows you."

"Anyway. Wait a day. Maybe he'll call you. And it just gives the guys over here more time to get flustered. Have you talked to them again?"

"Not since I told them you were looking around. When they want to talk new contract, we're ready. But you're going to listen to other people too. See what's out there."

"But, Joey, the more I think about it, your idea is brilliant. Perfect for me and perfect for them. If Everett Repton doesn't want to do it but the word gets around, maybe they'll do it here."

"They'll do it somewhere. The time is right. The news shows are dying on their feet, and look at the magazine numbers. Not just yours; all of them. And, don't worry, the word's getting around. I've dropped it in a couple of places."

"Terrific. Let's just wait a day or so and see what happens. Joey?" In an instant her voice could switch from warm and affectionate to cold and ominous. In one word. "Joey?"

"Yeah, I'm listening."

"The pictures you brought over. I noticed something. They were all there, as you said"—she sounded the way she did on her show, setting up the preamble before she nailed some slob—"they were all there, but one of the prints was actually two, stuck very close together."

"So?"

"So, it was the same one twice."

Steinman got a cold feeling in his stomach. "Well, what about it?"

"If this picture was printed twice, what about the others? Were they all printed twice? Was there a second set made?"

"God, no, I don't think so. The guy I dealt with, the detective, said this was all there was."

Ann's voice was its most seductive, melting. "Joey, you didn't keep a set yourself, did you?"

"No." He got out of it with a laugh. "I'd rather have pictures of you today than when you were a skinny kid."

"I trust you, Joey. But it makes me uneasy, thinking there might be some others out there. Why would just one picture have two prints?"

"It's a good question. I'll go back to the guy."

"You're a doll, Joey."

Steinman had not, after all, made a Xerox set for himself. He'd been tempted, then shied off, worried that she might know, might have them tested for fingerprints. Pretty farfetched, sure, but you never knew with her. But if he had made copies, he'd have found the duplicate. Her instinct, damn it, right as usual. It probably meant there *was* another set; that someone was holding back.

Being a feature reporter like Christopher Siefert was a succession of wooings, little seductions, then moving on, trying to establish rapport, ingratiate himself, lower the threshold of alarm all people felt when being questioned. Winning some trust. With Siefert, it worked far more often than it failed. His unthreatening, depleted appearance softened people. Interestingly, many of Grant's friends had responded to it with trust, like Don Evans, Laurie, and Teresa. Siefert didn't want to put it into words yet; he was holding even tentative conclusions at arm's length, keeping himself open to more impressions, but it was revealing that Grant had all these trusting friends.

He was still feeling the emotion of Teresa Weldon as he took the Seattle shuttle to San Francisco and rented a car for the drive out to Sonoma. Interesting that he'd responded with such sympathy to the people who liked Grant Munro, or loved him. He would have liked to spend more time with both women, so different; Laurie, the sardonic, lonely New Yorker, full of Jewish gemütlichkeit; he could imagine rainy Sunday afternoons with her, listening to Beethoven in Carnegie Hall. He could sense her yearning for a warm family life. He'd responded to Teresa too, not her outdoorsy, physical side (he quailed a little at where she might have led him); it was her womanliness that had appealed to Siefert. Her sexiness. As Laurie's had. He was drawn to the women who felt deeply for Grant. That hadn't happened in a profile before. He wondered how he'd react to Winona. He still had to set a date to meet her. He felt a sadness in having expended so much empathy putting these nice women at ease, making them want to talk to him, only to move on . . . and probably disappoint them in the end.

No profile ever satisfied those who loved the subject, including the subject himself.

THE ENTRANCE to Russian River Vineyard was a simple wooden arch over a dirt road winding among rows of vines, their pleasing geometry caressing the soft curves of the hills. And when he came to the house, dark within a shady grove of eucalyptus, it looked, as Teresa had said, like paradise. Low, with a mansard roof, it had a faintly Russian look in its wide clapboards, deep eaves, and long windows with curved tops. He was directed to another building, the business office, where he found Guy Ferris, a sun-dried, leathery man with a marked Aussie accent. They sat in a cool room across a table.

"We don't make wine, but the neighbors make it from our grapes. So we always have a drop on hand. It's a hot day. How about a sip of something cool?" He opened a small refrigerator. "Chardonnay, a Sauvignon Blanc, not terrific. A Pinot Gris."

"Thanks. What do you recommend?"

"The Chardonnay's all right."

He poured two glasses and sat down, pushing his hat back, and gave Siefert a disconcertingly direct look, considering how little blue actually showed through the squinting eyes.

"Grant tells me you're doing a cover on him."

"Him and the state of the industry."

"Bloody awful state, if you ask me."

"You were in it for many years? A cameraman?"

"I was. Worked with a lot of your *Time-Life* photographers over the years. Some great ones. And free-lancers whose stuff you used."

"Do you miss it?"

"Can't say I do. I was getting a little long in the tooth for it anyway, all that running around. You know what it's like."

"Yes," said Siefert. "I did a bit of running around myself."

Guy didn't say anything, and Siefert felt the silence lengthening. Whipping out a pocket recorder wasn't the same in front of a pro like this. But he pulled it out of his briefcase, raised it with a questioning gesture, got a nod, and put it on the table.

TRANSCRIPT:

FERRIS: I wasn't thrilled with the idea of talking to you. But Grant asked me to. I don't want to say anything that will end up hurting him.

CHRIS: I can't imagine you'd do that.

FERRIS: I can. I've got a bloody big mouth and it's always getting me into trouble. And I know your line of business.

CHRIS: What do you mean?

FERRIS: It's a rare bloke who comes out of one of your profiles, cover stories, with all parts of himself intact, not missing a few slices of his self-respect or worse. The North American Indians, some of them, used to tie a man up and take thin slices off him, very slowly.

CHRIS: I'm doing a piece that'll be true to him, that when you read it, you'll say, "That's fair."

FERRIS: Right, I know. I know. I've been there. I've heard it said a hundred times, said it myself. But it's different when you're on the outside. You see the trade differently. And what I see is a bunch of blokes, and women, however fair they intend to be, who have to show the viewer or the reader that they see through the bugger, so it won't be a puff piece that'll get 'em laughed at by their peers. And that's when the sharp knife comes out and the little slivers of flesh start coming off. Not now, when you're asking me questions, but when you're back, selecting what to put in, what to leave out, what to emphasize, turning the phrase so that it makes you sound smart and funny. That's where the knife comes in. (He took a sip of wine and gave the crinkled smile.) At least, so I've found.

CHRIS: This is no hatchet job. The more I hear about him, the more I find to admire about the man. He has a lot of friends.

FERRIS: And a few vipers, from what I hear.

CHRIS: Do you want to talk about that?

FERRIS: Better not.

CHRIS: You know the kind of thing I'm after. Good anecdotes. Good stories. Grant Munro in action. Things that show the kind of man he is.

FERRIS: Well, he's good to his friends. I'm proof of that. I'm the happiest man alive, thanks to him. Always wanted to make wine, but never had a tinker's chance of doing it.

CHRIS: But you don't actually make wine.

FERRIS: No, but we have plans to change that.

(He got up and took a bottle from a cupboard, pulled the cork, and poured a small amount of red wine into two fresh glasses.)

FERRIS: Tell me what you think of that.

CHRIS: I'm not an expert.

FERRIS: All the better.

CHRIS: It's good. Rich and smooth. I never learned the vocabulary. What is it?

FERRIS: A little Merlot I made from our grapes. An experiment. I think it's bloody good. Still too young, a little raw. But I have a few barrels we'll bottle in another six months or so. That should tell.

CHRIS: And if it's good, you'll go into production?

FERRIS: That's the idea. Where do you live, New York?

CHRIS: Yes.

FERRIS: What do you pay for a bottle of everyday wine, in a shop, I mean, not a restaurant? Red wine. Merlot, Cabernet?

CHRIS: I don't know. Fifteen dollars or less for everyday, not a special occasion.

FERRIS: Well, this bottle, with a fancy name and a pretty label and some nice chat in the wine trade, our little Merlot, could retail for thirty, thirty-five a bottle.

CHRIS: Gosh.

FERRIS: Even the big jug wine producers like Gallo are getting into the quality end of the trade, because the demand keeps growing. And no one can duplicate the conditions we're sitting on right here. So it makes sense. Have another drop.

(Obviously enjoying himself, Guy took off his battered hat and settled down in his chair. Resting on the table, his muscular, darkly tanned arms looked as if they could lift a full wine barrel.)

CHRIS: Presumably, it means a big capital outlay to create a winery.

FERRIS: It does.

CHRIS: Do you care to say how much?

FERRIS: To process our grape output, probably a few million, but gradually, you know . . . starting with the Merlot, continue selling the white wine grapes to others for a year or two, then bring some whites on line.

CHRIS: And can the business generate that capital?

FERRIS: Not all. It'll need some new investment.

CHRIS: Do you mind my asking, does that come from Grant?

FERRIS: Yes, he'll raise it.

CHRIS: How does your partnership work?

FERRIS: Well, that's where I started. How he treats his friends. He

234 ■

had the money, I had a little wine know-how. I was raised on a vineyard in Coonawarra, South Australia. Anyway, Grant bought this old winery, which had pretty well died during Prohibition. Bought it with my input, then got a lawyer and made us equal owners and partners. His money and my know-how given equal value. Well, a little of my money, too. Big gamble for him. All he had was my loud mouth to go on. And for that, I'm a half-owner of a vineyard that they'd eat their boots to see in Coonawarra. Even the gum trees grow better here. Equal shares. What does that tell you about him?

CHRIS: What's the business, the vineyard, worth now?

FERRIS: To sell it, I don't know. You'd have to ask people in the brokering business.

CHRIS: But it's a paying concern? Not a hobby vineyard?

FERRIS: Not since we got serious and began to run it well. Now it's profitable.

CHRIS: How closely does Grant involve himself?

FERRIS: He comes out five or six times a year. We talk as often as we need to.

(Siefert hesitated to raise the climbing accident, decided not to, then reversed himself.)

CHRIS: I gather he used to come more often before the accident on Chianti Spire.

(Guy gave him a mistrustful look.)

FERRIS: You getting into all that?

CHRIS: You don't think I should?

FERRIS: Raking it up again? I know, I know. Sitting where you are, I'd be doing it. Good story. Big drama. Tragedy. It's that when it happens to someone close to you, you wish the bloody media would leave it alone. Go away. Mind their own fucking business! I know all the arguments on the other side. I made my bloody living prying into other people's misfortunes. And I'm glad I'm out of it. Even Grant's show. Practically every night now they're peering into the President's sex life or some sordid detail of that murder in Wyoming because some perverted sod kills a little girl, and because her mother's a third-rate actress who never got so much publicity before. Even on Grant's show we're treated to all this leering stuff. God, I hate television now.

CHRIS: He tries to avoid that stuff.

FERRIS: I know he does. But he can't stop it. It's the name of the game.

(The idiom sounded strange, pronounced *nime* of the *gime.)*

CHRIS: Let me ask you, as someone who knows him very well, how did the accident, Tony Weldon's death, affect Grant? How did it change him?

(Guy offered the Merlot bottle. Siefert wanted to refuse. Too early to be drinking red wine, but it seemed a conciliatory gesture, so he nodded.)

FERRIS: Hard to say. Saddened him, obviously. They were nice people.

CHRIS: Teresa told me Grant invited them down here.

FERRIS: You talked to her?

CHRIS: I was there yesterday. Nice woman.

FERRIS: Great lady. And Tony was first-rate.

CHRIS: I gather Grant doesn't see her now.

FERRIS: Ah, you know.

CHRIS: She was remarkably unbitter about it.

FERRIS: As I say, she's a great lady. It's a terrible pity.

CHRIS: Grant and Teresa, was there something going on between them?

FERRIS: Why do you ask that?

CHRIS: I felt in her something . . . left over, some warm regret for him.

FERRIS (big laugh): Warm regret? A lot of ladies have felt warm regret for Grant Munro. I'd forget that line, mate. Nothing there.

CHRIS: He gave her money.

FERRIS: I told you that; he looks after his friends.

CHRIS: Was she that good a friend?

FERRIS: If you asked me that again, I'd say it's none of your fucking business, but since you haven't asked me, I don't have to say it. Now why don't we go up to my house and let the lovely Rosita give us some grub? She's a great cook.

SIEFERT PUT away the recorder and followed Guy out, a little woozy from the wine, his eyes aching in the bright sun. They drove a dusty Land Cruiser down a narrow track between flourishing vines. After a long silence, Guy said, "You asked about after the accident? Before that, I don't think he ever doubted himself. Not that I saw, anyway, and I saw him in all kinds of situations, over the years . . . Were you in Vietnam?"

"I covered it here."

"I see." Again Guy's sardonic, crinkled gaze. "Well, Grant and I were there. And other nasty places. Always knew his own mind, moved fast, instinctively, like an athlete, you know what I mean? Someone who knew how to move without thinking about it. I don't mean physically; I mean in life."

"And after the accident?"

"Much less sure of himself. Took it very hard. Blamed himself, which he shouldn't have done. He worries about it. In fact, he worries about a lot of things he doesn't need to . . . in my humble opinion."

"Like?"

But Guy stopped with a jerk and jumped down.

"Just have a look. These are the Merlot grapes you tasted. No, those were last year's. Same vines. Just look at these. Aren't they something?"

Siefert looked at the swelling green clusters under a sun that seemed to be focusing its attention on this glowing hillside, and at the proud grower's brown hand fondling a cluster as lovingly as he might a breast. More testimony to Grant Munro's attraction for likable friends.

46

Sherman Glass made the next move.

"I've got a way out. Bill Donovan becomes weekend anchor. Bryce Watson remains your weekday substitute. Perfect solution. The network gets a chance to see Bill in the anchor role; he gets the seasoning."

"Bryce loses the weekend shows."

"That's right. But I told you—sooner or later, he'll have to face the facts: he's never going to be your replacement. Too old-fashioned. Even if you went to the mat for him."

"You're a busy little guy, Sherman. You must have been burning up the phone lines with Donovan and Ev Repton."

"No need. We did it all in Washington. Ev was there, and I flew down for the day. We wrapped it all up and—"

"And the clause in my contract gives me no right of consultation on the weekend anchor, right?"

"That's right, or I'd have talked to you first . . . of course."

"Of course, Sherman."

"But the beauty thing about this"—his speech suggested that he was rolling one of his cigars around in his wet lips—"is that it removes the irritant with you. They know they screwed up by pulling that fast one with the substitution. We made them back down on Bryce."

"What do you mean *we*? I made them back down."

"Right. So the board's clear. We can deal again. The atmospherics are great, and I can go for the blockbuster deal. Five years at ten million per, or buyout."

"Buyout?"

"If they decide after a few years they want someone else, they have to buy you out at the full contract price. If it's three years to go, you'd get thirty million—"

"Jesus Christ! That sounds as if you're writing an invitation for them to get rid of me—a cancelation clause. We never had that before."

"No, but in reality they've always had it. They've always been able to cancel if they wanted to. They could right now, with two years to run, but then we'd have to haggle over the buyout figure. It wouldn't be the full bucks left in the contract; we'd have to settle for something less. What I'm proposing is that they have to pay you fifty million total, whether you work one year or five years, if they choose to get out. No different from now, only the guaranteed buyout."

"Who suggested the new language?"

"I did."

"What made you think about buyout?"

"Because you're going to be sixty. Because of the ratings. All the stuff we've talked about. It's an uncertain world, Grant."

"And because Bill Donovan is your client."

"Well, sure—"

"And buying out my contract would clear the way for him."

"Hey, Grant! You keep sounding like you don't trust me. You gotta knock that off. Listen to me; this is a dream deal. The whole scene's changing: all the new networks, all the new channels. The Internet. Who knows what anything's going to look like even three years from now? And I'm talking a seven-year deal. Present contract to year two thousand, plus five years at the biggest money anyone ever made as a network anchor."

"Until Ann Murrow—"

"Oh, her! Well, that's the beauty part. Whatever's cooking with her, this locks us in to two thousand five. She can twitch her little tush around all she likes, but this closes the door on your job."

"Unless they decide to cancel."

"They're not going to throw away all that dough, believe me."

"And Repton's on board?"

"No, but I think I can get him. Bill Donovan's new blood on Saturday-Sunday. Grant Munro, solid, reliable, respected: five days a week. It's a great package to ride into the twenty-first century."

"A team for the millennium?"

"Hey, great phrase! I'll use it with him."

"But you haven't got the weekend deal locked up?"

"It looks hot; I'm just waiting for the language."

"I want to see the language you're proposing for me, the buyout language. Write it up and send it over, with the present language too. So I can compare."

"OK. If you need to see it, I'll do it."

Grant had never bothered before, had scarcely even read his present contract. Now his instincts suggested a bad smell, and he wanted to sniff it out.

"What I don't get is Ann Murrow. The day before yesterday, you're in a sweat because you think Repton's talking to her; now, no sweat. What happened? Did he tell you he isn't talking to her after all?"

"No. He said he couldn't discuss it."

"And you're reassured by that?"

"Sure. Because this deal solves it all for him."

"What about her agent? Who is it?"

"Steinman. Joe Steinman."

"That guy who created all the buzz about her? Why should he think the door's shut?"

"Maybe he won't, but look, all he's doing is tossing the bait out there and seeing who bites. I don't think they're in serious talks with anyone. When people get together in real negotiations, they go quiet. He's still making too much noise."

"You certainly got reassured fast."

"Because I got the other part of the package. Trust me. You've gotta trust me. Who else are you going to trust?"

Good question.

Grant didn't care about weekend news. The real game was Monday to Friday. Who substituted there was important. If Bryce Watson was really short term, Grant wanted to be a player in naming his replacement.

•   •   •

LAURIE JACOBS came back raving about Fran Whitman. "She's really cool! Where did you *find* her?"

"I told you. Cleveland."

"She doesn't sound like Cleveland, or look it. Somebody's wised her up about a lot of things—her hair, her clothes."

"OK. But what about how she does the news? Remember that?"

"Pretty terrific. Was it your idea that she use one of our shows . . . your script?"

"Her idea. She had it done when I got there."

"How did she *ever* get you to look at it? There must be five hundred local anchor women who'd sell their—"

"Souls?"

"Sweetheart, I was actually thinking of something a little more tangible."

"You shock me, you liberated women."

"Well, whatever she did to you, it worked. Obviously she's smart. She looks terrific. And she doesn't have that local look. What's next?"

"I'm thinking. Marty Boyle or Ev Repton?"

"Repton. He must be smarting about Donovan. Do your charm act. Be nice to him. Show you're helping him think about the future— and your successor. His ally. Smart move right now, with Brenda Starr blazing in the heavens."

"Not Marty first?"

"Look, darling, Marty's had eighteen months, OK? Ratings flick-ered up for a few months and then slumped again. If heads roll, he'll go before Repton. And if Repton likes her, Marty will have to use her. What's her name?"

"Fran Whitman."

"Anything personal with you? Everyone's going to assume . . ."

"Nothing. You sent me to Cleveland, remember?"

"So I did, darling. Smart little me!"

• • •

GRANT WANTED another opinion and gave the tape to Don Evans. His take on Fran Whitman was subtler than Laurie's.

"Hate to sound snobbish, but I'll bet she went to a good private school. Maybe on scholarship, but probably family money. Milton, Phillips Andover, Groton—something like that. Then whatever university, probably Ivy League. There's a strong patina of confidence about her, and intellectual assurance."

"That's what I thought. I've got her résumé here. It says Harvard."

"Ah, the joys of egalitarian democracy! De Tocqueville, thou shouldst be living at this hour."

"You think this Whitman woman is network material?"

"Sure, I'd take a chance on her. Is she a particular friend of yours? *Une petite amie?*"

"Not at all."

"Not at all? Not even a tiny bit?"

"I just met her when I went to Cleveland."

"Of course I know what a model citizen you are in that department. But to come into New York on a whiff of scandal never did a young provincial any harm. What's your plan?"

"Show the tapes to Ev Repton."

"To block Ann Murrow?"

"To give the news department a chance to see some of the promising talent available out there in this great land of opportunity."

"Sounds as if you're understudying Al Gore. Before you sing the equal-opportunity hymn to me, check her high school. Privilege and elitism were still going strong the last time I checked."

"Thanks. And I'd like to keep this quiet for a while."

"I'm not going to read it in Carmody first?"

GRANT WAS beginning to enjoy this. The wind had shifted. Instead of bashing upwind, he had the breeze sweetly on his quarter. His tantrum about Donovan had cleared the air. When Grant stopped by Repton's office, Ev was positively affable.

"Sure, I'll look at her. What's the name?"

"Fran Whitman. She's from Pittsburgh."

"Pittsburgh!" New Yorkers uttered the names of hinterland cities as though they were peopled by Neanderthals.

"But she's been around. When you've looked, I have a suggestion to make."

"OK. I'll call you."

In midafternoon Laurie came by again. "Ev Repton called me in to ask what I know about Fran Whitman."

"What did you say?"

"Never heard of her."

Late afternoon, ten minutes before Grant went down to makeup, Sherman Glass called. "Who's this babe in Cleveland you've got the hots for? Ev Repton says you gave him some tape to look at."

"That's right."

"Who is she? You didn't tell me about her."

"I've got to go do the show. I'll tell you when there's something to tell."

Ev Repton had probably called ten people before he looked at the tape.

Cynthia, wiping a moist pad over Grant's face before applying the makeup, said, "You're looking more cheerful. More like yourself."

"Good."

"Have a touch of flu or something?"

"Just an attack of old age."

"If *you* start moaning about age, I'll drown myself." She lifted his chin and studied him in the mirror framed with lightbulbs. "Nothing a little facelift wouldn't remove. Here and here. Very simple. You should think about it."

ETHICALLY, before making his pitch to Repton, Grant had to talk to Bryce Watson.

"Grant, I can't thank you enough. I hear you turned it around, and I'm deeply grateful."

Bryce, with some Virginian or Border State Southern in his background, had good manners that were legendary.

"Well, I did my best, but I'm discovering I don't have a hell of a lot of clout. Have they talked to you about the weekends?"

"No?" And Grant could hear fresh anxiety as that one syllable faltered into a question.

He told Bryce what Sherman had said. "I have no say about that. Not in my contract. The weekends are different shows."

"I know. Yes, yes, I know."

"I think we're good for a while on the weekdays. To be honest, only for a while."

"What does that mean?"

"The press for younger people is on, Bryce. From what Sherman Glass says, clearly the move is on to think beyond me, and that means someone younger, a new generation, and I'm afraid I can't fight them on that."

"I see. I see."

"I also believe it's time they considered a woman. It's amazing that they haven't."

"You don't mean all the rumors about—"

"Ann Murrow? No, I think it's time. Also, I have a young woman in mind who might be brought along. I'm going to talk to Repton about her tomorrow."

"Anyone I know?"

"No. Not on any network."

"This is a hell of a lot to absorb in one phone call. I guess I have to thank you. No one else is ever as honest. I pick up the paper every morning expecting Carmody to know more about my future than I do."

Grant thought as he hung up the phone that Bryce was right. There seemed to be a sadistic pleasure in dealing behind peoples' backs, letting them find out good news and bad from leaks to the press.

www.hollygo.com

The inside word at Beige, in case you're curious, darlin, is that Gregory Peck has found himself a honey out in the boonies. The aging anchor, the dean of our current news stars, may not be as incorruptible as gossip always had it. But you never know how it strike a man touchin sixty, like he is, when there's not so much lead in the old pencil and the spring is gone from the step. I'm getting carried away, chilluns, the tears be wellin up, I'll ruin my mascara.

Lissen: Hollygo spies inform me that ever-compliant Gregory, always willin to carry the network's water, had to make a call on the turncoat affiliate that's just deserted Taupe for Beige in Cleveland. Don't it sound momentous when you put that way, honey? Taupe to Beige? Can't you hear the trumpets soundin? When the history of television is written . . . nobody will read it.

My Cleveland spy tells me old Gregory flies out there, does his duty, thrills the yokels to see a real teeveenews star in the flesh, but gets entrapped by an ambitious little number I'll call Country Fresh, like those sprays make your bathroom smell like a Maine mornin? Ms. Country Fresh, dewy-eyed and all agog over Mr. Network, flutters her lashes or her whatevers at him, and next thing you know he takin her tapes to New York.

Now may be some lil innocents or teevee wannabes out there in cyberspace don't know bout tapes. Well, here the facts. Everbody out there in teeveeland, smilin at you on the tube ever night, is actually always tryin to get the hell outta your city to a better place. Not heaven, chile; that another generation. A better place now is a bigger market. That heaven. You on teevee in Memphis, you like to move up to Nashville, you in Nashville, you want Atlanta, you in Atlanta, you got a big yen to get yourself to Chicago, L.A., or New York.

You play that game by makin up a tape reel showin you doin all that local teeveenews stuff. They put all their wares on cassettes and ship them out, like you'd send a résumé, to news directors in bigger markets. But Hollygo never heard of no network anchor, Mister Big, ever personally offerin to take tapes back to New York hisself, as Gregory Peck did for Ms. Country Fresh, *unless*—you can hear it comin, chilluns—unless they is a another motive than findin on-air talent, like because they different kinds of talent. Wanna bet? Next step will be, he'll invite her to New York to dazzle her even more. Move over, Horatio Alger. They's another installment comin.

Stay on line, or call me at www.hollygo.com for later developments. And mind! You heard it first from Hollygo!

Don'tcha luv it?

"Country Fresh? That's awful!" Laurie said to Grant. "But who knew?"

"Everybody knew. You told me Ev Repton started calling around the minute I gave him the tape. Right now, I've got Christopher Siefert. It's my turn again."

"I kind of like him," Laurie said. "I ran into him the other night and we had dinner together. I don't think we're in for a rough ride with him. What do you think?"

"I'd like to think that. How do you know until it comes out?"

Siefert, who had looked sickly when they first met, seemed decidedly healthier.

"You're looking well."

"Thanks. I feel better. Just getting out and doing some leg work has helped."

"Who've you been talking to? Laurie, I know. She said you had dinner."

"Yes. I enjoyed it. Nice woman."

"Who else?"

"I've talked to Everett Repton, Marty Boyle, Sherman Glass, Don Evans. And I've just come back from the coast, where I talked to Guy Ferris, as you know, and Teresa Weldon."

Siefert saw a noticeable stiffening.

"I didn't know you'd be seeing her."

"It is part of the record, I'm afraid, part of the story."

"How is she?"

"I'd say she's very loyal to you."

"Well, we were all close . . . before."

"So I gather."

Grant was tempted to ask, as though Siefert were a friend, what she had said. Siefert had that talent of dissolving the tension between reporter and subject.

"So you've covered a lot of ground."

"Yes. And there are some things I'd like to run by you. Just get this going . . ."

TRANSCRIPT:

CHRIS: First I'd like to pick up where we left off. You talked before about TV news going to hell, a loss of innocence, and so on. But *when* did the business go wrong—and why?

GRANT: Hell of a question. When and why? During my early years, the sixties, the tide was still coming in. The networks were gaining viewers, gaining respect and influence. At some point, the tide turned, and it's been going out ever since.

CHRIS: Can you identify any event, any date?

GRANT: When I look back at the big stories we covered . . . I think our priorities were right for a long time. I don't think we were grandstanding through Vietnam, or the turmoil of 'sixty-eight, the MLK and RFK assassinations, the moon landings, not through Nixon and Watergate . . . I'm trying to remember them all . . . the Yom Kippur war, Nixon's resignation, the surrender of Saigon, the CIA scandals, Carter's election, Camp David summit, Egyptian-Israeli peace, Khomeini overthrowing the shah, the hostage crisis—maybe there. But even after that, our priorities were still pretty much in place through the Reagan election, Salvador and Nicaragua civil wars . . .

(The voice rolled on. With these cadences, it sounded like a broadcast, Siefert thought, except that the famous anchor was leaning back in his chair, completely relaxed, with his feet on the desk.)

. . . the Reagan assassination attempt, Solidarity in Poland, Sadat killed, the Falklands War, AIDs epidemic. I'd say on through the eighties, important news still got treated as important: the marines killed in Beirut, Grenada, the Challenger disaster, Iran-Contra scandal, end of the cold war, fall of the Berlin Wall . . .

CHRIS: You said the Iran hostage story was a turning point.

GRANT: I guess that's the first time I felt uneasy, had a sense that we were putting our audience-building first. Remember "America Held Hostage," a show every night devoted to one story? No one did that in the Vietnam War, with hundreds of our guys dying every week. And that was before cable news got started. I was part of it; I take some responsibility for it . . .

CHRIS: Your job then was . . . ?

GRANT: White House correspondent, until I began anchoring full time and moved to New York, just after the Reagan inauguration. Maybe we were over the edge with the hostages, news judgment driven not by figuring what was the most important thing each day, but what we chose to stress . . . when one story became a campaign.

CHRIS: You didn't feel that way at the time?

GRANT: God, no! You know what that's like. In the thick of coverage on the White House beat, when there's a major story running, there's no time to think about anything. You're rushing to get a story together, attend briefings, milk your contacts, and every few minutes you're out on the lawn doing a standupper. You're on the air so much, scrambling and writing and talking so fast, it's like being in a battle, or a storm at sea. What's vital is the next thing you've got to do, and the next . . . Frantic days, always on call, always short of sleep, always expected to be available to sound off knowledgeably at any hour.

CHRIS: Do you think the Carter presidency was destroyed by the television attention to the story?

GRANT: No, no. Too many other factors. In the modern media age, a President has to decide what the wider U.S. interest requires. Maybe it's to *appear* driven by the TV pictures, using the public emotion we're whipping up. Maybe it's to dampen the emotion, direct national attention to some other issue.

CHRIS: But as I recall, Carter *did* divert attention. After the Soviet invasion of Afghanistan, the sanctions against Moscow, boycotting the Olympic Games.

GRANT: Sure, and he did order the aborted mission to rescue the hostages. But television mostly showed an impotent President, and, of course, that played well for Reagan.

CHRIS: There's a view that presidential conduct of foreign policy has been made much harder now because of what you're talking about.

GRANT: I know. I read that. But no President nowadays is a virgin in television. You don't get to be President unless you can manipulate television in your favor, by creating and dominating the news it has to cover. A modern presidency is a continuous P.R. campaign. The polling and the spinning never stop. To see him as the hapless victim of foreign coverage is to be naïve about his political skills. If he lets himself be driven by television, he's a weak President. He has to harness television. Of course, luck plays a big part, but a politician has to be able to make his own luck, as he seems to create his own weather. Jimmy Carter couldn't make the sun shine, and Reagan could.

CHRIS: So if you see the hostage crisis as the first sign, when did the tide really turn?

GRANT: Oh, the Gulf War and then O. J. Simpson, then Princess Di, then the presidential sex story. It gets more excessive each time.

CNN made such a meal of the Gulf War. They had a great scoop with the bombing of Baghdad, and from then on they played it like World War Three: constant, nonstop attention and hype: Armageddon just around the corner. I think we let CNN whip us up into a state of hysteria. The Gulf was important, but where does importance stop? It's the O. J. Simpson question on a different plane. Everything gets heightened, the stakes keep rising: the testing of U.S. nerve, the political will, the military power, the catharsis for Vietnam, the rehabilitation of soldiering, the moral re-masculinizing of the American soul. National theater. And in that orgy of patriotism we all unleashed, we let basic questions—how well it was done and what it really achieved—get smothered by the national celebration.

We all got a boost to our ratings, but I think the biggest impact was at cable news. Normally, few people watch, but the numbers leap with a big story. Lesson? Play any big story like the Second Coming. Keep the public excited and keep their eyeballs glued. And so—O. J. Simpson, where cable TV led all the rest of us down the garden path to a competition in speculation, to manipulation by the lawyers. We all chased the white Bronco and threw our news values out the window. And then sex in the White House.

CHRIS: But if you feel that way, as the managing editor of your show, why do you go along with it?

GRANT: Good question! It's tough to be clear about it in my own mind. And honest. And consistent. For all my disgust at what we were doing—and we had some real battles over leading with O.J. so often—I had to recognize the competitive sense, the competitive imperative. I agreed. I deplored and I agreed. We were in Havana ready to do the Pope and Castro, an important story, but we all rushed back for presidential sex! I deplored it, but I agreed at the time. Now we have all these cable channels with nonstop news as their commodity, plus the Internet, plus all the pseudo-news programs feeding the public. When the next hot story comes along, everyone will rush for a piece of it to hold their audience. And we can't afford to stay out of it. If no excess embarrasses us, what happens at the next *real* crisis?

CHRIS: Such as?

GRANT: You can imagine a foreign crisis with public hysteria fanned by competition to be sensational, to be first, to be dramatic, fed by politicians who might like to embarrass a President in office by saying his response was too weak, was not standing up to threats to our security . . . and so on.

CHRIS: How do you prevent that?

GRANT: With the restraint that comes from experience and the values of your network. You need experience when you're out there ad-libbing on a breaking story. There's a tendency to mouth off out of nervousness and the dread of empty air. There's the pressure to shine, to sound alert and knowledgeable, to appear calm, unflappable, reliable, and credible, yet get off a few phrases that your P.R. people can feed to the TV columns—it's not easy. You draw on every ounce of judgment and experience *not* to say something stupid.

CHRIS: But you didn't prevent the excess—going back to your RTNDA speech—a man of your experience sitting there?

GRANT: No, but perhaps I stopped it from being worse.

CHRIS: Or is this a rationale for not putting young guys like Bill Donovan in to substitute for people of your experience?

GRANT (laughing): You can read it any way you like.

CHRIS: I've been following your little saga on the Internet and in the gossip columns. What's the latest you can tell me on that?

GRANT: That's tricky.

CHRIS: Is it true you've found a young woman reporter you'd prefer to him? Or is that Hollygo stuff a joke?

GRANT: Look, I want to be straight with you. I have been, I am being, about all this stuff . . .

CHRIS: I realize that. I appreciate it.

GRANT: But it's delicate. It's internal and private, although it's hard to keep it that way. I'll tell you what: before you wrap this story up, I'll talk to you about it. Things will be further along then. That OK?

CHRIS: That's fine.

GRANT: Mostly I think we've lost the seriousness we used to have

■ 251

when we were confident that we and the audience—the thinking nation—were fundamentally in agreement about what was important. The ground rules weren't in dispute. Our job was to keep the nation informed about threats to security and American global responsibilities and the operation of a democratic society at home.

CHRIS: The ground rules have changed?

GRANT: Absolutely. The big difference is, we didn't have to hustle. (Hustle. Siefert had seen that recently in a Hollygo column.)

www.hollygo.com

    Those old networks, they like the hustlers in the vinyl minis tryin to snag the commuters into a quickie before the Lincoln Tunnel. How do you want it, darlin? We'll do it. You want O.J.? We'll give you O.J. until your eyes spin. You want titillatin little girl rape-murder in Wyomin? Just let me in the car, honey, and I'll give you as much as you want. You don't want no politics, sweetie? Don't want no foreign news? Neither do I! Come on, baby! Pretend like I'm Monica Lewinsky!)

GRANT: And there's another difference. I was certainly part of it, but after Nixon, the national press was born again, mean, suspicious, and unforgiving. When the network first hired me, we still tended to believe what government said until—unless—it was found to be lying. We didn't expect calculated deceit. Vietnam destroyed all that. It destroyed LBJ, destroyed Nixon, destroyed the trust that had given the national dialogue some civility.

Now we know how much that civility masked racism, sexual discrimination, corruption, and venality of various kinds in Washington, but exposing all that—having the President constantly under investigation—hasn't restored the trust either, the trust between press and government and people. Everybody simply distrusts everybody. I can remember the tone changing at the presidential news conferences . . . But look at the time! I've got to stop now. Have to pick it up next time.

(Siefert stopped the tape recorder, thinking that Grant understood the past well; it was the present that appeared to bewilder him.)

4 9

George White kicked himself. He should have spotted the two prints stuck together. Now they were suspicious, but so what? They'd even employed him again to watch the kid. This was turning into a moneymaker.

"Maybe the kid kept another set," he'd told Steinman. "We wondered about that before. You never replied to him, to that box number, right?"

"Right. Maybe you should watch him a little more to see what he's up to."

"I could do that."

"Like around that photo store."

"I can watch, but he may be scared off there for good. Maybe, maybe not. I can watch him for a few days. Same arrangement?"

"Yeah, OK. A thousand a day."

To Steinman, a few thousand more was a bargain to get it out of his mind for a while and Ann off his ass, when he had a deal worth millions cooking. "Call me in a couple of days and tell me what he's doing."

"OK. Will do."

As a matter of fact, White was curious himself to see what the kid was up to. He was beginning to admire him. He liked his resourcefulness. Would he give up now, or find some way to try again? And George had nothing else to do; it wasn't like his agency was swarming with customers. And if the great Ann Murrow was upset, wasn't that too bad? George had no idea what to do with the pictures he'd kept. Maybe something would come along. If it got risky, he could get rid of them in a second. But . . . an idea came to him. He could say he'd recovered them from the kid so that Steinman would want to pay for them. But not too soon. Not when he could make a thousand a day trailing the kid. The weather in June was nice for such a job.

50

"I haven't been to the Four Seasons for a while," Ev Repton said. "Thought we could try that. Car's waiting downstairs."

There was the customary fuss over Grant—"Ah, Mr. Munro. What a pleasant surprise!"—discreetly changing the table Repton had booked for one more prominent. If that irritated Repton, he hid it with searching questions about dishes on, and not on, the menu. All of which gave Grant time to look around, half expecting to see Sherman Glass or Ann Murrow. He knew she had lunch here occasionally. She was on his mind.

"Ev, what's going on with Ann Murrow?"

"What do you mean? I thought we were here to talk about this gal in Cleveland. What's her name?" He pulled out a piece of paper.

"Fran Whitman."

"Yeah, Fran Whitman. I think you're right. Good hunch you have there. She's got a lot of promise. Trouble is, I don't know exactly where to use her. We could probably fit her in somewhere, if you're that interested." He gave *interested* enough inflection to make it suggestive.

"Yes, I'm interested. But answer my question first. What in hell is going on with Ann Murrow?"

"Why do you think anything's going on? You make it sound like something ominous." Repton as usual evading the direct question.

"You are talking to her?"

"Look, I'll level with you. I got a call from Ken Walden. Apparently she cornered him the other night at the Museum of Broadcasting.

Came on strong. All he could do to be polite was say he'd look into it. Then he calls me, and I have to act as if I'm following up."

"What was her idea?"

"He wasn't clear. What does he know about programs? Something about a magazine concept. Nothing's going on."

"You haven't seen her yet?"

"No."

"Or her agent, Joseph Steinman?"

"Jesus, Grant! You're getting so goddamned suspicious!"

"Have you talked to Joseph Steinman about Ann Murrow?"

"Sure! I talk to a lot of agents who peddle their talent. It's my job to listen to them. I listen to Steinman; I listen to Sherman Glass. It's a way of keeping my ear to the ground. These agents know a hell of a lot."

Grant wasn't going to let him off the hook. "Have you seen Steinman recently? Since word got around that Murrow's in play again?"

"Yes, we talked a bit. You want to know where we had lunch? You and I were supposed to have fun. A good talk about your discovery. Ah, great, here's the food!"

Grant let Repton savor a few mouthfuls of delicately sliced breast of duck.

"Sherman Glass thinks Steinman's selling a strip of magazine shows, five nights a week, across the board."

"No kidding? I told you these agents know a lot."

"Steinman did lay that on you? Ann Murrow five nights a week?"

Repton sighed, wiped his lips, and sipped his white wine. "Grant, you and I are buddies. A long time, right? We go back together to when this was a different business. We've talked about that. Now I have to run this news department in the new real world. Personally, Ann Murrow gives me hives. She's not what we used to think of as news. She's a mutation, like cells gone wild. But she's part of the reality we face. Her shows kill our magazine. She's the hottest thing around. When they come calling, what does a news president say? No, I don't want to talk to you? I'd be crazy. On top of that I get a call from God. See this woman!"

"But it wasn't just because Walden called you. You were already discussing this stuff with Steinman."

"She didn't put the arm only on Walden. She's been onto members of his board!"

"Sounds like a real catch, Ev! Should really fit in well!" Grant thought he should touch some bases himself, urgently.

"Come on! Save the heavy irony. I'm talking to them because I have to talk. What's the worst that can happen? We end up with the biggest audience puller in the business, the bottom line looks better. Wall Street analysts like the stock; upstairs they love us, and ease the pressure on me to cut news-gathering costs, which helps us stay honest. In any event, she doesn't have a thing to do with 'The Evening News.' It doesn't affect you. It's a different universe. You satisfied?"

Grant saw no point in raising Sherman Glass's other hunch: a magazine strip to replace a dying "Evening News." Not now. He needed to talk about keeping it alive.

Repton said, "OK, you wanted to talk Fran Whitman. I looked at the tapes. I liked them. She may be good material. You've got an idea? So tell me."

"I've been thinking since our dust-up about Bill Donovan—and I want to come back to that—I've been thinking. I was sore about it. But also realize I wasn't thinking constructively about the future. Obviously, I'm not getting any younger."

Repton smiled and said nothing.

"And we do have to think about who comes after me. You were ahead of me on that. I hadn't thought of the future being so close. But I know now that I should be helping you think about it, plan for it; shouldn't be resisting it."

"I love it!"

"I'm saying, I want us to be partners in planning that future. It's dumb to be pulling in opposite ways."

"I welcome it. Let's do it." Ev reached over and shook hands. "We're partners!"

"But I have one condition."

"Sure!"

"No Bill Donovan."

"Now wait a minute!"

"Ev, keep listening a minute. The reason I flew off the handle about Donovan was partly that you'd surprised me, you didn't consult me—OK! I know, we've dealt with that. But the other part of it, much deeper, is that it gives me the creeps to think of that guy becoming my successor. You want the details, I can give them. But for now, take my word. I couldn't stomach the idea of his taking over our show—"

"That was never—"

"OK. Stay with me. Running into this woman in Cleveland, looking at her tapes—yeah, yeah, I know what it looks like, but it isn't—opened my eyes. There are alternatives. And a woman would be a hell of a good alternative. So here's my proposal: bring Fran Whitman in and try her out."

"She's had no network experience—"

"Ah, that doesn't work. Or if it works for her, it works for Donovan.

"But he's White House correspondent. He's getting real network experience."

"Because you gave it to him. Do the same with her. She's as smart as he is, if not smarter, and better. Listen to the way she uses the language."

"We don't have any slots. They're on my ass all the time to reduce the number of correspondents."

"They're also on your ass—you told me so yourself—to bring in younger people who cost less. Well, do it."

"Where would I put her?"

"You want my opinion? Reassign Donovan. Send him overseas, continue his seasoning."

"He's only been at the White House a few months."

"Actually, six months. You could move him soon. Say you're do- ing it to widen his experience. Bring Fran in and give her a shot at the White House, up to the next election, say. See how she does."

"Does Sherm Glass know about this?"

"Not yet. I haven't talked to anyone but you."

"What about Fran Whitman?"

"I haven't said anything. I said I'd show her tapes to people in New York. I haven't given her any answer."

"Sherm's pitching Donovan for the weekends."

"He told me you guys had it sewed up."

"I've been too busy with this other stuff."

"Anyway, my cards are on the table. I'm willing to work with you on an orderly changing of the guard . . ."

"And a timetable?"

"That can be part of it. Part of the contract talks Sherman's having with you. But one condition: not Donovan. He may be bril- liant. If so, he'll find his place. I'm not saying it has to be Fran Whitman. Just give her a chance. Maybe she'll be great, maybe not. Somebody else then."

"I've got to think about all this. So much is going on all at once. You want some coffee?"

"Sure."

"I like the idea of working together on the succession. It's a good idea. It's tricky. You've got to decide how long—"

"Before I get pushed?"

"No, of course not! But you have to think about that. That'll make it easier for everyone."

"I'm saying, it's easier if we think about it together."

"It's a deal. I'm glad we had this talk."

Grant went back to the office feeling he'd won a round on points. Beginning to negotiate his departure might be worth it, if it got Dono- van out. And by the end of the summer, the facelift healed, back from the so-called vacation, he'd look better.

The Ann Murrow business was another matter. He had to do

something. And that became still more obvious when he found Marty Boyle in a stew.

"Ann Murrow's got Samantha Robbins!"

"Who?"

"The mother of the Wyoming girl. The movie actress."

"So what?"

"The whole world's been trying to get her."

"We haven't."

"Sure we have! We've tried everything. But Ann Murrow's got an exclusive tonight, and they're running some bites on their news. They'll kill us!"

"This'll shock you, Marty, but I'm glad they got her, not us. It's not news. It's not serving our viewers; it's exploiting them."

"Grant, I respect you, but we can't be that square if we're going to survive. If we don't give the people this kind of thing, they won't *be* our viewers. They'll watch it somewhere else."

Grant logged on to his computer and found the wires already updating the Wyoming murder story with the Murrow interview, including quotes released by the network.

"I come into her bedroom every night and I look at her little empty bed," the actress said, sobbing, "and my heart just breaks all over again."

The Reuters story added: "Anchor Ann Murrow confided, 'It was the most difficult, the most harrowing, the most heart-rending interview I've had to do in all my years as a journalist.' "

"Bullshit!" said Grant to the computer screen. "Bull-fucking-shit!"

He looked up a number and dialed Clifton Matthews, the elderly lawyer who had partially retired after multiple careers in law, politics, and diplomacy. He'd taken an interest in Grant in the 1970s, and had been a sounding board and confidant ever since. More relevant, he was a member of the corporate board.

"Clif, could we get together in the next couple of days? There's something I need to discuss."

"Oh, I'm not so busy these days. A drink tonight?"

"I can't. We have a dinner right after the program."

"How about breakfast tomorrow morning?"

"Sure, fine."

"Why don't you meet me at the Racquet Club at eight? Is that too early?"

"No, that's good."

"You want to give me a hint so that I'm forearmed?"

"You know who Ann Murrow is?"

"Of course!"

"Ken Walden is putting pressure on the news department to bring her over here. And I gather some of your fellow board members are involved."

"Am I to take it that you think it's a bad idea?"

"I think it's a terrible idea."

"Well, let's discuss it in the morning."

"If you want to see what I mean, watch her show tonight. Ten P.M. She's interviewing the mother of the little girl raped and murdered in Wyoming."

"I hear you. I'll watch."

Angela said, "Sherman Glass has been trying you all day. Want me to get him?"

"No, let him wait. But see if Don Evans is around, will you?"

"He's out here at the news desk."

"Let me have a word with him."

"Afternoon, squire," said Don. "A sumptuous power lunch, I gather, at the Four Seasons."

"For Christ's sake, how do you know that?"

"Hollygo, of course. Log on to the Internet and you can read it yourself. One of her spies saw you there."

"Jesus! Soon I won't be able to go to the bathroom without a commentary on the Internet."

"Better get them to give you your own bathroom. Other anchors have them, and if it gets out that you haven't, we won't be able to hold our heads up in public. Head-to-head competition. I like it!"

"Push the door closed a minute, Don. I want to talk."

"A closed door! That'll get the tongues wagging out there."

"Let 'em wag. Look, I know you have connections up there."

"Depends how 'up there' you mean, old boy. I'm such a lapsed Episcopalian, I think I've burned my bridges at the top. But if you mean the more mundane, like our distinguished corporate owners, yes. I knew one member at college. I play bridge with another. And I know that you have friends in high places, too."

"Some. I'm curious as to what yours are hearing about Ann Murrow."

"Brenda Starr, ace reporter? I notice in Hollygo that she was putting the make on the chairman at the Museum of Broadcasting. Is it serious?"

"It's sounding serious. I gather she's mounting a campaign to come over here, and it may be working."

"Well, well! Mind you, I have such consummate faith in the recent bad taste of our leaders that it makes perfect sense. Let me look into it and see what I can rustle up."

51

For the second morning, Ernie Schmid spotted him when he came out of the rooming house. Just like yesterday, not even hiding, just leaning against a lamppost, reading the paper. Like he wanted to be seen, wanted Ernie to know he was watching him. The first sight of him yesterday had given Ernie a small lurch of fear. They'd found the money missing. They were watching to see him pull out one of the $100 bills so they could grab him. When Ernie crossed the street and turned the corner, he looked back and saw the man fold the paper and walk briskly after him. It made him nervous, but he tried to walk normally to the diner, buy his own paper outside, and order as always. Acting normal.

The security guy came in and had coffee while Ernie ate his regular breakfast, reading his paper, not making eye contact. The man left before Ernie finished and was down the street when he came out. Obviously waiting for him to go to the photo shop, where he'd nab him.

That's how it looked; watching to see if he'd go back and enter the shop illegally. Ernie hadn't dared go near the place in the week since White had surprised him and chased him away. Nothing to go for, anyway. All the photos and negatives were gone. The guard had grabbed them. No reason to risk going back.

After leaving the diner, Ernie walked around and the man followed. Ernie went to the library and killed an hour. He had lunch at Burger King. He did not go to the mailbox shop. That might be a giveaway. He got tired walking so much. He sat for a while in the park. So did the man. Then Ernie went home to his room and lay on the bed. The room was at the back and he couldn't see the street.

The security guard must've looked in the envelope; it wasn't sealed. So he knew what was in there. The color glossies of Ann Murrow. Two full sets. Had had a good look at them. And then what? Left them in the store as property that wasn't supposed to be taken out? If so, they might still be there.

It was getting to be late afternoon. He wondered if the man had gone away. He couldn't stand waiting any longer, not knowing, so he went out. At first he thought his watcher had gone, but then he spotted him near a tree across the street. Nervous, wondering what to do, Ernie set out at a fast walk, to look as if he knew where he was going. He'd go to a movie, eat later. This guy looked pretty old. Sooner or later he was going to get tired and leave him alone.

He could have taken the bus but decided to walk, because it'd tire the old guy out faster. Ernie still had enough for the movie, but soon he'd have to use one of the $100s. He hardly noticed which movie he was buying a ticket for. It was running when he went in. Arnold Schwarzenegger. A lot of action and crashes, explosions, shooting, noise. Ernie kept glancing around but couldn't see the man. Maybe he'd given up. Maybe he was outside, waiting. In the movies, guys on the run would go to the men's room and climb out the window. Get on a subway and off again just before the doors closed. Stuff like that. Down fire escapes. Across roofs. They always ran like they knew where they were going, knew where the ladder was, how far you had to jump, not like you were running scared, seeing it for the first time.

It was still light when he got out of the movie, and no sign of the shadow. Great; he'd given up. Ernie caught a bus back and had supper at the Chinese restaurant where John used to order takeout, around the corner from the photo store. Couldn't arrest him for that. Egg rolls. Chicken chow mein. You could get filled up for a few bucks.

The summer night was finally dark when he walked the few blocks to the rooming house. If the guy was hiding between the old houses, Ernie couldn't spot him.

But this morning, he was there again, by the lamppost, reading his paper. Shit. He followed Ernie to the diner. At breakfast, Ernie pretended to read the help-wanted ads but was sneaking covert looks to the side. He didn't look like a security guard; he didn't have any uniform. He looked like a middle-aged businessman or salesman, kind of fattish, half-bald. What was he up to? If he was guarding the photo store, would he be away from it like this? Following Ernie around all day, he couldn't be watching the store. A lawyer or something connected to John's death? Why would a lawyer be following a guy around the streets like this?

Ernie made a plan. The guy was heavy and probably couldn't run fast, so he'd give him the slip. Two streets away, in the block before the store, was an alley. It was a short cut Ernie used and had several ways out. He could duck around the corner and run like hell before the old guy made the turn. He was still drinking his coffee.

Ernie slid off the stool, paid the cashier, and left, walking innocently by the usual route. At the first corner he saw the man leave the diner. Ernie turned the corner and walked to the main street, then three blocks along to the first alley, where he ducked in and ran at top speed to the next turn, ran the half-block, turned again, and was back on the main street. He ran back to where the alley started and peeked down.

The old guy was peering up and down the side alley, made up his mind, and took the turn Ernie had.

Ernie rapidly crossed the main street, ran two blocks the other way, and boarded the first bus going downtown. He'd given the old guy the slip. He went first to the mailbox store and opened his box. He looked incredulously at a small postcard inside. It was the receipt for his package to Ann Murrow. Ernie got very excited. It wasn't all over! He could still hear from her. She must be thinking it over.

"I need to pay for the box another two weeks." He laid a $100 on the counter.

"You got anything smaller?"

"No. That's it."

"OK."

The guy made change and Ernie left, with $75 to spend. He felt rich again. He'd been scared of the hundreds, but they weren't so hard to use after all. He went next door for a coffee and to sit down and think. He could move. He should move. No need to have the old guy following him around. Move to another part of town. Out where his mother had lived; there were rooming houses there. If only he still had his car. Not that he had much to move. He could find a room, go back to his present room that night, pack his suitcase, call a cab from the pay phone on the landing, and get out. If the guy was watching, all he'd see was a cab drive away. He'd be off Ernie's tail.

Christopher Siefert was sitting in Elizabeth Deegan's kitchen, sipping a glass of wine, watching her finish the dinner for Grant and Winona. He'd convinced Grant that an informal meal at home would be easier than eating at a public restaurant, and Elizabeth had happily agreed.

"I'm developing a feeling about Grant," Siefert said. "See if you agree with me after tonight."

"You like him more than you expected to." Elizabeth's full apron made her figure look larger. She was easing a soft mixture into a baking dish, scouring the stainless steel bowl with a rubber spatula.

"I still do. He's smarter than I expected. A lot smarter. He's articulate. He has a sense of history. He's on the side of decency and restraint. But he just doesn't get it."

"Get what?"

"That the battle he thinks he's fighting is over."

"The battle for decency is over? That's pretty cynical! This looks thin to me." She dipped her finger. "Tastes all right, but it may be too moist." She looked back at the page of cookbook manuscript. "Add the orange juice and grated zest. That's all it says. We'll see! Did you pour me a glass?"

Siefert was growing very fond of this woman, who was so full of humor and good sense. If only she weren't so large. He fluctuated between letting it matter and not matter; between her arousing his returning desire and failing to. His problem, not hers. He handed her the wine, and she made her customary little kiss with her fingers from her lips to his, transferring a taste of chocolate soufflé, with orange flavoring.

"It may be too much when it's baked. We'll see. There's the bell. You let them in, and I'll tidy up."

Meeting Winona for the first time, Siefert was taken by the vivacity in her face, the engaging smile, the light-filled eyes. A beautiful woman whose energy and lithe figure reminded him of Laurie and Teresa and of desired women from his own past; a type that had always piqued Siefert's sexual curiosity.

"Come in. Come and meet Elizabeth in the kitchen."

"But what a kitchen!" Winona exclaimed at the large room with its tile floor and antique country furniture. "It's wonderful! It looks like Provence, and it's so big!"

"My hobby and my work. I edit cookbooks, so I like to try the recipes my authors come up with. And that's what it is tonight. Well, some of it.'' She shook hands with Grant. ''It's lovely to meet you. I'm sure everyone says this, but I do feel I know you well.''

''Thank you. It's kind of you to have us this evening.''

''What would you like to drink?'' Siefert asked.

''Some white wine would be lovely,'' Winona said.

''Grant?''

''A Scotch on the rocks, if I may.''

Winona took her wine and settled comfortably against a counter to watch Elizabeth. ''May I ask what book you're working on and what you're testing tonight?''

''This one's a book on favorite recipes from French country restaurants. The author's very reliable. Veal shoulder in a casserole. Some cognac, little white onions. Do you like to cook?''

''I like to but I don't much, I'm afraid. We're out, I'm working, Grant's late and, well, it's New York. You eat out; you order in. Sometimes on the weekends we cook. But when we entertain, usually someone caters it.''

''Oh, I'd love to know who you use.'' Elizabeth turned to Grant. ''Is the wine all right? I understand from Chris that you're in the wine business.''

''Just grape growers, not wine makers.''

Siefert said, ''But going to be right?'' To Winona: ''When I was there the other day, Guy Ferris gave me some of your test Merlot, plus the full argument for going ahead. He's really keen.''

Grant laughed. ''I think Guy has figured the story in *Time* should be a box on television news and a three-page spread on the great potential for Russian River wines.''

''Well, if you play your cards right . . .''

''Anyway, he's just about convinced me that we should try it.''

''I thought the Merlot was fine.''

''Let's sit down,'' Elizabeth said. ''Winona, if you sit here, then you can't see if I drop things on the floor. Incidentally, I love the name Winona. I know men are supposed to do these things, but can we just drink a toast to Winona and Grant and say how delighted we are to have you?"

"Thank you. Thank you."

"I say *we*. Chris and I have been spending a lot of time together in the last year. We knew each other years ago at *Time*, when he was an important writer and I was a lowly researcher. And then we got married—to other people—and things happened, and here we are! Chris spends part of his time here. It's wonderful to have the company and someone to try out food on, but he keeps his own place on West End Avenue and—"

"I commute," said Siefert. "I do my writing there."

"It's very handy, because he lives near Citarella and Fairway; I can fax him lists, and he delivers!"

Siefert admired how easily Elizabeth kept up this flow, putting the Munros at ease and adroitly defining their own relationship.

"Chris tells me—I'm afraid everything this evening starts with 'Chris tells me,' because he's been talking about you ever since he started this story—"

"You must be bored to tears with us," Winona said.

"Not bored at all! Fascinated. I've been watching your husband for years and years: political conventions, all the big special things—oh, the Diana funeral! You did that so beautifully! I got up up at four A.M. and sat there weeping, hour after hour. It was so sad and so beautiful . . ."

"Thank you," said Grant. "I'm not sure we didn't go a bit overboard. But it was one of those things where you feel your way along day by day. The intensity in London—you couldn't be there and not feel it."

"I don't think you went overboard one bit!" Elizabeth said. "Everyone I know wanted to see it all and have a good cry. And you let us do it."

Chris said, "You were there for the Churchill funeral. It's in your bio. Was that in your mind during the Diana coverage?"

"It was—a lot." Grant turned to Elizabeth. "The Churchill story was my first overseas assignment. I wasn't even a reporter, just a desk assistant. They sent me over to help out, and I carried messages, ripped wire copy, kept files for the correspondents. And for four nights I waited outside Churchill's home in Hyde Park Gate. It was freezing, but there was an amazing feeling. The film crews, British and foreign, with their tripods, film boxes, and ladders, were subdued and respectful, talking in low murmurs, drinking hot tea from thermoses, their cigarette ends winking in the dark, and I felt a real exhilaration at being present at the making of history."

"Like Berlin," Siefert said. "He was *in* Berlin when they started building the wall."

"Amazing!" said Elizabeth.

"Inside that brick house, one of the great men of the century was slipping away, and I felt important being with the small group waiting for the final word. Being there, on that spot. Today, if a Churchill were dying, there'd be electronic cameras outside, feeding satellite uplinks, ready to go live at any moment, but that's a different reality."

Grant couldn't keep his tone conversational, Siefert noticed, but habitually slid into a professional voice, as now, when he turned to Winona. "Do you remember when I took Sandy to that World Series game at Yankee Stadium? It was a big thrill, because he thought Reggie Jackson was God. But when the action stopped for a television time-out, the ballpark seemed like the wrong side of the moon."

To Siefert it sounded written out and memorized, an actor's lines.

"Where we were, a chill wind was blowing forlorn scraps of paper across the infield, while the players—all famous names, multimillion-dollar salaries—stood around awkwardly, getting cold, waiting for the television sun to rise on them again. It made me think how irrelevant things can seem when television turns away from them."

"Maybe," Siefert said, "the difference is that you're telling us what to feel—you, the television commentators, that is. You're shaping our feelings. Millions feel what you tell us it's appropriate to feel."

Elizabeth said, "Now nobody move. I'm going to change these plates. Chris, would you look after the red wine?"

Pouring wine, Siefert noticed the affection in Winona's voice as she said, "You've never told me the Churchill story like that. It's lovely. Full of atmosphere. And when you were there, I was still in Peru, right?"

"Right. Winona was in the Peace Corps."

"Oh, yes," Siefert said to Winona. "How you met. Grant said I should ask you. You watched him on television during the Kennedy assassination and called him up?"

"Yes, but that was the second time. We'd gone together for two years in college, then split up. Seeing him that weekend made me know I wanted to be with him."

"Oh, that's sweet!" said Elizabeth. "It's a bit like us. Don't stop. Tell us the story while I serve this."

As she took the lid from a casserole, an enchanting odor enveloped them.

"Mmm. Just smell that!" Winona said.

"Don't stop! Don't spoil the story."

Grant and Winona looked at each other, as if to ask who should begin.

Winona said, "I was a prig in college. Girls nowadays, like our daughter, Heather, would say Grant was only being a guy, taking a while to get it together. I was crazy about him, but I was convinced that he had no ambition."

Everyone laughed.

"It's true. I kept lecturing him about playing around with boats—that was his work in the summers—and not doing anything serious. I told him I had to have a man who wanted to go somewhere."

Grant smiled.

"So he said, fine, I'll go off with another woman. And he did."

"No, no, no!" said Grant. "Winona left me. Dropped me cold. That's when I started dating someone else."

"And someone else, and someone else," Winona added. "Grant was doing his sixties thing before the sixties began, and I was still back there in the fifties . . ."

Siefert noticed how they looked at each other as if prompting the other to tell. Grant was in much lighter spirits than Siefert had seen him.

Winona said, "I'd been going around with a man who was in the FBI—"

"I don't believe it!" Elizabeth shrieked. "In the Hoover days? Didn't they have to report to their bosses every time they . . ." She giggled.

"This is wonderful, Elizabeth. Simply delicious. The veal is melting."

"Ah, the recipe passes?"

"Absolutely."

"OK, I know! You got the FBI agent to trail Grant and see what skullduggery he was up to . . ."

"No, no. Nothing like that. My FBI friend was at work that day, November twenty-second. I was at the Peace Corps office, and we all sat there watching television, wrapped in horror. And then Grant came on, and as I watched him, I thought *that's* the man I'm interested in."

"What's your side of the story?" Siefert asked Grant.

"I didn't know anything about the FBI. I hadn't heard from Winona for five years or so. So it came out of the blue. She called on Tuesday, the day after the Kennedy funeral. I'd just had a bawling-out from the news director for taking his mobile unit—Christopher knows this story—but also I'd come down fast from the high of my reporting in Hyannis. I listened to this jerk with a sinking heart. He'd fire me. Back to looking for another entry-level job. Then, right after I left his office, the switchboard operator gave me a message, 'Winona called,' with a number in Washington. I remember wondering how to phone her. I didn't have credit cards or anything in those days. I was nervous about using a newsroom phone for a long-distance call. I futzed around for about five minutes and then told myself, The hell with it, and dialed the number."

Elizabeth asked, "And what did she say?"

Winona picked it up. "I said, I saw you a lot on television. You were really good."

Grant added, "And at that moment someone put a piece of paper in front of me: 'Al Williams, VP News, New York, on the line—FOR YOU!' The *for you* in caps. I told Winona I'd call her back, and five minutes later I was telling her, 'That was a guy with the network. Vice president of news. He asked me to come to New York to talk about a job!' "

"Oh, what a great story!"

Winona said, "Not all great. I was committed to go to Peru for the Peace Corps."

Grant said, "And my dad was dying."

Siefert asked about Grant's move to New York.

Grant laughed. "It's very corny. The moment I stepped out of Grand Central Terminal, I never wanted to live anywhere else. They were great to me at the network, gave me a tour, introduced me to people I'd seen on the air, and offered me a job as a desk assistant in the newsroom. I spent the rest of the day walking around Manhattan, all the obvious places, feeling a tremendous lift from the job offer, a mixture of fear of the city, and the sense that it belonged to me too. You've got a cliché about New York, I felt it."

Winona said, "He sent a telegram to me in Peru. A telegram seemed a very big deal in those days."

"And do you remember what you cabled back?" Grant said. " 'Hope big-time guy remembers small-town gal.' "

"Oh, that's so cute!"

"But it took us years. I was away, and then in graduate school, and then he was in Vietnam . . . It was a long time."

And Siefert could see the small-town kids re-emerging briefly from these sophisticated New Yorkers.

Elizabeth kept it going, putting Grant at ease with social chit-chat but eliciting lots of information.

"It must have been hard, being married and raising a family, with Grant's job . . . all the travel . . . all the demands."

"The credit is Winona's," Grant said in the voice Siefert was getting used to, when Grant didn't know how sententious he sounded. He responded to questions as though talking to an audience. And he sounded rehearsed.

"The anchor job looks sedentary—you have to be in the same city normally five nights a week—but you travel a lot of weekends to record or interview for a documentary, or there's a speech you can't turn down, or a conference you've got to go to. Or the big story—like Nelson Mandela's release from prison—when you move the whole operation to Johannesburg. Or a summit meeting, like Reagan and Gorbachev, in 'eighty-eight, when we did the whole show from Moscow for a week. Or the affiliates' meeting or the L.A. press tour to promote the new fall line-up. Or a hundred other things that come up. You don't own your life."

Elizabeth said, "If I go on listening, I'll burn the soufflé, and that won't be my author's fault. This may be a bit much for a summer night, but you can at least have a taste. The author's found a way of flavoring the chocolate with orange, so this is a real test!"

Siefert returned to business. "I'm interested in your idea that television creates its own reality; that that's where it takes us."

Grant said, "It does. Because institutions like baseball want the audiences and the money television brings, they're willing to reconstruct their reality to suit ours. It's like the political parties. Each presidential year they've adapted further. In 'ninety-six it reached a glorious absurdity. There we were, the networks, complaining that political conventions had become nothing but TV shows; that was to justify reducing our coverage to one hour of prime time. But the hour we did choose to be on the air, the parties ran their taped shows, so we tried to sound like political journalists not being sucked in by the party propaganda. The more we go on doing that, the more the print people will beat up on us for turning politics into entertainment!"

Elizabeth put the soufflé on the table. "There we are. I think it's all right. I was worried the orange would make it too wet. Tell me what you taste first, without the sauce."

"Mmm, delicious. Gorgeous. You can taste the orange."

"Yes, I suppose so," Elizabeth said. "But you could do the same with a little sauce. I don't know that it's such a big improvement."

"But the texture is perfect."

"It's a triumph!" Grant said. "I'd like to drink—"

"Oh, wait, wait!" Elizabeth ran to the fridge. "I forgot the dessert wine. Chris, sweetie, pour some, will you? I wish I could tape this and play it at my next dinner party. A toast from Grant Munro!"

"To Elizabeth, who clearly should be writing the cookbooks and not just editing them."

"Thank you. It was a pleasure having you as my guinea pigs. Now, it's mostly my fault, because I had to hear Grant talk, but we haven't heard a thing about Winona's work."

"My work? Well, it's two kinds. I have private clients for therapy, practical therapy, as commonsense and down to earth as I can make it. They're people like us, mostly women, with all the usual hang-ups. The other part is with people at the lowest end of everything. Defeated by life in every way. I see them at a clinic on the Lower East Side, most of them extremely poor, and the social morbidity is extreme." She shook her head. "Amazing contrasts. And then I come back to an idyllic setting like this, and it's two worlds. Or back to our own apartment, just across the park . . . I imagine you can almost see it from here."

Siefert asked, "Do any of your clients know who your husband is?"

"Some, but if they think that's relevant, I put them right, and if they persist, I drop them. Ninety-nine percent have no idea."

"Is it painful to work with so many disturbed and needy people?" Elizabeth asked. "Can you leave it behind when you go home, put on a party dress and have a night out?"

"If I feel I'm helping, then I really do get satisfaction from it. I love the work, but there are days when I feel burned out; then others when I feel wonderful."

"You *look* wonderful!" Elizabeth said. "Do you spend hours at a gym?"

"I have a trainer. He comes to the apartment three times a week. I'd never have the discipline to do it myself."

"How long are you both going to do what you do? I mean, it sounds perfect. But do you want to do it forever, or ease off? Or do you have plans to retire somewhere, like your vineyard in California?"

The loaded question, intended so innocently, made Siefert watch carefully and he noticed the first sign of tension: Winona and Grant each giving the other a long, wary look.

Winona replied, "Why not be honest? It's a very touchy subject at present."

Grant, embarrassed, added, "Christopher may know more about my future than I do. He's been talking to everyone." He glanced at his watch. "Look, I'm sorry to break this up, but I have to get to an early breakfast meeting . . . so if you'll excuse us. This was wonderful. You must come and have dinner with us."

"Oh, yes," Winona said warmly. "I can't promise cooking like this, but we'd love to have you."

"Did I ask the wrong thing?" Elizabeth said when the door had closed.

"It's the sixty-four-thousand-dollar question," Siefert said.

"Oh, I hope I didn't hurt his feelings. He's such a nice man, and she's divine, don't you think?"

"She's terrific." For the third time, a woman close to Grant had aroused that slight sexual current in Siefert. "But you got him to be more at ease and talk more personally than I've ever done. It was the perfect thing to do. Going to a restaurant would have made it much stiffer."

"Do you still think he doesn't get it?"

"Yes. I like him, but he doesn't get it. And he has almost no sense of irony about himself."

"Do you have to find *something* to put him down?"

"I wasn't doing that!"

"Well, I like him a lot. And her. And I think they're sweet together," Elizabeth said wistfully. "Watching them, I felt myself wishing that there wasn't your place and my place, but our place."

"That crosses my mind too."

"Does it? You've never said."

They kissed.

"The chocolate soufflé was a hit."

"You didn't like the veal?"

"The veal was fantastic."

"And the vegetables?"

"Right now I'm concentrating on the cook."

IN THE CAR, going up Central Park West, Winona said, "You rushed us out of there as though you'd been bitten by something."

"I'm sorry, but I'd just noticed what time it is. It's nearly ten. I've got to watch Ann Murrow at ten."

"You pulled us out of a nice evening to watch *her?*"

"I didn't want Siefert to know about it. There's a serious effort to hire her for our shop."

"I don't believe it. It's too crazy!"

"It's happening. Sherman Glass told me. Ev Repton confirmed it. She put the make on Kenneth Walden personally, and she's lobbying members of his board. I've got to do something to stop it. I'm seeing Cliff Matthews for breakfast."

"Well, remember what I said the other day. If they're willing to bring that woman in, you can walk out."

"I know. But first I want to fight. And I have to see her tonight to give me ammunition."

"Well, in that case I'll watch too!"

"You're a pal." He kissed her.

"I'm your pal," Winona said. "They're nice, Chris and Elizabeth, don't you think?"

"Yes, I do. It's still odd, knowing that he's mentally tucking everything away, even if he doesn't have his tape recorder running."

"But you don't think he's going to write anything bad, do you?"

"I hope not. You know, when he went out west to see Guy—and that was fine—he also went to Seattle and talked to Teresa Weldon."

"Is he going to bring all that up again?"

"I guess so, and in his shoes, I probably would."

Winona said, "Maybe I should call her and see how she feels about it."

"Good. I'd like to know what she told him."

"I'll bet you would. I often wonder whether you ever . . . you know . . . did anything with her."

"Come on!"

"You could have. It was obvious. Obvious to me. She was as crazy for you as for Tony. Maybe more."

Grant seemed not to hear her. "This Ann Murrow business is really getting to me."

ANN MURROW'S exclusive was heavily promoted during the ten o'clock station break; then she herself teased it at the opening of her show. She and the grieving actress-mother appeared together, looking at the mounds of flowers sent by strangers to cover the site of her daughter's murder. Over the pictures, Ann Murrow's unctuous voice: "An actress's all too real-life tragedy. Samantha Robbins takes us behind the brave public mask of her grief to her most private torments."

"I'm going to need a drink to get through this," Winona said.

"I'll get it. What would you like?"

"I don't know. I've had a lot of wine. What do you think I should have?"

"Sweetheart, I don't know. I'm going to have a Scotch on the rocks."

"I never know. Would I like a bourbon?"

"Maybe. Maybe you'd like a banana daiquiri."

"No, you're kidding."

A familiar conversation.

"I honestly don't want anything strong. Maybe I'll make a cup of tea."

"I'll do it."

"You'll miss the program."

"Don't worry, she'll save that goody to hold the audience. What kind of tea?"

"The usual. I'm going to get out of this dress. Why don't we watch in bed?"

"Fine with me."

The Wyoming segment, teased twice more, came third in the program. The set-up began in Ann Murrow's throaty, tragic tones:

"Michelle Robbins was born into a magic world, gorgeous movie actress Samantha Robbins, her mother, and stunning George Ackland, her daddy."

Pictures of the parents and little girl, tiny, then larger, posing, knowing the camera.

"Life was a fairy-tale world of beautiful homes and beautiful people."

Shots of houses with palm trees in the desert, and by the beach, filled with well-known actors.

"Then, last year, when she was nine, she loses her daddy. Samantha and George split up. Mother and daughter go to live at their idyllic ranch in Wyoming. Suddenly, in the middle of the night, Michelle runs to her mother's bed. She's sobbing from a frightening dream."

Cut to Samantha Robbins, in a flattering black jumpsuit, turtle-neck collar, bare arms, sitting on her large bed, a view of hills behind her, and Ann Murrow, in a black suit jacket and miniskirt, black stockings, and, touching detail, a black ribbon in her blond hair. She was prompting, "And when she snuggled into bed here with you . . . ?"

The actress, imitating a little girl's frightened voice, said, " 'Mommy, in my dream a big man came, and he took me out to the woods and he hurt me and he killed me.' So I calmed her down and told her it's just a dream, don't worry. Mommy'll look after you."

"Who were the men around the place at that time?" asked Ann, sympathetic friend.

"Just my stepson, Woodsy, you know, George's boy. He was staying with us, and my friend Scott Woolford was here sometimes, and the ranch hands."

"So there were real men Michelle could have been dreaming about?"

In the orgy of tabloid and television speculation, every male mentioned had already been suspected, found guilty, and discarded for another, including fifteen-year-old-Woodsy.

Ann led Samantha through the day of the crime.

"I'll never forgive myself for leaving her." She began to cry. "I had to go to L.A. overnight to re-shoot a scene in a miniseries pilot. Normally I took Michelle with me, but I thought it's such a quick trip . . . and then they called me. I was in the trailer . . ."

"Do you mind telling us . . ."

Samantha did not seem to mind. She dabbed her mascara-ed eyes and told. "They called and said they couldn't find her . . . and I said . . ."—her voice grew angry and shrill—" 'Well, what are you doing? Go look for her! Everyone, go look for her!' And then I had to do a take, and I couldn't keep my mind on it . . . and they called again . . . they'd found her . . ."

Now it dissolved to Ann and Samantha, two svelte figures in black, walking through trees, Samantha's voice continuing: ". . . they'd found her . . . here."

The shot zoomed out to a woodland glade piled with flowers.

"When they told me first, I thought maybe she'd fallen off her horse. She rode all the time . . ."

Home video shots of Michelle riding, blond ponytail flying, reining in, dismounting, patting her horse, smiling prettily.

Now the two women were back in the bedroom.

"And then," Ann Murrow said, "you learned the awful truth," and the word *awful* seemed to come from her deepest reservoirs of disgust. "Can you bear to tell us?"

Samantha could.

"Have you heard of this actress before?" Winona asked.

"Not until this. Small parts. Nothing big."

". . . and then the autopsy confirmed it."

Ann, helping her, "Confirmed . . . ?"

"Confirmed that she'd been raped . . ."

"Raped and . . . ?"

The actress's dry throat whispered, "Raped and sodomized."

"How ghastly!"

The actress was weeping uncontrollably.

"Is she acting, or is that genuine?" Grant asked.

"It could be both. Grief is a show."

Ann, asking, "And did you have any immediate suspicions your-self?"

"No, I couldn't imagine . . ."

"Not any of the ranch hands? Do you know them all?"

"Of course; they're wonderful men. They've always been sweet to Michelle. They taught her to ride."

"No one fired recently? No dispute over pay, anything like that?"

"The police asked all those type questions."

"Well"—Ann looked ingenuous—"do you ever, even for a moment, suspect someone *closer* to Michelle?"

"No, no. I know what they're saying, but it's not possible!"

"What are they saying?" Ann Murrow knew perfectly well what the tabs and tab TV shows were saying about Woodsy, the stepson, and Scott, the in-and-out lover.

"You know, Ann . . . that Scott . . . you know . . ."

"You tell *me,* Samantha," Ann cooed. "You tell *me.*"

"They're saying that Scott had an unnatural interest in her."

Now the film showed Scott, husky and tanned, riding a large horse, with little Michelle on the saddle in front of him, galloping away.

Cut back to Ann, looking artfully quizzical. "And how do you react when you hear that?"

"I don't believe it! I don't believe it for a minute. It's so unfair to Scott. He's a fine man, and now he can't even show his face in public."

"You never had any suspicions when . . ." The pictures of Michelle and Scott on horseback together reappeared. He got off, lifted the little girl from the tall horse, and put her on his shoulders to walk into the house.

"No, we're very close, Scott and I. He's been wonderful to me all through this . . ."

"What about George, Michelle's father? What about him?"

And the actress gave Ann a strangely unrehearsed look, as though she'd forgotten her lines. "Him? You mean—suspect him?"

"Well . . ."

"The police asked me that too."

"And what did you say?"

"I said George loved Michelle just like I did."

"But . . ." Ann insinuated.

"But . . . ?" Samantha raised her long lashes at Ann. "I didn't mean any buts. George was shattered, just like me."

The part that had been released to the wires and excerpted on the news was next. As they broke for a commercial, Grant asked Winona, "What did you mean, grief is a show?"

"Grief may be the biggest show some people ever get to put on. I see a lot of grieving people. This woman is probably deeply traumatized, and she also may be loving all this attention. Both understandable."

Ann Murrow reappeared, now in the studio, speaking to the camera intimately and tragically. "We asked Michelle's father and Scott Woolford to appear in this report, but they both refused. The sequence we're about to show you was personally, for me, the most difficult, the most harrowing, the most heart-rending interview I've had to conduct in all my years as a journalist."

The scene returned to the actress's bedroom. It began with a distant shot of the bank of flowers and slowly pulled back until you saw the two women. They had risen and were silhouetted, elegant figures against the picture window, looking out over a panoramic view, with the strewn flowers at the crime site becoming a speck in the distance.

Ann Murrow asked, "Samantha, how on earth do you go on, day by day, after this? Until they find who did it, you have no resolution, no closure."

The actress turned from the window. "I don't know. I never believed anything in this entire world could hurt so much."

And then the picture cut to a small frilly bed, with stuffed animals, obviously in the dead girl's room, and widened out to show Samantha leading Ann through the doorway.

"I come into her bedroom every night and I look at her little empty bed . . . and my heart just breaks all over again."

"I know . . ." Ann said soothingly, and picked up a furry animal from the bed. "What did she call this one?"

"That's her Woozie!" And the actress began freshly crying.

"And this?" Ann held up another.

"Uncle Benjie."

"Tell us how you like to remember Michelle."

Between sobs, the actress said, "She was the sweetest little girl . . . she loved all the animals . . ." The camera roamed the room, pausing on pictures of Michelle and her parents, on horseback, with Scott, with Woodsy, while her mother's voice continued, ". . . and there's just no more to say. She's gone. She's gone." She broke down and turned to Ann Murrow, who cradled her sobbing face on her shoulder and stroked her heaving back. The scene held for what seemed a long time, then faded out.

When the picture reappeared, Ann Murrow, chic and crisp, was in the studio again. She said to camera, "Nearly three weeks have gone by since the tragedy, and the police can't find the monster who did this? Give me a break! No arrests? No suspects? The people deserve better than this. And . . ."—her voice faltered, as if on a stifled sob—"and Samantha Robbins . . . I can't bear to think what she's going through tonight! I'm Ann Murrow. Good night."

"Jesus!" said Grant. "Did you ever see anything like that?"

"I don't know," Winona said. "Half of me wants to shout it's all a fake, and half wants to break down and cry. It seems so contrived . . . that stuff in the bedroom."

"Well, that had to be a set-up. The camera was in the room before they came in. Someone had to say, we're rolling, and cue them. Like the shot at the window. That long zoom back from the flowers. It's all crafted."

"She managed to imply that the little girl's father, her stepbrother, this woman's lover, all the ranch hands, all could be guilty. Who do you think?"

Grant said, "The biggest nudge she gave us was toward Scott, the boyfriend. But that was a weird moment about the husband."

"Well, I don't know. Does it make us feel pity? Maybe that's a good thing. Or does it make us voyeurs? I mean, she was laying it on pretty thick. All those suggestive questions. She practically had the boyfriend guilty of sexual abuse."

"What do you make of the dream?"

"If some man was abusing her, that might have been a clue. I think the actress—I mean, obviously she was acting, but we all act in public—she seemed pretty genuine. Yet there was something missing. If she was in my office, I could tell. You see it on television, they're here, they're there, that other woman is leading her to say things. How can you tell what's faked and what's genuine? Television fakes things. But it's probably going to keep me awake now, wondering about those people!"

Joe Steinman turned off the television. He was ecstatic. No question this would be a biggie. Say what you like about Ann—and privately Joe had cursed the woman as fervently as he'd worshiped her—he was dazzled by her worth as a client. In the lousy television racket, as

Don Imus said, it didn't get any better than this. The way she handled the stupid little actress, obviously torn apart between her moment of fame and her poor little girl—life was shitty sometimes—even worse for her knowing, probably knowing that one of the guys close to her, maybe even the guy she was sleeping with now, had done this. The fleeting instinct to call and offer to represent her was easy to suppress. She wasn't that electrifying. Ann Murrow, at least twenty years older than Samantha, showed twenty times more magnetism, more pure showbiz pizazz, from the moment they first appeared together. Besides, Hollywood actresses were a mess to represent. Even Ann Murrow was a breeze by comparison.

Tomorrow when they met, Everett Repton would have the New York overnights. What a set-up! This show had to be a blockbuster, maybe a record breaker. All news shows, network and local and cable, had obligingly promoted her interview by running excerpts she'd provided. What a transparent business! Get a story with ingredients like the Wyoming murder, and all the little media dogs have to come and pee on the same corner. Ann usually ignored the rest of them, or broke through with something stunning they all had to follow. Or even promote! You couldn't buy promotion like that: hour after hour, all day long, radio and television: "Actress Samantha Robbins told television's Ann Murrow . . . blah-blah-blah." And the obligatory pay-off for the right to use the quotes: "The interview will be seen in full at ten Eastern time tonight on . . ."

Ann always came up with a detail the lazy, copycat newspeople could not ignore. Like the kid's bedroom. The heart-wrenching toy animals she kept picking up and naming, echoing back in viewers' minds to the stud on the stallion riding with the little girl, reinforcing that in the bedroom shots with the photo of them on the horse. Cynically, Joe wondered whether that photo had been deliberately placed there. A little set decoration? Not beyond her.

So far he hadn't talked any numbers with Repton, just concepts. Tomorrow they would talk numbers—ratings numbers and dollars. Joe hadn't yet decided whether to go for the twelve mill he'd mentioned to

Ann, or a little more. He was happy to leave it to the intuition of the moment.

5 4

At the Racquet Club, Clifton Matthews rose to shake hands, thin, boyish in his late seventies, with a lock of hair loose on his forehead; so confident that he could wear this old seersucker suit and bow tie, brown oxfords cracked from age, obviously well mended, polished to a high gleam.

He asked Grant, "Your boat in the water? Been out at all?"

A late and reluctant convert to fiberglass hulls, Matthews sailed a large Hinckley.

"She's in," Grant said, "but we've only made it up to Boothbay one weekend, over Memorial Day. It's been too busy this spring."

"I know. I used to have the same problem. You should organize your life to make more time for yourself. You've earned it. Of course, you've got that place in California competing for your time. Russian River Vineyards, isn't it?"

"That's right."

"I'd like to have a look at that one day, if you'd let me, when I'm out on the coast."

"Love to have you. Just let me know. I'll try to be there myself."

"You and Winona likely to have any time this summer to come for a weekend on our boat? Over Labor Day, perhaps?"

"That's tempting. Let me have a look and talk to Winona."

"Are you going to eat some breakfast?"

"I'll just have an English muffin."

"Not me. I'm going for something solid. Corned beef hash with two poached eggs and rye toast," he told the waiter. "Now, you wanted to talk about this Murrow woman. I watched last night."

"What did you think?"

"Well, of course, it's not to my taste. The subject matter or the approach. It's always surprising to me to see what they get up to on television now. My old mother used to say—she was brought up in a very different time—'The trash our maids read!' She'd try to give them good books, but all they'd read was *True Romances*. She wasn't censorious; merely thought it incomprehensible that anyone would enjoy such cheap sensation. I suppose if people had maids today, they'd be watching shows like last night's. I gather millions of people do."

"Her show has one of the highest ratings on television."

"And what kind of a rating do you suppose the performance last night will garner?"

"Probably very high."

Matthews squished his poached eggs into the hash like a child mooshing his food together, ate a few mouthfuls, and had a bite of rye toast, before wiping his lips, sipping his coffee, and settling to talk.

"I made a few calls. Your information was correct. There's something afoot. Ken Walden's an old friend—we've done things together—so I can talk to him. He's not directly involved. Too many other things on his plate. But the Murrow woman accosted him personally at a dinner. He was a bit taken aback by her aggressiveness, but he said he'd follow up. And they've had some conversations with the news department man, what's his name?"

"Everett Repton, president of the news division."

"Repton; that's the name. It's still preliminary, as I understand, nothing firm, but, as you intimated, the lady hasn't left it there. At least one other board member has heard from her. And she's around and about, as you know. A few weeks ago, I found myself seated next to her at a State Department dinner. She's very personable. The aura she gives off . . . talking to a man, even as old as I am, she rivets you with those eyes, but her whole body seems to be informing you of—I have to say it—sexual potential. There, have I conveyed the message?"

The little recitation had raised the color in Matthews's gaunt cheeks and brightened his eyes as he attacked his eggs and hash again.

"I did, however, manage to keep my head and escape with my honor intact!"

"I'm glad to hear it."

"And I saw some of that power, if that's the word, on television last night. She upstaged and outshone that pathetic little actress. You'd have thought that Murrow was the Hollywood star. She has a strong presence."

"Let me explain the proposition they're putting to Repton."

"They?"

"Murrow and her agent, Joseph Steinman."

"Joseph Steinman? I don't know the name."

"The idea is this. Her programs appear in prime time. After eight P.M., when the audience is largest and where she does very well. The news programs appear well before prime time, say six-thirty, or earlier in some markets. The audience is smaller, and, frankly, our share of that audience is shrinking. Too many distractions, too many other channels, more entertaining channels for people to watch. She's now proposing a radical change. Put her magazine on our network for five nights a week. Same time every night. It's called a strip. At the start of each program, do a little hard news, then the magazine segments as you saw them last night. In a few years, if our straight news program loses more audience, just phase it out. Let the magazine strip perform that function."

"I understand your personal motive, but what's wrong with that as a business proposal?"

Grant was surprised to have the question put so objectively.

"I see it as a final surrender to the trend that's turning all news into entertainment. Without the evening news, and its journalistic disciplines, the values we've been trying to maintain would vanish. There'd be nothing to distinguish network journalism from the tabloids, from cable TV, from syndication. It means abandoning the tradition that began with the Paleys and Sarnoffs, with Edward R. Murrow, to make broadcasting a serious business, as well as a popular alternative to newspapers."

"How many years would it take to complete this transition?"

"Probably four or five, I'd guess. You'd have to get the magazines established, tinker with the amount of news you use at the top."

"In four or five years, you'll be how old?"

"Sixty-four; sixty-five."

"And where do you want your career to be then?"

"I'm wondering exactly that. We've just begun to negotiate a new contract. My agent is going for five years."

"And after that, what do you want to do?"

"I haven't settled that. Slip into a secondary role; commentator, maybe."

"Or get out and have time to sail, and so on."

"I can't see getting out. Not yet. Well, look at you. You don't want to stop completely."

"No, but I'm in a different kind of game. I can pick and choose things and people to keep me interested. The reason I ask you—and stop me if this is too personal—"

"No, no. I've always liked talking candidly with you. And I've always benefited from your advice."

"I see myself wearing two hats in this situation."

Grant imagined an old-fashioned straw hat hanging in the cloakroom downstairs, and one of Clif's floppy white sailing hats in a closet at home.

"One I wear as your friend. I enjoy our chats. I admire your serious approach to journalism. I can see it's becoming rare. Although, to be honest, that isn't where I go first for information. I look at your program, but I find it too chopped up for me now, too staccato, too light. On Sundays I like "60 Minutes" because it sticks to its last. To the degree that I stay informed day by day, I read the *Times* and the *Journal,* some periodicals and newsletters; you know the sort of thing. And when I'm at home having a drink, I'll watch Jim Lehrer and the public television people, because they take enough time with topics, and I find my pals watch it too, so it's something for us to talk about. I'm sorry to be blunt, but the programs like yours are more for the masses now, as I see it. I sympathize with your situation. You're the end of a tradition.

You uphold it honorably. But it may be fortunate for you that the years fall in your favor."

Grant was not happy with the trend of the conversation. He'd expected Clif Matthews to share his outrage at the excesses of Ann Murrow's performance, but, as usual, Matthews was talking in an entirely reasonable way, as, doubtless, he had talked to people far more important than Grant.

"Now I have to put on my other hat . . . as trustee, member of the board of your esteemed corporate employer, bound by law and honor to serve the interests of the owners, the shareholders in their thousands. You mentioned Paley and Sarnoff. I knew them. Never liked either of them much. But essentially they ran family businesses. New businesses. Formed by their entrepreneurial spirit, incidentally with a huge federal subsidy, in effect—use of scarce public airways—motivated by greed and also, given who they were, by a desire to be esteemed in their world, to have social position, political position. Businessmen as statesmen, if you like. Particularly after the rigged quiz scandals of the late fifties, they saw enormous political advantage in parading themselves as selfless public servants: running news operations for prestige, not profit, while they minted money on the entertainment side. Golden years. Golden profits. Golden reputations . . . excluding Paley's extramarital conduct . . . I could tell you a few stories there . . ."

Matthews smiled and looked aloft, as he might at a sail not drawing its fullest.

"Today, a different business. No family business anymore. But a big business, and part of ever bigger businesses. Each component of those businesses contributes to the overall health and profit. Prestige is a small commodity. Your corporation is like any other whose board I sit on. It is run, quite properly, for the bottom line, quarterly reports, analysts' expectations, stock price. So, I go back to Ken Walden. He's a shrewd man. Good CEO. You know him?"

"I've met him a few times."

"You should get to know him better. You'd like him. I'll have you to dinner soon. How about that? Or perhaps we could get the Waldens to sail with us over Labor Day. That'd be good. Like any good CEO, Ken has to watch each part of the company and see how it's performing. The television part comes up at every board meeting. The network's not doing as well as it was, as well as it could be doing, compared with the others. Overall ratings down. Advertising revenue down. Not only in news; across the schedule, with exceptions everyone knows about, the big hits. And they tinker with the programs from season to season. Now Ken is no Neanderthal. He's aware of the network's traditions, its past. He was excited with the takeover. There's still ego nourishment for a businessman to own a television network, you know, to hobnob with people like you, both his employee and a celebrity. But he's a businessman first. He hears of an idea that might lift the whole prime time schedule, at a relatively low cost. Thus, Ann Murrow. A network needs millions of people to watch its programs. If more people will watch her and he can afford her, it might make business sense to get her. And, as one of those who shares that fiduciary responsibility, I can't disagree. Not on taste grounds. The network hardly caters to my taste in any case. I read somewhere recently that in our culture taste has become irrelevant. That's the business as I see it. But I can tell I'm depressing you."

"Yes, you are."

"I regret that. But you're going to be all right. You haven't sacrificed your honor or dignity. Everyone respects you. You've won all the awards. Don't the universities shower you with honorary degrees?"

"Not very grand universities."

Matthews smiled knowingly. "And you've kept some modesty, too. I like that. But there are things you could do that would crown a marvelous career like yours. Like heading a great nonprofit in the arts, or medicine, or some humanitarian cause. Or becoming an ambassador. I'm sure that could be arranged."

"You have to buy your way into those."

"Some, true, but with your name it could be a very attractive appointment. I'd always be happy to put in a word here and there. If you were interested in politics . . . No? I thought not. But, Grant, you're still a young man, with shining prospects before you, glittering prizes, for which all you've done until now may have been the most valuable preparation."

Grant said, "Thanks for all that, but just to be clear: you won't lead a fight in the board to block Ann Murrow? To put it bluntly."

"No, I don't think that's a fitting role for a board member. It's a market, and the market should solve it. If I'm asked what I think of her performance on the grounds of taste, I might find something colorful to say—in private. 'Sleazebag,' I heard one of my grandchildren say recently. 'Sleazebag!' " He chuckled. "Would that fit the bill?"

"What if the market in this case is not good for the health of the democracy?"

Matthews smiled. "Are you asking whether Ann Murrow is bad for democracy?"

"Seriously, if the market keeps driving us to make the news more entertaining, to leave out the boring stuff, to make all politics into theater, ridiculing our institutions, including the presidency, treating it as scandal of the week, as a game, what happens to confidence in the system? To citizen participation? To all the things that make America work, in which journalists are supposed to play an important part?"

"Grant, do you know what I think we're going through? A period of little historical consequence. Of relaxation. Of consolidation. These are not great moments. There is none of the high state drama that attracts the masses. After decades, generations of struggle, life-and-death struggle, at times, the yoke of constant anxiety has been removed; the call to greatness is over. Over for a time, I trust, not over forever. And this time happens to coincide with the enormous leap in communications, the information revolution, most of it driven by business or popular entertainment. It's not surprising that the great bulk of it is trivial. Ordinary people don't feel the need to be as conscientious about the news as they were. You know what I suspect will happen? When things turn serious, the media will pay attention. You saw it during the Gulf War. The people will want to know. There'll be a market for responsible information at the popular level."

Matthews wiped his lips and sat back. "Of course, it could be that the tide has turned for America, that our civilization is on the way out. That's a pessimistic view. If it's the right one, it'll be decades, perhaps generations, before anyone knows whether we've had our heyday and it's the turn of the Chinese, or Asians generally, to supplant us. But I'm sorry to say, as distasteful as it may be, your network's hiring Ann Murrow won't advance or retard that process one jot or tittle."

55

www.hollygo.com

Academy Award performance, y'all! Last night, teevee's own Brenda Starr, in her starring role, doin all that cooin and cuddlin with that poor little Samantha Robbins? The real Hollywood starlet didn't have a chance! They always used to say, never act with children or animals, they'll upstage you. Better add Brenda Starr, darlins! By the way, didn't you love her eye makeup, that little tinge of purple in the corners? Now Princess Di, God rest her soul, could teach a girl a lesson there. Remember those wounded eyes in her great teevee interview? And no screen credit for Clinique?

But back to Brenda and all that eye-waterin stuff. Know what she made me think of? I'll date myself again, but think of Bette Davis in *The Little Foxes*. Sweet as pie but hard as steel underneath?

Such a big hit comes exactly when she needs it. Word is, things movin hot and heavy between Brenda and the biggies at Beige. Stand by for major developments! Don'tcha love it?

"Is that true?" Laurie asked Grant before the morning meeting. "I guess it is. But hot and heavy, I don't know."

"Morning meeting!" Angela called.

"Development in Wyoming. Police have called a news conference for twelve Eastern. We're covering."

Marty Boyle looked smug, as though the news conference, and the Ann Murrow show that had probably inspired it, vindicated him professionally.

Annoyed at the look, Grant said, "Everyone see the Ann Murrow show last night?"

Everyone nodded, or murmured, "Sure did!"

He looked around at the producers, writers, and associate producers—with a few exceptions like Don Evans, most of them under forty—looking expectant.

"I did too. What you thought about it is your own business, but I want to say it is not the kind of journalism, if that's what it was, that we practice. OK?"

There was a hubbub of "OKs" and "Sures," and everyone looked at Marty, then Grant, and back.

Don Evans said, "So should I cancel Samantha Robbins for tonight?" They laughed.

Grant asked, "Anything else happening?" He skimmed the AP budget in front of him and the assignment editor's list of stories they were covering or acquiring from other services.

On a hook-up from the White House press room, Bill Donovan said, "The President's announcing a major new initiative on Medicaid eligibility."

Marty groaned. "Medicaid! Gimme a break! We've been around that sucker a hundred times. And just because they say so doesn't make it a major initiative, Bill. They say that about everything."

Marty putting down his own protégé took Grant by surprise, and he found himself supporting Donovan. "Look, whatever they're doing, it affects millions of people and it's a hell of a lot more important than the news conference in Wyoming. If we're covering that, we can give a couple of minutes to this."

Marty protested, "A couple of minutes!"

Grant said, "Bill, flesh it out a bit more."

Donovan began talking statistics, obviously reading from the White House handout. Despite his authoritative voice, he didn't have the experience to make it a story, to put it in context. He made it sound boring. And Marty was right; eyes around the table were glazing over.

Marty said, "Only way to make that sexy is to carry the announcement today, sound bite of the president, Donovan wraparound, then find some examples out in the field. Come back in a few days with a 'Close to You' piece." He turned to Grant. "OK with you?"

"Sure, fine."

Marty assigned a producer.

Another skirmish won for seriousness.

5 6

Ernie Schmid woke up with an idea in his mind before he remembered he was in the new room. The house, farther out of town, was nicer. The room had a window that looked over a garden, the bed was firmer, and he'd slept well.

But he woke up thinking that if she'd got his letter with the sample photos in New York, she might be planning to get back to him, and if she did get back, what would he have to sell her? Nothing. The security guard had taken it, that strange guy who was still following him around. He'd said nothing was supposed to leave the store, so maybe he'd left the envelope there, like, lying on the counter, somewhere obvious. If Ernie could get back in, he'd see it in a second. Everything else had been put away. If the envelope was there, he'd have the prints and all the negatives, plenty to sell her. Getting back in was simple if the security guy wasn't looking. Unless they'd changed the code. And he'd know that the minute he punched the old code into the keyboard.

Obviously, the old guy couldn't watch the place all the time if he was following Ernie around. And this morning he wouldn't know yet that Ernie had moved last night. He was sure no one had been watching. After he'd called the taxi and taken his suitcase outside, he'd waited in the doorway shadow, standing very still, his eyes searching all the dark places where the guy could be lurking. Nothing. When the taxi came, he jumped in quickly and saw no one as it drove away. So the guy would still think he lived in the old place. Could be waiting there, like yesterday and the day before. And if he was there, he couldn't be watching the shop. If Ernie got to the shop early, like now, right away . . . Bright daylight, and it wasn't even six. He could dress, catch a bus downtown, and be there before seven. Approach cautiously. Check it out. If the guy wasn't watching, slip in, get the pictures and be out and away in a minute. While the guy was still waiting outside the old house. Ernie got out of bed and dressed fast, not worrying about how he looked.

When the bus let him off, he walked a different way to the store, approaching it from the opposite direction. At the corner opening into the alleyway to the back door, he looked carefully at all the doorways. The sun shone right down the alley so brightly it was obvious that no one was hiding on either side. Ernie hustled. With a trembling finger—half-expecting an alarm to go off—he punched the code, and the door opened. He turned to disarm the security system, but the indicator light showed green. It hadn't been reset. He locked the door, turned on the light, and looked around. The counters and work surfaces were completely tidy. No envelope. He turned off the light and opened the door to the front of the shop. Enough daylight through the venetian blinds to see. No manila envelope. He rapidly opened the cupboards under the cash register. Not there. Maybe the guy had put it in the filing cabinets.

Back into the lab room, he closed the door and turned the light back on. He pulled out the file drawers where he'd originally found Anna Malakoff's name. Nothing. Nothing under *M* for Murrow. No sign of anything recently jammed in. The envelope wasn't there. The guy who'd said he was a security guard had taken them, or someone who'd come in since. Now Ernie needed to get out of the store and out of this part of town. He resisted the habit of re-arming the security system. Better leave it as he'd found it. He pulled the door shut and got out of the alley fast.

GRANT: That was fun last night. I'm sorry we had to leave so early.

CHRIS: Elizabeth figured you wanted to watch Ann Murrow.

GRANT: Smart lady! And a great cook.

CHRIS: You did watch?

GRANT: Yes. Did you?

CHRIS: After Elizabeth suggested it, I thought I'd better see what you were watching.

GRANT: And?

CHRIS: I thought I was interviewing *you.*

GRANT: I don't discuss my colleagues' work.

CHRIS: For background?

GRANT: No. Any way you'd use it, the context would point to me. But I did tell our people in the morning meeting that it's not the kind of journalism we practice.

CHRIS: Full stop?

GRANT: Full stop.

CHRIS: Why isn't it your kind of journalism?

GRANT: I think it speaks for itself, and our work does too.

CHRIS: Some people might say it's just a difference of degree. You cover the Wyoming story too.

GRANT: Differences of degree can be wide. Both Americans and Germans were guilty of anti-Semitism; the differences of degree were pretty colossal.

CHRIS: Are you saying Ann Murrow's work is different on that gross a scale?

GRANT (laughs): No. I'm saying differences of degree are important. We all draw lines somewhere in our professional conduct. Most journalists do. By your reputation, I know you do. There are some things we don't stoop to.

CHRIS: And she does?

GRANT: Look, you're trying to tease a harder quote out of me, and I'm not going to say anything more.

CHRIS: Yeah, I was. Anyway, that's fine. How serious are the talks she's reportedly having with your guys?

GRANT: I know there are talks. I don't know how serious they are.

CHRIS: They don't confide in you about such a big move?

GRANT: They've told me they're talking to her.

CHRIS: What would you think about her coming here?

GRANT: Let's put that in the category of Bill Donovan. It's all fluid right now. Before you have to close your story, I'll tell you what I can. That'll save us both a lot of time.

CHRIS: But to follow up for a minute . . . If you say you don't practice her kind of journalism, yet your bosses are negotiating to bring her into your shop, isn't there going to be a major incompatability?

GRANT: I'd rather not speculate about it.

CHRIS: Do they know, Everett Repton and company, how you feel about her work?

GRANT: No comment.

CHRIS: Anyway, big changes may be coming?

GRANT: Let's wait and see. You've got a few weeks?

CHRIS: Maybe. All the speculation about her has our people wondering whether they should move faster with your story.

GRANT: And change the emphasis?

CHRIS: Now, you know the game as well as I do. Anyway . . . let's proceed as we were, and when I'm right on deadline and have to write, I'll come back for what you can tell me.

GRANT: Fine.

CHRIS: OK, changing the subject. I'm curious about your father. What kind of a man was he? What sort of atmosphere did you grow up in?

GRANT: We didn't communicate very well. He was a bitter guy. Wanted to be a writer, a scholar. He thought the literary establishment rejected him because he had only a teacher's education. He taught high school English.

CHRIS: He died quite young.

GRANT: He was forty-eight. He had lung cancer. He took a dim view of my sailing work. And he resented it that everything seemed to come easily to me.

CHRIS: And has it? Was he right?

GRANT: Yeah, he was right. I was pretty lucky. One nice thing seemed to lead to another.

CHRIS: Until . . .

GRANT: What do you mean?

CHRIS: I was wondering whether you feel the tide of good fortune has turned for you.

GRANT: No . . .

(Pause)

(Long pause)

"AND FOR THE first time," Siefert told Elizabeth, "I felt the tiniest crack in his self-assurance."

"But, honey, it's kind of a killer question."

"I didn't mean it that way."

"What did he say?"

"He said *no* sort of automatically, and stopped, and he looked at me as if he hadn't seen me, or maybe himself, before. Then he recovered his normal broadcasting voice and kissed it off with a kind of a laugh. And he went into a long thing about his father."

• • •

WHEN THEY got into bed, Grant told Winona, "He asked me whether I felt the tide of good luck, good fortune, has turned for me."

"That's interesting. Very perceptive."

"It kind of rattled me to hear it asked like that."

"Well, you do think that, don't you?"

"Do I? I haven't put it like that to myself."

"But isn't that what you've been implying these last few weeks? That's how it sounded to me . . . things have turned against you. I couldn't believe my ears when you told me about the facelift. I still can't quite believe it. Worried about Bill Donovan? And that Murrow woman? It's not like you. I've been wondering whether you're a bit depressed."

"No. I'm just . . . I don't know. When I used to feel like this, kind of tied up inside, getting out on the boat or going climbing, something hard and physical, would wash it away."

"So go and do something."

"I think I've had it with climbing. For obvious reasons. And I'm way out of shape for that."

After a silence, Winona said, "You've still got the boat, but you almost never use it."

"I know. Something always seems to get in the way."

"Well, as I tell clients every day, you set the priorities, buster. You're going to take a whole month for the facelift. If that wasn't a priority, you could spend it on the boat."

"The surgery—I hate the word facelift—is a career matter. It's not a vacation!"

"You haven't gone on a real cruise for years. Maybe Sandy would go with you."

Grant lay back and closed his eyes. His heart used to leap at the prospect of taking off on his boat. He'd fall asleep imagining all the details. Now he couldn't find any trace of that excitement. The ketch *Winona,* beautifully maintained, lay on its mooring off their place in Boothbay, and he paid a guy—like himself forty years old—to row out and wash the seagull droppings off the sail covers. What a waste!

He had to get the cosmetic surgery over with. Behind him. And move on.

"I need to make a date with the doctor in San Francisco. All this waiting around, on top of the stuff with Repton and everyone, is bugging me."

"Don't forget we have the White House dinner on Saturday."

"Dumb time to have the Fourth of July, on a Saturday."

"That's not the Clintons' fault."

"Ruins the weekend though, doesn't it?"

"What did you tell Siefert when he asked that?"

"Oh, I laughed it off."

"I'll bet."

"I told him a lot more about Dad than I ever thought I would. He picked up on that."

"He picks up on a lot," Winona said.

"And it all just came out."

"Maybe it's good for you to talk to him."

"Yeah, but I've got to remember he can publish anything I say."

TRANSCRIPT:

CHRIS: I was wondering whether you feel the tide of good fortune has turned for you.

GRANT: No . . .

(Pause)

(Long pause)

GRANT: You want to know about my father? He was an old unreconstructed man of the left. He was smart about Vietnam. In the summer of 'sixty-three, he was grumbling about the stupidity of getting involved after the French had been forced out of Indochina and Eisenhower had the sense not to go in. "We'll only be seen as neo-colonialists," Dad said. "We'll play into the hands of the communists, like the Japanese and the French."

CHRIS: With judgment like that, he'd look pretty smart today.

GRANT: Right.

CHRIS: Why didn't he like your working on sailboats?

GRANT: I think he connected it with my admiration for John Kennedy, and there was a sort of connection. In the two trips to Hyannis I made before the assassination, I felt right at home with the people there. When I saw Kennedy's sailboat on a mooring, I knew I could handle it perfectly well.

CHRIS: So you felt at home there.

GRANT: I did. Of course, the Kennedys lived a life style far richer than most of their neighbors, but in Hyannis it was cleverly subdued. You know, those weathered beach houses, the cute kids, the beautiful women, doting grandparents, ordinary enough cars, all the stuff that looked within reach of most better-off Americans. And that's what they wanted the world to see, the kind of middle-class tip of their enormous hidden iceberg of money.

But Dad was one of those who saw through the ordinariness. His son, budding TV reporter, fell for the publicity image so skillfully managed by the Kennedys. And I thought Dad's personal hang-ups blocked his judgment. He couldn't feel what even Kennedy's opponents had begun to notice by the time he died: JFK made Americans feel good about their country and see the possibility of a future without nuclear war. In fact, he gave us the first glimpse of the world we live in today. He was right, despite Vietnam, and he might have been right there too, if he'd lived long enough to get smart and pull out.

CHRIS: Sounds as if you feel some ambivalence now. Some of your father's views creeping in?

GRANT: Well, it'd be interesting now to talk to Dad, if he'd lived to be eighty-two. All the things that have happened since he died. I'd love to be able to tell him that television made it possible for a second-rate actor to serve two terms in the White House and end the cold war. What can astonish us anymore? I wonder what my son Sandy would have to tell me if I popped back from the dead forty years from now? With my father, the emotional distance between us made me indifferent to whatever he thought or felt.

CHRIS: Have you bridged that emotional distance with your own children?

GRANT: Oh, I think so. Certainly tried.

CHRIS: How would you feel about being so successful if your father were alive?

GRANT: I don't know. Mixed. Proud. Maybe a little embarrassed.

CHRIS: Because you've become as rich as the people your father despised?

GRANT: Maybe envied, too. Look, I'm afraid we've run out of time for this session.

ANGELA SAID, "Grant, noon meeting's started. We need to do the mail, and I've got a lot of calls. Sherman Glass is getting really frantic. Three calls this morning."

"OK. Later."

When he took his place at the table, Marty did a quick recap. "Our producer in Wyoming says they've arrested Scott Woolford, the boyfriend Ann Murrow fingered last night. That's why they've called the news conference."

"So?"

"So, it's the first arrest!"

"Well, I guess we'll report it, Marty. OK?"

"Sure. And just so's you know, we're building a package from there. Maybe the police chief will play, and we've got the two legal analysts lined up for you to interview."

"What have they got to say?"

"Don't know yet. Should have some pre-interviews in a couple of hours. But, hey, what can I say? It's the big story. And it's hard news."

"What else is there?"

"Just the White House thing Donovan pitched this morning. Remember, we decided to kiss that off with a sound bite and come back in a coupla days with a 'Close to You' piece. Right?"

"Right. Do they have any evidence on the boyfriend? Or are they arresting him because Brenda Starr says so?"

"Good question, Grant. Good to ask the experts."

Christopher Siefert was standing quietly in the corner, taking notes. When the meeting broke up, he said, "Angela tells me you're going to the President's Fourth of July dinner. You don't mind if our White House photographer grabs a few shots of you and Winona with the President?"

"No, that's fine."

Marty called out, "Grant, we're ordering from the Afghan place. You want in?"

Grant turned to Siefert. "Are you free for a bite?"

"Sure."

"No, thanks, Marty."

The prospect of talking to Siefert was more congenial than hearing Marty churn the Michelle Robbins story.

"Just give me a few minutes to make some calls."

Siefert said, "Fine. I'll go over and talk to Laurie."

Grant called Sherman Glass.

"What've I got, B.O. or bad breath? Everyone's giving me the cold shoulder. You don't answer my calls. Ev Repton won't talk to me. I can't get to him to pitch the Donovan thing, and until I do that I can't get your contract talks started. I've got to talk to you."

"Just cool it, Sherman. Repton told me. He's up to his ass in talks about Ann Murrow. Got the word from the CEO himself."

"I told you they're serious. I hear she's asking for fourteen million!"

"How do you hear stuff like that, Sherman?"

"You don't believe I've got contacts?"

"I can't believe the people who knew it would tell you that unless they wanted it blabbed around. And why would they want it blabbed around?"

"The usual. Creates more buzz. Ups the ante. Raises the expectations."

"And you're helping them do that?"

"Come on! I'm helping you."

"How in the hell do you figure that?"

"Simple. The buzz about the bucks she's asking raises your value. If she's worth fourteen, you're worth nine or ten."

"Thanks a lot. It was ten a while ago."

"Sure, ten, maybe eleven."

"You just said nine or ten, Sherman."

"But all that's not worth a pinch of shit if I can't reach Repton to talk, so you've got to help me."

"Forget it for now. There's no point while they're going through this. If they hire her to do a magazine strip, the whole thing changes. I don't even know what I'd want to do."

"What do you mean?"

"How do I hang around and do my thing if they're spending millions for a show that will kill it? I mean, how? You're the one who had the scenario. Strip the magazine with a hard news top, and the news show will wither away."

"But not for years. Not for five years. And in those years we pick up fifty million."

"What do you think it's going to be like, working in the same news department, down the hall from that?"

"So she's a pain in the ass! But she's hot. Maybe she'll pump up the ratings and you'll all be better off."

"Sherman, there's no point talking about it until we know what's up."

"Hey, I picked up some dope on the babe you flipped for in Cleveland, Frannie Whitman?"

"What dope?"

"She's loaded. Comes from an old Pennsylvania family. Steel, hardware, defense stuff, you name it."

"And?"

"People who know her in Cleveland tell me she's great. A real pro. And I guess she's going to need an agent."

"She told me she had one, Sherman."

"No shit. Who is it?"

"She didn't tell me that. Maybe Joe Steinman. Why don't you ask him when he's filling you in on Brenda Starr."

Grant hung up, angry. "Tell Chris Siefert I'm ready to go to lunch."

"You'll be a lot of fun to eat with!" Angela said. "Don't forget I've got a pile of mail."

5 8

George White kept a box of disposable rubber gloves like those he'd used when he was a cop handling evidence. With difficulty he pulled a pair over his large hands and removed the prints from the envelope he'd taken out of the safe. Handling them carefully by their edges, he arranged them all on his desk and studied each one. He was aroused, not by the cheap sex, but by the power they represented.

The detective racket was slow. No-fault divorces had cut badly into the work. Sure, the occasional wife still wanted a husband watched; now and then a suspicious husband would hire him. He'd served parents worried about who their kids were hanging out with; fathers investigating the backgrounds of their daughters' fiancés; employers verifying references for executive prospects. So many Americans were rootless now that people didn't have the usual sources for good information, and White could often supply it. It was a living, but the money he had from Steinman, $50,000 plus the $1000 per diems, would double what he could piece together in a year. And staring him in the face were twenty-two- or twenty-three-year-old pictures that could double that again. Maybe more. From people who could easily afford it. There were stories saying she made eight million a year and was looking for more. What in God's name did anybody do with that kind of money? Or deserve it? By getting the pictures back to her, through Steinman, he'd be doing her a favor. Relieving anxiety. Besides, she'd brought it on herself, using her ass like that to get her career started. Not that that was unknown elsewhere, but it was only fair she should pay a little for it. And he'd kept quiet about finding her at it with the press secretary. Even after she became famous. Now was different . . . the supermarket tabloids paid big for stories like this about celebrities. But he needed a story for Steinman.

He could say:

I followed the kid like you said. He switched rooming houses on me but I caught him again going to his mailbox. Guess what? He's been hiding the pictures there all the time. Pretty smart, don't you think? A little risky maybe. But smart. He came out with this envelope. Must've been getting nervous. I followed him. Carefully. He walks almost everywhere except when he grabs the bus to go home . . .

Have to work the rest out to make the story ring true. Like . . .

Mr. Steinman, I got an idea. I left a note in his mailbox telling him I had instructions from the lady to discuss buying the pictures from him. Set a date for him to meet me. Not my office. A hotel lobby. He came. Pretty nervous kid. Scared when he recognized me from the photo shop. I said, Let me see what you've got. We went outside. Place by the river. No one around. Showed me the prints. And, you know, it's the matching set he must have made at the same time, with one print missing, the one that was stuck to another one. I asked him if there were any others. He said no. He couldn't make any more because I'd taken the negatives . . .

And so on through bargaining with the kid, coming up with a figure, and settling it with Steinman. Plausible, maybe, but not such a great idea. Best he could probably say he'd agreed with the kid would be $25,000. But these pictures could be worth a lot more. He needed another story . . .

The kid has the pictures, right? I follow him. He goes to this small magazine office. I wait. He comes out without the pictures. I go in, smooth-talk the guy, who looks like he never had a thousand bucks to his name. What'd the kid get paid? I want to buy them back. I'll go higher. How high? Well, what'd you pay him? He says I'm not going to play that way; how high will you go? I say the kid didn't have the right to sell them. He stole them. They're hot. Get you in trouble. Sell 'em to me, and no questions asked. I'll forget where I got them. Who am I? Someone interested in recovering the pictures. So he says fifty thou. I say that's preposterous. Unheard of. He says there's magazines would pay two or three times that. I say, but they don't buy stolen stuff and wouldn't have the right to publish. Make a long story short, he settles for forty thousand. I pay him out of what you paid me. Cash transaction. No receipts. No paper. So I can send 'em to you for forty thousand plus my per diem, plus whatever you think for my trouble. And that'll be the end of it.

NOT A BAD STORY, considering Steinman wouldn't want to check too hard in case the details got around.

But the story could be better. George studied the pictures some more. If it was known that they existed, maybe they'd be worth more. Wouldn't the price go up? If the word was out, there'd be big boys like the *National Enquirer* sniffing around, maybe with hundreds of thousands of bucks. Not that he'd sell to them. Too risky. Much safer to get Steinman to pay a fair price to keep them out of print. Drive up the price in his mind. And in Murrow's. Need to put the word in the right place so it'll slip out; word that the pictures existed.

In New York. Had to be there, where she'd see it and freak out. The media in New York. And then it was obvious. Go back the same route Steinman had used to find him. Not the rogue cop himself but the network of ex-cops and Larry, buddy of a buddy, half-owner of the club downtown George had visited on his night in New York. Too smoky, music deafening, but one of the places the gossip reporters trolled for titbits among the models and P.R. people. Favors in the past. Remember, I owe you one, OK? That was the way.

59

Leaving the office, Grant said, "In any restaurant around here we'll have a hard time talking. My driver's outside. We can go up to the apartment and have a sandwich there."

"Fine with me." Siefert wanted to see the apartment.

In the car, Siefert said, "I get the impression from that meeting just now that it's harder and harder for you to hold back the tide, because you're a swimmer in the same currents. You can't say no Wyoming story every day, because the Wyoming stories are now the bread-and-butter of all the shows. You can't buck that current."

Grant wanted to say no, no, it wasn't like that. But it was. "As we said earlier, it's a matter of degree. Small degrees make big differences. I correct the steering when I can."

Siefert could hear him sliding into the voice that made even casual utterances sound like public addresses.

"In a sailboat, if you steer one degree off course for an hour, you can be a tenth of a mile wrong. Multiply that hour after hour, day after day, say you were sailing to Bermuda, you could miss it altogether. You could end up in a different country, across the Atlantic. Of course, in practice, in a boat you keep correcting all the time, so the course you actually make good is an average of many little corrections. I try to make little corrections so that we're not totally at the mercy of the prevailing winds."

"But can your corrections keep the ship from ending up in a different country, or are you drifting that way?"

"That's the big question."

They arrived, and Siefert vacuumed details of the apartment into his memory: the elegant entryway, the elevator exclusive to one apartment on each floor, the curved staircase to the second floor, windows above the tree line with views over the park, gracious rooms indicating professional decoration, although understated and relaxed. Elizabeth would know the names of these fabrics and furniture.

Grant led him into the kitchen, a Viking six-burner stove and Sub-Zero refrigerator suggesting its cost. Siefert refused beer or wine for water. Grant took off his jacket and made sandwiches from ham, cheese, and lettuce. Made them well, with Dijon mustard; obviously practiced. Perhaps Siefert had been fantasizing too extravagantly about Grant's wealth, assuming a resident cook or housekeeper.

"Do you have a housekeeper?"

"There's a woman who comes in the mornings to keep the place clean."

Grant carried the sandwiches into the library, which he enjoyed showing off, and told the Barzini story. Siefert had mixed feelings: the room was exquisite, but felt too purchased, too immaculate, a decorator's magazine layout.

"My library is my office, and it's a mess," Siefert said. "Bookshelves overflowing. Books stacked on the floor. Unfiled papers in boxes piled up. How do you keep this so neat? There isn't a book out of place."

"I wish I had time to read them," Grant said unaffectedly, and Siefert thought, You could worry less about keeping it tidy, for one thing. The pristine room made Grant's life itself seem dumbly serene, uncluttered, uncomplicated, so why shouldn't he have time to read?

"And I have a little office upstairs," Grant said, "where I can work."

"May I see it?"

"Sure."

On the second floor they passed bedrooms and more glimpses of Central Park.

"How many rooms do you have altogether?"

"Fourteen. One of the big old apartments. Of course we got it long before prices are what they are now."

Of course, Siefert thought, and now probably worth three or four million. Should check with a real estate agent.

The study had a desk with a computer, some files, and every inch of wall space covered with framed awards, citations, honorary degrees, and photographs of Grant with Presidents and other heads of state. Behind the door were shelves bearing a parade of Emmys and other awards.

"What a collection! I'm curious to know why they're here, where no one can see them, and not in your office."

"It got to seem like showing off, I guess. Even here. Winona asks if I really need to remind myself who I am."

"What's the answer?"

"When I put them up, I guess so. Now, I don't know."

"Teresa Weldon said you have a climbing wall. Do you mind if I see that?"

Grant said, "Oh, sure," in a voice that suggested the contrary, but he led Siefert to the end of the bedroom corridor, past walls of photographs of tanned and happy-looking people on skis, on sailboats, hiking on mountains.

He stopped. "These are my kids. I guess that's the most recent. That's Sandy leading a NOLS group. And that's Heather a couple of years ago."

"Great-looking kids."

"Yeah, thanks. So this is it." They entered a large room containing an exercise bicycle, Nordic Track and gym mats, a ballet barre in front of a large mirror, and a wall covered with sculpted shapes, the upper half angled inward.

Grant touched some of the hand-holds lightly. "I used to use it to strengthen my hands, fingers, wrists, legs, pretty well everything, but I haven't for a while. I'm not in that kind of shape now."

Siefert wanted the climbing discussion on tape, so he eased out, saying, "Thanks, now I know what one looks like," and headed for the stairs.

Grant's mind teemed. So many irritations, unresolved matters clamoring—Ev Repton, Ann Murrow, Bill Donovan, Sherman Glass, Fran Whitman—but he pushed them away. This was the priority, the biggest chance he might get to put the record straight. Mustn't skimp it. Besides, he liked Siefert, his subtlety, his curiosity. It was soothing to talk to him. The other stuff could wait.

Back in the library, Siefert set the recorder running.

TRANSCRIPT:

CHRIS: How long have you got?

GRANT: Let's see. If we leave here at two, I'm OK. Let's say an hour and a quarter.

CHRIS: Good. (Pause) I wanted to ask about some things the others have told me. For instance, Teresa Weldon. I won't quote her. She asked me not to, and I didn't take any notes. She said a couple of things . . . She said in your world if you wanted anything, you got it, when it suited you. It was habit. Everything was possible to you. Talk about that. Do you see yourself that way? Is it a habit that comes from your work, your success?

GRANT: I didn't think I appeared that selfish.

CHRIS: No, she said you were far from selfish, very considerate, but it was the way your world worked. Everything was possible.

GRANT: Uh-huh.

CHRIS: She also said you were so used to people doing what you wanted, you thought you could make anything happen. Another way of saying the same thing.

GRANT: Well, I know what's behind your question. The accident. Tony getting killed. How much it was my fault. I felt it was; I said so at the time. I told Teresa.

CHRIS: She doesn't think it was your fault. It was as much his.

GRANT: But I was the one who pushed it, against his better judgment. We shouldn't have been on the mountain that day.

CHRIS: Tell me what it was like.

GRANT (A long sigh): It was like a nightmare . . . when something awful threatens and you can't make your muscles move to run away. You're powerless. At a certain point I was powerless to do anything.

CHRIS: Can you describe it?

GRANT: The helicopter put us on the glacier seventy-six hundred feet up, just below the four-hundred-foot spire. Tony led all the way, because he was the expert climber and in perfect shape. It was tough going for me, and I was much slower working each pitch after him. If we'd gone at Tony's speed, we'd have made it all the way. There's a good ledge after the fourth pitch, and I badly needed a rest, so we sat there, ate a candy bar, and drank some water while we admired the view. But what had been a nice day was rapidly clouding over, so we hurried to tackle the fifth pitch. I belayed him from an anchor on the ledge, and he climbed the two-inch crack. The wind grew stronger; just standing there handling his rope, I began to get cold, but I didn't want to stop him to put on more clothes. He was getting even harsher wind up higher, and he shouted a couple of times that he was cold. There's a tricky bit where the two-inch crack gives out and a four-inch begins. There's a bolt there.

CHRIS: What's a bolt?

GRANT: Fixed protection. A steel bolt. Somebody had drilled a hole in the rock and screwed it in, with a ring outside to take a carabiner. Tony shouted he was going to tie onto the bolt for a minute and put on some warmer clothes, so I might as well tie him off and do the same. He clipped on and hung there, fishing his stuff out of his backpack and putting it on while I did too. Then he got going again, with me belaying him. Finally he reached the top of the pitch, tied off, and belayed me while I started up, clipping my rope into the protections he'd set. As soon as I got above the ledge and out in the real wind, I knew it was much colder, and just as I got to the fixed bolt, it began to rain. Soon the rain began freezing on everything, making it tough to get a grip. Tony shouted, "It's no good. Too risky. We've got to go down. Fast as we can, but very carefully." He said the bolt looked good, but because I was the heavier one, to be safe I should back it up with another good anchor, and then set up to rappel down to the ledge. He said, "I've got you until you're ready, and when you're down I'll follow."

Where he was, higher up, the mountain top narrowed so the winds were coming at him with no protection; he must have been even colder than I was. And he had to wait. I had trouble getting my numb fingers to work, to unhook the anchor from my rack and set it, tie the sling to equalize the strain with the bolt. Stuff kept slipping out of my grip, and it took an agonizingly long time, and my whole body got colder. I had to clip two carabiners on the sling, then take my rope and feed it through to the halfway point. I was beginning to get scared. I was so cold and so stiff, I worried about making a mistake in setting the rappel device, or getting it confused with the line Tony was belaying. And all that time—maybe half an hour—Tony was stuck there, above me, waiting and freezing. Finally I was ready. I put my weight on the rappel rope, unclipped from Tony's rope, and went down. The icy rain on the rope made it go faster than I wanted, but I made it to the ledge and immediately was out of the worst wind. I signaled to Tony, and he climbed down to the bolt—I don't know how he downclimbed in those conditions—hooked himself on to the rappel, then cleared his own rope and sent it down to me. It was very tough grabbing it with the wind blowing it away, but I got it, pulled it down, and coiled it on the ledge, ready to set the rappel down the next pitch. Tony came down, but when he hit the ledge, I thought he looked only half awake. His lips were blue, and he was shivering violently.

He said, "Can't stay here; we'll lose it. Set the rappel; I'll clear my rope."

He began pulling his rope down, and when I turned to watch him for a second, I realized he hadn't tied in.

I shouted, "Tie in!" And he looked at me with a kind of dawning. "Oh, yeah," he said, but casually, and like a sleepwalker he grabbed a bight of the rope he was pulling down and began tying a figure eight through his harness. I looked away, expecting him to go on and tie himself into the anchor. Then, out of the corner of my eye, I saw him flicking the rope above him to pull it clear, and suddenly he was over the edge and out of my sight. Heart-stopping to me but normally OK, because he'd stop in a few feet. But his rope kept whizzing out until it sprang taut. And then I knew that he hadn't tied in. Only the safety knot in the end of the rappel rope had stopped him by catching in the anchor above us. I grabbed a sling and fixed it around his rope. I was terrified the knot would slip through above and send him crashing down to the glacier. I called, but couldn't hear anything in the wind. I was trembling, shaking all over. I untied enough to give me some slack so I could see over the ledge. Tony was sixty to seventy feet below. He looked unconscious, his body splayed out, his head hanging strangely. I sat back into the ledge and pulled out the radio the helicopter pilot had given us to call him back. My fingers wouldn't move. It took me a long time to make it work and even longer to raise him. He said he thought we'd be calling when the weather turned bad. I said it was an emergency, Tony looked unconscious, maybe badly injured, and I needed help fast.

I crawled back to the edge to look down at Tony and shouted, but he looked inert. I had to get down to him. You can't leave an injured climber dangling like that. I didn't dare try to hoist him up, because I was scared his rope would fray on the rocky ledge. So I had to go down to him. Only thing to do.

I'd already fixed the rappel rope, but I was terrified that I'd make a mistake and fall too, so I checked everything over and over, then forgot whether I'd checked something and had to do it all over again. Finally, I eased off over the edge. I hate a free rappel when you're hanging in space and you can't steady yourself with your feet against the mountain. But there was no choice. My hands were numb on the rope as I inched down and eventually reached Tony. He looked dead. Nobody hangs like that unless his neck is broken. I clipped our lines together and felt for his carotid artery. I couldn't feel any pulse. Even inside his clothes, his neck was cold. There was thin ice on his face and hair where the rain had frozen. His eyes were glassy. I tried slapping him, rubbing his face. Nothing. I swung him around and tried blowing into his mouth. It was cold, like ice. No good.

Then there was nothing to do but hang there with him, the wind blowing us both, wondering if I was going to freeze to death before they came. My body temperature was so low, I had trouble thinking. I tried to get the radio out again, but my fingers were useless. I don't know how long it was until they came. I must have fallen asleep or lost consciousness.

CHRIS: That's a terrifying story. Have you ever told it before like this?

GRANT: I told Teresa. I told Winona. My kids. The police. The people who record climbing accidents. Not publicly.

CHRIS: You must have asked yourself why the better climber, the younger man, had an accident and died, and you survived.

GRANT: Because if he hadn't been slowed down by me, he'd have been off that mountain fast. He was looking after me. It was only three hundred feet or so down to the glacier. He'd have made it. But waiting for me all that time, not able to move and stay warm . . . that did it.

CHRIS: But you risked your life going down to him in those conditions.

GRANT: It was too late. It was Tony who'd risked his life—and lost it.

CHRIS: Tony could have said no. He was the expert.

GRANT: I wish to God he had.

CHRIS: Teresa said you told her you shouldn't have been on the mountain that day.

GRANT: I shouldn't have been on that mountain, period.

CHRIS: Why did you want to be there, if it was so tough?

GRANT: Why do middle-aged guys do all kinds of dumb things? Ask a shrink. Ask Winona.

CHRIS: Maybe because they want to show someone?

GRANT: I think climbing was always to show myself I could do something that was hard to do.

CHRIS: Because everything else came so easily to you?

GRANT: Maybe.

CHRIS: As your father thought?

GRANT: Yeah . . . maybe.

CHRIS: I saw the tape of the rescue at the station in Seattle. It looked terrifying.

GRANT: Sickening. I was so out of it when they came, I didn't notice the news chopper. But I'd got our chopper through the station, so they knew right away.

CHRIS: What did it feel like, watching the tape of your own rescue? Being a news story yourself?

GRANT: Embarrassing, awful.

(There was an angle, Siefert thought: the star newsman's career bookended by two helicopter rescues on camera, Vietnam and the mountain: the heroic, the humiliating. Maybe get the videotapes and blow up stills from each.)

CHRIS: Tell me about the settlement you made for her.

GRANT: It's private. I won't talk about it.

CHRIS: Someone else told me, but Teresa confirmed it. Half a million dollars is the right figure?

GRANT: I know it's your call, but I want to ask you, as a personal favor, not to use it.

CHRIS: She hasn't done anything with it. Just put it in the bank.

GRANT: Did she seem OK?

CHRIS: She seemed fine. She's a nice woman.

GRANT: She is.

CHRIS: You have terrific women in your life: Winona, Teresa . . .

GRANT: Teresa wasn't "in my life." She was Tony's wife. We were all buddies.

CHRIS: Laurie Jacobs . . .

GRANT: Laurie? She's not in my personal life. Just work.

CHRIS: I know, but like Teresa, she's very attached to you.

GRANT: Well, don't imply—

CHRIS: No, no. I didn't mean that. I was thinking that you obviously inspire strong loyalty, maybe devotion's the word. I'm also thinking of Guy, of Tony, and I'm sure there are others. Many people charmed by you.

GRANT: (laughs): Yeah? And some who aren't. I'm sure you've met them too.

CHRIS: Not really. Do you think . . . I don't know how to ask this . . . I wonder whether you left your sense that everything was possible back there on that mountain?

GRANT: Jesus, what a question!

CHRIS: Guy Ferris said before then you'd never doubted yourself, and since then you've been less sure of yourself; you worry about a lot of things you don't need to.

GRANT: Well, maybe. I don't know. But I thought we were going to talk about other things.

CHRIS: Just one final question. How do you think that experience on the mountain has affected you personally, and your work?

GRANT: I don't know. I really don't know. It's hard for me to see any difference.

CHRIS: But you've told me it's a struggle to keep things on course, and it didn't used to be.

GRANT: It's not I who's changed; it's the business.

CHRIS: But using Teresa's phrase, you could make anything happen. You can't do that now?

GRANT: I can't because the whole context of what we do has changed. I've told you that. We've been all over it.

CHRIS: And you're convinced that you haven't changed?

GRANT: Convinced? I don't know. I thought we were dropping this. Talk to Winona. She's the professional therapist. She always has me figured out far better than I do.

60

www.hollygo.com

Thank you darlins for all your e-mails on Brenda Starr. Seems all anyone want to talk about is her comin deal with Beige. The lady herself look like she gone to earth since her Oscar-quality performance with Samantha Robbins. Maybe she slipped off to Canyon Ranch for a little shapin-up for her new bosses, if she decide to switch. Or dropped outta sight for a little cosmetic surgery, though can't be much that gal ain't had nipped or tucked already.

She may be keepin quiet, but believe me, muchachas, every-one else in the business talkin like they got nothin else to do.

Here some of the better titbits.

First at Taupe, where Brenda the big star: you think they wailin and gnashin they teeth because she fixin to leave? You be wrong, sister, you be dead wrong. No, sir! They is gigglin and screamin and dancin on the desks, I hear, at the chance she may be goin. Her network execs may be going ape-shit over losin her, foamin at the mouth thinkin she'll take all that audience over to Beige. But her co-workers, least those who blitzin my e-mail, just delighted, honey. A day without Brenda be like a month in the country, one of them told Hollygo. She make our life a hell around here. Please take her away, they beggin me. Take her anywhere!

But at Beige, what they thinkin about their big coup? They

got the Brenda-Starr-comin-I-better-be-leavin-town blues. I tell you. Nobody got it worse than Gregory Peck, lookin more like the statesman of teeveenews ever day. You watch him on the news tonight, see if he don't look crushed, all the wind taken outta his sails. And he know what that mean, cos he a big-time sailor. Word is he fit to be tied.

Gregory Peck sashay into the editorial meetin this mornin (people tell me everythin) and he say to the assembled news geniuses: "Anyone here see the Ann Murrow show last night?" Everybody, includin the janitor, raise his hand. "Well, that ain't the kind of journalism *we* practice, no how!" says Gregory. I'm so proud of him! Didn't add nothin. Just left it there for them to mull over. Leavin the Power Ranger blushin like a Jersey tomato.

Those Beige folks even speculatin where her office would be and how far away from her they could relocate theyselves. They talk to the Taupe people; they know what to expect.

But you know what so funny about all this? Them networks spendin millions and millions ever year, year after year, fixin who they are in the minds of the public. Hire big advertisin firms to figure out logos or colors or slogans. Millions! And you wanna know the awful secret? 'Course you do, honey! Ain't one person in five really know one network from another. That's why I say Beige or Taupe or Bisque, don't make a dime's worth of differ-ence to me, cos don't make no difference to America. Gregory Peck been waggin them sexy eyebrows at us from the Beige anchor desk for seventeen years now. But go out on the street and ask the brothers and sisters which network he work for? They won't know. And won't care none, neither. Only people care is advertisers, and they hunt with any old dog got the best ratins.

And that's the truth. Don'tcha love it?

61

Everett Repton made Joe Steinman uneasy. Never a hint of anti-Semitism, yet he reeked of it. His aftershave, the silk polka dot tie and matching handkerchief in the breast pocket of his Prince of Wales check suit, the big teeth when he smiled, the watery blue of his eyes behind the oversize glasses, all signaled hostile goy. In New York, they said, think Yiddish, dress Briddish. But Steinman could buy the same suit at Paul Stuart, put the same affected silk hanky in the pocket, order the same Turnbull and Asser shirt from London, splash his face with the same Floris lime aftershave, and still feel centuries of difference between them.

In Repton's presence, Steinman thought of himself as Joey, and hated himself for feeling so insecure. He didn't like Repton, didn't trust him, but he could play him like a dream.

Steinman did not fish, but he knew about it. He could imagine himself casting and hooking and playing a lively trout.

Repton was hooked, but playing coy, the coy goy, now refilling his wine glass with Corton-Charlemagne. This superb Burgundy Steinman had carefully researched but touched only to moisten his lips from politeness, because he did not drink. And he ate at places like Lutèce only to gratify gulls like Everett Repton, who enjoyed it hugely.

"Of course, a deal like this is not something I can decide myself."

"Ev, let me tell you something: don't make the mistake of underestimating your influence," Steinman said.

"No. But we'd better be clear about this. I'll be the ball carrier—and I'm enthusiastic, no question—but I'm going to need network and corporate on board for a deal, for a change as big as this. The kind of money you're talking about. That's just not going to play. Fourteen million is not in the cards."

"Ev, will you listen to me? If you've got a strip with Ann Murrow that brings you big Nielsens five nights a week, first hour of prime time—it's better than football—fourteen million for the star who gives you those ratings would be cheap. I'm probably selling her short, but I'm talking introductory offer, with options for the future."

"You didn't mention options. What options?"

"Maybe stock?"

"We don't do that. Never done that with talent."

"This may be the time to start. Or profit-sharing. Take the average rating for a quarter, or a year, whatever, and bonus up by so much, a percent for every point of improvement on your present rating—"

"You're joking. Nobody's ever done that for news anchors."

"Ev, we're not talking news anchors anymore! We're talking a whole new dimension in information-entertainment television."

Steinman sensed that Repton was struggling to keep his tone cool, skeptical.

"Of course, the big question, for me and for my guys upstairs, is what guarantees that all the pizazz she has on her air now will carry out five nights on our air? Unknown factor, right?"

"But with strong probabilities built in."

"Maybe yes, maybe no. It'll be a gamble. Do the kind of people who like her now want to see the same stuff five nights in a row? We have no experience of that. The other thing is what the network will have to bump."

Steinman noticed the *will*, not *would*.

"Some of our shows are well-established hits and doing great."

Steinman said, "Ev, you're a great persuader. I'll bet you were a great debater at college—Princeton, right?"

"I did some debating—"

"—and a terrific negotiator. It's why you're where you are. But you're focused on news. I've studied your prime time schedule. I have my own research. Nothing you've got brings in so much audience, eighteen to forty-five, so inexpensively, with network-owned product, and sells so much advertising, and at premium rates, as Murrow does. It's there in the figures. The other thing, unprecedented in the business, it gives Everett Repton, president of the news division, control over five more hours of prime time, the keystone hours. And a major source of network profit. Think what that does to the news division? Up there with sports. Up there with the entertainment guys on the coast, and you'd have more owned product than they do."

Repton sipped his Burgundy and wiped his lips. Did his hand tremble slightly?

"Well, Joe, I've told you I'm enthusiastic. Now I'll have to see what the reaction is and analyze it myself. It means a whole different budget structure for the news department to produce five new magazines a week, and I also have to figure what to do with our own magazine."

"It's dead. I'd kill it." Steinman said.

"Come on! It's a fine show and profitable."

"You know," Steinman said, as if he'd just thought of a whole new slant, "I think you should meet Ann herself. Hear what she has to say about it. You'll be swept away by her enthusiasm."

"Of course I'd like that, before this goes much further."

"Done! I'll fix it up. I'll get some dates and call your assistant. We could do dinner, just meet for a drink, a lunch. Whatever. She's incredibly busy—she's had to take the Concorde over to England for a few days—but she'd make this. She's dying to meet you. She thinks you're the best news head in the business."

"Where did she pick up that idea?"

"Ev, since you're going to be dealing with Ann, never be surprised at what information she picks up, who she talks to, who she can get on the phone in a minute, who she socializes with . . ."

"Oh, I know, I know. As they say, she's a bombshell."

"Bombshell does not do her justice. Believe me, I've been looking after her interests for nineteen years. This lady is a phenomenon of our time. She's like those women who made the wheel of history turn, Helen of Troy, Cleopatra—"

"You're going to say Joan of Arc?"

"That's amazing! I was! I know, it all sounds like agent talk, my client's the greatest stuff—sure! But you're a very smart man. Don't take my word for it. Meet Ann, talk with her, get to know her."

"What's happening at her place? Why are they sitting on their hands? It's out that she's talking to us, isn't it? Why aren't they doing something to keep her?"

"Well, of course they are. They're not dumb. They know what they could be losing."

"Where are you with them?"

"We're negotiating."

"Same deal. Five-night strip?"

"Same deal."

"But if you can get it there, why come and offer it to us?"

"Can I be honest with you? I mean confidential? No leaks?"

"Yes."

"We're not sure they have the imagination or the boldness of heart to do this. We think you have."

"What's the timetable with them?"

"No deadlines. I mean, she's got six months' contract time to go, and it can extend after that. No pressure."

"Why didn't they start negotiating a long time ago?"

"Frankly, we didn't want to."

"Have they made an offer?"

"That's getting a little close to the bone for me to discuss. But after last night's ratings, I think they'll be beating down the door."

"I need to know what kind of time pressure I'm under to come up with our offer."

"I'll tell you what. Take your time. Take a few days. If it gets down to the wire with them, I'll let you know."

"A few days isn't much time."

"Do what you need to do, OK?"

"OK. Thanks for a great lunch. Really terrific."

"Oh, tell me one thing, Ev. I'm curious. I read all this speculation. What's happening with Grant Munro?"

"Well, nothing. What do you mean?"

"Oh, I just mean the rumors. I'm wondering what your plans are for . . . let's say, future investment?"

"In fact, I'm about to get into that. I have to find out what Grant wants to do. But Ann is my number one priority."

"I see." Steinman got up and held Ev Repton's chair before the waiter could reach it.

Walking downstairs, Steinman said, "Hey, I just thought! Are you going to the White House Fourth of July dinner? Because Ann's going to be there. Chance for you to meet."

"No, I'm not going."

"Oh, OK." Steinman knew how to play Everett Repton.

As they came into the sunshine on Fiftieth Street, a motor-driven camera whirred, and Repton saw a photographer by the curb, taking their picture.

"Jeez," Steinman said, "I wonder who that's for?" A somewhat rhetorical question, since his office had tipped off "Page Six."

"Phone calls or mail first?" Angela asked when Grant got back to the office.

"Who are the calls from?"

"Sherman Glass again. *New York Post, Variety, USA Today*. They all want to talk about Ann Murrow. Is she really coming here?"

"Maybe. They're talking to her."

"That is gross!"

"Give me a minute to look at the wires, and then I'll do mail. And ask Laurie to come over."

The wires were re-topping the Wyoming story with the news conference announcing an arrest warrant for actor Scott Woolford. Grant flipped his remote control through the all-news cable channels. The ever-ready legal pundits were already chattering away. He stopped on a replay of Woolford's lawyer reacting in L.A. to a forest of mikes, and clicked on the sound. The lawyer was preening in the attention, Johnnie Cochrane sugarplums dancing in his head.

"No! We protest this outrageous injustice. My client was not on the Robbins ranch at the time the little girl was killed."

"So where was he, Brad?" Using the lawyer's first name, a reporter already angling for the personal relationship he might need. "Where was he?"

"Scott was on private business in the Los Angeles area at the time."

"What private business, Brad?"

"My client would prefer not to disclose that at this time."

"There's talk he's been seeing the actress Natasha Rusoff. Was he with her?"

"My client wishes to keep his private life out of this."

"Have he and Samantha split up?"

Questions about Woolford's dating, sex life, recent whereabouts, and current movies crescendoed until the lawyer waved his arms.

"That's all now, ladies and gentlemen, please! We have protested to the Wyoming court over this wholly unwarranted action against Scott Woolford. We are preparing legal action to reverse it. It's a disgrace to the American justice system to have this awful tragedy besmirched with this trial by media. Thank you."

A chorus of shouted questions as he turned away: "When will he turn himself in? Today? Have you told the police who he was with? When did he leave the ranch?" And the channel switched back to a pair of young anchors clearly stimulated by the excitement, recapping what Grant had missed. The lawyer had said the actor would comply if forced to by the court, but the warrant was being challenged and he had not yet surrendered to police. The anchors promised frequent updates and went to commercial with a bumper showing adorable Michelle Robbins and the caption *American Tragedy*.

"Jesus!" Grant muttered.

Angela said, "So what about the mail?"

"OK."

"This just came. Brunch at Katharine Graham's on Sunday after White House dinner."

"Sure. We'll just get a later shuttle back."

"I have your tickets, the White House cards, and the reservation confirmed at the Four Seasons. I'll give you that Friday night. But to order a car in Washington, I need to know what shuttle you're taking."

"OK. Let me check with Winona."

"And you'll keep the same car on call for the White House and the brunch Sunday."

"Fine."

"OK. Committee to Protect Journalists. Annual dinner. Will you be on the committee and will you speak? The other anchors will."

"Sure, I usually do, that's fine. Mark it in the diary."

"Yale Political Union. Talk to their members in your office. One hour. A Wednesday morning, November. You said no last year, but told them to ask this year, so they're asking."

"Oh, OK."

"League of Women Voters. Meeting Washington, October nineteenth. Will you moderate a panel?"

"No. No, nicely."

"Professor in Illinois, writing a book on television news, wants to interview you. Any time convenient?"

"OK, I guess. Find a date."

"Man in Texas, doing Ph.D. Will you write a few pages on—"

"No."

"You didn't hear what about."

"I don't need to. Let him write his own crummy thesis."

"Chairman FCC, coming to New York, inviting you, other news anchors to breakfast, July twenty-third. You're free."

"What's it about?"

"Doesn't say."

"OK."

"Japanese ambassador to the UN. Lunch for visiting Japanese editors. July seventeenth. You're free."

"I'll skip that."

"That agent for the cruise lines again. Do you want to be their guest, your choice, anywhere in the world, ten days? First-class air out and back, you and guest, and you give one lecture."

"When is it?"

"You can choose. Sounds dreamy to me."

"Sounds dreamy until you get cornered for ten days with jerks who want to tell you about the liberal conspiracy to slant the news."

"So, no?"

"So, no thanks. Maybe when I'm retired."

"Oh, when's that?"

"Don't get your hopes up. Not until you're married with three kids and a dog in Englewood."

"That'll never happen."

"Anything else?"

"Bunch of benefit dinners."

"Give me the stack. I'll look through them."

Laurie stuck her curly head in the door. "I've got a pile of calls about Brenda Starr. They want to talk to you. Did you really say this morning we don't practice her kind of journalism?"

"Yes."

"Well, it's on Hollygo already."

"Goddamn it!"

"They all want confirmation and more quotes."

"Say I'm not talking to anyone now. I'd blow my stack even more. Just say I have no comment."

"OK, darling, I'll pull up the drawbridge and scurry up to my room in the tower. Any more about Brenda?"

"Nothing."

"A little bird told me her agent, Joseph Steinman, and Ev Repton had lunch today at Lutèce."

"No kidding?"

"Can I get serious a minute?"

"Sure. Sit down."

Laurie drew a chair close to his desk. "Seriously, if they make a deal to bring Brenda over, would you stay here?"

"Seriously, if Ann Murrow comes here . . ." Grant leaned back in his swivel chair.

Marty came in, big and breathless. "We can get an interview with Woolford! Down the line to L.A. You OK for a pre-tape?"

"I don't want to interview him."

"You mean, get someone else to do it?"

"I mean, I don't want us interviewing him."

Marty was shocked. "Grant, nobody's talked to him. He's in hiding. They want to talk before he surrenders. Our exclusive. But we got to say yes right away. We don't, they'll go with another network. Come on, Grant! It's news!"

"I don't want us to play this cheap game! It's all manufactured shit."

"Grant, please, just listen a minute, OK? I know you don't like the story. We keep sparring about it. But this is big. We need it. This is the game we're in. We gotta go for it. How're we going to stay competitive if we don't play the same game everyone else is playing?"

Grant looked at Laurie, who for once was not smiling. The moment crystalized everything. In one moment. One decision.

"Don't interview him!"

"I don't believe you're saying this!"

"Don't interview him. Understood?"

"Yup. But I'm gonna have to go to Ev Repton on this one. It's too important, Grant. I can't work like this. We're in the news business. This is the hottest news of the day."

"It's not news!"

"We'll get creamed by the opposition, because they'll grab it in a second. When you start being the show that doesn't get the biggies, you don't get offered the next time. And then you're the show that doesn't get it—period! I'm going to Ev."

"Go ahead. My contract says I have editorial control."

"And mine says I'm the executive producer. If the ratings go to hell, it's my ass on the line!" His face was so red, it obscured his freckles. Marty stormed out.

"Wow!" said Laurie, letting out her breath. "You were great! I loved it!"

"Better forget you heard it."

"I'll remember it the rest of my life! This office was like an electrical storm."

Don Evans came in, smiling. "Hail to the Chief! Everyone heard it out there. Great stuff!"

Angela scurried in as though nothing had happened. "Are we going to get to the phone calls?"

"Just a minute." He dialed Ev Repton's extension. "It's Grant. Important. Let me talk to him. Yeah, well, let me talk anyway. Hi. You talking to Marty? Yeah, yeah, I know. OK, fine. Thanks." He put the phone down. "We don't interview Scott Woolford."

Laurie clapped, and Don Evans smiled. "Great moments in journalism and You Were There!"

But a small voice in Grant's head whispered: Maybe that wasn't the right decision. He could hear Marty saying, "This is the game we're in."

Angela returned with a handful of pink message slips. "I've got sixteen."

"Give all the newspaper people to Laurie. She'll call them back. I'll take the rest."

But first, after Angela left, he took out his wallet and removed the card with Dr. Friedland's number in San Francisco. For privacy he had not put it in the Rolodex on his desk.

"Hello. I thought maybe you'd dropped the idea."

"No, I just needed to sort things out. I'm looking at my calendar. Would you be able to do it, say, the seventh of August?"

"Let me check. No, the seventh is full, and the sixth, and the fifth. I have a morning free on the third."

"Fine. Let's settle on that."

"All right. I'll put it down. But we need to talk about it more, and I'm busy right now. When can I call you?"

"I'd prefer to call you later. Just give me a time."

He'd have to tell Winona that he'd set the date. And send memos to Marty and Repton and Bryce Watson, announcing his vacation dates. And tell Guy and Maria Luisa. August third would give him through Labor Day to recover.

He went though the program on automatic pilot. Marty had constructed the Wyoming story in a manner that seemed to advertise No Woolford Interview. With Grant, before and after the show, Marty kept a pouty silence.

6 3

www.hollygo.com

This gotta be the most popular web site goin, things comin so hot and heavy, hollygo can't hardly keep up with the traffic. They steamin, chile. They hittin my site like crazy! More'n I can say for my sex life, chiquita. Ever since hollygo zoomed up to critic of major importance in the world of teeveenews, ain't had no time for nuthin. And I mean nuthin.

So here goes, chérie! (That French for darlin, stupid.) To put it real simple, so's y'all can understand, things is *steamin* at Beige!

First off, freshen your lipstick, girlfriends: it's PRINCIPLE time in journalism. Like the announcers say, the heartwarmin story of one man's lonely fight against the forces of greed and evil, one courageous man's struggle to bring back the wholesome values of yesteryear! You thought the only teeveeman hung up on principle these days was the Bus Driver over at PBS, the Public Bus

Station? Wrong, honey. A trusted informant tells me old Gregory Peck *absolutely refused* to interview Hollywood's Scott Woolford, now co-starring with Samantha Robbins in teevee's Sex Crime of the Century. Woolford wanted to talk before he went to jail? Well, Gregory Peck refused as A Matter of Principle! The Matter of Principle was that Woolford was fingered last night as prime suspect by fearless crime reporter Brenda Starr over at Taupe. You think Gregory Peck gonna make Brenda look more legit when she might be bout to take over Gregory's Beige network? Yeah, honey, rumors at boilin point that Brenda goin to slip the surly bonds at Taupe, and Beige gonna hire the Blond Bombshell for a five-night strip (no, not what you think, darlin!), that is five magazines, Monday to Friday. Only thing stripped there is da greed, baby!

But you live by principle, you gonna die by principle be my philosophy. (Y'all ever hear of a black drag queen with philosophy? No! Attitude? Plenty!) Others ain't so particular.

Here the scene reported to Hollygo in the Beige newsroom while Gregory Peck is off in the studio doin "The Evening News." No one ain't hardly watchin Gregory, cos all eyes is glued to the other monitors to see which net will stoop to do the Woolford interview. His lawyer was shoppin that dude around this afternoon like a two-bit whore. Sure nuff, up he pops with Grecian Formula on the Bisque "Nightly News," sayin he willin to take a DNA test to prove he not the killer of little Michelle Robbins. Said he loved that chile like she was his own daughter. And he deeply resent the foul insinuations certain teevee people been broadcastin about him. "Certain teevee people" means Brenda, naturally. Sensation in the Beige newsroom! Power Ranger sayin', "And *we* could have had that! Dammit, *we* could have had it!"

Just so no speck of doubt is left in any the dirty minds out there in teeveeland, Grecian Formula had a brace of legal eagles spell it out for us. Very dignified, very serious, he skillfully drag out of the lawyers what they clearly pantin to tell him: a DNA test means comparin Scott Woolford's semen with that found in the murdered child. Got it? And this was network news, muchacha. Imagine what they sayin on the tabteevee!

Don'tcha luv it?

64

Grant was tired of thinking about it, but he had to face Winona. As it used to happen in his parents' house, even in this grand apartment unpleasant talks took place in the kitchen.

Always so calm and rational, Winona was near tears. "I was sure all along you'd change your mind. Don't you see there's an enormous gap between your perceptions and everyone else's? Doesn't that make you wonder? I mean, *Guy* called me!"

"Yeah, I thought he would," Grant said.

"Because he cares about you. As I do. He said, 'You've got to talk him out of it!' Well, I haven't tried to do that . . ."

"Sure you have."

"Only a little. But what do you think about that?"

"About Guy?"

"No! About everyone else, including me, thinking you look great for your age. But you—you alone—are obsessed with the idea that you look too old."

"Obsessed? Anyway, it isn't *everyone* else."

"You said even the doctor in San Francisco thinks you could pass for much younger. And she makes her living doing cosmetic surgery! At least she sounds honest."

"And there's the audience survey stuff I showed you. Younger audiences think I look old."

"Oh, honey, for heaven's sake! Of course they do! We look old to

Sandy and Heather. It's natural. They're in their twenties, and we're nearly sixty. Of course we look old to them!"

"But that's the demographic the networks are losing, *our* show is losing."

"And you think you're going to keep people in their twenties and thirties watching you because you get a facelift? I know you have more sense than that. I've never seen you like this. I think it's irrational. Like Bill Donovan. You actually threatened to resign over him, and you've never done that over anything else, over journalism issues—"

"Donovan *is* a journalism issue!"

"Even when you were outraged over the O.J. coverage, or the White House last winter, you didn't march into Repton and threaten to quit. I think you're letting this distort your sense of values. Everyone, you know, has periods of irrationality, when they feel under stress. It's not uncommon in men your age, any more than in women, and that's an old story."

Grant was grimly silent.

Winona sounded defeated, a rare state for her. "What do you feel like eating?"

"I don't care. I'm worn out. I came back here for lunch with Chris Siefert and made a sandwich, to have a quiet place to talk."

"I saw the plates."

"He's asking if you'll talk to him alone."

"Oh, I suppose so, if you think it's important. But how am I going to avoid talking about all this—the facelift and your anxiety about age?"

"You don't have to bring it up."

"And if I don't, I'll be hiding the most important thing going on with us. How are the changes in television news affecting your husband? It's that! What does he feel about younger competition, like Bill Donovan? It's that! In my work, I don't have to lie. I don't want to lead that kind of a life."

"It isn't lying."

"It's dishonest."

Grant sighed and turned away, but Winona continued. "If he asks about our vacation plans this summer, it's still *that!* Don't you see? To support you in this I have to come out to California, where it's blistering hot in August, when I'd much rather be in Boothbay."

"Well, if it suits you, *be* in Boothbay!" Grant said sharply.

Winona looked at him carefully. "I'm getting the feeling there are things going on that I don't understand."

"Like what?"

"I talked to Teresa. She said Siefert asked her about the money. What money?"

There was a long silence. Then, lamely, Grant said, "I sent her money after the accident."

Amazed, Winona asked, "Why?"

"I felt bad about her, about Tony, about . . . everything."

"It's very strange you didn't tell me. Why was that?"

"I asked her to keep quiet about it."

"But why didn't you tell *me?*"

"I don't know."

"I guess you did sleep with her, after all."

Another silence.

"I did. A couple of times."

"Oh, honey!" She began to cry. "How much did you give her?"

Grant said it as quietly as he could. "Half a million dollars."

"My God! What? And how many times did you go to bed with her?"

"Twice."

"Well, that's some rate! Damn it. Damn it!"

"Of course the money wasn't for that."

"Oh? And how would I know that? You're only telling me now, about both things together."

"I felt so awful about Tony. And her. I couldn't think of anything else to do. The money was something to do. I went up to see her. She refused the money. She was in a terrible state. I tried to comfort her. I stayed talking to her very late, drinking some wine. When she calmed down, she got amorous. She said she'd always wanted to make love with me. So we did. And again the next day. And then I left. I haven't seen her since then."

"How long ago?"

"About a year and a half. In the fall after the accident."

"And you sent her the money anyway? Half—a—million—dollars?"

"I felt so goddamned guilty. I'd taken her husband away!"

"I *wondered* whether the facelift had another meaning. Is that it?"

"It has absolutely nothing to do with it. I told you I saw her eighteen months ago. Not since. What happened then happened. I'm sorry about it. But it was all over the weekend it happened."

"I can't eat anything tonight," Winona said, and abruptly left the kitchen, leaving Grant dazed, incredulous. In two minutes his emotional life had been turned inside out. He had blurted out what he'd intended never to tell—because he did not wish to hurt her, because it was in the past and didn't matter, because it wasn't important enough to cause such damage. He couldn't remember when they'd last had a fight. He could hear parts of this conversation repeating themselves, more painful with each repetition.

He went to the pantry, where they kept drinks, took ice from the icemaker and poured a Scotch, then moved into the library and sank wearily into the inviting leather sofa. The Scotch when he sipped was still raw, undiluted by any melted ice. His eyes fell on the shelf of his father's books. He could hear his father saying, contemptuously, "Women!" Grant didn't feel that way. He was sad and exhausted.

Again, as on the night before his flight to California, he felt the presence of his father, enveloped by unfamiliar sympathy for him; a pain in the soul both paternal and filial, for the man who had left the world so much younger than Grant was now. The emotion seemed to dissolve the kernel of harsh memories that had constituted his father's image in the thirty-five years since his death, dissolving Grant's indifference to the pain of being so much less in the world's eyes than in one's own; feeling at this moment quite the reverse; so much less in his own eyes than in the world's.

How stupid he'd been to keep the money a secret from Winona, fearing disclosure would lead precisely where it had in these past few moments. He hadn't slept with Teresa out of sudden compassion; he'd always been tempted, and Winona knew it, and he knew that she knew. And, as became clear that weekend in Seattle, Teresa knew. He thought he had since wiped it out by putting it behind him, the distance erasing the guilt, until it erupted tonight. He was not used to such direct emotional exchanges. They were too dramatic, too much like actors overacting. Their marital style had always been light, good-humored, with the deep feelings secure and understood.

He wanted to explain to Winona, tell her not to be hurt. This shouldn't be something that hurt her. It was so as not to hurt her that he had kept quiet . . . but all he could imagine was that the farther he waded into such efforts to dispel it, Winona's skepticism would grow deeper.

In this mood he finally went to bed. He found her asleep, or pretending to be, facing away from him. For the first time in years, they went to sleep without speaking or touching.

65

Siefert awoke feeling the warm haunch of Elizabeth against his thigh, and he slid a grateful hand along her hip, his fingers now more aware of her finely textured skin. They had turned off the air conditioner and opened the window. He could hear summery morning traffic on Central Park West and the rumble of the subway. The sweet texture of the morning and of her sensuous presence rose in him, making his caress a trifle more determined; but she was deeply asleep, and he desisted.

His need wasn't urgent; indeed, there was satisfaction simply in knowing it had returned and could be satisfied. He related that directly to the women around Munro.

Elizabeth was still lying as she had been when they'd fallen asleep, with him curled around her.

Yesterday he'd been considering how to frame his understanding of Grant Munro. It was hard to find metaphors for the hero who lets things slip away, the affectless hero, the man whom no experience touches deeply. Even Tony's death and Grant's professed guilt. There was stoicism that could endure great pain, and there was behavior that looked stoic but harbored no pain; in fact, seemed inoculated against feeling.

Something there to pursue. He liked the affectless anchor hero, marching through all humanity's woes untouched; richer, more celebrated, adjusting his own standards with equanimity; complaining but ultimately accommodating.

Did anybody ever quit, he wondered? Did any of these guys ever tell their networks to stuff it? The anchor did that in Paddy Chayevsky's *Network,* but in real life? Principled resignation was not part of the culture, any more than in Washington. Remember McNamara, bewildered when reporters asked: But why didn't you resign?

The phone rang on Elizabeth's side; she answered and passed him Dick Schoenfeld.

"Sorry to call you there, but I got the machine at your apartment."

"No, it's fine. What's up?"

"I hate to do this, but I'm in a bind. The Ann Murrow story's getting bigger every minute. I'm worried we'll get blind-sided by some big announcement, and I need options. I want you to drop Munro for now and crash on Murrow."

"Jesus!" Siefert said.

"I know, I know, but what am I going to do? We'll look pretty dumb if the biggest story in TV news breaks over the weekend, and we're committed to a profile of a has-been."

"He isn't a has-been. He's an important player."

"You know what I mean."

"I forbear to remind you who made the assignment."

"Forget the forbearance! I reminded myself already."

"And, believe it or not, Munro's getting really interesting. Good story. The whole TV news revolution personified in one bewildered guy."

"Yeah, that's the piece I'd hoped for. Maybe you can stitch some of it into the Murrow piece."

"Yeah, maybe."

"But you've gotta hustle for me, Chris. I need a crash profile on the lady by Saturday night, absolute deadline, reading as if we'd known all along and had planned it. OK? I've got a back of the book cover on changing patterns of home ownership, and I can hold the space until Sunday morning if necessary. We can decide which cover to go with, depending on how it breaks."

"Guts ball!"

"Now I've gotta find some sexy pictures of her."

"OK, I'll give it a try."

"You're the one who suggested doing her instead of Grant Munro, remember?"

"Yeah, so I did."

"If you could wangle an interview with her, even better. At the least we could run it in a box."

"I've been trying while working on Munro, but no luck. Even her agent won't talk to me."

"Maybe he'll talk if she's the story."

66

When Grant awoke to find the bed empty beside him, his memory instantly reproduced the scene of the night before, and the sick feelings it had left in him returned.

He had to do something to repair it before they both left for work. He got out of bed and met Winona coming into the bedroom with two mugs of coffee.

"We'd better talk this out a bit, and it's easier for me before I get dressed. Here." She put a mug on his bedside table, carried the other around to her side, and got into bed. So did he.

He said, "Did you sleep?"

Winona said, "After a long time. I heard you come to bed. When you fell asleep, I was really mad that, after all that, you could just doze off with a clear conscience and I couldn't. So I went to Heather's room and took a Halcion."

"I didn't have a clear conscience. I felt terrible about it, but I guess I was exhausted."

"I hear this kind of thing from clients every day. Every day stories like this, and I see all the raw emotions. But of course I don't *feel* them. My job is to help them deal with the emotions and get on with their lives. Usually by the time I see them, things are bad, and undoing the situation is very difficult, sometimes impossible. So—since this is what I do—I've been trying to think what my approach would be if I were a client, or we were, as a couple. One of the first things I would ask me, as a client, would be: Do you still love your husband?"

"And the answer would be?"

"Oh, of course the answer is yes. And I would ask him whether he loved her."

"And the answer would be yes, of course."

"And I would say: That's good. I would ask me: Do you want to go on living with him? And I would say: Of course, then ask whether he wants to."

"Of course."

"So then I'd say, if you both want that, we have to work on it. Are you willing to help us find out why communications between two people who love each other broke down so badly and do what we can to restore them? Right?"

"Right."

"I'm not kidding. When I go to the office I'm going to be doing stuff like this all day. But I give the clients hours and hours of attention.

We rarely pay that much attention, you and I, to what the other thinks and feels."

"You're saying we have to."

"I am."

"Well, I agree."

"I've been thinking this morning about what you told me last night, and how I would have felt if you'd told when it happened, if you'd asked my advice about giving her money, at least. You were unlikely to ask my advice about the other, which I always suspected, anyway."

"What would you have thought about the money?"

"I don't know. It's strange. I want to say it's not the amount. But it *is* the amount. It is so large, and that it could be so big, and that you would think to give so much, and could afford to give so much—I'm not questioning that—but the amount itself reveals how distorted our values have become, that we can deal—calmly, even emotionlessly—with a sum of money that would be earthshaking for most people. It isn't the money; it's the warped values that so much money brings—and, inevitably, what you go through to *get* so much money. And that brings us right back to where we are. You're the prisoner of those values, or you'd never consider the facelift thing; and I'm the prisoner, too, because of jealousy of you, insecurity about my own aging, attractiveness, all that. Do you see at all what I mean?"

"Yes, I do."

"It's not that you slept with her. It's that you don't sleep with me very much anymore . . . and all that."

"I know."

"So we've got a lot to work through. Last night I felt we were coming apart; that after all these years I didn't know you anymore. I'm worried you don't know yourself right now. You'll go out to San Francisco and do this and really regret it later. I know the strain you're under. But how about we don't let it destroy the marriage. OK?"

"OK. I agree."

"Unless you're planning more compassionate sex with Teresa?"

"I am not. I told you last night. It's over."

"What about other Teresas lurking in the wings, more acts of charity pending?"

"There are none."

"What about this lady in Cleveland?"

"Nothing."

"Then you may kiss the bride, although she hasn't brushed her teeth."

After she got dressed, Winona said, "I'll talk to Chris Siefert. I can fake it on the facelift."

"That's great. Thank you."

"I really liked him and Elizabeth. I'd like to have them over."

Grant said, "Look how the *Times* is playing the Woolford story! Front page, two columns. I turned that interview down. It's made real news."

"Because the *Times* prints it?"

"I wondered right afterward whether it was the right decision. Marty kept saying: This is the game we're playing. We've got to play it."

"What is real news anymore?" Winona asked.

"Good question."

"Sorry, got to go. Friends?"

"Friends."

"See you tonight. I love you."

"I love you too."

FROM THE office Grant called Siefert about Winona.

"Hey, really sorry. I was going to call. Dick Schoenfeld hauled me off your story for now. I've got to crash on Ann Murrow. It's lousy, but the news is pushing us. You know what it's like."

"Sure," Grant said, hardened fellow professional.

"Since I've got you, you said you'd talk about her when I got on deadline, so what can you tell me?"

"What d'you want to know?"

"Crucial question: Is Everett Repton going to sign a deal with her, and when?"

"I honestly don't know. I need to ask him myself."

"From all the speculation, it sounds imminent."

"I know."

"He's not taking any calls, and she's overseas. Do you think you'll know more later today? I mean, if you're going to talk to him yourself?"

"Maybe."

"Can I check back later and find out?"

"Sure."

"Is it true you refused, on principle, to interview Scott Woolford last night?"

"I don't know about principle, but I did refuse. Where'd you hear it?"

"Hollygo. I'm not on the Internet, but a researcher has downloaded her stuff for me."

It was stupid, childish to feel so crushed. As a reporter, Grant had done this often; dropped a subject he'd courted avidly because the news dragged him elsewhere; feeling the exhilaration of that imperative. Sorry, but something else has come up. He knew it well, yet he felt like a jilted date.

Then Sherman Glass.

"Hey, Grant, things must be pretty hot over your way!"

"You're the one with the hot sources. What's your buddy Steinman got to say about my future?"

"The way I see it, not a cloud in your future. Blue skies. Murrow will give your whole place the lift it needs. Make them stop penny-pinching the news department, your show . . ."

"So you think the deal's set? What do you know?"

"I guess it's set, or as good as set."

"You guess or you know?"

"I don't know for dotting *i*'s and crossing *t*'s, for God's sake. But they've gone quiet. And when negotiators go quiet, it's a sign they're there. I bet we'll have an announcement before the weekend. Anyway, I called for something else. Could be a whole new thing for you."

"Like what?"

"Like CNN."

"Oh, come on!"

"No, listen to me. Sure, they've been sniffing around before, but this is different. They see it a different way now. They know they can't buy one of you guys with a conventional offer—"

"You remember what they said, Sherman? They actually said it. It's easier to buy a big-name anchor to boost their numbers than to start another Gulf War. They actually said it."

"Sure, but then they found it's not so cheap. I've been talking to them—"

"Who told you to do that?"

"Sometimes I have to take the initiative."

"Did you initiate it or did they?"

"They did, and me a little."

"Jesus Christ!"

"And here's the deal."

"Sherman, there isn't any deal!"

"No, but here's what the deal could be: a totally unique financial package that would make networks look like pikers."

"Sherman, knock it off! I don't want to hear it!" Grant slammed down the phone. Whatever the surface bullshit, Sherman's subtext was clear: Murrow's arrival was not good news for Grant.

And that looked even more certain after he talked to Ev Repton.

Although none was visible, there was an air of champagne and congratulatory flowers in Ev's office. Repton's face was flushed, exultant.

"I've been neglecting you, and I apologize. I know we have an agenda, your gal in Cleveland, and I want to get to that, and I want to get to Sherm Glass on the rest of the issues. But, believe me, it's been too hectic. The biggest thing I've ever been involved in."

"Does that mean it's done? You've got a deal?"

"Between you and me, I have a deal. As near as damn it. Just waiting for network approval and a green light from Ken Walden and his board. And I expect that soon."

Repton smiling, stretching like a big contented cat in his chair, hands behind his head, expensive loafers crossed on the desk.

"Soon means when?"

"Could be today; could be tomorrow."

"And you'd announce it when?"

"Maybe tomorrow, or maybe Monday. Come on, buddy! You look like a funeral! Believe me, it's going to be a hell of a shot in the arm for this news department; this is going to pay off. As good for you and 'The Evening News' as it'll be for everything else. More attention, more audience, more control, more money in the department."

"Funny, Sherman Glass just fed me the same line."

"It's not a line! And as an old friend, Grant, I'd strongly advise you, don't take a sour line with this when we go public. It wouldn't be smart to bad-mouth her. You hear me?"

"I hear you, Ev. And you know what I hear? I hear you rationalizing a deal that, deep down, you probably feel stinks as badly as I do. I mean, talking journalism. Talking business, I don't know. And you probably don't know either. I mean, you can't be sure, can you?"

"You're wrong. I'm sure."

"So what do I say? Congratulations?"

"Easy on the irony. I've known you too long."

"You probably won't be with us long. Big coup like this pays off, you'll find yourself running the whole network."

Repton smiled complacently. "Nothing farther from my mind."

"So I have to start thinking of Ann Murrow as a colleague?"

"Uh-huh."

"Have you ever met her?"

Repton, slightly uncomfortable. "Not yet. She had to fly to London for something."

"You made the deal without seeing her?"

"That's the way I had to do it."

"Well, the rumor mill about her is wild. Get someone to print out the Hollygo stuff."

ANGELA SAID, "You haven't forgotten the Overseas Press Club tonight?"

"God, that's all I need."

"I checked with Winona. She hasn't. And you can't very well skip it when they're giving you the award and expecting you to talk ten or fifteen minutes. You ever get tired getting awards?"

"Probably about as tired as you get with guys telling you they love you."

"That's not the same; they just want sex. Your guys want speeches. Anyway, black tie, Hyatt. Cocktails at seven. Dinner, eight. Program at nine. You want to prepare something or wing it?"

The OPC deserved something thoughtful, and he felt empty of any thoughts, his mind overwhelmed. Absurd night to be honored for the career that seemed to be crashing around him. Or maybe appropriate. Like the RTNDA a few months earlier, the OPC was recognizing life-time achievement. This time it had a terminal ring.

He had no choice; he had to get up on his feet and say something that made sense. Another imperative of the job. The discipline was now so ingrained that, whatever his mood, however depleted his optimism, he had to perform—and he would.

He keyed into Word Perfect and began typing in a few notes. In a quarter of an hour he had two pages of key phrases. A talk. With any luck, he'd think of a few funny asides to help the medicine go down. He saved the file, printed the pages, and stuck them in his briefcase to take when he went home to change and pick up Winona. Then, noting the time, he tabbed into the rundown for tonight's show to look for any changes and to edit copy written for him. The Scott Woolford interview was still generating new angles. No way the show could ignore them. All the mainstream media were caught. A sudden impulse made him call Marty, who came in looking wary. "Yeah?"

"I've been thinking about yesterday. You were right. I should have done that interview. I wanted to tell you."

"OK, OK. Thanks, Grant. I hear you."

"I guess there's no way to be a little pregnant, right? Or pregnant one day and not pregnant the next."

After all, he had to go on working with this guy.

A FEW minutes later, Shirley Trattner called.

"I'm sorry to bother you so close to air, but is the grapevine right about Ann Murrow?"

"I'm afraid so. Ev told me it's wrapped up. He's going to announce it Monday at the latest."

"Great moments in journalism! What are you going to do?"

"I don't know yet. I'm still shellshocked."

"Well, I had already decided, but if I hadn't, this would have pushed me over the edge. I'm going to Bryn Mawr."

"Congratulations. I think you're smart. But I'm going to miss you."

"Come down and see us. I'll give you an honorary degree."

CHRISTOPHER Siefert called to follow up about Ann Murrow, and Grant decided to be straight with him; the deal was done, just getting clearance up top, an announcement Friday or Monday.

"You pretty sure of that?"

"I'm just repeating what Repton said, but not for attribution, OK? Use network sources or something. No quoting me or him. Agreed?"

"No, that's fine. It's a big help. Between us, Schoenfeld's still wavering on whether to go with a Murrow cover or not. He's got the back-up ready to roll, so I guess we'll sweat it out down to the wire. Now, do you want to tell me how you feel about this momentous event in the history of American journalism?"

"I'm going to back off that one. I need some time to sort out my own feelings."

"Can I use that?"

"I'd prefer you didn't quote me at all right now."

"But you did say yesterday you'd told your staff. That's not the kind of journalism we practice."

"Yeah, I did."

"You want to elaborate now?"

"No, I really don't. I've got to go on working here."

"OK, then. Thanks a lot. Mind if I check back with you over the next couple of days, in case anything changes?"

"Yeah, sure."

THE OPC, unlike most awards dinners, was exhilarating, just to be reminded that American journalism hadn't fully lowered the blinds on the world; that there were live reporters out there doing their thing. Grant was impressed by the range of datelines and the youth of the award winners, men and women, some of whom glanced at him admiringly as they came up to the platform. The outside world was still a place where young correspondents could make a name. These people weren't all pining to be anchors, sitting in a studio, a non-place, reciting the news from nowhere. Obviously, they got a thrill from what they did and cared passionately about it.

The citation for his lifetime award recited all the big stories he'd covered overseas and called his reporting "always competitive and always distinguished." The applause was long and warm, and in the moment of rising to accept, he decided to scrap his notes.

Instead, he talked about the moment he first discovered the excitement of foreign reporting. With as much detail as he'd given Siefert, he recounted the story of the Berlin Wall, his accidentally becoming an assistant to the BBC crew, and how that had launched his career. Then the thrill of going back, thirty-eight years later, as a network anchor, with his own army of assistants, to cover the fall of the wall. He knew he was telling it well, speaking softly and personally, close to the micro-phone, very intimately. He could tell from the thick quality of the silence how the audience was soaking it up. The applause was rapturous. He'd touched them because he'd touched himself.

With Winona's hand in his, he took a long time working through all those who wanted to shake hands. Then they reached the entrance and found their driver.

"You were wonderful!" Winona said in the car, and gave him a warm kiss. "Just wonderful. They loved it. And so did I."

"It was fresh in my mind because I'd told it all to Siefert. I hate to spoil a nice evening, but he's been pulled off our story to do a quick piece on Ann Murrow."

"Oh, no!"

"Very apologetic, but they have to go with the news. And the news is, Ev Repton told me, he's made a deal with her. They'll announce it by Monday."

"What are we going to do?"

"I don't know. I'd better let my feelings cool down and think it through carefully. I get so furious when I think about what they're doing, I don't trust myself to make any sound decisions."

"Well, nobody there tonight would have guessed for a minute that you had all that on your mind."

"I didn't. When I got up there, I forgot about it."

Winona tucked herself closer against him. "Well, let's go home and forget about it some more!"

67

By Friday, to Joe Steinman's satisfaction, the storm of speculation about Ann Murrow's future had burst out of the gossip columns into all mainstream media. Even the *New York Times*'s "TV Notes" acknowledged what was universally assumed, that Ann Murrow was about to switch networks for a financial package said to break new ground in levels of compensation for network news personalities. An announcement was expected on Monday. Neither Ms. Murrow, who was abroad, nor her agent, nor executives at her new network could be reached for comment, and her present employers were silent.

The New York Post kept running its exclusive picture of Steinman with Everett Repton outside Lutèce in sizes and captions that grew with the story, from *The Ann Murrow Negotiators* to *$14 Mill Lunch Rocks TV!*

The $14 million figure did not rock Steinman, because he had leaked it to the *Post* reporter. By daring to leap to fourteen, he had raised Ev Repton to where, only in his wildest scenario, Steinman had hoped to end up. Repton had spluttered, "Of course, fourteen million is not in the cards!" But later settled for twelve.

Steinman had another reason for leaking the fourteen: to be sure Murrow's present employers were paying close attention. And, gratifyingly, they were. But so were CNN and Fox and Barry Diller. Their interest, too, had found its way into print, goading Everett Repton into anxious calls—"I'm nearly there!"—intended to reassure Steinman but making Repton sound desperate.

The silence from Minneapolis—it had now dragged into the fourth day—made Steinman uneasy. Otherwise, he concluded, gazing down as he liked to do at the busy square in front of the Plaza, things were going very well.

His phone had been ringing incessantly. The more he held off the press—the *Times, Time* magazine, the *New York Observer, TV Guide* were all clamoring for interviews—the more the appetite grew. Time to unleash her after the announcement. But no announcement until the cat was in the bag.

With the full resources of *Time* magazine on the case, the problem for Christopher Siefert was too much information. It took hours to sift through the mass of material from the file as well as the new stuff being faxed and e-mailed in from *Time* staffers across the country, hurriedly reassigned to dig up background. He couldn't begin writing until he'd glanced at everything, rejecting a large and growing stack, reserving only items on which he'd circled a fact or a quote.

The work with Grant Munro had given him all the context he needed. Murrow's story quickly crystalized as the antithesis of Munro's, through the looking glass of his world: not the industry Grant saw going to hell by surrendering to entertainment values, but an industry creatively discovering new ways to blend information and entertainment in audience-pleasing formats.

He thought of Hamlet's remarks about the Players: "They are the abstracts and brief chronicles of the time." In the pre-journalism era, they were actors; in the post-journalism era, they were actors again.

At the back of Siefert's mind, not yet verbalized as a sentence he'd be happy to publish, was the thought: It's her world now, not his. Each media generation produced its own formula and stars, its own legitimacy. If Grant Munro was one media generation past Walter Cronkite, Ann Murrow was two. The very magazine he was writing for had undergone its own serial metamorphoses. Luce's austere magazine of the thirties and forties bore little resemblance to the seductive covers and busy formats that competed with television today.

Fortunately, Elizabeth had steered him into watching Ann Murrow on the Wyoming child murder, the highest rated of any prime time magazine show and a prime demonstration of her style and technique. Siefert had no doubt about his own attitude: the woman was appalling. But he would hold that opinion aside, using it like an electrical charge to bring power to the piece, to balance it with effusions from the audience that adored her and the business heads that shook in wonderment at the dough she made for them.

There was no shortage of negative material. While entertainment writers gee-whizzed about Murrow, and celebrity magazines milked her for the same bitchy nectar they squeezed from supermodels and film stars, the television critics were almost uniformly snide and the journalism pundits scathing. If you took hollygo seriously, co-workers hated her. So Siefert had enough quotes to make Murrow sound like the Wicked Witch of the West Side. And that wasn't the assignment. It was to don the mantle of journalistic gravitas to do, with literary flourishes, what all the others did: celebrate celebrity and success. And when success and celebrity came with the body and face of a movie star or a fashion model, celebrate that too. If a little vinegar leaked into your prose, that gave you ironic distance.

What he didn't have was an interview. Steinman kept promising, "Later." Clever P.R. to let the mystery build up.

69

Whenever they had time alone now, Winona made Grant keep talking. At the Four Seasons in Washington, she was sitting on the bed, putting studs and cuff links into his dress shirt, as she had for years.

"I know you'd feel a lot better if you'd talk to someone, find a therapist. I suggested it after Tony's accident, but you didn't want to. That was a lot to absorb. Years and years of positive vibrations from the world, being Mr. Wonderful, and suddenly Fate shows you a hole in the fabric."

"I live with a therapist. Why do I have to pay one?" Grant, out of the shower, wearing the hotel's terrycloth robe, sat in an armchair across the room. "I get therapy morning, noon, and night."

Winona said, "You're going to pay the plastic surgeon. With what she'll cost, you could buy a year of therapy. Anyway . . ." She got up and hung the shirt on a chair back. She was wearing the silky robe she always traveled with. She came and sat on the footstool against his bare feet. "I've thought a lot more about all this. If you were a client of mine, I'd know what to say . . . if you want to hear it. The difference between you and a client is that you know I love you. Right?"

"Right. So?"

"So, to a client I'd say something like this . . . You've been used to people admiring you. You do live with a pretty amazing level of admiration. Everywhere you go, getting on the shuttle this afternoon, arriving at the hotel, people stop to tell you how wonderful you are. And constant praise is habit-forming. It gets to be like a mood-altering drug. I think you handle it well. We've seen plenty of TV people grow into monsters. You know who I mean."

"Yeah."

"All the same, even for a well-integrated guy with his feet on the ground, it's hard being taken off the drug. He can hallucinate. He can imagine plots and conspiracies. And if you told any therapist all this was happening to a man about to be sixty, he'd say: Of course! On top of that, I know you haven't got over Tony's death. Leave Teresa out of it. Just being the survivor in a situation like that can be traumatizing. If you don't deal with it, the stress can become unbearable, affecting your whole life."

She stopped to watch his reaction.

"So?"

"Does this make any sense to you?" She stroked his foot. "Or just upset you, hearing things you don't want to hear?"

"Since I always hated the idea of letting the celebrity stuff change me, it's not so great hearing that I'm drugged on it."

"Don't exaggerate. All I said was that a diet high in praise must addict you a little, make you expect it, so when there's even small withdrawal of praise, you may overreact."

"And you think my feelings about Bill Donovan and Ann Murrow are overreactions?"

"Yes—especially the facelift."

"What would a normal reaction be? Should I be laughing it all off?"

"Maybe see your feelings in a little different perspective."

"Perspective! You haven't mentioned that all these supposed over-reactions of mine are tied exactly to that—a wider perspective. Not my personal vanity or whatever—probably a lot of that—but the business I've been in for thirty-five years. What's a normal reaction to what these people are doing to our business?"

"I know, I know."

"Do you know? All these years I've thought I played a part in how the country operates; that behind all the nonsense in politics and government and journalism, we helped make the system work. When I talk about it—say, with Siefert—it comes out sounding corny and stupid."

Winona held up her hand gently to stop him. "Let me tell you something I feel. Not talking about you, for a moment, but about me. It scares me a little. I've told you, you get a facelift and maybe look forty-five; more important you'll probably try to *think* like forty-five. Where does it leave me? Looking sixty and thinking worse! As if I've grown up and you haven't. I'm going to live forever with the Eternal Boy? You see what I mean? All mental health comes down to knowing yourself, knowing what you are, and I think that means knowing how old you are, and acting it. Unless—"

"Unless what?"

"Unless you're still not being honest with me and you're lusting after some young woman or having an affair, and that's what's driving you."

"You know that's not true."

"If I knew, would I raise it?"

"How do I convince you?"

"I told you. By wanting to make love to *me* more often, which you don't very much. You're not the only one at an insecure age. How about *my* sexual confidence? Since we're being frank about it, that's why I thought you had something going with Teresa, because since that happened, your libido has taken a real slump in my direction."

"I don't know why; I don't feel like it as much."

"With me!"

"With anybody."

"I even thought—talk about neurotic—I even thought Tony might have died not deliberately, but unconsciously, maybe, the great altruistic gesture, to take himself out of the way."

"Come on; that's sick!"

"Sick, I don't know. Jealous, I know."

Her robe had parted, disclosing a stretch of thigh, and he reached to stroke it. "What are you doing right now? You busy?"

She leaned forward to kiss him. "You play your cards right, and I could spare a few hours."

BEING AT the White House reinforced Grant's awareness of age. Whatever storms blew around him, the President exuded youth and vitality, as did the service officers, men and women serving as social aides, all dismayingly young.

As they waited in the receiving line, watching the President and First Lady in evening dress, Grant said to Winona, "It's the first time I've been older than a President. Funny feeling. Like being older than my father. Older than Kennedy."

Shaking hands, the President raised his chin and smiled at Grant. "Gadarene swine! I liked that! I really liked that."

GRANT DID NOT see Ann Murrow until they were seated for dinner, and she made a late entrance, a willowy progression among the tables, bestowing looks of girlish contrition on the President and First Lady. She was wearing a white evening dress that left her fine arms and shoulders bare. Winona caught his eye across the table and winked.

"Vera Wang dress," said the woman on Grant's left, the elegant wife of the Wall Street type beside Winona. "I tried it on. Would you believe twenty thousand dollars? But it sure makes her look innocent."

"Then it's quite a bargain," Grant said, and the woman laughed.

"She can wear it. Look at those shoulders. And your wife's dress is gorgeous."

"Not twenty thousand dollars."

"She's a beautiful woman."

"Thanks. I agree."

"I guess there's nobody with Ann Murrow," his dinner companion said. "No escort. That's quite a statement."

"A statement that says what?" Grant asked.

"Total availability or total unavailability. Or both! Who knows? Maybe total confidence."

During dinner, Grant's eyes strayed repeatedly to Murrow's table, observing how quickly she commanded it, maintaining one conversation, absorbing them all into her space, not she into theirs. Even in these quick glimpses, he caught her in a variety of poses—girlish, insouciant, frivolous, flirtatious, then dignified, the intelligent debater, the earnest listener.

Grant had met her in the past, but had never exchanged more than a nod or a word or two. He'd recently constructed such an image of driving ambition that he'd forgotten how fragile and feminine she looked, how appealing.

After the President's Independence Day toast, dancing began, and just as the press and television cameras were let in for a photo op, Ann Murrow was dancing with the President.

Winona, dancing with Grant, said in his ear, "Doesn't miss a trick, does she? She looks fabulous, damn her! You're sure she isn't the one you've got the secret hots for? Saying all this negative stuff about her to put me off the scent?"

Grant danced with the other women at the table. They sat down again for dessert. Then Winona went to the ladies' room, and, still standing, Grant found Ann Murrow at his side—disturbing, disconcerting in the flesh.

"Hi, it's me!"

She did not hold out a hand in greeting, but took his arm quickly, intimately, and said, "We should talk. Let's do it dancing." And led him to the floor.

She was slighter than Winona, her body more flexible; the bare skin of her back felt satiny and inviting under his hand, her perfume something delicious. But what transfixed him were her eyes . . . of the palest blue, like ice in a glacial crevasse, and impenetrable, unreadable.

"Grant, I want to tell you how honored I will feel, if things work out, to be your colleague."

"Well, thanks. I gather things are headed that way."

"Well . . ."—she glanced away disdainfully—"I leave all that to the people who negotiate." She then flicked her pale eyes back to his and smiled. He noticed that even her teeth were beautiful.

Leaning back coquettishly against his right hand, she looked up. "I want you to know how much I've always admired your work. You're the one who sets the standards in our business!"

Hardened to compliments, Grant received this with emotions so conflicted he could scarcely hear. He was dancing with—physically holding, touching, feeling, smelling—this woman, whose work aroused feelings close to disgust, whose schemes seemed about to destroy his career, yet who was, as a woman, breathtaking.

What could he say to her? He said, "You must be very pleased with the success of your programs, the audience, the ratings."

And she said, with her ice blue eyes on his, "Grant, I have learned one thing about the American people. And you know what it is? Sincerity. They demand absolute sincerity!"

Stunned, he said, "I guess so. It's pretty complicated, what they want sometimes."

"I must let you go, but I have to say one more thing. I heard you refused to interview Scott Woolford. And you know, I admired that! People like you and I have to maintain some standards, or this business we love will sell out everything! Everything! Woolford is scum. I respect you for your dignity!" She gave him a quick, proprietary pat on the arm and was gone.

Grant wandered back to his table, nodding at people who smiled in recognition, and found Winona.

"You see, the minute my back is turned!"

He sat beside her. "You won't believe what that woman said to me."

"I'll believe anything, after what I just heard in the ladies' room."

"What?"

"You first."

"Ms. Murrow believes absolute sincerity is what the American people insist on. Number one. Number two, she respects my work. Number three. If people like us—she said 'like you and I'—don't maintain standards, they'll sell out everything."

"And she's so cute, you swallowed every word of it?"

"She's like something in a sci-fi movie, where aliens invade human bodies, displace the soul, steal the identity. Unbelievable!"

"Hi, Grant!"

Behind them was Bill Donovan, tanned, vital, dark eyes glittering.

Grant got up and introduced Winona, who said, "What a coincidence! I was just talking to your wife, Mary Kay. She's very sweet."

"She's pretty excited. So am I. It's really something, isn't it? I suppose you two have been to lots of these dinners over the years." No sarcasm evident.

Grant said, "Yeah, a few."

"I saw you earlier but didn't get a chance to come over and say hi. Then I saw you dancing with Ann Murrow. She's something, isn't she? So what's the word in New York? Is it set with her?"

"Ev Repton told me it is. He's just waiting to get it approved up the line."

"Boy, we'll sure have a powerhouse with her, don't you think?"

"She's a powerhouse, all right," Grant said. "How are you liking the White House beat?"

"It was pretty exciting, getting here just as the sex story broke. When that's off the boil, it's harder getting on the air. Well, you know. Oh, thanks for putting in a good word the other day when Marty wanted to shoot down my story."

"It was an important story."

"Kind of boring, I thought, but if the President does it, I guess it's news. Well, it was a pleasure to meet you, Winona. First woman I ever knew with that name, apart from Winona Ryder. It's a real cute name."

"Thanks. Nice to meet you."

"I'd better be getting back to Mary Kay."

"Real cute!" Winona said. "Real jerk. Where do they find these people?"

In the car going back to the hotel, she said, "You know what Mary Kay told me? She's a sweet little thing, from Atlanta, very wide-eyed about being here. How exciting it is just to be in Washington, to be at the White House. She calls him Billy. 'Billy is so thrilled to be at the network. He works so hard. He'll do anything to get ahead. He's so ambitious. Do you know what he did before we left Atlanta? He thought his eyes were a little bit puffy for television? So he marched out and had cosmetic surgery? It came out real good, don't you think?' "

Grant said, "At *his* age? He can't be more than thirty!"

"You'll never catch up with that. But who would want to?"

Grant slumped back in the seat. "I don't know what to think. I don't understand any of this anymore. If those two are the future of the business . . ."

Winona took his hand and was quiet even when they reached the hotel and were bowed into the lobby. In their room, Grant took off his dinner jacket and bow tie. "I'm going to have a drink." He found Scotch in the mini-bar and ice in the bucket. "What would you like?"

"I don't know. What should I have?"

"Well, there's brandy and Kahlúa and B and B and—"

"I'll have a brandy!"

"Wow!"

"The President didn't ask me to dance tonight, although he has before. He was charming in the receiving line, but he didn't ask me to dance."

"You could have asked *him,* like you know who."

"I'm glad you can see it a little bit funny. You looked catatonic when you came back to the table."

Grant slipped his shoes off and sat beside her on the bed, leaning against bunched-up pillows.

"I always thought his eyes looked funny. Donovan's. Too piercing. Too wide-awake."

"You said his eyes were impertinent. It's a good description."

"And you know, close up, Ann Murrow's eyes look fake."

"Maybe she's wearing those colored contact lenses."

"I think they're her own eyes, but unreal, like Siberian huskies' white-blue eyes."

"Don't insult huskies. They're nice."

Grant sipped his drink. "What in hell are we going to do?"

"Remember the woman anchor at a local station in Chicago? When they brought in that jerk to be a commentator—

"Jerry Springer. Her name is Carol Marin."

"She quit in protest. And everybody applauded her. And a few days later Springer was gone."

"Now he's an even bigger star, and where did it leave her? She didn't go back to her job."

"Well, do you blame her? Why would she want to work for people who did that to her?"

Grant was silent.

70

In the morning, having breakfast in their room, reading the Sunday *Washington Post* and *New York Times,* Winona said, "There's a picture of her dancing with the President."

"No kidding?"

Winona held the paper up to him, then crushed it on her lap. "Honey, you don't want to go to Kay Graham's and have Murrow flaunting it there too, condescending to you again."

"You're right. Let's skip it."

"I'll call tomorrow and apologize. Let's go back to New York; go somewhere fun for lunch and find a movie afterward. Forget all this stuff for a while."

"So if we want to be in town by what? Twelve-thirty? We should take the—"

The phone rang and Winona answered.

"Oh, hi, how are you? No, it's OK. He's here. It's Laurie Jacobs."

"Hi, Grant. I'm sorry to hit you this early on a Sunday—"

"No problem. We were up."

"It's so sad, Grant! Don Evans died last night."

"Oh, no!"

"His sister called me. You knew he lived with her? She got home last night late and found him slumped over his computer. He'd had a heart attack."

"Oh, God." Grant turned to Winona. "Don Evans died. The senior writer on our show. He had a heart attack. His sister found him last night."

"Oh, I'm sorry."

To Laurie, Grant said, "God, he was just my age—"

"No, no!" Laurie said. "Darling, he was seventy! Didn't you know that? Don was seventy."

"I never knew that. I thought we were the same age. We were such rivals years ago, I assumed we were the same age."

"He looked good because he'd worked at it. And remember, he had a big facelift a long time ago."

"A facelift?"

Winona looked up and caught his eye.

Laurie said, "I spent some time with him when I first came to work here. He told me a lot."

"For God's sake! That's incredible. I'd better call his sister. I don't think I've ever met her."

"Her name's Caroline. Nice woman. She's a big deal in a firm on Wall Street. As smart as Don and just as witty. Oh, I'm going to miss him! He made it fun to come to work."

"Give me her number, and I'll call. We're coming back this morning."

"How was last night? Or should I ask? I saw Brenda's picture dancing with the playboy of the western world."

"I'll tell you later. I can't believe it's all happening."

"Brave new world, darling."

He put the phone down and told Winona, "Don Evans was actually seventy years old. Laurie said he'd had a facelift years ago. It certainly fooled me."

"Did it help him, looking ten years younger? I liked him. And I know you did. But behind all his cleverness, he seemed sad. A man out of place. He wasn't married?"

"He was. Years ago. They had a couple of kids and then split up. I don't know what happened to her. Laurie says Don was living with his sister."

"Sometimes, these days, it seems our marriage is the only one that hasn't fallen apart."

He and Winona looked at each other until Grant said, "I know what you're thinking."

"What am I thinking?"

"You're thinking, facelifts don't save careers."

"I'm thinking, it'd be nice if you called his sister. And asked if we can come to see her when we get back to New York. Maybe this afternoon?"

Caroline Evans said he was sweet to call. She had to take care of funeral arrangements in the afternoon; would they come and have a drink with her at six? She had something particular to ask him.

And so it happened that for many hours after the news broke, the whole country knew, but Grant did not. He and Winona got the eleven A.M. shuttle. His usual driver met them at La Guardia and took them to the Café des Artists, on West Sixty-seventh, where they slipped into a favorite hideout, the last table behind the bar, and dawdled over lunch with a bottle of wine. The subdued lighting, the wine, the knowledge of Evans's death, coupled with whole dismaying chain of events, seemed to suspend reality, dissolve time.

"It's like those lunches we used to have in Paris when there was no news and you had afternoons to kill."

"Maybe I'll have that again—afternoons to kill."

"We used to kill them in bed, remember?"

"Sure. It was thirty years ago."

"Meaning?"

"Meaning I was a young guy."

"I remember." She sipped her wine with a dreamy smile. "That was the year everyone was reading *Portnoy's Complaint.*"

"You've got sex on the brain."

"That isn't where I've got it."

"It's funny, when we were in college I was always pestering you about it."

"I was terrified of getting pregnant. I can't believe I lived before the pill! Anyway, I'm not pestering you now."

"We never had anywhere to go then."

"We do now. We have more beds than we know what to do with."

"You want to go home?"

"I don't think I'm in the mood for a movie."

They took a taxi across the park, found the suitcases their driver had delivered, went to bed, and made love.

"I feel like a man out on bail, waiting for his sentence to begin."

"You don't have to serve any sentence at all if you don't want to."

They fell asleep for a short time, showered, dressed again, and went back to the West Side to Caroline Evans's corner apartment in the Beresford, overlooking Central Park and the Museum of Natural History.

Don's sister thanked them for coming and said, "Would you mind if we have a private word before we join the other people?" She took them into a small room with bookshelves, a desk, and a computer.

"This is where I found him last night, at the computer. He loved being on the Internet, and I haven't a clue about it. Grant—I feel as if I know you—Don had such admiration for you. I wonder whether I can ask a favor?"

"Of course!"

"Would you deliver a tribute at his funeral? It'll be Tuesday, at noon, at Saint Thomas's on Fifth Avenue. I know he'd be pleased if it was you. It doesn't have to be long."

"Well, yes, I'd be honored." And the private professional reflex: a speech to work up in the middle of all this other stuff. "Yes, of course."

"Thank you. It's a great comfort to know I can relax about that. You're kind. Now, please come in and have something to drink."

As they entered a living room brilliant with summer evening light, he saw Laurie Jacobs notice him and let an amazing smile break over her face.

"Isn't it unbelievable!"

"What?" asked Grant.

"About Brenda!"

"What about her?"

"You don't know!" Laurie squealed, pulling Grant and Winona back into the study.

"She's not coming! She's not coming! Isn't it fabulous! The announcement's been out for hours and hours. It's all over everywhere,

CNN, everything. I'm so happy, I can't stand it!" She threw her arms around Grant and kissed him and then did the same to Winona. "Sit down. I'll tell you. Where on earth have you been? I left all kinds of messages."

"We didn't look at the answering machine. We came back from Washington—"

"Never mind. Around eleven o'clock, I got a call from Chris Siefert. There was a statement all over the wires, the Internet, and cable. It said, after careful consideration of all her options, Ann Murrow has decided for career reasons to stay where she is. They made her an offer she can't refuse. She's deeply grateful for the interest all the other distinguished broadcast news organizations have shown in her . . . blah, blah, blah . . . but this is her true journalistic home, and their renewed confidence will be an inspiration for years to come."

"Well, I'm—I don't know what the hell I am!" Grant said. "What do you suppose happened? Did Ev Repton's deal get slapped down upstairs?"

"No one's divulging the amount of the contract, but some source told the AP—we'll have all this in the office for you—the deal was better than Repton offered her. Not only better money, but more air time."

"It's unbelievable. Everything that's happening is unbelievable." Grant reached out and took Winona's hand.

Laurie's lively face was radiant.

"But Don Evans is dead," Winona said. "Why don't we go back and pay our respects; then we can go and celebrate. Would you like to come with us and have some supper?"

"Oh, that's lovely. But I feel I should stick around with Caroline. I'm kind of family. Grant, call Chris Siefert when you get a chance. They pulled their cover on Brenda. And they were all set to use the shot of her dancing with the Prez!"

"Jesus!" Grant said. "Now I feel like the guy sentenced to death who gets a last-minute reprieve."

"I'll bet you one thing," Laurie said. "Ev Repton will be a lot more receptive to Fran Whitman. He'll be lucky if he isn't fired himself for getting sucked in so publicly."

WHEN GRANT found him at Elizabeth's, Christopher Siefert said, "I tried to reach you. We were right down to the wire. It took Dick Shoenfeld about two minutes to decide to go with his back-up and pull her cover off the magazine. He said, 'Ann Murrow doesn't change networks? What kind of a story is that? What are we, her press agents?' So he has egg on his face with the money guys, because it costs a hell of a lot to do that, but he avoids mega eggs in running a Murrow cover and a non-story. He pushed the button in time to hit about ninety percent of the circulation."

Grant said, "Do you know what happened? Why she pulled back? I saw her last night at the White House, and it sounded all but sewn up. She was talking about becoming my colleague."

"I don't know. Steinman won't talk, and they say only that she'll talk later in the week. I don't know; what's your hunch?"

"Haven't got a good one. I'll talk to a few people. Maybe tomorrow I'll know something."

"Please call. By the way, your story's alive again."

Grant said to Winona, "Siefert says we're alive again . . . in Time's eyes. What d'you think of that?"

"In Time's eyes . . . sounds like a Shakespeare sonnet."

"I want to sleep on it and see what I pick up at the office in the morning. It alters everything . . . but really doesn't change anything."

The next morning, when Grant began calling around, Clif Mat-thews said, "I suppose even today it's a lady's prerogative to change her mind . . . if *lady* is the operative term in this case. I did put in my two cents' worth, but I gathered they were going ahead with it. I suppose you're delighted?"

"Relieved, sure. Not delighted that so many of my loyal colleagues and bosses were prepared to disregard my advice."

"Anyway, I did talk to Ken Walden. He and Betty can join us sailing over Labor Day. How about you and Winona? Now it's defi-nitely time you got to know him better."

"I'm almost certain we can. I'll confirm it with her, but I'm sure she'd love to."

THEN THE corporate chairman himself called. "Grant? Ken Walden. I gather we're going to see you and Winona on Clif's boat over Labor Day. That's great. But why don't we and our wives have a quiet dinner soon? There's a lot more I'd like to know about things in the news area. Have you got an evening free, this week or next?"

"I'm sure we do. I'll check with Winona and call you back. We'll look forward to it."

SHERMAN GLASS, still unquenchable, said, "Brilliant play by Steinman. The guy's a genius."

"What do you mean?"

"The way I figure it, he must've planned it this way all along. Create a huge storm, everyone and his brother trying to get her, and then he raises the price where she is."

"Sherman, I suggested that when you first sounded the alarm about her."

"Yeah? So great minds think alike! Look what he gets. No disruptions. No risk in changing networks. Who knows, she might have bombed with you guys. Almost double the money, and more air time. He's golden. You got to hand it to him."

"If it kept her out of here, I guess I do."

"Now, buddy, we've got to talk. You want to push this gal in Cleveland?"

"Yes, I do."

"Well, Ev Repton's never going to be a softer touch than right now. And I think Murrow's deal makes ten mill easy pickings for us."

Grant couldn't listen anymore. "I'll talk to you soon, Sherman. I've got some thinking to do."

"Don't be gloomy. This is a great day for us! OK?"

"OK."

EVERETT REPTON looked like a balloon that had leaked air overnight. He said to Grant, "I suppose you're happy as hell."

"What happened?"

"I don't know. One minute we have a great deal, everyone happy, no problems upstairs as far as I know. We're crafting the release for Monday morning, and this bombshell bursts on Sunday morning."

"Sherman Glass thinks Steinman intended it all along. Just negotiated to jack her price up over there."

"Sure, sure. Makes me look pretty naïve. One thing I wondered about, I even talked to you about it, and that's your own attitude. Maybe that got around. Maybe she felt it wouldn't be comfortable, working here with you bad-mouthing her."

"Really? For the record, Ev, I spoke with the lady Saturday night at the White House. In fact, I danced with her, and she told me she admired my attitude. Jesus! You going to blame this on me?"

"It's as plausible as any other reason."

Later, Laurie leaned in her usual way around Grant's door. "Got a sec?"

"Sure."

She came in quickly and closed the door.

"Top secret. Understood?"

"OK. What is it?"

"Last night when people left, Caroline Evans asked me to turn off Don's computer. It had become symbolic by then, as if he weren't quite dead while it was on. The screen saver was still running. I pushed the space bar to stop it, and guess what I found? It was open to a web site with a half-page written. I printed it out." She handed over a sheet of paper. "This is what he was working on when he died."

And Grant read:

www.hollygo.com

Now Brenda Starr bout to be undisputed Queen of the Airwaves, may be trouble up there in paradise. All you chicks know Hollygo got a million sources. Everone like to lay a little knowledge on me. Well, stand by, as they say in teeveenews, and all you queens out there fix up your mascara, cos we got news! One my lil informants just dyin to tell me bout a rumor she pick up in the clubs. Not the meat locker clubs you frequent, you eager bitch, but the clubs where the gossip reporters hang out all night, kissin ass with celebs and publicity agents, hopin some crumbs'll drop from the gossip table.

Way it come to me, from a source I'll call a Liz Smith Wannabe, is this: Brenda Starr be in a tizzy, a Princess Di–class tizzy, cos some dude come across a mess of hot pictures Brenda don't want to see the light of day. No way, no how! Pictures taken when she just a teevee weather girl in Minneapolis, place so cold a gal got to work overtime to keep her tush warm. And that what Brenda doin: posin for sex pictures. Don'tcha luv it?

Now, way we heard it, the dude that found the pictures want to sell them to *Penthouse* or *Hustler* or some other high-culture magazine UNLESS Brenda pay him serious money. We talkin big bucks. Trouble is, Brenda think she already paid the dude off, but he ain't gone away. He back with more pictures! Out there in the mean, racist, penis-driven, patriarchal, white world, that known as blackmail, chilluns. I call it extortion in any color. But what's a teevee anchor to do, if she made her way up the hard way . . .

Grant looked up at Laurie. "Don Evans was Hollygo?"

"I guess so. And it fits, doesn't it?"

"Well, goddamm it!"

"All those lunch times he'd disappear and say he was walking? Probably slipping home to be Hollygo."

"And you didn't know?"

"I swear I didn't!"

Grant looked at her skeptically.

"Darling, I swear!"

"And what about this sex picture stuff? Is that supposed to be serious?"

"Hollygo seemed to be right about everything else."

"But if Don knew about it, the chances are someone else knows."

"Uh-huh."

"Could this be what made her pull out?"

"Maybe there's no connection," Laurie said. "Don never got his story onto the Internet. He hadn't finished it."

"But someone else may."

"Could be some reporter a little shy of publishing himself slips it to Hollygo; figures once she's out there with it, he can quote it, make it seem more legit."

"And you really didn't know, all along?"

"I promise you. But I said top secret, right? So his secret's safe with us?"

Grant said, "OK."

"Shake?" She held out her hand.

"Shake."

"Don'tcha luv it?" Laurie said.

368 ∎

• • •

WHEN SHE LEFT, Grant sank back comfortably into his chair and put his feet on the desk to think.

There was Winona's option: get out and good riddance to them. Why work for people who had tried to stick it to him like this?

The other was to hang on. Hang on and fight it. Do as well as he could, giving way when he had to, staring them down when he could.

But he was sure of one thing. He called Winona and kept his voice light. "Social notes."

"OK."

"Ken Walden, the corporate chairman, wants us to have dinner some evening this week or next. Just the four of us. His wife's name is Betty."

"Trying to make nice all of a sudden, as they say in New York?"

"Looks like it."

"Well, we're free. Sure."

"And Clif Matthews has asked if we'd join a party on his boat, with the Waldens, over Labor Day."

"What is this, the wooing of Grant Munro?"

"Or choosing the default position, as they say in computers."

"No default position for me!"

"And I was wondering . . . how'd you like to go sailing—with me, the newly popular Grant Munro—for the month of August?"

Silence from Winona for a moment. "I thought you had a big date in San Francisco."

"I think I'll forget that. Maybe I should be the only person in the business *without* a facelift."

72

As George White settled into a first-class seat for his second flight to New York, he was thinking that he really owed the kid something. Not money. Didn't want him to think blackmail paid off. Too dangerous. George could say: I was hired to find the pictures and put them in safe hands. And I did.

The kid was sharp and fast and young. He'd make a great leg man for a middle-aged detective. He could be hired and trained. Teach him the trade. Keep him out of trouble. Put him on a straight path. The idea was appealing. Just have to wait outside the mailbox store the kid was still haunting and have a straight talk with him. Cancel the mailbox. Nothing to wait for anymore. You're lucky it's over like this. Blackmailers are criminals. They get caught and spend a long time in jail. No place for a young guy who's never been in trouble. What you need is a job.

Yeah. He'd enjoy that conversation.

JOE STEINMAN reached Ann Murrow.

"We've got the other set of pictures. You were right, there was another set, minus the print you have. George White got them from the kid. He's bringing them to me in person. He doesn't want to tell me exactly how he got them, and I don't think we want to know. But he's certain it's the end. There are no more prints."

"Do you trust him?"

"Sure. We don't have much choice."

"What did it cost?"

"Another fifty thousand."

"A hundred altogether. Isn't it fishy to you, Joey? That's just what the kid demanded in the first place. Maybe they're in it together."

"It's possible. The important thing is, we're out of it. It's over. No bad publicity. Considering your new deal, a hundred thousand bucks is cheap."

"Maybe. Anyway, I have some good news for *you.*"

"What's that?"

"Deep secret, OK?"

"Sure. OK."

"No one knows until it's in the can, OK?"

"OK."

"Balmoral Castle, the royal retreat in Scotland, one whole day's taping in August, exclusive with Prince Charles—"

"Fantastic!"

"Wait a minute . . . with Prince William and Prince Harry joining us for part of the interview. First interview since the death of Princess Diana. What do you think of that, Joey?"

"I'm thinking fantastic! I'm thinking special, prime time, blockbuster special."

"So am I."

"I'm thinking produced by you. You own the rights."

"Even better."

"You know what I'm also thinking? You own this business now."

ABOUT THE AUTHOR

Robert MacNeil was, until his retirement in
October 1995, the coanchor of PBS's "The
MacNeil/Lehrer NewsHour." A lifelong love
of language has inspired him to write, and his
previous books include two volumes of
memoirs (*The Right Place at the Right Time* and
Wordstruck), the bestselling tie-in to his PBS
series "The Story of English," and two novels,
Burden of Desire and *The Voyage*. He lives in
New York City.